献给爱自然，爱诗歌的大小朋友们！

——Abby

美国童诗桂冠诗人 ［美］J.帕特里克·刘易斯　主编
Abby F. Yehenola ✿ 张原平 ✿ 和览　编译

NATIONAL GEOGRAPHIC
美国国家地理

book of nature poetry

最美自然诗集 1

（汉英对照）

200首诗歌
和会漂浮
会穿越，
会开花
的精彩图片

河南科学技术出版社
·郑州·

千山鸟飞绝，
万径人踪灭。
孤舟蓑笠翁，
独钓寒江雪。

这是唐朝柳宗元的《江雪》。短短的20个字，便成功捕捉一幅美丽的风景画。当时的孤冷静谧与雪白世界，似乎透过这首诗被永久封存，美丽了好几千年，不曾消逝。

《最美自然诗集》的出版，重新带给我这样的震撼与感动。随着时代的变迁，生活节奏的加快，文字阅读耗费时间，致使读者更为钟情图像阅读。不过图像阅读与文字阅读所获得的乐趣，无法互相取代。纵使是对同个风景的描绘，使用新诗文字创作与照片图像创作，让读者感受到的乐趣亦是截然不同。若是舍弃文字的阅读，全都转向图像阅读，实在相当可惜。《最美自然诗集》却完美解决了这个问题：这本诗集的每首诗，都是一张照片加上一首诗，使得文字文本和图像文本相互合作对话，形成一支精彩的双人舞。

这本书真的让我重新认识美丽的地球！在大自然中，随着四季的交替、地形的差异、气候的更迭，每一刹那的风景都是独一无二、稍纵即逝的。照片是静态的叙事，透过摄影师的镜头，有意识地捕捉吉光片羽，所以一张张的美照，是摄影师透过自身的美学哲学与镜头的选择所决定的，也可以说照片是摄影师眼中的美景。

而诗的创作，则是透过诗人纤细善感的心思，触景生情，把当时的生命状态转化成诗句，以情寓景，让景物多了一股人情的芬芳，不少美景在诗句的化妆下，变得充满情韵，让人印象深刻。

除此之外，这本书的编者扮演着隐形创作者的角色，因为他们成功媒合了照片与诗句，让作品更有一层乐趣。诗句的意象让静态的照片翩然生动，仿佛可以听见照片中的潺潺流水声，让读者宛若身临其境，感受照片里的一草一木，让读者悠游在每幅照片之中。阅读《最美自然诗集》，需要最好的领航员同游，我们的译者充分领会了编者的匠心独运，十分用心地录制了200首音频，恰是《最美自然诗集》最好的导读。

这本诗集让读者感受到三种美学：文学之美、摄影之美以及想象之美。透过诗句，让读者感受到文字透过意象诠释的美学；透过摄影照片让读者感受到强烈的视觉盛宴。当今的科技，无论是手机、电视还是穿戴科技等等，均试图以科技的力量，让读者感受到身临其境的感官盛宴，增强读者的视觉与听觉震撼，产生娱乐感，但是与此同时，相对地也剥夺了读者想象之美的权利。而《最美自然诗集》在照片与文字当中，保留了相当多的空白，并分类为“感叹自然”“凌空”“渊洋”“生灵”“山川”“美植”“灾难”“四季”“奇景”“敬畏自然”，让读者可以发挥想象，感受编者所安排的想象之美。因此，阅读这本书让读者经历一场美学盛宴，沉醉在大自然的洗礼之中。

最后，从这本书中也可以看出编者对于环境保护的意识。人类过度开发，使得环境被破坏，导致气候异常，很多珍稀动物濒临灭绝，大自然也不再美丽。希望这本诗集，能唤起人类对于大自然的重新思考，思考如何与环境共生。

透过这本最美丽的诗集，让我们回忆起我们曾经的美好！伟哉自然，伟哉生命！

林文宝

· 译者序 ·

翻开这本书，也就拉开了赞叹大自然的篇章！本书由13首感叹大自然的诗歌和23首细致刻画天空的诗歌组成。

佩姬·吉福德的开篇诗意境把我震撼了，我在翻译之前就在嘴里像嚼口香糖一样嚼了好几遍她的诗，当看到最后地球变蓝了时，我笑崩了。

美国土著诗人莫马戴的一首《石树男孩的欢歌》可以用如此简单的语言，调动起如此巨大的力量来赞美他所爱的土地。

如果你啃不下拜伦的长诗，那就来尝尝这篇节选，你同样会知道他有多么爱大自然。

莫菲特的一首小诗把我们带入微观的世界，你必须进入那叶间的宁静才可以真正了解大自然。

罗马尼亚著名诗人马林·索里斯应和着莫菲特，说你要研究一棵草，直到成为研究小草的博士。

《吗哪》一诗，诗人抬头看天，漫天的雪花让他想起上帝对人类的应许，他是位供应者。

《逸情》一诗道出了现今茫然且忙忙碌碌的人，竟然连发呆的时间都没有。

日本著名诗人小林一茶的四首俳句诗融合花、虫和生活中的小事，原来这一切才是真。

埃米莉·迪金森这位走在时代前列的女诗人将自然用来看、听、理会，一首小诗也可以气势磅礴。

当人老了，回乡还走在一条未曾改变的路上，估计就如诗中写的，肯定边走边哭了。

松尾芭蕉是日本另一位著名的俳句诗人，这四首俳句诗写了闪电、猴子、冬日等，一切常见却不寻常的事物。

埃米莉·迪金森的另一首诗中，说到秋日的早晨都比平常更温柔，诗人不禁戴起一枚胸针与其媲美。

谁都有焦虑的时候，当被世界的纷扰困住时，如诗中所写，来到大自然中，看野鸭孤芳自赏，这就是解药。

再来读读凌空的诗意：

我太喜欢这三首关于夜晚的诗了，有太阳和月亮倒班的童趣，有著名诗人威廉·布莱克笔下夜的宁静，更有乔伊斯·西德曼诗中夜的喧嚣和派对。

你想过月亮什么时候过生日吗？你见过月亮人的脸吗？你想过天上挂着的其实是一轮萝卜吗？快来读读这三首创意无比的诗！

有些事情，想通了就好办了，连太阳都会死亡，何况人呢？来读这首老太阳的诗。

一首象形诗，把两朵雪花如何碰面，如何恋爱，又如何殉情，表现得好巧妙。

对于孩子来说，可以对下雪充满想象，想知道雪和鸟是什么关系？来读这首诗。

地球这颗行星的确挺奇怪的，一会儿绿，一会儿白，从太空看会是什么样子？来读这首诗。

天空若没有星星的点缀就不会如此有趣，四首诗从不同的侧面来描述星星的可贵。

当你抬头看天，第一眼看到的一定是白云，但你想过云的反义词是什么吗？

《雨》这首诗是国外孩子们耳熟能详的一首，朗朗上口，来咬一口。

你可会把风比作什么？书中的两首诗把风比作赛马，真够劲儿。

有多少人为云作诗，又有多少人会为云间的蓝天作诗，这首诗写得好巧妙。

什么都挡不住诗人对大自然的探索，哪怕是今天有明天没的冰凌，都会被诗人赋予生命。

雾，总是一个捉摸不定的题材，本书有首诗是《最美动物诗集》中《雾》的续写，雾如猫，潜入夜。

Abby 2017年10月于昆明

THE WONDER OF NATURE 感叹自然

IN THE SKY 凌空

J. PATRICK LEWIS HAS WRITTEN MORE THAN 95 PICTURE AND POETRY BOOKS FOR YOUNG READERS. IN 2011 HE WAS APPOINTED U.S. CHILDREN'S POET LAUREATE, AND WAS GIVEN THE NATIONAL COUNCIL OF TEACHERS OF ENGLISH AWARD FOR EXCELLENCE IN POETRY FOR CHILDREN.

HENRY DAVID THOREAU was one of America's truly Big Thinkers on a little pond—Walden Pond. It was there in 1853, in a self-built cabin not far from his Massachusetts family home, that he wrote: "I have a room all to myself; it is nature."

From his tucked-away cottage, Thoreau produced some of the most profound thoughts on Mother Nature. But poets from centuries past rarely wrote about the more exotic natural wonders. They never saw them, never knew they existed. Many of the most fascinating phenomena that we often take for granted today—thanks to the convenience of travel, books, or photographs—were seldom brought to the attention of the classical poets.

How would William Shakespeare or John Keats have described in a poem the grandeur of the Grand Canyon? One can only imagine Emily Dickinson, transported to the scene, painting on an easel built of words a picture of an Asian tsunami or an African drought. What immortal verse might William Wordsworth have written after a day's walk in the Amazon rain forest instead of the English countryside? What picture would Kobayashi Issa or Li Po paint after a submersible dive to the ocean deep?

And yet a poet does not have to be there! You needn't leave your chair to write a poem about the wilder shores of creation. A book is your ticket to ride; a photograph is rapid transit to the brain. What kind of poem would you write if all you had in front of you was an image, like one of the breathtaking pictures in the *Book of Nature Poetry* you are now holding?

Better yet, let your eyes be your camera, taking incredible pictures your brain will thank you for. Get up and go there! Explore the woods, a cave; climb a mountain; go scuba diving; or simply make a friend of a grasshopper in a field on a windy summer day. You might even imagine you *are* that dragonfly trying to escape a swift, or a lucky salmon that has wiggled through the legs of a grizzly bear.

Travel by photograph or on foot, but go quickly before nature disappears. Every day more than 70 animals, plants, or other living things, like fungi, roots, and molds, vanish forever. The *Book of Nature Poetry* seeks to capture the ever changing nature of nature, so that gone is not forgotten. Besides, when more of us care for nature, more can help save it.

However and wherever you greet the world outside your window, listen again to Mr. Thoreau for the last and best words of advice:

"It's not what you look at that matters.
It's what you see."

—J. Patrick Lewis,
former U.S. Children's Poet Laureate

MALACHITE BUTTERFLY
孔雀石蝴蝶

J. 帕特里克·刘易斯已经为孩子们创作了95部图画书和诗集。2011年，他荣获了美国童诗桂冠诗人奖，并被美国国家英语教师委员会授予杰出童诗奖。

·前　言·

亨利·戴维·梭罗是美国真正的大思想家之一，他曾隐居在瓦尔登湖。

1853年，在离马萨诸塞州家不远的自建小木屋里，他写道："我有一个只属于我自己的房间——大自然。"

就在这世外桃源般的小木屋里，梭罗萌发出一些关于大自然的极其深刻的思想。但是这几百年来，诗人们却很少再去描写更独特的自然奇观。他们从来没见过，甚至都不知晓它们的存在。很多今天我们习以为常的，可以从旅行、书籍或照片中轻松获取的绝世美景，以前却很少能引起古典诗人们的关注。

试想，莎士比亚和济慈会怎样用诗歌去描绘大峡谷的壮美？可想而知，若埃米莉·迪金森能亲临亚洲海啸或非洲干旱现场，她将会用文字绘制出怎样的一幅画卷。那华兹华斯呢？如果他有机会走在亚马孙雨林中，而不仅仅是在英国乡间小道徘徊，他的笔下会写出怎样的诗句呢？若小林一茶或李白能乘潜艇探访大洋深渊，他们诗作的意境又将是怎样的呢？

然而，诗人并非一定要身临其境。你不需要离开椅子才能去写沧海桑田。一本书可以带你去遨游，一张照片可以带你去穿越。如果你拥有的只是面前的一幅图，就像你手里的《最美自然诗集》中的任意一幅惊艳的美图一样，你能写出怎样的诗句呢？

更棒的是，去旅行，让眼睛成为你的照相机，让眼前的美景滋养你的大脑。去吧，去森林中历险，去探索一个洞穴，去勇攀一座高峰，去潜入海底，甚至去野地里和一只蚱蜢交个朋友，任夏风轻抚。你甚至可以去想象自己就是那只努力躲过雨燕的蜻蜓，或是那条幸运地游过灰熊两腿之间的三文鱼。

无论是借着照片观光还是身临其境，请尽早，赶在自然景观消失之前。每天，都有超过70种生物在地球上永远消失。《最美自然诗集》力图捕捉到大自然瞬息万变的属性，让逝去的不再被遗忘。同时，当有更多的人开始关心大自然时，便会有更多的人来拯救她。

无论你在哪里，用怎样的方式来向窗外的世界致敬，请你再一次，也是最后一次聆听梭罗先生的警世良言："重要的不是你眼前的，而是你心里的。"

——J. 帕特里克·刘易斯，美国童诗桂冠诗人

AURORA BOREALIS
北极光

The Thing Is the Thing Is Green

The thing is the thing is green and the green is green and by green I mean real mean green. I mean electric-eel green, alligator, iguana, anaconda green. I mean this thing has got all things green. It's got green turtles in turtle-green ponds and grasshoppers springing from groomed-green lawns and a green tree frog on a girl's left arm. It's got dark and dangerous greens. Greens you've never even seen greens. Ocean floor greens. Tornado sky greens. Tiger's eye greens. Eat-your-broccoli greens. Watermelons sparkling in the sun greens. Way beyond evergreen, this thing leaves green geckos on green leaves feeling green and green moths in the green dark and preying mantises on their thin green knees. It's a great and gorgeous green a light-bright-just-right-watch-it-grow-it-says-go shade of green. Have you guessed yet? Do you need another clue? Think rolling waves of grain green. Thick arms of vines climbing tall green trees. Mountains and mountains of green billions of waves reaching out of dark green seas all wrapped in one green ball and hung, an ornament in the sky. What a thing it must be to see the whole green thing floating by. It's true. The thing is the thing is green . . .

except when it's blue.

—Peggy Gifford

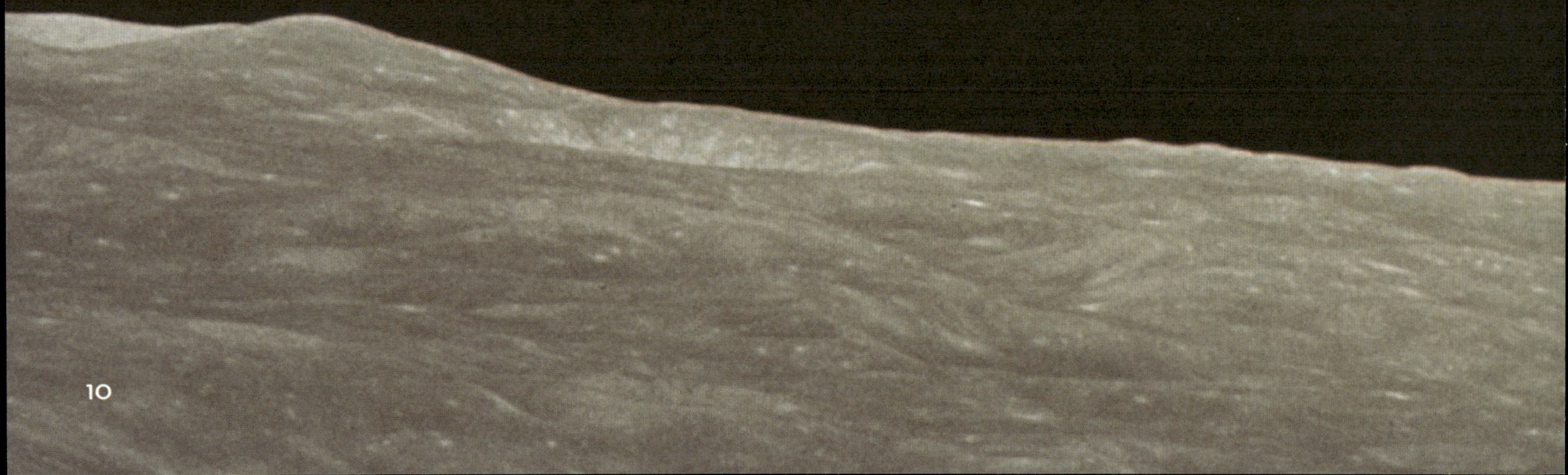

它要多绿就有多绿

要多绿就有多绿，绿就绿它个透心绿，就是这么绿，实打实的绿。我讲的是电鳗绿、鳄鱼绿、蜥蜴绿、蟒蛇绿，我说的这种绿把所有东西都染绿了。瞧那绿龟徜徉在龟绿色的池塘里，蚱蜢从刚修绿的草坪里一跃而起，一只绿树蛙停歇在女孩的左臂。有时候，它绿得阴森，绿得凶险，绿得其实你从未见过。大洋底的深渊绿，龙卷风的虐绿，老虎眼底的幽绿，“吃完西兰花”的郁闷绿，西瓜在阳光下的闪耀绿。比常绿植物更绿的，是绿叶上享绿的绿色壁虎、沉绿夜空的绿色飞蛾、紧绷双膝的绿色螳螂。它绿得伟大，绿得华丽，那“趁着阳光正好赶快生长说长就长”的一抹绿。还没有猜出来吗？还需要再来一点提示吗？想想那绿色的麦浪翻滚，想想那粗壮的藤蔓攀上绿色的参天大树。连绵不绝的绿色山峦，深绿海洋中的滔天巨澜，竟都被包在一个绿色的球里，独具一格地装点着天空。能亲眼看见这大绿球飘过该是一件多么大的幸事啊。没错，它要多绿就有多绿……

除非它变蓝了……

——佩姬·吉福德

THE WONDER OF NAT

URE

BEES AND LOTUS
蜜蜂与荷花

The Delight Song of Tsoai-talee

I am a feather on the bright sky
I am the blue horse that runs in the plain
I am the fish that rolls, shining, in the water
I am the shadow that follows a child
I am the evening light, the lustre of meadows
I am an eagle playing with the wind
I am a cluster of bright beads
I am the farthest star
I am the cold of the dawn
I am the roaring of the rain
I am the glitter on the crust of the snow
I am the long track of the moon in a lake
I am a flame of four colors
I am a deer standing away in the dusk
I am a field of sumac and the pomme blanche
I am an angle of geese in the winter sky
I am the hunger of a young wolf
I am the whole dream of these things

You see, I am alive, I am alive
I stand in good relation to the earth
I stand in good relation to the gods
I stand in good relation to all that is beautiful
I stand in good relation to the daughter of Tsen-tainte
You see, I am alive, I am alive

—N. Scott Momaday

from Childe Harold's Pilgrimage

There is a pleasure in the pathless woods,
There is a rapture on the lonely shore,
There is society where none intrudes,
By the deep Sea, and music in its roar:
I love not Man the less, but Nature more.

—George Gordon, Lord Byron

PESCADERO STATE BEACH, CALIFORNIA, U.S.A.
佩斯卡德罗州立海滩，加利福尼亚州，美国

To Look at Any Thing

To look at any thing,
If you would know that thing,
You must look at it long:
To look at this green and say
"I have seen spring in these
Woods," will not do—you must
Be the thing you see:
You must be the dark snakes of
Stems and ferny plumes of leaves,
You must enter in
To the small silences between
The leaves,
You must take your time
And touch the very peace
They issue from.

—John Moffitt

Perseverance

I shall look at the grass
Till I obtain the degree
Of Doctor of Grass.

I shall look at the clouds
Till I become a Master
Of Clouds.

I shall walk beside the smoke
Till out of shame
The smoke returns to the flame
Of its beginning.

I shall walk beside all things
Till all things
Come to know me.

—Marin Sorescu

Translated by D. J. Enright
and Joana Russell-Gebbett

Manna

Everywhere, *everywhere*, snow sifting down,
a world becoming white, no more sounds,
no longer possible to find the heart of the day,
the sun is gone, the sky is nowhere, and of all
I wanted in life—so be it—whatever it is
that brought me here, chance, fortune, whatever
blessing each flake of snow is the hint of, I am
grateful. I bear witness, I hold out my arms,
palms up, I know it is impossible to hold
for long what we love of the world, but look
at me, is it foolish, shameful, arrogant to say this,
see how the snow drifts down, look how happy
I am.

—Joseph Stroud

BLACK LOCUST TREE
刺槐树

Leisure

What is this life if, full of care,
We have no time to stand and stare.

No time to stand beneath the boughs
And stare as long as sheep or cows.

No time to see, when woods we pass,
Where squirrels hide their nuts in grass.

No time to see, in broad daylight,
Streams full of stars, like skies at night.

No time to turn at Beauty's glance,
And watch her feet, how they can dance.

No time to wait till her mouth can
Enrich that smile her eyes began.

A poor life this if, full of care,
We have no time to stand and stare.

—W. H. Davies

ELWHA RIVER, WASHINGTON, U.S.A.
埃尔瓦河，华盛顿州，美国

Four Haiku

I
Don't worry, spiders,
I keep house
casually.

II
How *much*
are you enjoying yourself,
tiger moth?

III
In this world
we walk on the roof of hell,
gazing at flowers.

IV
Even with insects—
some can sing,
some can't.

—Kobayashi Issa

Translated by Robert Hass

PRAYING MANTIS
螳螂

Tiger Got to Hunt

Tiger got to hunt,
Bird got to fly;
Man got to sit and wonder
"Why, why, why?"
Tiger got to sleep,
Bird got to land;
Man got to tell himself he understand.

—Kurt Vonnegut

BENGAL TIGER
孟加拉虎

BIRCH LEAVES
白桦树叶

"Nature" Is What We See

"Nature" is what we see—
The Hill—the Afternoon—
Squirrel—Eclipse—the Bumble bee—
Nay—Nature is Heaven—
Nature is what we hear—
The Bobolink—the Sea—
Thunder—the Cricket—
Nay—Nature is Harmony—
Nature is what we know—
Yet have no art to say—
So impotent Our Wisdom is
To her Simplicity.

—Emily Dickinson

WOODS, GOUGANE BARRA, IRELAND
树林，古迦巴拉，爱尔兰

Four Haiku

I

How admirable!
to see lightning and not think
life is fleeting.

II

First winter rain—
even the monkey
seems to want a raincoat.

III

Winter solitude—
in a world of one color
the sound of wind.

IV

What fish feel,
birds feel, I don't know—
the year ending.

—Matsuo Basho

Translated by Robert Hass

LIGHTNING STORM
雷暴

The Morns Are Meeker Than They Were

The morns are meeker than they were,
The nuts are getting brown;
The berry's cheek is plumper,
The rose is out of town.

The maple wears a gayer scarf;
The field a scarlet gown.
Lest I should be old-fashioned,
I'll put a trinket on.

—Emily Dickinson

EUROPEAN CRANBERRY BUSH
欧洲越橘丛

The Peace of Wild Things

When despair for the world grows in me
and I wake in the night at the least sound
in fear of what my life and my children's lives may be,
I go and lie down where the wood drake
rests in his beauty on the water, and the great heron feeds.
I come into the peace of wild things
who do not tax their lives with forethought
of grief. I come into the presence of still water.
And I feel above me the day-blind stars
waiting with their light. For a time
I rest in the grace of the world, and am free.

—Wendell Berry

GREAT BLUE HERON
大蓝鹭

IN THE

SEAGULLS, SAMUT PRAKAN, THAILAND
海鸥，沙没巴干，泰国

sky

Changing of the Guard

In their twice-a-day meeting
Sun and moon exchange
The same greeting,
"Hello," "Goodbye."
With a nod of the head,
One's off to work,
One's off to bed.

—Charles Waters

from Night

The sun descending in the west,
The evening star does shine;
The birds are silent in their nest,
And I must seek for mine.
The moon, like a flower
In heaven's high bower,
With silent delight,
Sits and smiles on the night.

—William Blake

SEASTACKS, OLYMPIC NATIONAL PARK, WASHINGTON, U.S.A.
海栈，奥林匹克国家公园，华盛顿州，美国

Welcome to the Night

To all of you who crawl and creep,
who buzz and chirp and hoot and peep,
who wake at dusk and throw off sleep:
Welcome to the night.

To you who make the forest sing,
who dip and dodge on silent wing,
who flutter, hover, clasp, and cling:
Welcome to the night!

Come feel the cool and shadowed breeze,
come smell your way among the trees,
come touch rough bark and leathered leaves:
Welcome to the night.

The night's a sea of dappled dark,
the night's a feast of sound and spark,
the night's a wild, enchanted park.
Welcome to the night!

—Joyce Sidman

FIREFLIES IN WOODS
树林中的萤火虫

Old Man Moon

The moon is very, very old.
The reason why is clear—
he gets a birthday once a month,
instead of once a year.

—Aileen Fisher

FULL MOON OVER SOMOSKÓÚJFALU, HUNGARY
匈牙利Somoskóújfalu的满月

The Man in the mOOn

He used to frighten me in the nights of childhood,
the wide adult face, enormous, stern, aloft.
I could not imagine such loneliness, such coldness.

But tonight as I drive home over these hilly roads
I see him sinking behind stands of winter trees
and rising again to show his familiar face.

And when he comes into full view over open fields
he looks like a young man who has fallen in love
with the dark earth,

a pale bachelor, well-groomed and full of melancholy,
his round mouth open
as if he had just broken into song.

—Billy Collins

Write About a Radish

Write about a radish
too many people write about the moon.

The night is black
the stars are small and high
the clock unwinds its ever-ticking tune
hills gleam dimly
distant nighthawks cry.
A radish rises in the waiting sky.

—Karla Kuskin

The Aged Sun

Whether our star, the sun, grows old
By turning into liquid gold

And dripping down invisible space
To some celestial fireplace,

Expands, like science says it must,
And turns its planets into dust,

Or simply ups and disappears
Like some ascending-ending spheres,

I do not think it matters much.
Great things collapse, depart, lose touch

When slow time reckons they are done—
And so it will be with the sun.

—*Anonymous*

Two Falling Flakes

Two falling flakes by chance did meet,
Lived happily ever after
Till they hit the street.

—Douglas Florian

GEESE IN NEW ENGLAND, U.S.A.
新英格兰的大雁，美国

Snow

In the gloom of whiteness,
In the great silence of snow,
A child was sighing
And bitterly saying: "Oh,
They have killed a white bird up there on her nest,
The down is fluttering from her breast!"
And still it fell through that dusky brightness
On the child crying for the bird of the snow.

—Edward Thomas

Looking Through Space

If people are living
on Venus and Mars
and looking through space
at the planets and stars,
I wonder if Earth
seems a queer sort of thing,
with whiteness in winter
and greenness in spring.

—Aileen Fisher

EARTH'S ATMOSPHERE AS SEEN FROM SPACE
从太空观测到的地球大气层

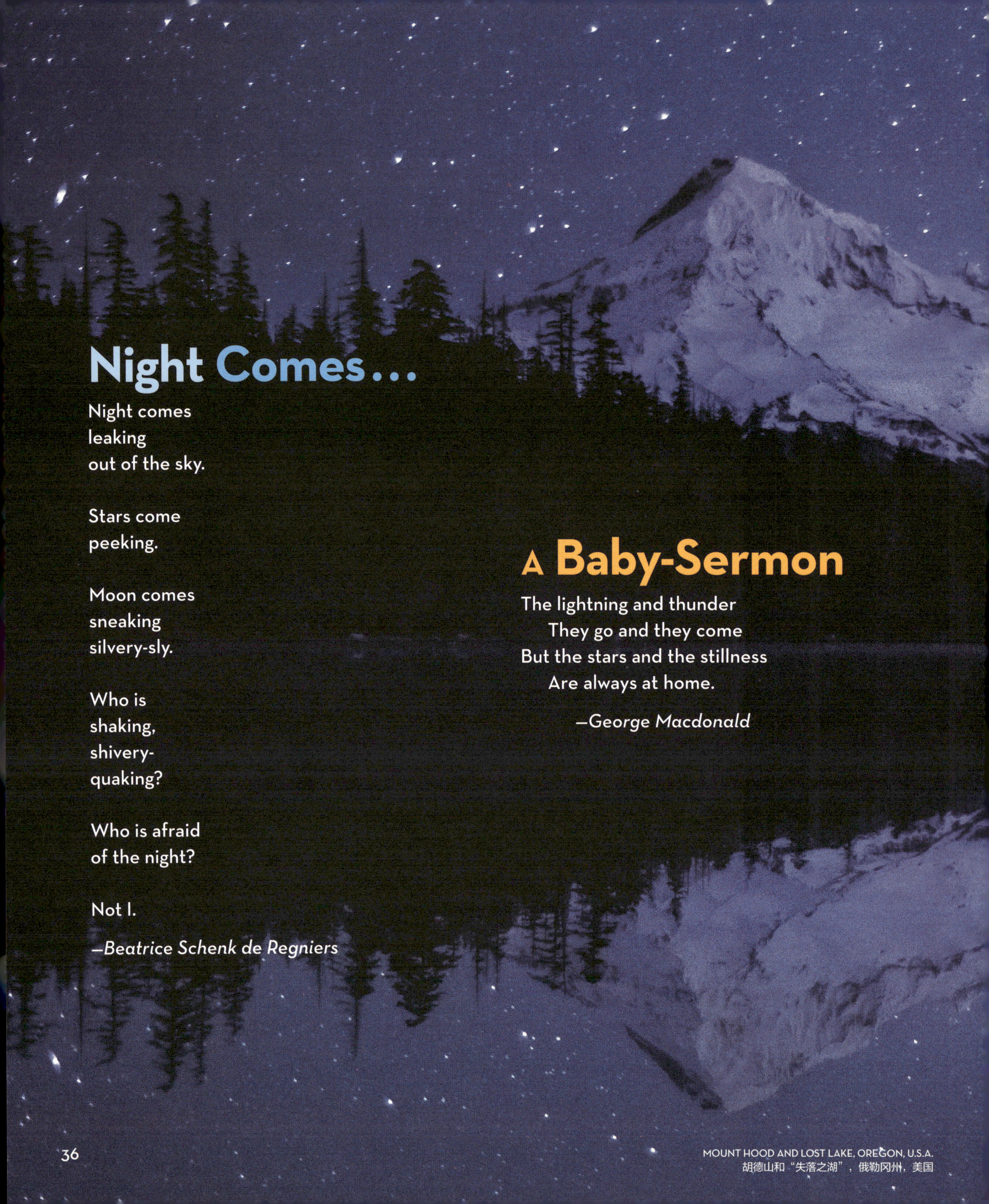

Night Comes…

Night comes
leaking
out of the sky.

Stars come
peeking.

Moon comes
sneaking
silvery-sly.

Who is
shaking,
shivery-
quaking?

Who is afraid
of the night?

Not I.

—Beatrice Schenk de Regniers

A Baby-Sermon

The lightning and thunder
They go and they come
But the stars and the stillness
Are always at home.

—George Macdonald

MOUNT HOOD AND LOST LAKE, OREGON, U.S.A.
胡德山和“失落之湖”，俄勒冈州，美国

Stars

Stars, I have seen them fall,
But when they drop and die
No star is lost at all
From all the star-sown sky.
The toil of all that be
Helps not the primal fault;
It rains into the sea,
And still the sea is salt.

—A. E. Housman

When I Heard the Learn'd Astronomer

When I heard the learn'd astronomer,
When the proofs, the figures, were ranged in columns before me,
When I was shown the charts and diagrams, to add, divide, and measure them,
When I sitting heard the astronomer where he lectured with much applause in the lecture-room,
How soon unaccountable I became tired and sick,
Till rising and gliding out I wander'd off by myself,
In the mystical moist night-air, and from time to time,
Look'd up in perfect silence at the stars.

—Walt Whitman

SOUTH SISTER AND SPARKS LAKE, OREGON, U.S.A.
南姐妹火山和火花湖，俄勒冈州，美国

The Opposite of a Cloud

The opposite of a *cloud* could be
A white reflection in the sea,
Or a huge blueness in the air,
Caused by a cloud's not being there.

—Richard Wilbur

Rain

The rain is raining all around,
It falls on field and tree,
It rains on the umbrellas here,
And on the ships at sea.

—Robert Louis Stevenson

RAINDROPS
雨滴

Windy Nights

Whenever the moon and stars are set,
Whenever the wind is high,
All night long in the dark and wet,
A man goes riding by.
Late in the night when the fires are out,
Why does he gallop and gallop about?

Whenever the trees are crying aloud,
And ships are tossed at sea,
By, on the highway, low and loud,
By at the gallop goes he.
By at the gallop he goes, and then
By he comes back at the gallop again.

—Robert Louis Stevenson

The Wind

The wind stood up and gave a shout.
He whistled on his fingers and
Kicked the withered leaves about
And thumped the branches with his hand
And said that he'd kill and kill,
And so he will and so he will.

—James Stephens

ARABIAN HORSE
阿拉伯马

The Blue Between

Everyone watches clouds,
naming creatures they've seen.
I see the sky differently,
I see the blue between—

The blue woman tugging
her stubborn cloud across the sky.
The blue giraffe stretching
to nibble a cloud floating by.
A pod of dancing dolphins,
cloud oceans, cargo ships,
a boy twirling his cloud
around a thin blue fingertip.

In those smooth wide places,
I see a different scene
In those cloudless spaces,
I see the blue between.

—Kristine O'Connell George

PONDEROSA PINE
美国黄松

Icicles

Swell
and
grow,

put on
your
mighty show

this bitter-bold,
brutal-cold,
howling,
windy-wintry
day—

'cause
you
cannot
know

tomorrow's
tad
of sunshine prey

will
stalk

to
take

your
breath
away.

—Lee Bennett Hopkins

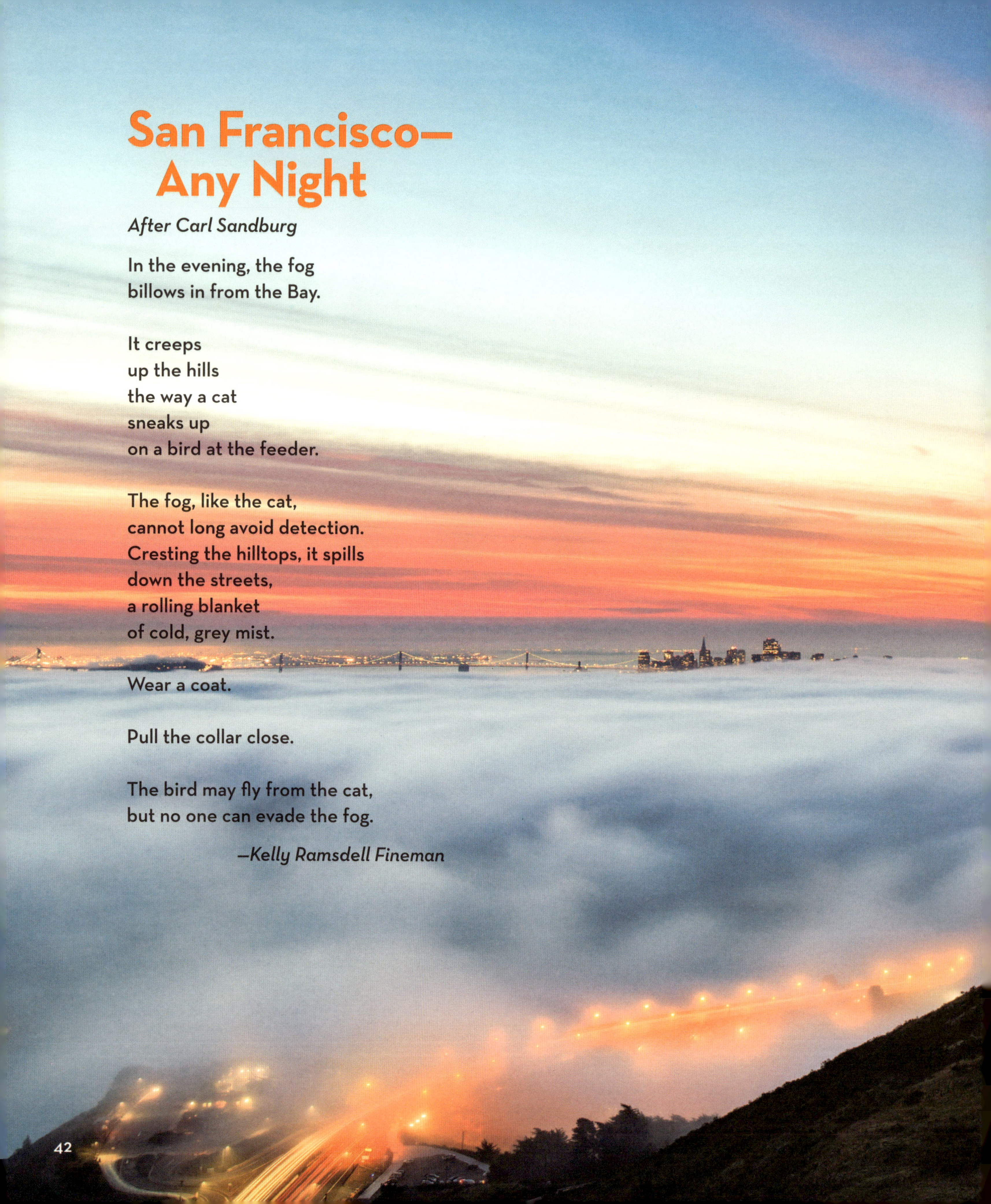

San Francisco— Any Night

After Carl Sandburg

In the evening, the fog
billows in from the Bay.

It creeps
up the hills
the way a cat
sneaks up
on a bird at the feeder.

The fog, like the cat,
cannot long avoid detection.
Cresting the hilltops, it spills
down the streets,
a rolling blanket
of cold, grey mist.

Wear a coat.

Pull the collar close.

The bird may fly from the cat,
but no one can evade the fog.

—Kelly Ramsdell Fineman

The Sun and Fog

The Sun and Fog contested
The Government of Day—
The Sun took down his Yellow Whip
And drove the Fog away.

—Emily Dickinson

This Is My Rock

This is my rock,
And here I run
To steal the secret of the sun;

This is my rock,
And here come I
Before the night has swept the sky;

This is my rock,
This is the place
I meet the evening face to face.

—David McCord

SAN FRANCISCO, CALIFORNIA, U.S.A.
旧金山，加利福尼亚州，美国

THE WONDER OF NAT

感叹自然

URE

BEES AND LOTUS
蜜蜂与荷花

The Delight Song of Tsoai-talee

P14

石树男孩的欢歌

我是明空中飞舞的羽毛，
我是平原上狂奔的蓝色骏马，
我是河流中闪耀欢跳的鱼，
我是紧随孩童的身影，
我是黑夜的光洁，草原的亮泽。
我是与风嬉戏的雄鹰，
我是一簇闪烁的露珠，
我是天空中最遥远的星。
我是黎明的清冷，
我是暴雨的怒吼，
我是雪晶的跃动，
我是湖中的月光，拖着长长的尾巴，
我是四色的火焰，
我是暮色中眺望的雄鹿，
我是漆树成林，芜菁连连，
我是冬日里列队翱翔的雁，
我是饥肠辘辘的狼崽，
我是万物的幻境。

你瞧，我是鲜活的，我是鲜活的！
我与地球相伴，
我与神明共存，
我与万物之大美琴瑟和鸣，
我与白马帅之女甜蜜依偎，
你瞧，我是鲜活的，我是鲜活的！

——N. 斯科特·莫马戴

from Childe Harold's Pilgrimage

P15

《恰尔德·哈罗尔德游记》选段

愉悦在罕迹森林，
狂喜在寂寞海畔。
和谐在无人入侵，
深海之岸，天籁交响在其波澜：
我喜人类，但更恋自然。

——乔治·戈登·拜伦勋爵

To Look at Any Thing

P16

来赏物

来赏物，
你若愿领悟它，
必久久地体会它，
领会这片绿，
只说“我在林中得见春天”是不够的，
你须化为它：
你须化为绕枝而上的阴郁茎蔓、蕨草的细羽，
你须化为栖于叶片间小小的静谧，
你须化为淡然轻抚其源原的安宁。

——约翰·莫菲特

Perseverance

P17

恒心

我须注目小草，
直至获得小草的博士学位。

我须明察云彩，
直至成为研究云彩的大师。

我须穿梭烟雾，
直至走出自惭形秽，
烟雾退回火焰始燃。

我须伴行万物，
直至万物与我相交。

——马林·索里斯

（原诗由 D. J. 恩赖特和乔安娜·拉塞尔－格贝特译为英文）

Manna

P17

吗哪

四面八方，四面八方，雪花散落，
泛白的世界，一片寂静，
这一日再也无法寻回，
太阳走了，天空无处可寻，
我的一生——诚心所愿——顺其自然吧，
无论我是因何而来，机缘，命运，
无论每片雪花带着怎样的祝福，
我都心存感激。
我见证，我张开双臂，掌心向上，
我知道我们不能贪恋地上的一切，
但瞧我，说这话的时候多么愚蠢、多么可耻、多么傲慢，
定睛看雪花飘落，
我心喜乐。

——约瑟夫·斯特劳德

Leisure

P18

逸情

当，满怀愁苦，人生何旨，
我们无暇驻足凝视。
无暇驻足枝叶下的阴凉，
无暇久久凝视全地牛羊。
无暇林中驻足，
窥视藏果松鼠。
无暇留意，阳光洒满，
溪水波光，宛如星空灿烂。
无暇顾及美人一瞥，
双脚跃起，舞姿摇曳。
无暇等候她嫣然一笑，
始于双眸，盛在嘴角。
我们无暇驻足凝视，
当，满怀愁苦，人生无旨。

——W. H. 戴维斯

Four Haiku

P19

俳句四首

Ⅰ
别担心，蜘蛛，
我打扫房间时会
草草了事的。

Ⅱ
虎蛾、虎蛾，
告诉我，告诉我，
你到底有多开心？

Ⅲ
在这世界上
我们走在地狱的
屋顶，赏鲜花。

Ⅳ
即使是昆虫，
有的会婉转歌唱，
有的则不能。

——小林一茶

（原诗由罗伯特·哈斯译为英文）

Tiger Got to Hunt

P20

老虎要捕猎

老虎要捕猎，
鸟儿要飞翔，
人坐地苦想：
“为什么？为什么？为什么？”
老虎要睡觉，
鸟儿要降落，
人则自言自语：明白了。

——库尔特·冯内古特

“Nature” Is What We See

P21

所见“自然”

所见“自然”，
山冈、午后、
松鼠、月食、大黄蜂，
不仅如此，大自然是天堂，
大自然是我们所听到的，
食米鸟、海洋、
雷鸣、蟋蟀，
不仅如此，大自然是和音，
大自然是我们心领神会的，
却无以言表。
人类的智慧相比大自然的朴素，
黯然失色。

——埃米莉·迪金森

RETURN

P22

返乡

那时，林子还小，
那时，我刚刚离开家，
我航行在未知的海岸，踏遍苍茫的平原，
向着乐土和传说，向着陌生的一切。
而如今，我重返乡途，
风尘仆仆，但心潮澎湃，
只因纳入眼帘那怀旧的青苔，那熟悉的石头，
阳光穿透勾勒着天空的树叶，不曾改变，
但小树们，已长大。

——佩奇·陶勒

Four Haiku

P23

俳句四首

Ⅰ

太佩服你了！
看到闪电都不觉
生命的短暂。

Ⅱ

第一场冬雨——
连猴子都好像要
穿一件雨衣。

Ⅲ

冬日的孤寂——
就在单色的世界，
也在风声中。

Ⅳ

鱼什么感觉，
鸟儿呢，我不知道——
一年到头了。

——松尾芭蕉

（原诗由罗伯特·哈斯译为英文）

The Morns Are Meeker Than They Were

P24

早晨比往日更温情

早晨比往日更温情了，
坚果比棕色更深。
浆果的脸颊更饱满了，
玫瑰花落纷纷。
枫树戴上围巾，欢畅无比，
牧场红得更真。
我怕赶不上这秋色的时尚，
一枚首饰戴在身。

——埃米莉·迪金森

The Peace of Wild Things

P25

安享生灵的宁静

当对世界的绝望蔓延在我心，
哪怕是一丁点声音都会把我惊醒。
因着为自己和孩子们的未来而恐慌，
我躺卧在野鸭孤芳自赏的水边、白鹭觅食的岸际。
我安享在生灵的宁静中，
它们从不透支未来的哀伤，
我沉浸于静水的存在。
仰面，犹如白昼般的繁星用它们的光芒守候着我。
那一刻，我安息在世界的恩典救赎之下，瞬时解脱。

——温德尔·贝里

凌空 IN THE SKY

SEAGULLS, SAMUT PRAKAN, THAILAND
海鸥，沙没巴干，泰国

P28

Changing of the Guard

轮班守卫

每天两次会合，
日月互换相同的问候，
“你好”，“再见”。
点头微笑，
一个来上班，
一个去睡觉。

——查尔斯·沃特斯

P29

Welcome to the Night

快来，享受夜色

嘿，所有爬行的、蠕动的，
嗡嗡叫的、叽叽喳喳的、聒噪的、啾啾叫的，
所有黄昏醒来，却倒头又睡的：
快来，享受夜色。

你呀，令山林欢唱，
你呀，轻翼矫捷，闪弧疾降，
你呀，鼓翼、盘旋，当仁不让：
快来，享受夜色！

来享受微风拂面，色彩斑斓，
来穿梭林间，嗅出对来路的期盼，
来抚摸粗糙的树干，观层林尽染：
快来，享受夜色。

夜，是黑海，斑斑驳驳，
夜，是声宴，闪闪烁烁，
夜，是迷园，含情脉脉。
快来，享受夜色！

——乔伊斯·西德曼

P28

from Night

《夜》选段

落阳西天逃，
夜空星灿灿；
鸟群静归巢，
吾于何处安。

明月娇如花，
绽放天堂塔；
静谧而欣喜，
莞尔落夜席。

——威廉·布莱克

Old Man Moon

P30

月亮老爷爷

你知道吗？月亮年龄好大好大啦。
知道为什么吗？很简单——
他不是每年过一次生日，
而是每个月过一次。

——艾琳·费希尔

Write About a Radish

P31

写写萝卜吧

月亮都被写滥了，
写写萝卜吧。

夜色漆黑，
渺小的星辰遥不可及，
钟表也放慢了滴答作响的脚步。
山峦无助地时隐时现，
远方夜鹰啼鸣，
一轮萝卜升起在迫不及待的天空。

——卡拉·库斯金

The Man in the mOOn

P31

月中人

他好吓人，小时候的每个夜晚都让我恐惧，
一张成熟的脸，又大又宽，又严厉，又高远。
我无法想象那般寂寞、那般冷酷。

今夜，当我行驶在蜿蜒的山路时，
瞥见他沉入冬日林海，
又时而再现。

然而当来到开阔空地，他终于显露无遗，
宛如一个年轻人，不可救药地爱上了夜幕中的大地。

面色苍白的单身汉啊，衣冠楚楚，多愁善感，
微微张开他的唇，
依稀仿佛，耳畔响起醉人的情歌。

——比利·柯林斯

The Aged Sun

太阳老了

我们的太阳老了，
化成金灿灿的水流走了，

一滴一滴，穿过暗处，
落进宇宙的壁炉，

膨胀，有如科学所讲，
化行星为灰尘模样，

抑或仅仅飘上去，不见了，
像一些星球，飘着飘着，消失了。

我认为这一切都没关系，
再伟大的东西也会烟消云散、杳无踪迹，

万物耐不住岁月蹉跎，
太阳也逃不过。

——无名氏

Two Falling Flakes

两片雪花

两片雪花一见钟情，
从此幸福快乐地生活在一起，
忠贞不渝，直至撞在地面。

——道格拉斯·弗洛里安

Snow

雪鸟

在白白的朦胧暮色中，
茫茫雪原，万籁俱寂，
一个孩子唏嘘感叹："哦，
有人杀了一只巢中白色的鸟，
鸟儿胸口的白羽毛飘啊飘！"
白羽毛飘啊飘，穿过那忧郁的光，
飘落在为雪鸟而泣的孩子身上。

——爱德华·托马斯

Looking Through Space

P35

远远望着

如果咱都住在
金星和火星,
远远望着
那些星球,
心里会犯嘀咕:
地球是否有点违和?
冬天变白,
春天变绿。

——艾琳·费希尔

Night Comes...

P36

夜,来了……

夜,来了,
从天空
流泻。

星,来了,
暗中偷窥。

月,来了,
透着银色的
鬼祟。

谁
在发抖,
瑟瑟发抖?

你怕了吗?
才没有。

——比阿特丽斯·申克·德雷尼尔斯

A Baby-Sermon

P36

短训

雷和电,往而返,
星和静,在家园。

——乔治·麦克唐纳

Stars

P37

星

我曾亲眼看着星星坠落,
　　但随着它们落下,消亡,
天空依旧星火灼灼,
　　没有一颗星失丧。
所有的努力,
　　也无法弥补起初的过错。
就这样倾入了海浪,
　　怎奈大海仍苦涩如昔。

——A. E. 豪斯曼

When I Heard the Learn'd Astronomer

P37

那博学的天文学家在演说

那博学的天文学家在演说，
成山的数据罗列在我眼前，
图纸、表格，加、减、乘、除，
震耳欲聋的掌声响彻礼堂，
我却莫名其妙地疲乏了、困倦了，
我起身溜出去，
沉浸在夜幕里，神神秘秘的，潮潮润润的，
我时不时地望向寂然无声的星河。

——沃尔特·惠特曼

Rain

P38

雨

雨，落满全地，
飘落在田间、树上，
滴答在行人的雨伞上，
轻敲着海上的船舱。

——罗伯特·路易斯·史蒂文森

The Opposite of a Cloud

P38

云的反义词

云的反义词是——
海中的白色倒影，
或是天空中的那块巨蓝，
只因云不在天。

——理查德·威尔伯

Windy Nights

P39

夜起，风行

每当星月升空，
每当风声正起，
又黑又潮，夜色正浓，
他，马不停蹄。
午夜，灯火熄了，熄了，
他为何还在飞奔，飞奔？

每当森林在狂吼，
每当船只在海上摇荡，
他，在大道奔走，又沉又吵，
他，信马由缰。
他，疾驰而过，
他，驰骋而回。

——罗伯特·路易斯·史蒂文森

The Wind

P39

风

风，起身，嚎叫。
他吹着口哨，
踢踹着枯叶乱飘，
双手把树枝猛摇，
喊着：杀呀！杀呀！
我来啦！我来啦！

——詹姆斯·斯蒂芬斯

The Blue Between

P40

云间蓝

人人都爱看云，
都能说出看到了什么生物。
我却不看云，
偏看云间大蓝锦簇。

蓝妈妈拽着倔强的云孩子满天跑。
蓝色长颈鹿伸长脖子把云朵捞。
一群海豚跃动长空，
云海，货船，
还有小男孩
纤纤蓝色指尖搅动乾坤。

在那大块大块的平坦之地，
风景不同，
在那无云处，
我看云间蓝。

——克里斯廷·奥康奈尔·乔治

Icicles

P41

冰柱

膨胀，
疯长，
快快
呈上
你的
锋芒。

虐啸，
寒峭，
风嚎，
寒冬
腊月天。

谁知
明日
哪怕
些许
阳光
都能
暗中
折磨你，
只留下
唏嘘不已。

——李·贝内特·霍普金斯

San Francisco—Any Night

P42

旧金山——潜入夜

续写卡尔·桑德堡的《雾》

夜，雾从海湾汹涌而来，
它悄悄地爬上山头，
如猫儿偷偷靠近忙食的鸟儿。
雾，猫，
都无法躲过被发现。
漫过山顶，
倾泻在街头，
一张冰冰的灰暗雾毯
翻滚而来。
披上外套，
紧紧衣领。
鸟儿或许可以躲过猫儿一劫，
但没人可以幸免于雾。

——凯利·拉姆斯德尔·法恩曼

The Sun and Fog

P43

太阳与雾

太阳和雾来较量，
看谁能做白天的主——
只见太阳拿出大黄鞭，
三下两下把雾驱逐。

——埃米莉·迪金森

This Is My Rock

P43

这，是我的磐石

这，是我的磐石，
我从这里起跑
窃取烈日的奥妙。

这，是我的磐石，
我行迹匆匆，
趁夜幕尚未席卷长空。

这，是我的磐石，
在此，
我与黑夜面对面 。

——戴维·麦科德

Who is mother nature?

When Mother Nature's near—in waterfalls, rivers, rainbows, meadows, or oceans—her admirers react with love, awe, curiosity, even fear, if she decides to reveal her grumpier side. The lady can be seen through telescopes or microscopes, from mountaintops or ravines, with the wind in our hair, soil in our hands, or sand in our toes. For those who aren't hopelessly city-bound, looking out a window will do.

Driven to explore the *science* behind the wonder of it all, Charles Darwin filled scores of notebooks about what was then the unexplored wildlife of the Galápagos Islands. Countless nature writers have followed his courageous example. Others have put themselves in nature, like naturalist John Muir, who once rode out a northern American windstorm by cocooning himself in the branches of a sky-high Douglas spruce. (Muir is famous—or should be—for saying, "The clearest way into the Universe is through a forest wilderness.")

Some humans, however, have no use for wild places, a view once expressed by Woody Allen with his typical wit: "I love nature. I just don't want to get any of it on me." For some, their love for animals extends only as far as Fido or Sweet Pea. That we share the Earth equally with other creatures is a notion as foreign and irrelevant to them as the disappearance of the rain forests or the melting of the ice caps.

But Mother Nature doesn't care who likes her. Nor is she bothered about being ignored. A midwife at the birth of creatures large and small, she will go on making waves by making waves, assembling forests, flowering deserts, and beautifying gardens. We can embrace her or resist her charms; it is of no concern to her.

Who is the mysterious lady known as Mother Nature? She is the material world, the environment of trees, plants, animals, everything under and over the sun. In short, she equals the world around us and includes whatever is not built by human hands.

Mother Nature is where we live. In other words, she is

a refuge to the lost,
a magnet to the curious,
a dare to the daring,
the cradle of rapture,
the university of the universe,
the glory of a morning and of a morning-glory,
not a whale but the idea of a whale,
a sign rewriter: I Welcome All No Trespassing,
the best cure for couch disease,
an opera performed by birds, bullfrogs on drums,
the sound of silence . . . amplified
to the symphony of the spheres, and ____________
____.

Can you add another short description of Mother Nature to this poem?

The poets and photographers who have come together to produce National Geographic's *Book of Nature Poetry* would agree with John Keats, who defined their abiding faith: "The poetry of earth is never dead."

THREAD-WINGED ANTLION
线翅蚁狮

自然之母是谁？

当自然之母靠近的时候——在瀑布中，在河流中，在彩虹中，在草地或是海洋中——她的爱慕者用爱、敬畏、好奇来回应，甚至如果她显示暴躁的一面时，则用恐惧来回应。这位女士可以用望远镜或是显微镜来观察，从山顶到深谷，风在我们的发丝中穿过，泥土在我们手中漏出，沙在我们的脚趾中渗出。对于那些不喜欢住在城里的人来说，只要看一看窗外就行。

为了探索自然奇观背后的科学道理，查尔斯·达尔文把加拉帕戈斯群岛未知的野生动物记满了几十本笔记本。难以数计的自然主义作家跟随着他，以他为榜样。其他人则让自己融入自然。例如自然主义者约翰·缪尔，曾经用高耸入云的道格拉斯云杉的枝叶包裹着自己，经受住了北美的风暴。（缪尔由于下面这句话而知名——或应该知名——“融入宇宙最清晰的方式莫过于通过荒野森林”。）

然而，也有一些人，觉得野外毫无用处，这也是伍迪·艾伦用他特有的机智曾经表达的观点：“我爱自然，但是一点也别弄到我身上来。”而另一些人，他们对动物的喜爱只限于“菲多”或是“甜豌豆”。对他们来说，我们与其他生物平等地分享地球的观念，和雨林正在消失、冰层正在融化这样的概念一样，是未知而不重要的。

但自然之母并不关心谁喜欢她。她对这种忽视也毫不在意。她是大大小小各种生物出生时的产婆，她将不断在波浪中创造波浪，让森林遍地，让花朵在沙漠开放，让花园变得更美。我们可以接受或是抗拒她的魅力，她对此却毫不关心。

这位被人称为自然之母的神秘女士是谁？她是物质世界，也是植物、动物的环境和阳光下所有的一切。简言之，她就是我们周遭的世界，人类双手无法创造的世界。

自然之母在我们生活的地方。换句话说，

她是：
迷失者的庇护，
好奇者的磁石，
勇敢者的挑战，
狂喜者的摇篮，
宇宙的教化者。
她是：
清晨的光辉，
牵牛花的光，
并不是鲸鱼，
而是这创意。
她重新写了一个标记：我欢迎所有的非擅自闯入者。
她是：
沙发病的良药，
鸟儿、牛蛙在鼓上演奏的歌剧，
是寂静之声……被放大，
而成为万物的交响曲，
也是 ____________________________

你可以在这首诗后面加上一段描写自然之母的短句吗？

共同创作《最美自然诗集》的诗人和摄影家们会同意约翰·济慈的话，他道出了他们永恒的信仰：“地球的诗篇永远不会消亡。”

LOTUS AND BEES -WUQIANG
荷花与蜜蜂（吴强）

美国国家地理学会是世界上最大的非营利科学与教育组织之一。学会成立于1888年，以"增进与普及地理知识"为宗旨，致力于启发人们对地球的关心。美国国家地理学会通过杂志、电视节目、影片、音乐、电台、图书、DVD、地图、展览、活动、学校出版计划、交互式媒体与商品来呈现世界。美国国家地理学会的会刊《国家地理》杂志，以英文及其他33种语言发行，每月有3800万读者阅读。美国国家地理频道在166个国家以34种语言播放，有3.2亿个家庭收看。美国国家地理学会资助超过10 000项科学研究、环境保护与探索计划，并支持一项扫除"地理文盲"的教育计划。

Acknowledgments
To the entire National Geographic team for their enthusiasm and dedication in the making of this book, and to all the poets whose deserving work, regrettably, could not be squeezed into its pages.—JPL

The publisher gratefully acknowledges the heroic efforts of Natalie Turner in securing permissions, as well as the invaluable research assistance of Alyson Foster.

图书在版编目（CIP）数据

最美自然诗集 / （美）J. 帕特里克·刘易斯主编；Abby F. Yehenola，张原平，和览编译. —郑州：河南科学技术出版社，2018.1
ISBN 978-7-5349-8952-0

Ⅰ. ①最… Ⅱ. ①J… ②A… ③张… ④和… Ⅲ. ①儿童诗歌-诗集-美国-现代 Ⅳ. ①I712.82

中国版本图书馆CIP数据核字(2017)第269830号

出版发行：河南科学技术出版社
地址：郑州市经五路66号　邮编：450002
电话：（0371）65737028　65788613
网址：www.hnstp.cn
特邀策划：Abby F. Yehenola
策划编辑：马艳茹　韩雅楠　于凯燕
责任编辑：于凯燕
责任校对：徐小刚
整体设计：吴豆豆
责任印制：张　巍
印　　刷：北京盛通印刷股份有限公司
经　　销：全国新华书店
幅面尺寸：232 mm × 276 mm　印张：3.75　字数：94千字
版　　次：2018年1月第1版　2018年1月第1次印刷
全套定价：588.00元

To poets, nature, and nature poets everywhere.—JPL

献给诗人、自然和全世界写自然的诗人。

——J. 帕特里克 · 刘易斯

献给爱自然，爱诗歌的大小朋友们！

——Abby

美国童诗桂冠诗人［美］J.帕特里克·刘易斯　主编
Abby F. Yehenola ❁ 张原平 ❁ 和览　编译

NATIONAL GEOGRAPHIC
美国国家地理

book of nature poetry
最美自然诗集 2

（汉英对照）

200首诗歌
和会漂浮
会穿越，
会开花
的精彩图片

河南科学技术出版社
·郑州·

千山鸟飞绝，
万径人踪灭。
孤舟蓑笠翁，
独钓寒江雪。

这是唐朝柳宗元的《江雪》。短短的20个字，便成功捕捉一幅美丽的风景画。当时的孤冷静谧与雪白世界，似乎透过这首诗被永久封存，美丽了好几千年，不曾消逝。

《最美自然诗集》的出版，重新带给我这样的震撼与感动。随着时代的变迁，生活节奏的加快，文字阅读耗费时间，致使读者更为钟情图像阅读。不过图像阅读与文字阅读所获得的乐趣，无法互相取代。纵使是对同个风景的描绘，使用新诗文字创作与照片图像创作，让读者感受到的乐趣亦是截然不同。若是舍弃文字的阅读，全都转向图像阅读，实在相当可惜。《最美自然诗集》却完美解决了这个问题：这本诗集的每首诗，都是一张照片加上一首诗，使得文字文本和图像文本相互合作对话，形成一支精彩的双人舞。

这本书真的让我重新认识美丽的地球！在大自然中，随着四季的交替、地形的差异、气候的更迭，每一刹那的风景都是独一无二、稍纵即逝的。照片是静态的叙事，透过摄影师的镜头，有意识地捕捉吉光片羽，所以一张张的美照，是摄影师透过自身的美学哲学与镜头的选择所决定的，也可以说照片是摄影师眼中的美景。

而诗的创作，则是透过诗人纤细善感的心思，触景生情，把当时的生命状态转化成诗句，以情寓景，让景物多了一股人情的芬芳，不少美景在诗句的化妆下，变得充满情韵，让人印象深刻。

除此之外，这本书的编者扮演着隐形创作者的角色，因为他们成功媒合了照片与诗句，让作品更有一层乐趣。诗句的意象让静态的照片翩然生动，仿佛可以听见照片中的潺潺流水声，让读者宛若身临其境，感受照片里的一草一木，让读者悠游在每幅照片之中。阅读《最美自然诗集》，需要最好的领航员同游，我们的译者充分领会了编者的匠心独运，十分用心地录制了200首音频，恰是《最美自然诗集》最好的导读。

这本诗集让读者感受到三种美学：文学之美、摄影之美以及想象之美。透过诗句，让读者感受到文字透过意象诠释的美学；透过摄影照片让读者感受到强烈的视觉盛宴。当今的科技，无论是手机、电视还是穿戴科技等等，均试图以科技的力量，让读者感受到身临其境的感官盛宴，增强读者的视觉与听觉震撼，产生娱乐感，但是与此同时，相对地也剥夺了读者想象之美的权利。而《最美自然诗集》在照片与文字当中，保留了相当多的空白，并分类为“感叹自然”“凌空”“渊洋”“生灵”“山川”“美植”“灾难”“四季”“奇景”“敬畏自然”，让读者可以发挥想象，感受编者所安排的想象之美。因此，阅读这本书让读者经历一场美学盛宴，沉醉在大自然的洗礼之中。

最后，从这本书中也可以看出编者对于环境保护的意识。人类过度开发，使得环境被破坏，导致气候异常，很多珍稀动物濒临灭绝，大自然也不再美丽。希望这本诗集，能唤起人类对于大自然的重新思考，思考如何与环境共生。

透过这本最美丽的诗集，让我们回忆起我们曾经的美好！伟哉自然，伟哉生命！

林文宝

· 译者序 ·

25首关于大海的诗，给我们带来了海的声音、海的腥味、海的清凉。

海边总会是一个有故事的地方，这里有会签名的海潮、来淘金的小鸟和让我们不想离开的风景。

诗人总喜欢把大自然的某些精神寄托在人的身上，例如《黑人兄弟论江河》，如江河澎湃般将黑人的历史和精神表达出来，真难得。

这首关于密西西比河的诗真是不一般，译者竟然用虞美人的词牌把它翻译了出来。

你去过加拉帕戈斯群岛吗？这里有番茄一样红的螃蟹、身着锦缎的大蜥蜴、亮黄色的嘲鸫……读完这首诗，你一定想去那里看看。

你听说过圣埃尔莫之火吗？这种被水手神化了的火焰据说可以保佑他们的平安，到底是怎么回事？请读这首诗。

罗马尼亚有一个瀑布群，被称为世界必去的地方，水如牙线一般落下来，这首诗告诉你它们是怎么形成的。

加拿大的亚伯拉罕湖底有条会喷火的龙，一到冬天就吐泡泡，可是，泡泡却被冻在冰层中。去不了？没关系，读诗就算去过了。

卡明斯堪称一名奇葩诗人了，所谓的奇葩就是想怎么写就怎么写，语法、标点什么都不在乎，来读读这首关于海边小姑娘们的诗。

克里斯蒂娜 · 罗塞蒂是我非常喜爱的诗人，这首诗只有四句，可却把真理写得如此深入人心。

死海的形成可不是个神话，这首诗可以作证，而且还告诉了你更多的科普知识。

美国土著人的历史和河流分不开，虽然土著文化在消失，可是他们给河流留下了美丽的名字，一首诗让你熟练掌握这些名字。

《一个孩子的诗园》堪称英文童诗历史上的必读，本书关于小船的这首诗就出自于此。

有首关于沼泽的诗真是给我的翻译工作带来了极大的困难，而一旦翻译出来了，就对这首诗爱不释手。

《最美自然诗集》中终于来了一首关于中国景观的诗，可却又出现了一个大乌龙，快扫二维码听听我采访当地人揭开这个错误的秘密。

在圣诞岛上，每到繁殖季，漫天遍野的红色小螃蟹从森林里爬到海边约会，然后再爬回去，这个景观你如果不去就很难领略到，除非你来读读这首诗。

大蓝洞一直是潜水爱好者的宝地，本书有两首诗，从不同角度告诉我们大蓝洞是如何形成的。

Abby 2017年10月于昆明

IN THE SEA

渊洋

J. PATRICK LEWIS HAS WRITTEN MORE THAN 95 PICTURE AND POETRY BOOKS FOR YOUNG READERS. IN 2011 HE WAS APPOINTED U.S. CHILDREN'S POET LAUREATE, AND WAS GIVEN THE NATIONAL COUNCIL OF TEACHERS OF ENGLISH AWARD FOR EXCELLENCE IN POETRY FOR CHILDREN.

HENRY DAVID THOREAU was one of America's truly Big Thinkers on a little pond—Walden Pond. It was there in 1853, in a self-built cabin not far from his Massachusetts family home, that he wrote: "I have a room all to myself; it is nature."

From his tucked-away cottage, Thoreau produced some of the most profound thoughts on Mother Nature. But poets from centuries past rarely wrote about the more exotic natural wonders. They never saw them, never knew they existed. Many of the most fascinating phenomena that we often take for granted today—thanks to the convenience of travel, books, or photographs—were seldom brought to the attention of the classical poets.

How would William Shakespeare or John Keats have described in a poem the grandeur of the Grand Canyon? One can only imagine Emily Dickinson, transported to the scene, painting on an easel built of words a picture of an Asian tsunami or an African drought. What immortal verse might William Wordsworth have written after a day's walk in the Amazon rain forest instead of the English countryside? What picture would Kobayashi Issa or Li Po paint after a submersible dive to the ocean deep?

And yet a poet does not have to be there! You needn't leave your chair to write a poem about the wilder shores of creation. A book is your ticket to ride; a photograph is rapid transit to the brain. What kind of poem would you write if all you had in front of you was an image, like one of the breathtaking pictures in the *Book of Nature Poetry* you are now holding?

Better yet, let your eyes be your camera, taking incredible pictures your brain will thank you for. Get up and go there! Explore the woods, a cave; climb a mountain; go scuba diving; or simply make a friend of a grasshopper in a field on a windy summer day. You might even imagine you *are* that dragonfly trying to escape a swift, or a lucky salmon that has wiggled through the legs of a grizzly bear.

Travel by photograph or on foot, but go quickly before nature disappears. Every day more than 70 animals, plants, or other living things, like fungi, roots, and molds, vanish forever. The *Book of Nature Poetry* seeks to capture the ever changing nature of nature, so that gone is not forgotten. Besides, when more of us care for nature, more can help save it.

However and wherever you greet the world outside your window, listen again to Mr. Thoreau for the last and best words of advice:

"It's not what you look at that matters. It's what you see."

—J. Patrick Lewis,
former U.S. Children's Poet Laureate

MALACHITE BUTTERFLY
孔雀石蝴蝶

J. 帕特里克·刘易斯已经为孩子们创作了95部图画书和诗集。2011年，他荣获了美国童诗桂冠诗人奖，并被美国国家英语教师委员会授予杰出童诗奖。

·前　言·

亨利·戴维·梭罗是美国真正的大思想家之一，他曾隐居在瓦尔登湖。

1853年，在离马萨诸塞州家不远的自建小木屋里，他写道：“我有一个只属于我自己的房间——大自然。”

就在这世外桃源般的小木屋里，梭罗萌发出一些关于大自然的极其深刻的思想。但是这几百年来，诗人们却很少再去描写更独特的自然奇观。他们从来没见过，甚至都不知晓它们的存在。很多今天我们习以为常的，可以从旅行、书籍或照片中轻松获取的绝世美景，以前却很少能引起古典诗人们的关注。

试想，莎士比亚和济慈会怎样用诗歌去描绘大峡谷的壮美？可想而知，若埃米莉·迪金森能亲临亚洲海啸或非洲干旱现场，她将会用文字绘制出怎样的一幅画卷。那华兹华斯呢？如果他有机会走在亚马孙雨林中，而不仅仅是在英国乡间小道徘徊，他的笔下会写出怎样的诗句呢？若小林一茶或李白能乘潜艇探访大洋深渊，他们诗作的意境又将是怎样的呢？

然而，诗人并非一定要身临其境。你不需要离开椅子才能去写沧海桑田。一本书可以带你去遨游，一张照片可以带你去穿越。如果你拥有的只是面前的一幅图，就像你手里的《最美自然诗集》中的任意一幅惊艳的美图一样，你能写出怎样的诗句呢？

更棒的是，去旅行，让眼睛成为你的照相机，让眼前的美景滋养你的大脑。去吧，去森林中历险，去探索一个洞穴，去勇攀一座高峰，去潜入海底；甚至去野地里和一只蚱蜢交个朋友，任夏风轻抚。你甚至可以去想象自己就是那只努力躲过雨燕的蜻蜓，或是那条幸运地游过灰熊两腿之间的三文鱼。

无论是借着照片观光还是身临其境，请尽早，赶在自然景观消失之前。每天，都有超过70种生物在地球上永远消失。《最美自然诗集》力图捕捉到大自然瞬息万变的属性，让逝去的不再被遗忘。同时，当有更多的人开始关心大自然时，便会有更多的人来拯救她。

无论你在哪里，用怎样的方式来向窗外的世界致敬，请你再一次，也是最后一次聆听梭罗先生的警世良言：

“重要的不是你眼前的，而是你心里的。”

——J. 帕特里克·刘易斯，美国童诗桂冠诗人

AURORA BOREALIS
北极光

The Thing Is the Thing Is Green

The thing is the thing is green and the green is green and by green I mean real mean green. I mean electric-eel green, alligator, iguana, anaconda green. I mean this thing has got all things green. It's got green turtles in turtle-green ponds and grasshoppers springing from groomed-green lawns and a green tree frog on a girl's left arm. It's got dark and dangerous greens. Greens you've never even seen greens. Ocean floor greens. Tornado sky greens. Tiger's eye greens. Eat-your-broccoli greens. Watermelons sparkling in the sun greens. Way beyond evergreen, this thing leaves green geckos on green leaves feeling green and green moths in the green dark and preying mantises on their thin green knees. It's a great and gorgeous green a light-bright-just-right-watch-it-grow-it-says-go shade of green. Have you guessed yet? Do you need another clue? Think rolling waves of grain green. Thick arms of vines climbing tall green trees. Mountains and mountains of green billions of waves reaching out of dark green seas all wrapped in one green ball and hung, an ornament in the sky. What a thing it must be to see the whole green thing floating by. It's true. The thing is the thing is green . . .

except when it's blue.

—Peggy Gifford

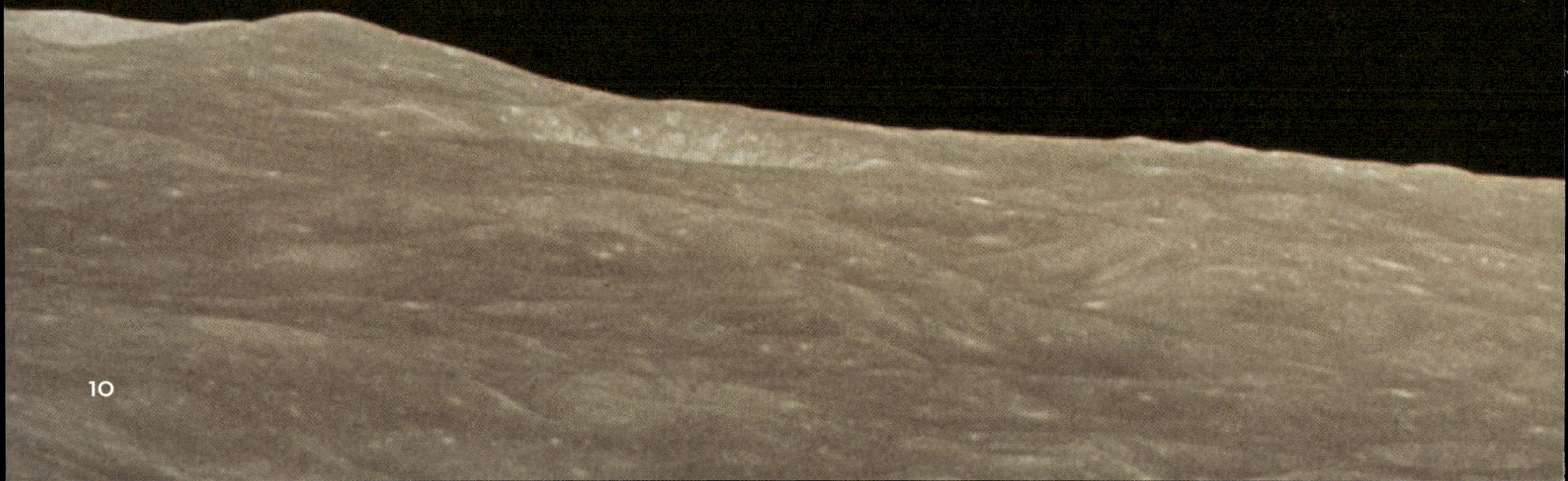

它要多绿就有多绿

要多绿就有多绿，绿就绿它个透心绿，就是这么绿，实打实的绿。我讲的是电鳗绿、鳄鱼绿、蜥蜴绿、蟒蛇绿，我说的这种绿把所有东西都染绿了。瞧那绿龟徜徉在龟绿色的池塘里，蚱蜢从刚修绿的草坪里一跃而起，一只绿树蛙停歇在女孩的左臂。有时候，它绿得阴森，绿得凶险，绿得其实你从未见过。大洋底的深渊绿，龙卷风的虐绿，老虎眼底的幽绿，“吃完西兰花”的郁闷绿，西瓜在阳光下的闪耀绿。比常绿植物更绿的，是绿叶上享绿的绿色壁虎、沉绿夜空的绿色飞蛾、紧绷双膝的绿色螳螂。 它绿得伟大，绿得华丽，那“趁着阳光正好赶快生长说长就长”的一抹绿。还没有猜出来吗？还需要再来一点提示吗？想想那绿色的麦浪翻滚，想想那粗壮的藤蔓攀上绿色的参天大树。连绵不绝的绿色山峦，深绿海洋中的滔天巨澜，竟都被包在一个绿色的球里，独具一格地装点着天空。能亲眼看见这大绿球飘过该是一件多么大的幸事啊。没错，它要多绿就有多绿……

除非它变蓝了……

——佩姬·吉福德

IN THE

GHOST CRAB, BAHIA, BRAZIL
沙蟹，巴伊亚，巴西

SEA

Tideline

Ocean draws on the sand
with trinkets of shell and stone,
the way I write on the sidewalk
with a stick of chalk at home.

She signs her name in letters
long and wavy and clear,
saying, "Don't forget me—

I was here,
    wasss h e r e
        wasssss h e r e . . ."

—Kate Coombs

By the Sea

The visitors strolling the sand
Look like they're willing to pay—
Though the ocean isn't selling
And the sun is closing for the day.

Still the walkers keep trolling
The purple shore, bags in hand,
And the sinking sun keeps tossing its gold
Recklessly on the sand.

We will scurry home with our haul tonight,
Dreaming of golden sand,
While the sea keeps throwing its treasures
Out as far and as fast as it can.

—Liz Rosenberg

At Seacliff Cottage

The breeze breezing me.
The sun sunning me.

The gulls arching.
The mist prancing over the waves.

The salted caramel spray
tanging the air.

The train whistling by,
low and wistful.

Some bird I've never heard before
wistfulling back.

A dragonfly
glinting by . . .

Who knew heaven could be rented?
Not I.

—Sonya Sones

SURF IN HAWAII, U.S.A.
夏威夷的海浪，美国

Haiku

bass
picking bugs
off the moon

—Nick Virgilio

LARGEMOUTH BASS
加州鲈

The Negro Speaks of Rivers

To W. E. B. DuBois

I've known rivers:
I've known rivers ancient as the world and older than the flow of human blood in human veins.

My soul has grown deep like the rivers.

I bathed in the Euphrates when dawns were young.
I built my hut near the Congo and it lulled me to sleep.
I looked upon the Nile and raised the pyramids above it.
I heard the singing of the Mississippi when Abe Lincoln went down to New Orleans, and I've seen its muddy bosom turn all golden in the sunset.

I've known rivers:
Ancient, dusky rivers.

My soul has grown deep like the rivers.

—Langston Hughes

MISSISSIPPI RIVER, MISSISSIPPI, U.S.A.
密西西比河，密西西比州，美国

The Mississippi

I heard it creep down from the north
at first in whispers, then it clapped
a river tune, and danced to steam—
blue tributaries bounding forth
from where geography had mapped
itself a continental stream.

I sat along the sandy bank,
like many a cane pole country boy,
to watch the waters lazing by.
Who cared if our red bobbers sank?
This mirror river of Illinois
reflected the enormous sky.

—Anonymous

Galápagos: Hood Island

Here's what I saw today:
a dazzling display of exotic wildlife
quietly sunbathing
side by side on the rocks:
Sally Lightfoot crabs, vivid as ripe tomatoes;
languid black lizards;
marine iguanas in dark brocade coats
now swathed
in turquoise and red;
seabirds swooping overhead;
pert yellow mockingbirds investigating the beach;
and sea lions of all sizes
snoozing, snuggling, swimming—
large eyes curious
velvety fur inviting
the forbidden touch of fingertips.
This is, I thought,
growing as fearlessly relaxed as the animals,
"The Peaceable Kingdom."

—*Bobbi Katz*

SALLY LIGHTFOOT CRAB, GALÁPAGOS, ECUADOR
莎莉飞毛腿蟹，加拉帕戈斯，厄瓜多尔

NORTH SEA BLUE PEBBLES
北海蓝鹅卵石

St. Elmo's Fire

On the deck of the frigate
Sailors dropped to their knees.
As lightning flashed out of the west,
All eyes rose toward heaven.
Thunder drummed the skin of the sky.

The main masthead threw blue flames
While they whispered *spirit candles*
And crossed themselves—
St. Elmo's divine lantern
Come to light their way.

—Georgia Heard

Old Man Ocean

Old Man Ocean, how do you pound
Smooth glass, rough stones round?
Time and the tide and the wild waves rolling
Night and the wind and the long gray dawn.

Old Man Ocean, what do you tell,
What do you sing in the empty shell?
Fog and the storm and the long bell tolling,
Bones in the deep and the brave men gone.

—Russell Hoban

Bigar Cascade Falls, Romania

It's possible
a frost giant
tossed a
stony saucer
across the river
and left a fossil
faucet on
in a rocky posture of
loss,
awesome and
austere,
still glossy with
moss
and a docile
jostling of waterfall
floss.

—Steven Withrow

BIGAR CASCADE FALLS, ROMANIA
比加尔瀑布，罗马尼亚

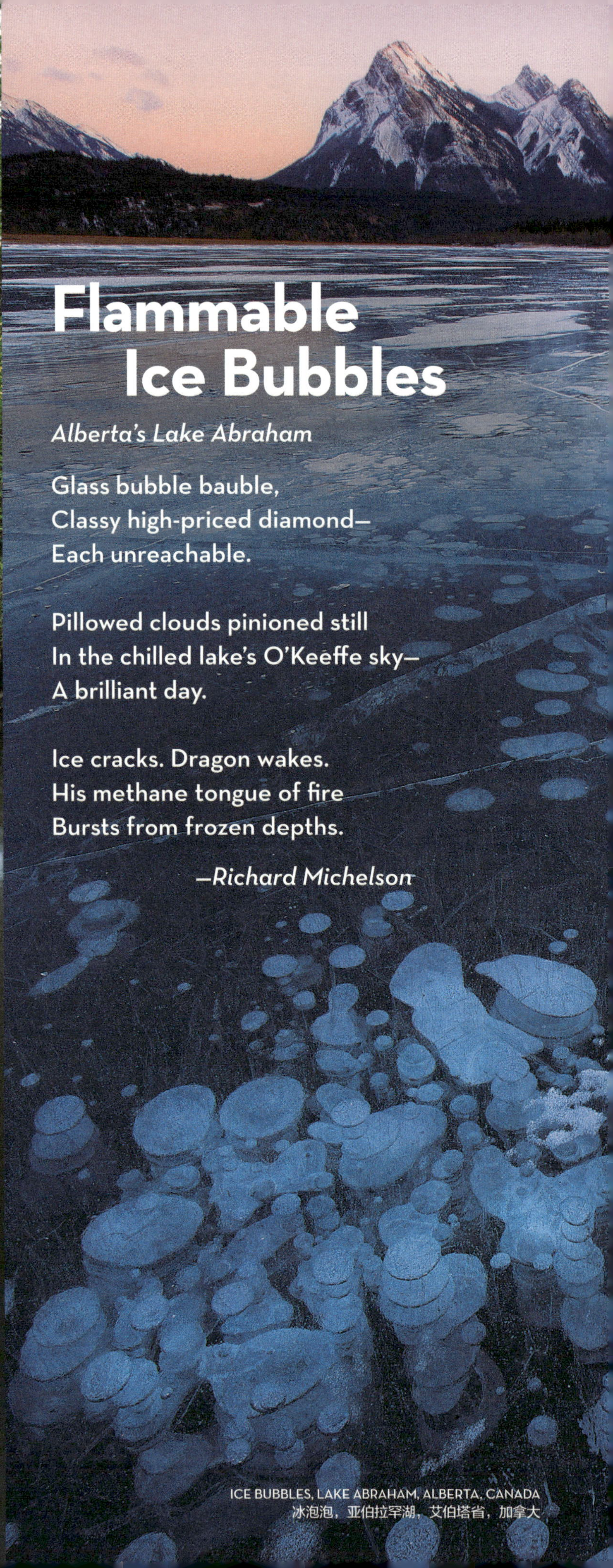

Flammable Ice Bubbles

Alberta's Lake Abraham

Glass bubble bauble,
Classy high-priced diamond—
Each unreachable.

Pillowed clouds pinioned still
In the chilled lake's O'Keeffe sky—
A brilliant day.

Ice cracks. Dragon wakes.
His methane tongue of fire
Bursts from frozen depths.

—Richard Michelson

ICE BUBBLES, LAKE ABRAHAM, ALBERTA, CANADA
冰泡泡，亚伯拉罕湖，艾伯塔省，加拿大

Lost Giant

A wetland spans a continent
across to such an elephant
as I, who knows the nomad bird
alone can fly him to the herd.

—Mariel Bede

AFRICAN ELEPHANT, MAPUTO ELEPHANT RESERVE, MOZAMBIQUE
非洲象，马普托大象保护区，莫桑比克

maggie and milly and molly and may

maggie and milly and molly and may
went down to the beach(to play one day)

and maggie discovered a shell that sang
so sweetly she couldn't remember her troubles,and

milly befriended a stranded star
whose rays five languid fingers were;

and molly was chased by a horrible thing
which raced sideways while blowing bubbles:and

may came home with a smooth round stone
as small as a world and as large as alone.

For whatever we lose(like a you or a me)
it's always ourselves we find in the sea

—*e. e. cummings*

BLUE SEA STAR AND BAITFISH
蓝海星与饵鱼

Until I Saw the Sea

Until I saw the sea
I did not know
that wind
could wrinkle water so.

I never knew
that sun
could splinter a whole sea of blue.

Nor
did I know before,
a sea breathes in and out
upon a shore.

—Lilian Moore

What Are Heavy?

What are heavy? Sea-sand and sorrow:
What are brief? To-day and to-morrow:
What are frail? Spring blossoms and youth:
What are deep? The ocean and truth.

—Christina Rossetti

The Dead Sea

A salt lake bordering Jordan to the east
and Israel and Palestine to the west

Somewhere down and down below
at the bottom of the bottom, this place
claims no skeletons or bones
under its brackish face;

it spits a rain of brimstone
in a sulphur somersault,
from out of the dark it bubbles
with salt
        and salt
                and salt.

—Rebecca Kai Dotlich

SALT CRYSTALS, DEAD SEA, ISRAEL
盐结晶，死海，以色列

Like Ghosts of Eagles

The Indians have mostly gone
but not before they named the rivers
the rivers flow on
and the names of the rivers flow with them
    Susquehanna   Shenandoah

The rivers are now polluted plundered
but not the names of the rivers
cool and inviolate as ever
pure as on the morning of creation
    Tennessee   Tombigbee

If the rivers themselves should ever perish
I think the names will somehow somewhere hover
like ghosts of eagles
those mighty whisperers
    Missouri   Mississippi.

—Robert Francis

BLUE SPRING, MISSOURI, U.S.A.
蓝泉，密苏里州，美国

Ammonites: Sculptures of the Sea

Nestled in the outermost chamber
of their self-sculpted spirals,
ammonites sleep deep till nightfall,

safely ascend to the ocean surface—
letting air into each chamber—
then scavenge till daylight

signals them to silently sink
back down on their sides
like rugged handmade plates.

—Betsy Franco

AMMONITE SPIRAL SNAIL FOSSIL
鹦鹉螺化石

Where Go the Boats?

Dark brown is the river,
Golden is the sand.
It flows along for ever,
With trees on either hand.

Green leaves a-floating,
Castles of the foam,
Boats of mine a-boating—
Where will all come home?

On goes the river
And out past the mill,
Away down the valley,
Away down the hill.

Away down the river,
A hundred miles or more,
Other little children
Shall bring my boats ashore.

—Robert Louis Stevenson

The Mill Back Home

Logs drowse in the pond
Dreaming of their heroes
Alligator and crocodile

—Vern Rutsala

ROCK CREEK, WASHINGTON, D.C., U.S.A.
罗克溪，华盛顿州，美国

BAYOU SAUVAGE NATIONAL WILDLIFE REFUGE, LOUISIANA, U.S.A.
苏瓦吉河口国家野生动物保护区，路易斯安那州，美国

In the Salt Marsh

How faithfully grass holds the shape of the sea it loves,
how it molds itself to the waves, how the dried salt
peaks into cowlicks the combed mane of the marsh.
Tousled by tides, it pitches tents, breaks into turrets
and coxcombs and whorled nests and green baskets
for the bleached armor of fiddler crabs, like earrings
hung by the sea on lobes of darkness. Could I lay my ear
on that darkness where the tide's trowel smooths islands
and scallops the sand, moon-tugged, till it slows
and turns? Could I keep the past in the present's eye?
Could I know what the grass knows?

—Nancy Willard

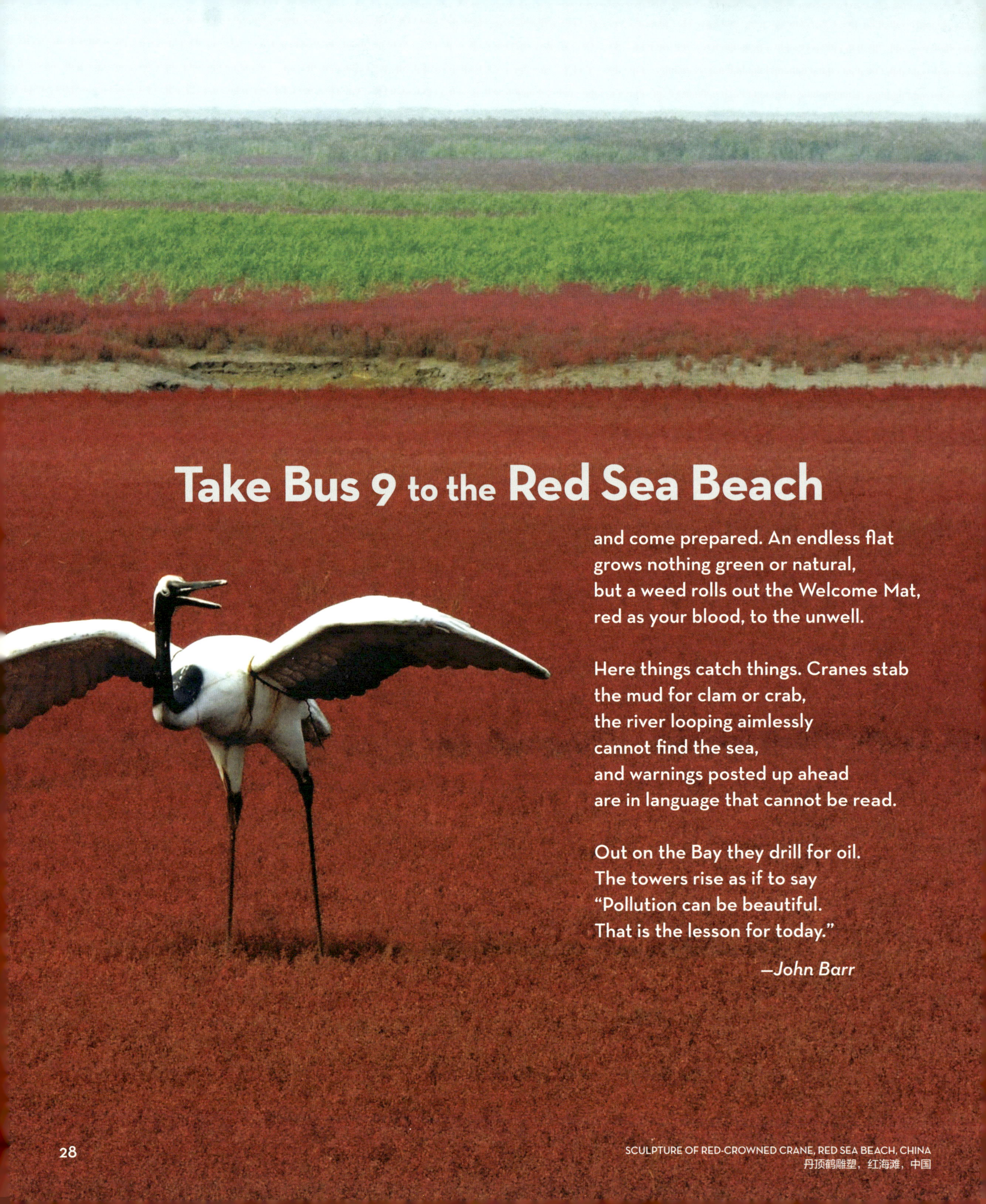

Take Bus 9 to the Red Sea Beach

and come prepared. An endless flat
grows nothing green or natural,
but a weed rolls out the Welcome Mat,
red as your blood, to the unwell.

Here things catch things. Cranes stab
the mud for clam or crab,
the river looping aimlessly
cannot find the sea,
and warnings posted up ahead
are in language that cannot be read.

Out on the Bay they drill for oil.
The towers rise as if to say
"Pollution can be beautiful.
That is the lesson for today."

—John Barr

SCULPTURE OF RED-CROWNED CRANE, RED SEA BEACH, CHINA
丹顶鹤雕塑，红海滩，中国

CHRISTMAS ISLAND RED CRABS, CHRISTMAS ISLAND, AUSTRALIA
圣诞岛红蟹，圣诞岛，澳大利亚

The Red Crabs of Christmas Island

From the forest, males are sprawling.
Over craggy cliffs, they're crawling,
scuttling toward the sea.

Into sandy shores, they furrow,
digging a protective burrow,
near the sounding sea.

Now the frantic females hurry.
To the waiting males they scurry,
skittering toward the sea.

Eggs are laid where water's creeping.
Waves come closer, sweeping, sweeping
egg sacs out to sea.

Baby crabs, born in the ocean,
synchronize their sideways motion.
Millions leave the seas,

and head back to the trees.

—B. J. Lee

The Great BLUE HOLE

Off the coast of Belize

Dark, dead, no current
four hundred feet deep

Rise now from the bottom, peer into
an ancient, gaping cavern as you ascend, touch
stalactites hanging like monstrous jungle vines, meet
sleek reef sharks circling, shadows in shallows, feel
the reassuring slope of sandy limestone shelf, spot
sunlit coral fringe, turtles, tropical fish, and

Break through! Breathe air! Surface
into the last ice age, witness
water carve cave from rock, gasp
as the sea rushes in, tremble
as a dry roof collapses, flee
as formation drowns, marvel

as it is sucked into vast chasm
abyss of blue intensity born

—Donna Marie Merritt

I Owe It All to Water

The Great Blue Hole, Belize

Back in the ice age,
I became a cave.
In my hollow heart, I meditated
on my maker.

Water's three little atoms have such power:
dripping steadily,
grinding microscopically,
sculpting artistically.

Suddenly
(or so it seemed)
the oceans rose, my ceiling fell, and I was completely
submerged. Filled to the brim. Literally.

Now I am a deep, indigo blue. A circular
sapphire in a turquoise sea: singular.
Breathtakingly spectacular.
And I owe it all to water.

—Mary Lee Hahn

HOLTUN CENOTE, MEXICO
荷顿岩洞，墨西哥

IN THE

GHOST CRAB, BAHIA, BRAZIL
沙蟹，巴伊亚，巴西

渊洋

SEA

P14

Tideline

浪的杰作

海水爱画画，
贝壳、石子，玲珑剔透，
画在沙滩上。
就像我一样，
抄起一支粉笔挥洒在人行道上。
她的签名长长的、弯弯的、清清楚楚的，
写道："别忘了我——
我来过，
我——来——过——
来——过——"

——凯特·库姆斯

P15

At Seacliff Cottage

我的海崖小屋

来，微风轻抚，
来，太阳光照，
来，海鸥跳跃，
薄雾欢腾于海波之上，
空气中弥漫着咸咸的焦糖味儿。

列车呼啸而过，低沉而惆怅，
听，陌生的鸟儿伤感地回应。
看，一闪而过的蜻蜓，
天堂能被租借吗？
当然不能。

——索尼娅·索恩斯

P14

By the Sea

海边

访客在沙滩踱来踱去，
看起来想要买点什么。
可大海不想卖了，
太阳也要打烊了。

漫步者继续寻寻觅觅，
在迷紫的海岸，收获满满，
下沉的太阳依旧不在乎地
向沙滩投撒金币。

今晚我们将满载而归，
梦回金色海滩，
大海依然
又快又远地将财宝抛撒。

——利兹·罗森堡

P16

Haiku

俳句·鲈鱼

鲈鱼
帮月亮
捡虫子。

——尼克·维尔吉利奥

The Negro Speaks of Rivers

P16

黑人兄弟论江河

献给 W.E.B. 杜波依斯

我知江河：
我知世界命立之际的江河，
远早于人类脉动中流淌的血液。

我的灵魂，
如江河般深奥难寻。

我出浴在幼发拉底河时，
黎明尚且稚嫩。
我落脚于刚果河畔，
潺潺翻动哄我入眠。

我放眼尼罗河，
将一座座金字塔矗立其上。
我听过密西西比河的欢唱，
伴着林肯的大军直下新奥尔良，
我也曾看到它沾满污泥的胸膛翻身挺起，
在落日的余晖中闪着金光。

我知江河：
古老，幽暗的江河。

我的灵魂，
如它般深奥难寻。

——兰斯顿·休斯

The Mississippi

P17

虞美人·密西西比

源流淙淙顺北来，拍岸和蒸腾。
碧波款款奔东西，勿忘母江盘绘大陆基。

乔装垂钓卧沙岸，静赏悠水踱。
谁人觉察鱼咬钩，只缘庞空争投明鉴流。

——无名氏

Galápagos: Hood Island

P18

加拉帕戈斯的胡德岛

这是今天映入我眼帘的景象，
一排眼花缭乱的奇异海洋生物，
悠然地肩并肩在石头上晒太阳。
莎莉飞毛腿蟹，通红得有如熟透了的番茄，
懒洋洋的黑蜥蜴来做陪衬，
海鬣蜥一改往日的暗黑锦袍
将红红绿绿尽情往身上裹，
海鸟从头顶俯冲而下，
牛哄哄的黄色嘲鸫负责地盘查着海滩，
大小各异的海狮
睡睡觉、游游泳、你侬我侬——
大眼睛灵光闪烁，
缎子般的皮毛充满诱惑，
摸一下，怎么样？
我想，所谓“和平王国”，
不正是像这些动物那样
无畏而悠闲地生活？

——鲍比·卡茨

St. Elmo's Fire

P19

圣埃尔莫之火

水手们的双膝跪拜在
舰艇的甲板上，
闪电划破了西天，
众人仰望天堂，
响雷轰打着天空的皮膜。

桅顶瞬时喷出蓝色火焰，
水手默念着灵火，
胸前画十字——
来吧！圣埃尔莫的神圣火盏，
来光照我们的前程吧。

——乔治娅·赫德

Old Man Ocean

P19

老人海

老人海，
你如何将光滑玻璃、粗糙石块
拍打至圆润？
老人海，
时光、潮汐，狂澜翻腾，
黑夜、大风，黎明灰暗。

老人海，
空空的贝壳中，
有你怎样的诉说和吟唱？
老人海，
大雾、暴风，哀钟长鸣，
白骨深葬，勇者已殇。

——拉塞尔·霍本

Bigar Cascade Falls, Romania

P20

罗马尼亚比加尔瀑布

想想肯定是这样：
一个满头白霜的大巨人
把一个大石盘扔过河，
一不小心
忘了关那化石级别的水龙头，
却歪打正着，
朴实而宏伟，
布满青苔，
却光泽有加，
含蓄的水流，
推推搡搡，
垂丝落下。

——史蒂文·威思罗

Flammable Ice Bubbles

P20

燃烧吧，冰泡泡！

艾伯塔省的亚伯拉罕湖

晶莹剔透的小泡泡，
上等的昂贵钻石——
你就是够不着。

枕头般的云朵被冻在
奥基夫画笔下的刺骨寒湖——
天气不错。

冰裂开，
龙醒来。
沼气火舌
冲破冰封的深渊。

——理查德·米切尔森

Lost Giant

P21

走失的巨象

湿地横贯大地，
巨象隔岸孤立，
迷象如我，
知牧鸟亦可独影渡其归。

——玛丽埃尔·比德

maggie and milly and molly and may

P22

玛吉、米利、莫莉和梅

玛吉、米利、莫莉和梅
一起去沙滩玩，

玛吉找到一个会唱歌的贝壳，
甜美的歌声让她忘记一切烦恼。

米利交了个搁浅的朋友，
是只懒洋洋的海星。

莫莉被一个怪物追得乱跑，
横冲直撞还满嘴泡泡。

梅带回家一块又滑又圆的石头，
小不过世界，大不过自己。

不管我们丢了什么（哪怕是个你，哪怕是个我），
总会在海里找回自己。

——e. e. 卡明斯

P23

Until I Saw the Sea

见到海之前

见到海之前，
我不会知道，
风
可吹皱大水，凸凸凹凹。

我亦可疑惑，
阳
可打碎大蓝，闪闪烁烁。

我从不清楚
海
可喘息至岸，一吸一吐。

——莉莲·穆尔

P23

What Are Heavy?

何为深重？

何为深重？海沙和痛苦。
何为短暂？今日和明天。
何为脆弱？春花和年轻。
何为深奥？大洋和真理。

——克里斯蒂娜·罗塞蒂

P24

The Dead Sea

死海

一汪咸水湖东坐约旦肩，
西投巴以怀

水之深，深不可测，
渊之深，深不见底，
苦涩的湖面下从未存留任何遗骸。

翻腾之间，
喷吐出硫黄火舌，
暗中，它沸腾出
盐，
盐，
还是盐。

——丽贝卡·卡伊·多特里奇

P25

Like Ghosts of Eagles

印第安人要走了，
走前没忘给河流取好名字。
河流奔流向前，
它们的名字也随波逐流，
萨斯奎哈纳、谢南多厄。

河流已被污染，侵吞，
但名字没有，
依然镇定自若，神圣不可侵犯，
圣洁，有如创世之初，
田纳西、汤比格比。

若河水枯竭，
名字却冥冥中犹如鹰的灵魂，
盘旋上空，
这些庞然大物窃窃私语着
密苏里、密西西比。

——罗伯特·弗朗西斯

P25

Ammonites: Sculptures of the Sea

鹦鹉螺：海中雕塑

鹦鹉螺，海中的能工巧匠，
休憩在亲自打造的螺旋闺房。
鹦鹉螺，一睡睡到夜幕降临，
稳稳当当升到海平面，
给每间屋子都充充气，
接下来，扫荡晚餐直到天亮，
阳光示意小房子们悄悄落下，
侧躺下，就当是纯手工的粗糙餐盘吧。

——贝齐·佛朗哥

P27

In the Salt Marsh

盐碱滩的故事

草海如此忠贞不渝地拥抱着彼此，
如此把自己塑造成海浪，
沼泽刚刚打理好鬓发，干涸的盐块就偷偷躲进乱翘的杂毛。
潮汐来袭，
草海扎营、筑垒、织巢、编篮……
全为了招潮蟹们旧得泛白的盔甲，
就像大海用来装扮黑暗的耳环。
我能否在暗中倾听？
倾听潮汐削平岛屿，轻踏沙滩？
倾听月亮轻轻拉扯，渐缓渐落？
我若能将过去尘封在今天的眼眸中该多好！
我若能和草海知道的一样多该多好！

——南希·威拉德

P26

Where Go the Boats?

小船都去哪儿了？

黑沉的是河，金黄的是沙，
无休止地流淌，树儿两岸驻扎。

绿叶来飘摇，泡沫筑城堡，
小船尚在途中，何时把它们盼到？

顺着河水，行过磨坊，
漂过峡谷，穿过山冈。

就这么漂走了，
渡过万水千山，
其他小伙伴啊，
一定把它们带上岸。

——罗伯特·路易斯·史蒂文森

P26

The Mill Back Home

老家的磨坊

朽木在池水中昏昏欲睡，
睡梦中与它们的英雄相会——
各种鳄鱼……

——维恩·拉特萨拉

Take Bus 9 to the Red Sea Beach

P28

9路车直达红海滩

准备好了！
一眼望去，无绿，无自然景观，
只有这种红草来迎接你，
红得像血，像生病了一样。

在这里，生物之间互相厮杀，
仙鹤在泥里戳来戳去找贝壳、螃蟹，
河流瞎转圈圈，找不到大海，
警示牌上写的啥也看不懂。

远处的海湾里，有人在钻井打油。
高昂着头的钻井台好像在说：
“给你上一课，
污染也可以很美。”

——约翰·巴尔

The Red Crabs of Christmas Island

P29

圣诞岛红蟹

走出森林，公蟹们一路蔓延开来，
越过崎岖的峭壁，它们爬行，不辞辛劳，
迫不及待地冲向大海。

沙滩上，它们连日劳作，
连挖带刨打造保护窝，
紧临轰鸣的大海。

狂躁的母蟹们疾走如飞，
向翘首企盼的公蟹们急追，
轻快地奔向大海。

孵卵正值海水涨溢，
一浪，一浪，一落，一起，
把卵囊通通扫进大海。

螃蟹宝宝，海里出生，
齐刷刷天生横行。
成千上万离开大海，
返回森林，它们的家。

——B. J. 李

The Great BLUE HOLE

P30

大蓝洞

位于伯利兹外海

暗沉，死气，无水流过，
深至四百英尺。

从底部启程，
一边上升，一边探究
这古老的大洞穴，
触摸着如藤蔓般垂下的钟乳石，
偶遇光洁的礁鲨盘旋，投影至浅滩，
感受坚实的石灰岩沙坡，
瞥见洒满阳光的珊瑚礁边缘、海龟、热带鱼。

冲上来！喘口气！
漂浮在上个冰川纪，
目睹大水切石成洞，
惊叹海水倒灌，
震慑穹顶坍塌，
逃离巨阵淹溺，

感慨一切尽吸于大洞，
赞叹墨蓝深渊的降生。

——唐娜·玛丽·梅里特

I Owe It All to Water

P31

一切归功于水

伯利兹，大蓝洞

冰川世纪，
我成了一个洞。
内心空空如也，
我冥想于造物主。

水的三个小原子竟然有如此能量，
坚持不懈地滴落，
一丝不苟地琢磨，
美轮美奂地镌刻。

突然
（起码看上去是这样），
海水上腾，我的屋顶坍塌，
我完全被淹没，
水溢至洞口。

如今，我深沉，靛蓝，
碧蓝大海上的一颗圆形蓝宝石，独一无二。
举世奇观，令人惊叹，
一切归功于水。

——玛丽·李·哈恩

Who is mother nature?

When Mother Nature's near—in waterfalls, rivers, rainbows, meadows, or oceans—her admirers react with love, awe, curiosity, even fear, if she decides to reveal her grumpier side. The lady can be seen through telescopes or microscopes, from mountaintops or ravines, with the wind in our hair, soil in our hands, or sand in our toes. For those who aren't hopelessly city-bound, looking out a window will do.

Driven to explore the *science* behind the wonder of it all, Charles Darwin filled scores of notebooks about what was then the unexplored wildlife of the Galápagos Islands. Countless nature writers have followed his courageous example. Others have put themselves in nature, like naturalist John Muir, who once rode out a northern American windstorm by cocooning himself in the branches of a sky-high Douglas spruce. (Muir is famous—or should be—for saying, "The clearest way into the Universe is through a forest wilderness.")

Some humans, however, have no use for wild places, a view once expressed by Woody Allen with his typical wit: "I love nature. I just don't want to get any of it on me." For some, their love for animals extends only as far as Fido or Sweet Pea. That we share the Earth equally with other creatures is a notion as foreign and irrelevant to them as the disappearance of the rain forests or the melting of the ice caps.

But Mother Nature doesn't care who likes her. Nor is she bothered about being ignored. A midwife at the birth of creatures large and small, she will go on making waves by making waves, assembling forests, flowering deserts, and beautifying gardens. We can embrace her or resist her charms; it is of no concern to her.

Who is the mysterious lady known as Mother Nature? She is the material world, the environment of trees, plants, animals, everything under and over the sun. In short, she equals the world around us and includes whatever is not built by human hands.

Mother Nature is where we live. In other words, she is
a refuge to the lost,
a magnet to the curious,
a dare to the daring,
the cradle of rapture,
the university of the universe,
the glory of a morning and of a morning-glory,
not a whale but the idea of a whale,
a sign rewriter: I Welcome All No Trespassing,
the best cure for couch disease,
an opera performed by birds, bullfrogs on drums,
the sound of silence . . . amplified
to the symphony of the spheres, and ____________
____.

Can you add another short description of Mother Nature to this poem?

The poets and photographers who have come together to produce National Geographic's *Book of Nature Poetry* would agree with John Keats, who defined their abiding faith: "The poetry of earth is never dead."

THREAD-WINGED ANTLION
线翅蚁狮

自然之母是谁?

当自然之母靠近的时候——在瀑布中，在河流中，在彩虹中，在草地或是海洋中——她的爱慕者用爱、敬畏、好奇来回应，甚至如果她显示暴躁的一面时，则用恐惧来回应。这位女士可以用望远镜或是显微镜来观察，从山顶到深谷，风在我们的发丝中穿过，泥土在我们手中漏出，沙在我们的脚趾中渗出。对于那些不喜欢住在城里的人来说，只要看一看窗外就行。

为了探索自然奇观背后的科学道理，查尔斯·达尔文把加拉帕戈斯群岛未知的野生动物记满了几十本笔记本。难以数计的自然主义作家跟随着他，以他为榜样。其他人则让自己融入自然。例如自然主义者约翰·缪尔，曾经用高耸入云的道格拉斯云杉的枝叶包裹着自己，经受住了北美的风暴。（缪尔由于下面这句话而知名——或应该知名——“融入宇宙最清晰的方式莫过于通过荒野森林”。）

然而，也有一些人，觉得野外毫无用处，这也是伍迪·艾伦用他特有的机智曾经表达的观点：“我爱自然，但是一点也别弄到我身上来。”而另一些人，他们对动物的喜爱只限于“菲多”或是“甜豌豆”。对他们来说，我们与其他生物平等地分享地球的观念，和雨林正在消失、冰层正在融化这样的概念一样，是未知而不重要的。

但自然之母并不关心谁喜欢她。她对这种忽视也毫不在意。她是大大小小各种生物出生时的产婆，她将不断在波浪中创造波浪，让森林遍地，让花朵在沙漠开放，让花园变得更美。我们可以接受或是抗拒她的魅力，她对此却毫不关心。

这位被人称为自然之母的神秘女士是谁？她是物质世界，也是植物、动物的环境和阳光下所有的一切。简言之，她就是我们周遭的世界，人类双手无法创造的世界。

自然之母在我们生活的地方。换句话说，

她是：

迷失者的庇护，

好奇者的磁石，

勇敢者的挑战，

狂喜者的摇篮，

宇宙的教化者。

她是：

清晨的光辉，

牵牛花的光，

并不是鲸鱼，

而是这创意。

她重新写了一个标记：我欢迎所有的非擅自闯入者。

她是：

沙发病的良药，

鸟儿、牛蛙在鼓上演奏的歌剧，

是寂静之声……被放大，

而成为万物的交响曲，

也是 ______________________

你可以在这首诗后面加上一段描写自然之母的短句吗？

共同创作《最美自然诗集》的诗人和摄影家们会同意约翰·济慈的话，他道出了他们永恒的信仰：“地球的诗篇永远不会消亡。”

LOTUS AND BEES-WUQIANG
荷花与蜜蜂（吴强）

美国国家地理学会是世界上最大的非营利科学与教育组织之一。学会成立于1888年，以“增进与普及地理知识”为宗旨，致力于启发人们对地球的关心。美国国家地理学会通过杂志、电视节目、影片、音乐、电台、图书、DVD、地图、展览、活动、学校出版计划、交互式媒体与商品来呈现世界。美国国家地理学会的会刊《国家地理》杂志，以英文及其他33种语言发行，每月有3800万读者阅读。美国国家地理频道在166个国家以34种语言播放，有3.2亿个家庭收看。美国国家地理学会资助超过10 000项科学研究、环境保护与探索计划，并支持一项扫除“地理文盲”的教育计划。

著作权合同备案号：豫著许可备字-2016-A-0212

Acknowledgments

To the entire National Geographic team for their enthusiasm and dedication in the making of this book, and to all the poets whose deserving work, regrettably, could not be squeezed into its pages.—JPL

The publisher gratefully acknowledges the heroic efforts of Natalie Turner in securing permissions, as well as the invaluable research assistance of Alyson Foster.

图书在版编目（CIP）数据

最美自然诗集 /（美）J. 帕特里克·刘易斯主编；Abby F. Yehenola，张原平，和览编译. —郑州：河南科学技术出版社，2018.1

ISBN 978-7-5349-8952-0

Ⅰ.①最… Ⅱ.①J… ②A… ③张… ④和… Ⅲ.①儿童诗歌-诗集-美国-现代 Ⅳ.①I712.82

中国版本图书馆CIP数据核字(2017)第269830号

出版发行：河南科学技术出版社

地址：郑州市经五路66号　邮编：450002

电话：（0371）65737028　65788613

网址：www.hnstp.cn

特邀策划：Abby F. Yehenola

策划编辑：马艳茹　韩雅楠　于凯燕

责任编辑：于凯燕

责任校对：徐小刚

整体设计：吴豆豆

责任印制：张　巍

印　　刷：北京盛通印刷股份有限公司

经　　销：全国新华书店

幅面尺寸：232 mm × 276 mm　印张：2.75　字数：69千字

版　　次：2018年1月第1版　2018年1月第1次印刷

全套定价：588.00元

To poets, nature, and nature poets everywhere.—JPL

献给诗人、自然和全世界写自然的诗人。

——J. 帕特里克 · 刘易斯

献给爱自然，爱诗歌的大小朋友们！

——Abby

美国童诗桂冠诗人［美］J.帕特里克·刘易斯 主编
Abby F. Yehenola ❁ 张原平 ❁ 和览 编译

NATIONAL GEOGRAPHIC
美国国家地理

book of nature poetry
最美自然诗集 3
（汉英对照）

200首诗歌
和会漂浮
会穿越，
会开花
的精彩图片

河南科学技术出版社
·郑州·

自然最美

千山鸟飞绝，
万径人踪灭。
孤舟蓑笠翁，
独钓寒江雪。

这是唐朝柳宗元的《江雪》。短短的20个字，便成功捕捉一幅美丽的风景画。当时的孤冷静谧与雪白世界，似乎透过这首诗被永久封存，美丽了好几千年，不曾消逝。

《最美自然诗集》的出版，重新带给我这样的震撼与感动。随着时代的变迁，生活节奏的加快，文字阅读耗费时间，致使读者更为钟情图像阅读。不过图像阅读与文字阅读所获得的乐趣，无法互相取代。纵使是对同个风景的描绘，使用新诗文字创作与照片图像创作，让读者感受到的乐趣亦是截然不同。若是舍弃文字的阅读，全都转向图像阅读，实在相当可惜。《最美自然诗集》却完美解决了这个问题：这本诗集的每首诗，都是一张照片加上一首诗，使得文字文本和图像文本相互合作对话，形成一支精彩的双人舞。

这本书真的让我重新认识美丽的地球！在大自然中，随着四季的交替、地形的差异、气候的更迭，每一刹那的风景都是独一无二、稍纵即逝的。照片是静态的叙事，透过摄影师的镜头，有意识地捕捉吉光片羽，所以一张张的美照，是摄影师透过自身的美学哲学与镜头的选择所决定的，也可以说照片是摄影师眼中的美景。

而诗的创作，则是透过诗人纤细善感的心思，触景生情，把当时的生命状态转化成诗句，以情寓景，让景物多了一股人情的芬芳，不少美景在诗句的化妆下，变得充满情韵，让人印象深刻。

除此之外，这本书的编者扮演着隐形创作者的角色，因为他们成功媒合了照片与诗句，让作品更有一层乐趣。诗句的意象让静态的照片翩然生动，仿佛可以听见照片中的潺潺流水声，让读者宛若身临其境，感受照片里的一草一木，让读者悠游在每幅照片之中。阅读《最美自然诗集》，需要最好的领航员同游，我们的译者充分领会了编者的匠心独运，十分用心地录制了200首音频，恰是《最美自然诗集》最好的导读。

这本诗集让读者感受到三种美学：文学之美、摄影之美以及想象之美。透过诗句，让读者感受到文字透过意象诠释的美学；透过摄影照片让读者感受到强烈的视觉盛宴。当今的科技，无论是手机、电视还是穿戴科技等等，均试图以科技的力量，让读者感受到身临其境的感官盛宴，增强读者的视觉与听觉震撼，产生娱乐感，但是与此同时，相对地也剥夺了读者想象之美的权利。而《最美自然诗集》在照片与文字当中，保留了相当多的空白，并分类为“感叹自然”“凌空”“渊洋”“生灵”“山川”“美植”“灾难”“四季”“奇景”“敬畏自然”，让读者可以发挥想象，感受编者所安排的想象之美。因此，阅读这本书让读者经历一场美学盛宴，沉醉在大自然的洗礼之中。

最后，从这本书中也可以看出编者对于环境保护的意识。人类过度开发，使得环境被破坏，导致气候异常，很多珍稀动物濒临灭绝，大自然也不再美丽。希望这本诗集，能唤起人类对于大自然的重新思考，思考如何与环境共生。

透过这本最美丽的诗集，让我们回忆起我们曾经的美好！伟哉自然，伟哉生命！

林文宝

· 译者序 ·

在自然诗集里面能读到动物的诗歌是不是很惊喜！如同重温《最美动物诗集》一般，这本书中，有21首关于动物的诗歌。动物也是自然的一部分，因着这些生灵的存在，自然界充满了勃勃的生机。

一只鹤会和一只青蛙有怎样的对话？不管它们说什么，这对冤家的对话你肯定要来围观一下。

你知道小丑鱼和海葵是亲密无间的朋友吗？海葵会蜇人，但对小丑鱼却一直友好，怎么回事呢？快来瞧瞧吧。

生活中处处有惊喜，诗人在路边遇到两匹马，很简单的一件事，却变成了他的幸事。

你见过美洲鸵吗？和鸵鸟差别不大，只是整了容。什么！整了容？赶紧读诗。

有一首诗把世界上最大的蝴蝶写得如此流光溢彩，快来领略一下。

再翻一页，你会看到几种奇异的小生物，例如会做俯卧撑的小蜥蜴、可以点亮整个纽约城的电鳗及会吟诗的蛐蛐和蟋蟀。

谁说美国人没有“旧”可怀，每每说到土著人，美国人就很怀旧，一首关于吃花长大的牛的诗道出了一切。

青蛙和蟾蜍有什么区别呢？原来青蛙爱吻公主，蟾蜍爱吻什么呢？读诗见答案。

杰克 · 普里卢斯基的一首《致生灵》堪称描写生灵的一绝，世上所有的生物都有自己的美，非同寻常的美。

翻到下一页，你会读到三首关于小鸟的诗，有不怕人的鹌鹑、死就死但从不自怜的鸟儿、用爱筑巢的主红雀。

如果你还在纠结是不是要减肥，这首关于鲸鱼的诗一定会让你释然。

这首尖嘴鱼的诗写得很巧妙，整首诗被排成了尖嘴鱼的形状。

当哲人要问大问题的时候，让他去问牛、羊、猪吧，回答一定会让其满意的。

一条大蛇旁边有三首诗，有关于横行霸道的蝎子的、关于会炼金术的蜈蚣的，还有让你看见就喊妈的巨蟒的。

Abby 2017年10月于昆明

ON THE MOVE 生灵

J. PATRICK LEWIS HAS WRITTEN MORE THAN 95 PICTURE AND POETRY BOOKS FOR YOUNG READERS. IN 2011 HE WAS APPOINTED U.S. CHILDREN'S POET LAUREATE, AND WAS GIVEN THE NATIONAL COUNCIL OF TEACHERS OF ENGLISH AWARD FOR EXCELLENCE IN POETRY FOR CHILDREN.

HENRY DAVID THOREAU was one of America's truly Big Thinkers on a little pond—Walden Pond. It was there in 1853, in a self-built cabin not far from his Massachusetts family home, that he wrote: "I have a room all to myself; it is nature."

From his tucked-away cottage, Thoreau produced some of the most profound thoughts on Mother Nature. But poets from centuries past rarely wrote about the more exotic natural wonders. They never saw them, never knew they existed. Many of the most fascinating phenomena that we often take for granted today—thanks to the convenience of travel, books, or photographs—were seldom brought to the attention of the classical poets.

How would William Shakespeare or John Keats have described in a poem the grandeur of the Grand Canyon? One can only imagine Emily Dickinson, transported to the scene, painting on an easel built of words a picture of an Asian tsunami or an African drought. What immortal verse might William Wordsworth have written after a day's walk in the Amazon rain forest instead of the English countryside? What picture would Kobayashi Issa or Li Po paint after a submersible dive to the ocean deep?

And yet a poet does not have to be there! You needn't leave your chair to write a poem about the wilder shores of creation. A book is your ticket to ride; a photograph is rapid transit to the brain. What kind of poem would you write if all you had in front of you was an image, like one of the breathtaking pictures in the *Book of Nature Poetry* you are now holding?

Better yet, let your eyes be your camera, taking incredible pictures your brain will thank you for. Get up and go there! Explore the woods, a cave; climb a mountain; go scuba diving; or simply make a friend of a grasshopper in a field on a windy summer day. You might even imagine you *are* that dragonfly trying to escape a swift, or a lucky salmon that has wiggled through the legs of a grizzly bear.

Travel by photograph or on foot, but go quickly before nature disappears. Every day more than 70 animals, plants, or other living things, like fungi, roots, and molds, vanish forever. The *Book of Nature Poetry* seeks to capture the ever changing nature of nature, so that gone is not forgotten. Besides, when more of us care for nature, more can help save it.

However and wherever you greet the world outside your window, listen again to Mr. Thoreau for the last and best words of advice:

"It's not what you look at that matters. It's what you see."

—J. Patrick Lewis,
former U.S. Children's Poet Laureate

MALACHITE BUTTERFLY
孔雀石蝴蝶

J. 帕特里克 · 刘易斯已经为孩子们创作了95部图画书和诗集。2011年，他荣获了美国童诗桂冠诗人奖，并被美国国家英语教师委员会授予杰出童诗奖。

·前　言·

亨利·戴维·梭罗是美国真正的大思想家之一，他曾隐居在瓦尔登湖。

1853年，在离马萨诸塞州家不远的自建小木屋里，他写道：“我有一个只属于我自己的房间——大自然。”

就在这世外桃源般的小木屋里，梭罗萌发出一些关于大自然的极其深刻的思想。但是这几百年来，诗人们却很少再去描写更独特的自然奇观。他们从来没见过，甚至都不知晓它们的存在。很多今天我们习以为常的，可以从旅行、书籍或照片中轻松获取的绝世美景，以前却很少能引起古典诗人们的关注。

试想，莎士比亚和济慈会怎样用诗歌去描绘大峡谷的壮美？可想而知，若埃米莉·迪金森能亲临亚洲海啸或非洲干旱现场，她将会用文字绘制出怎样的一幅画卷。那华兹华斯呢？如果他有机会走在亚马孙雨林中，而不仅仅是在英国乡间小道徘徊，他的笔下会写出怎样的诗句呢？若小林一茶或李白能乘潜艇探访大洋深渊，他们诗作的意境又将是怎样的呢？

然而，诗人并非一定要身临其境。你不需要离开椅子才能去写沧海桑田。一本书可以带你去遨游，一张照片可以带你去穿越。如果你拥有的只是面前的一幅图，就像你手里的《最美自然诗集》中的任意一幅惊艳的美图一样，你能写出怎样的诗句呢？

更棒的是，去旅行，让眼睛成为你的照相机，让眼前的美景滋养你的大脑。去吧，去森林中历险，去探索一个洞穴，去勇攀一座高峰，去潜入海底，甚至去野地里和一只蚱蜢交个朋友，任夏风轻抚。你甚至可以去想象自己就是那只努力躲过雨燕的蜻蜓，或是那条幸运地游过灰熊两腿之间的三文鱼。

无论是借着照片观光还是身临其境，请尽早，赶在自然景观消失之前。每天，都有超过70种生物在地球上永远消失。《最美自然诗集》力图捕捉到大自然瞬息万变的属性，让逝去的不再被遗忘。同时，当有更多的人开始关心大自然时，便会有更多的人来拯救她。

无论你在哪里，用怎样的方式来向窗外的世界致敬，请你再一次，也是最后一次聆听梭罗先生的警世良言：“重要的不是你眼前的，而是你心里的。”

——J. 帕特里克·刘易斯，美国童诗桂冠诗人

AURORA BOREALIS
北极光

The Thing Is the Thing Is Green

The thing is the thing is green and the green is green and by green I mean real mean green. I mean electric-eel green, alligator, iguana, anaconda green. I mean this thing has got all things green. It's got green turtles in turtle-green ponds and grasshoppers springing from groomed-green lawns and a green tree frog on a girl's left arm. It's got dark and dangerous greens. Greens you've never even seen greens. Ocean floor greens. Tornado sky greens. Tiger's eye greens. Eat-your-broccoli greens. Watermelons sparkling in the sun greens. Way beyond evergreen, this thing leaves green geckos on green leaves feeling green and green moths in the green dark and preying mantises on their thin green knees. It's a great and gorgeous green a light-bright-just-right-watch-it-grow-it-says-go shade of green. Have you guessed yet? Do you need another clue? Think rolling waves of grain green. Thick arms of vines climbing tall green trees. Mountains and mountains of green billions of waves reaching out of dark green seas all wrapped in one green ball and hung, an ornament in the sky. What a thing it must be to see the whole green thing floating by. It's true. The thing is the thing is green . . .

except when it's blue.

—Peggy Gifford

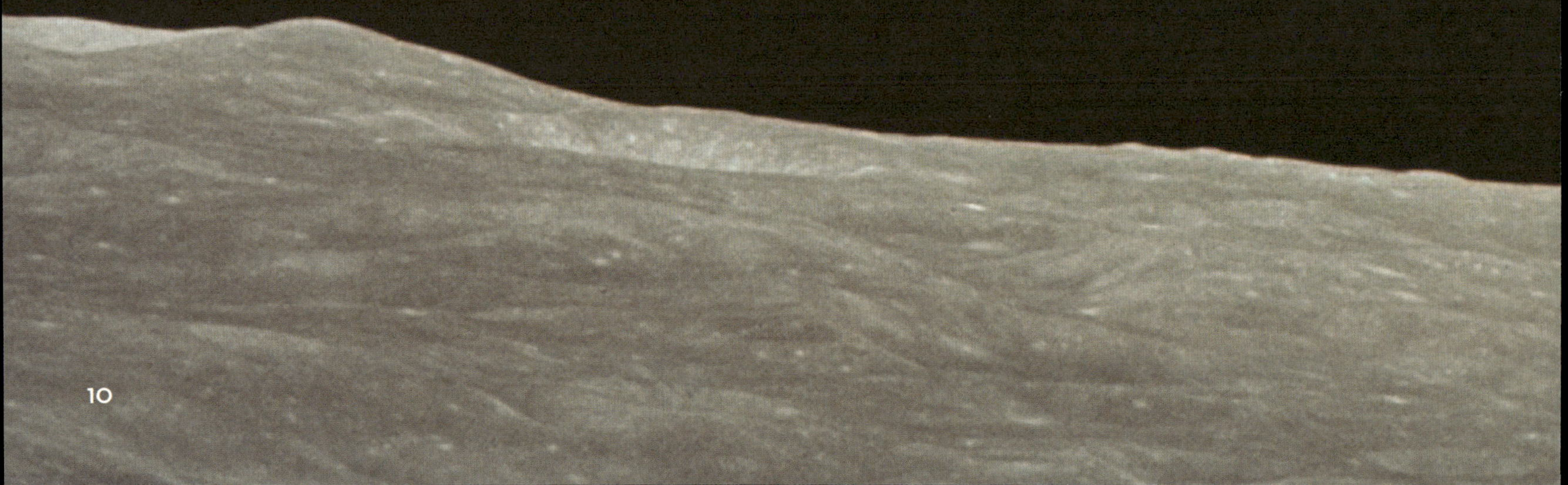

它要多绿就有多绿

要多绿就有多绿，绿就绿它个透心绿，就是这么绿，实打实的绿。我讲的是电鳗绿、鳄鱼绿、蜥蜴绿、蟒蛇绿，我说的这种绿把所有东西都染绿了。瞧那绿龟徜徉在龟绿色的池塘里，蚱蜢从刚修绿的草坪里一跃而起，一只绿树蛙停歇在女孩的左臂。有时候，它绿得阴森，绿得凶险，绿得其实你从未见过。大洋底的深渊绿，龙卷风的虐绿，老虎眼底的幽绿，“吃完西兰花”的郁闷绿，西瓜在阳光下的闪耀绿。比常绿植物更绿的，是绿叶上享绿的绿色壁虎、沉绿夜空的绿色飞蛾、紧绷双膝的绿色螳螂。 它绿得伟大，绿得华丽，那“趁着阳光正好赶快生长说长就长”的一抹绿。还没有猜出来吗？还需要再来一点提示吗？想想那绿色的麦浪翻滚，想想那粗壮的藤蔓攀上绿色的参天大树。连绵不绝的绿色山峦，深绿海洋中的滔天巨澜，竟都被包在一个绿色的球里，独具一格地装点着天空。能亲眼看见这大绿球飘过该是一件多么大的幸事啊。没错，它要多绿就有多绿……

除非它变蓝了……

——佩姬·吉福德

ON THE

MOVE

GRAY WOLF
灰狼

Advice for a Frog

(Concerning a Crane)

Watch out, Old Croaker.
Here comes Stick Walker,
here comes Pond Poker,
here comes Death.

Take a breath, Slick Skin.
Muck down, sink in.
Don't make bubbles.
Good luck, Grin Chin—

here comes Trouble.

—Alice Schertle

FLORIDA SANDHILL CRANE
佛罗里达沙丘鹤

The Clown Fish

Is not an enemy
of anemone;
in fact, it is anemone's maid,
for which anemone
stings its enemies.
And that's how friends are made.

—David Elliott

CLOWNFISH AND ANEMONE
小丑鱼和海葵

A Blessing

Just off the highway to Rochester, Minnesota,
Twilight bounds softly forth on the grass.
And the eyes of those two Indian ponies
Darken with kindness.
They have come gladly out of the willows
To welcome my friend and me.
We step over the barbed wire into the pasture
Where they have been grazing all day, alone.
They ripple tensely, they can hardly contain their happiness
That we have come.
They bow shyly as wet swans. They love each other.
There is no loneliness like theirs.
At home once more,
They begin munching the young tufts of spring in the darkness.
I would like to hold the slenderer one in my arms,
For she has walked over to me
And nuzzled my left hand.
She is black and white,
Her mane falls wild on her forehead,
And the light breeze moves me to caress her long ear
That is delicate as the skin over a girl's wrist.
Suddenly I realize
That if I stepped out of my body I would break
Into blossom.

—James Wright

ICELANDIC HORSES
冰岛马

The Rhea

The rhea rheally isn't strange—
It's just an ostrich, rhearranged.

—Douglas Florian

Queen Alexandra's Birdwing

This largest and loveliest, last of its kind,
is the jewel of the jungle. Its wings unveil
iridescence that flies off the radiance scale.
Emerald and sapphire so finely designed!
Butterfly rarest and hardest to find.

—Avis Harley

QUEEN ALEXANDRA'S BIRDWING BUTTERFLY
亚历山大女皇鸟翼凤蝶

Everything Old Becomes New

Everything old becomes new before it dies.
Chrysalis, a moment before the butterflies
stretch those limp and limpid wings,
makes a sound, almost sings,
exchanges breath with its quaking new life.
Egg about to crack before the beak's sure knife
remembers warmth inside the hen.
Mountain crumbles into its own ravine.

And you walking the Devon hills
remark the old year, watching the spills
of winter sun blaze the ancient landscape there
before the turning of the fading year.
Everything old, dear friend, anew.
Even me, even you.

—Jane Yolen

Gym on a Rock

I watch a lizard
doing push-ups in the sun—
a tiny buff man.

—*Sonya Sones*

FOREST CRESTED LIZARD
棕背树蜥

Electric Eel

Some think Electric Eel lacks looks,
But others find it stunning.
A homegrown battery it packs
To keep its shocker running.

Why, you could light all New York's streets
And skyscrapers and stuff
With one Electric Eel alone
If it were long enough.

—*X. J. Kennedy*

ELECTRIC EEL
电鳗

On the Grasshopper and Cricket

The poetry of earth is never dead:
When all the birds are faint with the hot sun,
And hide in cooling trees, a voice will run
From hedge to hedge about the new-mown mead;
That is the Grasshopper's—he takes the lead
In summer luxury,—he has never done
With his delights; for when tired out with fun
He rests at ease beneath some pleasant weed.
The poetry of earth is ceasing never:
On a lone winter evening, when the frost
Has wrought a silence, from the stove there shrills
The Cricket's song, in warmth increasing ever,
And seems to one in drowsiness half lost,
The Grasshopper's among some grassy hills.

—John Keats

GRASSHOPPER
蚱蜢

The Flower-Fed Buffaloes

The flower-fed buffaloes of the spring
In the days of long ago,
Ranged where the locomotives sing
And the prairie flowers lie low:—
The tossing, blooming, perfumed grass
Is swept away by the wheat,
Wheels and wheels and wheels spin by
In the spring that still is sweet.
But the flower-fed buffaloes of the spring
Left us, long ago.
They gore no more, they bellow no more,
They trundle around the hills no more:—
With the Blackfeet, lying low,
With the Pawnees, lying low,
Lying low.

—Vachel Lindsay

BUFFALO, GRAND TETON NATIONAL PARK, WYOMING, U.S.A.
水牛，大蒂顿国家公园，怀俄明州，美国

The Difference Between Frog and Toad

The look-alike of *frog* is *toad*;
They have a similar dress code.
A *frog* has skin that's smooth and slimy;
A *toad*'s complexion's warty and dry;
A *frog* would like to kiss a princess;
A *toad* prefers to kiss a fly.

—*Anonymous*

RED-EYED TREE FROG
红眼树蛙

BALD EAGLE
秃头鹰

The Ways of Living Things

There is wonder past all wonder
in the ways of living things,
in a worm's intrepid wriggling,
in the song a blackbird sings,

In the grandeur of an eagle
and the fury of a shark,
in the calmness of a tortoise
on a meadow in the dark,

In the splendor of a sea gull
as it plummets from the sky,
in the incandescent shimmer
of a noisy dragonfly,

In a heron, still and silent
underneath a crescent moon,
in a butterfly emerging
from its silver-spun cocoon.

In a fish's joyful splashing,
in a snake that makes no sound,
in the smallest salamander
there is wonder to be found.

—Jack Prelutsky

Quail's Nest

I wandered out one rainy day
And heard a bird with merry joys
Cry "wet my foot" for half the way;
I stood and wondered at the noise,

When from my foot a bird did flee—
The rain flew bouncing from her breast
I wondered what the bird could be,
And almost trampled on her nest.

The nest was full of eggs and round—
I met a shepherd in the vales,
And stood to tell him what I found.
He knew and said it was a quail's,

For he himself the nest had found,
Among the wheat and on the green,
When going on his daily round,
With eggs as many as fifteen.

Among the stranger birds they feed,
Their summer flight is short and low;
There's very few know where they breed,
And scarcely anywhere they go.

—John Clare

QUAIL EGGS IN NEST
巢中的鹌鹑蛋

Cardinal Nest

Tiptoe up and look real closely
made with sticks and straw but mostly
made with love and lots of care
a little tree house in the air.

—Charles Ghigna

Self-Pity

I never saw a wild thing
sorry for itself.
A small bird will drop frozen dead from a bough
without ever having felt sorry for itself.

—D. H. Lawrence

WHALE

A whale is stout about the middle,
He is stout about the ends,
& so is all his family
& so are all his friends.

He's pleased that he's enormous,
He's happy he weighs tons,
& so are all his daughters
& so are all his sons.

He eats when he is hungry
Each kind of food he wants,
& so do all his uncles
& so do all his aunts.

He doesn't mind his blubber,
He doesn't mind his creases,
& neither do his nephews
& neither do his nieces.

You may find him chubby,
You may find him fat,
But he would disagree with you:
He likes himself like that.

—Mary Ann Hoberman

SPERM WHALE
抹香鲸

Sips of Sea

the
pipe
fish
seems
to
me
to
be
a
straw
to
draw
up
sips
of
sea

—Avis Harley

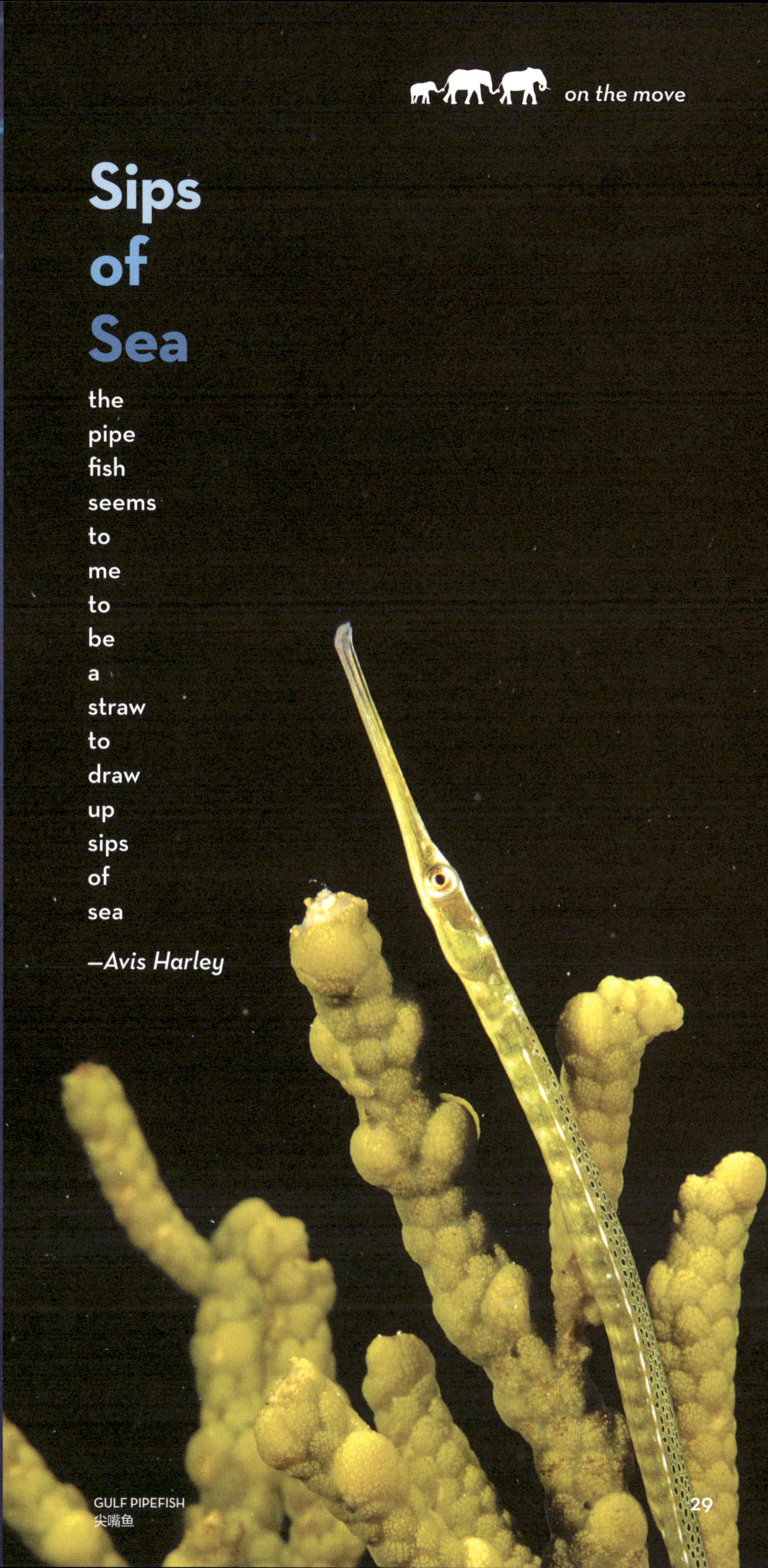

GULF PIPEFISH
尖嘴鱼

The Answers

"When did the world begin and how?"
I asked a lamb, a goat, a cow:

"What's it all about and why?"
I asked a hog as he went by:

"Where will the whole thing end, and when?"
I asked a duck, a goose, a hen:

And I copied all the answers too,
A quack, a honk, an oink, a moo.

—Robert Clairmont

HEREFORD COW
海福特牛

Advice from the Scorpion

Do not be afraid, *amigo*.
Walk softly through the silent crowd
Of cactus men and cholla boys—
The touch-me-nots of the desert.
Here in scrub country,
I am a touch-me-not too—
The Land Lobster, sideways-dancing.

Do not be afraid, *amiga*.
The screaming you hear
Is only the yellow-breasted chat
Scolding the purple-mad sky.
Even in the Land of Little Rain,
Five-legged Lightning
Can break Moon's heart.

—J. Patrick Lewis

Centipede

Beneath the lawn, on the slimy bottoms
of logs and stones,
among the fallen, rotten, and sodden,
where every root
hoards the alchemy of sunbeams,
the centipedes
create the planet's future, turning
what once had been
into what yet might be: an aspen,
a milkweed pod,
a pumpkin, or a field of beans.

—Michael J. Rosen

The BOA

Just when you think you know the boa,
There's moa and moa and moa and moa.

—Douglas Florian

BOA CONSTRICTOR
大蟒蛇

ON THE

生灵

MOVE

GRAY WOLF
灰狼

Advice for a Frog (Concerning a Crane)

P14

给青蛙的忠告

（来自鹤的温馨提示）

你，呱呱叫的，当心，
我，踩高跷的，来了，
我，池塘挑事的，到了，
死神，到了。

深呼吸，滑溜溜的东西，
钻进去，沉下去，
别吐泡泡，
祝你好运，爱笑的大嘴巴——

麻烦，来了。

——艾丽斯·舍尔勒

The Clown Fish

P15

小丑鱼

不是海葵的敌人，
而是海葵的朋友，
海葵专蜇敌人，
真是不打不相识。

——戴维·埃利奥特

A Blessing

P16

幸事

一路狂奔至明尼苏达的罗切斯特，
薄暮轻柔地弹跃在脚前的草地上。
两匹印第安矮马的眸子
深沉而友善。
它们欣然走出柳树丛，
来迎接我和我的朋友。
我们跃过带刺铁丝网来到牧场，
它们整日在此孤独地吃草。
它们焦急地踱步，按捺不住内心的喜悦，
我们终于来了。
它们俯首，如湿漉漉的天鹅，
它们爱着彼此，
从未见过这般的寂寞。
回家了，
它们咀嚼着黑暗中春天的嫩草。
让我把那瘦弱的拥入怀抱，
因她向我走来，
用鼻轻拱我的左手。
她黑白交杂，
鬃毛在额前野性地垂挂，
怎奈轻轻微风怂恿我爱抚她的长耳，
肤如凝脂，白皙如姑娘的手腕。
我突然意识到：
若我跳出这躯壳，定会像花儿一样怒放。

——詹姆斯·赖特

The Rhea P18

美洲鸵

美洲鸵的样子真的一点都不囧，
其实它还是鸵鸟，只不过整了容。

——道格拉斯·弗洛里安

Everything Old Becomes New P19

万象更新

万事逝去之前必焕然如新。
正如蝴蝶诞生之前必经茧，
奋力展翅，晶莹剔透，
呢喃细语，欲展歌喉，
喘息在微弱的新生。
蛋未裂，鸟喙犀利，却未曾
忘记母亲怀中的温存。
山峦崩塌，倾注于深谷。
漫步于德文郡山路，
回顾过去的一年，
观冬日残阳将旧景点燃，
陈年褪去的绚烂。
亲爱的，凡事历久弥新，
如我，如你，如今。

——简·约伦

Queen Alexandra's Birdwing P19

亚历山大女皇鸟翼凤蝶

最后这一只，最大，最美，
是丛林之宝石。它飞起来的时候
简直是彩虹乍泄的节奏。
祖母绿、宝石蓝，如此精致，仿若天成！
稀世珍宝就是它，毋庸置疑。

——阿维丝·哈莉

Gym on a Rock P20

石头上健身

太阳下，蜥蜴
拼命地做俯卧撑——
迷你健将。

——索尼娅·索恩斯

Electric Eel P20

电鳗

有些人说电鳗其貌不扬，
但有些人觉得它美得震慑四方。
随身携带的自产电池
可时刻保持气场最强。

天啊，你甚至能点亮全纽约城的
街道与大楼。
只要一条电鳗
足够长。

——X. J. 肯尼迪

On the Grasshopper and Cricket P21

致蚱蜢与蟋蟀

地球的诗句永不消亡：
当所有的鸟都被曝晒晕厥，
藏匿于清凉之荫，
一个声音响彻草坪，
从这篱到那篱，
这就是蚱蜢——奢华夏日的领唱。
他从不因悦己而歌，
当兴致退去，
休憩于安逸的野草下。

地球的诗意永不泯灭：
冬日孤寂的夜晚，
冷霜携来静谧，
炉旁传来蟋蟀的锐音歌唱，
温暖骤然上升，
倦意减半，
蚱蜢已在山间草中。

——约翰·济慈

P22

The Flower-Fed Buffaloes

吃花的牛

很久很久以前，
春天的那些吃花的牛
游牧在火车头轰鸣、
野花遍布的草原。
那些舞动的、绽放的、扑鼻馨香的野草
被小麦一扫而空，
机轮翻过，一翻，一翻，一翻，
在这个依旧甘甜的春天。
然而，吃花的牛已远去，
早已远去。
它们不再打斗，不再低吼，
不再漫步山间。
和黑脚族一样，沉默，
和波尼族一样，沉默，
沉默。

——韦切尔·林赛

P23

The Difference Between Frog and Toad

青蛙蟾蜍比一比

蟾蜍是青蛙的仿版，
从着装上就可见一斑。
青蛙的皮肤又平又黏，
蟾蜍好干，疙瘩连连。
青蛙要吻则吻公主，
苍蝇才是蟾蜍之爱恋。

——无名氏

The Ways of Living Things

P25

致生灵

致超越一切奇迹的奥秘，
万物生灵的受造全然可畏，
致小虫坚韧的蠕行，
致画眉甜美的歌声，

致苍鹰的雄壮，
致残鲨的暴烈，
致陆龟的恬淡，
夜幕中草甸的光洁，

致海鸥，
横空俯冲的豪迈，
致蜻蜓，
躁狂炙热的光彩，

致苍鹭，
新月下的沉静，
致蝴蝶，
银丝茧中的浮映，

致游鱼水中戏玩，
致蛟蛇行踪轻轻，
致蝾螈娇小玲珑，
只待其奥秘显明。

——杰克·普里卢斯基

Quail's Nest

P26

鹌鹑小窝

一日雨天散步，
我听见一只鸟欢愉无比，
“小脚湿了！”欢呼一路，
我纳闷这声音，甚是惊奇。

的确有只小鸟从我脚前飞过，
雨水从她胸前飞落，
我想知道这到底是什么鸟，
差点绊到鸟窝摔一跤。

鸟窝里全是圆圆的蛋，
我在山里遇到一个牧羊人，
把我所见与他交谈。
“肯定是鹌鹑，不用问。”

原来他也曾找到过鸟窝，
就在麦田间、草地上，
每天都从这里过，
数数刚好十五个。

跟各种鸟一起觅食，
夏季的飞程短而低，
没人知道它们在哪儿繁殖，
更不知道它们要去哪里。

——约翰·克莱尔

Self-Pity P27

自怜

我从没见过任何一只动物
顾影自怜。
哪怕是一只小小鸟，
从树枝上掉下，
冰冷，僵硬，
也从未替自己惋惜过。

——D. H. 劳伦斯

Cardinal Nest P27

主红雀巢

轻手轻脚走近一瞧，
材料不止树枝乱草，
更有呵护爱加倍，
小小树屋空中垒。

——查尔斯·吉格纳

WHALE P28

鲸

鲸的中间粗壮，
两头粗壮，
他的全家粗壮，
朋友也都粗壮。

他很高兴他是个大块头，
他很得意他重千斤，
女儿们都这样，
儿子们都如此。

他饿的时候就吃，
想吃啥吃啥，
叔叔们都是这般，
婶婶们都是那样。

他不介意膀大腰圆，
也不介意沟壑纵横，
外甥们也满不在乎，
侄女们也熟视无睹。

不管你说他胖乎乎，
还是肥嘟嘟，
他都不敢苟同：
就这样正好，心满意足。

——玛丽·安·霍伯曼

P29

Sips of Sea

尝尝海

尖嘴鱼鱼嘴尖，尖尖一吸尝到海。

——阿维丝·哈莉

P30

The Answers

答案

“世界何时诞生？怎样诞生的？”
我问小羊、山羊、牛。

“世界到底是怎么回事？又为什么是这么回事？”
我问了一头刚走过的猪。

“世界到底到哪里是个头？什么时候结束？”
我问鸭、鹅、鸡。

我也用它们的方式来回答，
咩咩，哼哼，哄哄和嘎嘎。

——罗伯特·克莱尔蒙特

Advice from the Scorpion

P31

听蝎子的话

朋友，别害怕。
轻轻走过，
尖尖的他和刺刺的他，
别碰。
矮树王国里，
也别碰我，
旱地龙虾，横行霸道。

别怕，小姑娘。
你听见的撕心裂肺，
只是黄胸巨莺在责骂
气得发紫的天空。
即便是少雨国，
五只脚的闪电，
也可以伤透月亮的心。

——J. 帕特里克·刘易斯

Centipede

P31

蜈蚣

草坪下面，
木头、石头湿滑的底部，
落叶中、朽木中、湿花中，
阳光赋予了每个树根魔力，
蜈蚣则创造了地球的未来，
使得过去演变成将来：
无论是一棵白杨、一粒乳草荚、
一个南瓜，还是一整田的豆子。

——迈克尔·J. 罗森

The BOA

P31

蟒

你确定跟蟒很熟?
"哎呀妈呀，妈呀，妈呀，妈呀。"

——道格拉斯·弗洛里安

Who is mother nature?

When Mother Nature's near—in waterfalls, rivers, rainbows, meadows, or oceans—her admirers react with love, awe, curiosity, even fear, if she decides to reveal her grumpier side. The lady can be seen through telescopes or microscopes, from mountaintops or ravines, with the wind in our hair, soil in our hands, or sand in our toes. For those who aren't hopelessly city-bound, looking out a window will do.

Driven to explore the *science* behind the wonder of it all, Charles Darwin filled scores of notebooks about what was then the unexplored wildlife of the Galápagos Islands. Countless nature writers have followed his courageous example. Others have put themselves in nature, like naturalist John Muir, who once rode out a northern American windstorm by cocooning himself in the branches of a sky-high Douglas spruce. (Muir is famous—or should be—for saying, "The clearest way into the Universe is through a forest wilderness.")

Some humans, however, have no use for wild places, a view once expressed by Woody Allen with his typical wit: "I love nature. I just don't want to get any of it on me." For some, their love for animals extends only as far as Fido or Sweet Pea. That we share the Earth equally with other creatures is a notion as foreign and irrelevant to them as the disappearance of the rain forests or the melting of the ice caps.

But Mother Nature doesn't care who likes her. Nor is she bothered about being ignored. A midwife at the birth of creatures large and small, she will go on making waves by making waves, assembling forests, flowering deserts, and beautifying gardens. We can embrace her or resist her charms; it is of no concern to her.

Who is the mysterious lady known as Mother Nature? She is the material world, the environment of trees, plants, animals, everything under and over the sun. In short, she equals the world around us and includes whatever is not built by human hands.

Mother Nature is where we live. In other words, she is

a refuge to the lost,
a magnet to the curious,
a dare to the daring,
the cradle of rapture,
the university of the universe,
the glory of a morning and of a morning-glory,
not a whale but the idea of a whale,
a sign rewriter: I Welcome All No Trespassing,
the best cure for couch disease,
an opera performed by birds, bullfrogs on drums,
the sound of silence . . . amplified
to the symphony of the spheres, and __________
______________________________ .

Can you add another short description of Mother Nature to this poem?

The poets and photographers who have come together to produce National Geographic's *Book of Nature Poetry* would agree with John Keats, who defined their abiding faith: "The poetry of earth is never dead."

THREAD-WINGED ANTLION
线翅蚁狮

自然之母是谁？

当自然之母靠近的时候——在瀑布中，在河流中，在彩虹中，在草地或是海洋中——她的爱慕者用爱、敬畏、好奇来回应，甚至如果她显示暴躁的一面时，则用恐惧来回应。这位女士可以用望远镜或是显微镜来观察，从山顶到深谷，风在我们的发丝中穿过，泥土在我们手中漏出，沙在我们的脚趾中渗出。对于那些不喜欢住在城里的人来说，只要看一看窗外就行。

为了探索自然奇观背后的科学道理，查尔斯·达尔文把加拉帕戈斯群岛未知的野生动物记满了几十本笔记本。难以数计的自然主义作家跟随着他，以他为榜样。其他人则让自己融入自然。例如自然主义者约翰·缪尔，曾经用高耸入云的道格拉斯云杉的枝叶包裹着自己，经受住了北美的风暴。（缪尔由于下面这句话而知名——或应该知名——“融入宇宙最清晰的方式莫过于通过荒野森林”。）

然而，也有一些人，觉得野外毫无用处，这也是伍迪·艾伦用他特有的机智曾经表达的观点：“我爱自然，但是一点也别弄到我身上来。”而另一些人，他们对动物的喜爱只限于“菲多”或是“甜豌豆”。对他们来说，我们与其他生物平等地分享地球的观念，和雨林正在消失、冰层正在融化这样的概念一样，是未知而不重要的。

但自然之母并不关心谁喜欢她。她对这种忽视也毫不在意。她是大大小小各种生物出生时的产婆，她将不断在波浪中创造波浪，让森林遍地，让花朵在沙漠开放，让花园变得更美。我们可以接受或是抗拒她的魅力，她对此却毫不关心。

这位被人称为自然之母的神秘女士是谁？她是物质世界，也是植物、动物的环境和阳光下所有的一切。简言之，她就是我们周遭的世界，人类双手无法创造的世界。

自然之母在我们生活的地方。换句话说，

她是：
迷失者的庇护，
好奇者的磁石，
勇敢者的挑战，
狂喜者的摇篮，
宇宙的教化者。
她是：
清晨的光辉，
牵牛花的光，
并不是鲸鱼，
而是这创意。
她重新写了一个标记：我欢迎所有的非擅自闯入者。
她是：
沙发病的良药，
鸟儿、牛蛙在鼓上演奏的歌剧，
是寂静之声……被放大，
而成为万物的交响曲，
也是 ______________________

你可以在这首诗后面加上一段描写自然之母的短句吗？

共同创作《最美自然诗集》的诗人和摄影家们会同意约翰·济慈的话，他道出了他们永恒的信仰：“地球的诗篇永远不会消亡。”

LOTUS AND BEES -WUQIANG
荷花与蜜蜂（吴强）

美国国家地理学会是世界上最大的非营利科学与教育组织之一。学会成立于1888年，以“增进与普及地理知识”为宗旨，致力于启发人们对地球的关心。美国国家地理学会通过杂志、电视节目、影片、音乐、电台、图书、DVD、地图、展览、活动、学校出版计划、交互式媒体与商品来呈现世界。美国国家地理学会的会刊《国家地理》杂志，以英文及其他33种语言发行，每月有3800万读者阅读。美国国家地理频道在166个国家以34种语言播放，有3.2亿个家庭收看。美国国家地理学会资助超过10 000项科学研究、环境保护与探索计划，并支持一项扫除“地理文盲”的教育计划。

Acknowledgments
To the entire National Geographic team for their enthusiasm and dedication in the making of this book, and to all the poets whose deserving work, regrettably, could not be squeezed into its pages.—JPL

The publisher gratefully acknowledges the heroic efforts of Natalie Turner in securing permissions, as well as the invaluable research assistance of Alyson Foster.

图书在版编目（CIP）数据

最美自然诗集 /（美）J. 帕特里克 · 刘易斯主编；Abby F. Yehenola，张原平，和览编译. —郑州：河南科学技术出版社，2018.1
ISBN 978-7-5349-8952-0

Ⅰ. ①最… Ⅱ. ①J… ②A… ③张… ④和… Ⅲ. ①儿童诗歌-诗集-美国-现代 Ⅳ. ①I712.82

中国版本图书馆CIP数据核字(2017)第269830号

出版发行： 河南科学技术出版社
地址：郑州市经五路66号　邮编：450002
电话：（0371）65737028　65788613
网址：www.hnstp.cn
特邀策划： Abby F. Yehenola
策划编辑： 马艳茹　韩雅楠　于凯燕
责任编辑： 于凯燕
责任校对： 徐小刚
整体设计： 吴豆豆
责任印制： 张　巍
印　　刷： 北京盛通印刷股份有限公司
经　　销： 全国新华书店
幅面尺寸： 232 mm × 276 mm　**印张：** 2.75　**字数：** 69千字
版　　次： 2018年1月第1版　2018年1月第1次印刷
全套定价： 588.00元

To poets, nature, and nature poets everywhere.—JPL

献给诗人、自然和全世界写自然的诗人。

——J. 帕特里克 · 刘易斯

献给爱自然，爱诗歌的大小朋友们！

——Abby

美国童诗桂冠诗人［美］J.帕特里克·刘易斯 主编
Abby F. Yehenola ✿ 张原平 ✿ 和览 编译

NATIONAL GEOGRAPHIC
美国国家地理

book of nature poetry

最美自然诗集 4

（汉英对照）

200首诗歌
和会漂浮
会穿越，
会开花
的精彩图片

河南科学技术出版社
·郑州·

自然最美

千山鸟飞绝，
万径人踪灭。
孤舟蓑笠翁，
独钓寒江雪。

这是唐朝柳宗元的《江雪》。短短的20个字，便成功捕捉一幅美丽的风景画。当时的孤冷静谧与雪白世界，似乎透过这首诗被永久封存，美丽了好几千年，不曾消逝。

《最美自然诗集》的出版，重新带给我这样的震撼与感动。随着时代的变迁，生活节奏的加快，文字阅读耗费时间，致使读者更为钟情图像阅读。不过图像阅读与文字阅读所获得的乐趣，无法互相取代。纵使是对同个风景的描绘，使用新诗文字创作与照片图像创作，让读者感受到的乐趣亦是截然不同。若是舍弃文字的阅读，全都转向图像阅读，实在相当可惜。《最美自然诗集》却完美解决了这个问题：这本诗集的每首诗，都是一张照片加上一首诗，使得文字文本和图像文本相互合作对话，形成一支精彩的双人舞。

这本书真的让我重新认识美丽的地球！在大自然中，随着四季的交替、地形的差异、气候的更迭，每一刹那的风景都是独一无二、稍纵即逝的。照片是静态的叙事，透过摄影师的镜头，有意识地捕捉吉光片羽，所以一张张的美照，是摄影师透过自身的美学哲学与镜头的选择所决定的，也可以说照片是摄影师眼中的美景。

而诗的创作，则是透过诗人纤细善感的心思，触景生情，把当时的生命状态转化成诗句，以情寓景，让景物多了一股人情的芬芳，不少美景在诗句的化妆下，变得充满情韵，让人印象深刻。

除此之外，这本书的编者扮演着隐形创作者的角色，因为他们成功媒合了照片与诗句，让作品更有一层乐趣。诗句的意象让静态的照片翩然生动，仿佛可以听见照片中的潺潺流水声，让读者宛若身临其境，感受照片里的一草一木，让读者悠游在每幅照片之中。阅读《最美自然诗集》，需要最好的领航员同游，我们的译者充分领会了编者的匠心独运，十分用心地录制了200首音频，恰是《最美自然诗集》最好的导读。

这本诗集让读者感受到三种美学：文学之美、摄影之美以及想象之美。透过诗句，让读者感受到文字透过意象诠释的美学；透过摄影照片让读者感受到强烈的视觉盛宴。当今的科技，无论是手机、电视还是穿戴科技等等，均试图以科技的力量，让读者感受到身临其境的感官盛宴，增强读者的视觉与听觉震撼，产生娱乐感，但是与此同时，相对地也剥夺了读者想象之美的权利。而《最美自然诗集》在照片与文字当中，保留了相当多的空白，并分类为“感叹自然”“凌空”“渊洋”“生灵”“山川”“美植”“灾难”“四季”“奇景”“敬畏自然”，让读者可以发挥想象，感受编者所安排的想象之美。因此，阅读这本书让读者经历一场美学盛宴，沉醉在大自然的洗礼之中。

最后，从这本书中也可以看出编者对于环境保护的意识。人类过度开发，使得环境被破坏，导致气候异常，很多珍稀动物濒临灭绝，大自然也不再美丽。希望这本诗集，能唤起人类对于大自然的重新思考，思考如何与环境共生。

透过这本最美丽的诗集，让我们回忆起我们曾经的美好！伟哉自然，伟哉生命！

· 译者序 ·

这本书用18首诗来歌颂地球上壮丽的山川，有草场、山间、山丘、洞穴、沙漠、荒野、峡谷、林间小道……颂扬的歌声从地球各地传出，听：

第一首诗竟然来自中国著名的唐代诗人李白，诗人向往自然的宁静，想远避喧嚣的情怀用英文也可以表达出来。

如果你来描写太阳，你会用怎样的方式呢？诗人把不同时间段的太阳比作女孩儿、待燃的火、受伤的小鹿和苍老的鹰。

对于埃米莉·迪金森来说，什么都不是难事，一个草场，靠冥想就能做成。

你爬到过山顶吗？你是否被山顶的景色折服到一言不发？两位诗人同时表达出在山顶心满意足的感受。

爱德华·托马斯，这位著名的诗人，在参军牺牲之前，写下了《爱德斯托镇》这首诗。人们也因着这首诗，把这个小小的火车站当成了祭奠他的胜地。

“山不在高，有仙则灵”，那洞穴呢？有蝙蝠则灵啊！诗人妙笔生花，把蝙蝠翅膀的扇动比喻成黑色的肺。

沙漠不是亘古不变的黄色，某些瞬间也有花蕾的绽放、生灵的攒动，来读这首诗，参加沙漠大派对。

一直特别喜欢《在加拿大边境没有国家纪念碑的地方》这首诗，我们一般只关注战场，但很少关注平安之地，那些没有被破坏的寸土，是不是也值得我们缅怀？

有没有曾经想过自然界的颜色都是如何形成的？一首诗让我们知道大自然的颜色配比的秘密。

在加利福尼亚的一个国家公园里，许多块大石头拖着各个方向的长尾巴，安息在荒漠中，谁也不知道它们是从哪里来的？尾巴又是什么情况？快听听这首诗的译者讲解吧。

有这么一首诗，它告诉我们钟乳石是如何形成的，又告诉我们什么是钟乳石之吻。

诗人给峡谷写了一封信，为了感谢它的存在。快去看看人家大师的信是怎么写的吧。

深秋，漫步在刚割的草地上，会不会让你黯然神伤？罗伯特·弗罗斯特的一首凄凉而略带甜蜜的诗献给你。

3首有关山间的诗让我们的心瞬时安静下来：叶芝的诗让我们尝到了恋爱的感觉，另外两首，仿佛是山峦在给我们唱摇篮曲。

Abby 2017年10月于昆明

ACROSS THE LAND 山川

J. PATRICK LEWIS HAS WRITTEN MORE THAN 95 PICTURE AND POETRY BOOKS FOR YOUNG READERS. IN 2011 HE WAS APPOINTED U.S. CHILDREN'S POET LAUREATE, AND WAS GIVEN THE NATIONAL COUNCIL OF TEACHERS OF ENGLISH AWARD FOR EXCELLENCE IN POETRY FOR CHILDREN.

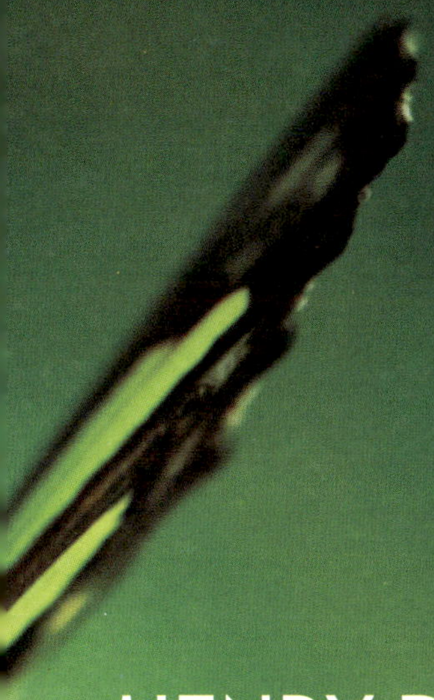

HENRY DAVID THOREAU was one of America's truly Big Thinkers on a little pond—Walden Pond. It was there in 1853, in a self-built cabin not far from his Massachusetts family home, that he wrote: "I have a room all to myself; it is nature."

From his tucked-away cottage, Thoreau produced some of the most profound thoughts on Mother Nature. But poets from centuries past rarely wrote about the more exotic natural wonders. They never saw them, never knew they existed. Many of the most fascinating phenomena that we often take for granted today—thanks to the convenience of travel, books, or photographs—were seldom brought to the attention of the classical poets.

How would William Shakespeare or John Keats have described in a poem the grandeur of the Grand Canyon? One can only imagine Emily Dickinson, transported to the scene, painting on an easel built of words a picture of an Asian tsunami or an African drought. What immortal verse might William Wordsworth have written after a day's walk in the Amazon rain forest instead of the English countryside? What picture would Kobayashi Issa or Li Po paint after a submersible dive to the ocean deep?

And yet a poet does not have to be there! You needn't leave your chair to write a poem about the wilder shores of creation. A book is your ticket to ride; a photograph is rapid transit to the brain. What kind of poem would you write if all you had in front of you was an image, like one of the breathtaking pictures in the *Book of Nature Poetry* you are now holding?

Better yet, let your eyes be your camera, taking incredible pictures your brain will thank you for. Get up and go there! Explore the woods, a cave; climb a mountain; go scuba diving; or simply make a friend of a grasshopper in a field on a windy summer day. You might even imagine you *are* that dragonfly trying to escape a swift, or a lucky salmon that has wiggled through the legs of a grizzly bear.

Travel by photograph or on foot, but go quickly before nature disappears. Every day more than 70 animals, plants, or other living things, like fungi, roots, and molds, vanish forever. The *Book of Nature Poetry* seeks to capture the ever changing nature of nature, so that gone is not forgotten. Besides, when more of us care for nature, more can help save it.

However and wherever you greet the world outside your window, listen again to Mr. Thoreau for the last and best words of advice:

"It's not what you look at that matters. It's what you see."

—J. Patrick Lewis,
former U.S. Children's Poet Laureate

MALACHITE BUTTERFLY
孔雀石蝴蝶

J. 帕特里克 · 刘易斯已经为孩子们创作了95部图画书和诗集。2011年，他荣获了美国童诗桂冠诗人奖，并被美国国家英语教师委员会授予杰出童诗奖。

·前　言·

亨利·戴维·梭罗是美国真正的大思想家之一，他曾隐居在瓦尔登湖。

1853年，在离马萨诸塞州家不远的自建小木屋里，他写道：“我有一个只属于我自己的房间——大自然。”

就在这世外桃源般的小木屋里，梭罗萌发出一些关于大自然的极其深刻的思想。但是这几百年来，诗人们却很少再去描写更独特的自然奇观。他们从来没见过，甚至都不知晓它们的存在。很多今天我们习以为常的，可以从旅行、书籍或照片中轻松获取的绝世美景，以前却很少能引起古典诗人们的关注。

试想，莎士比亚和济慈会怎样用诗歌去描绘大峡谷的壮美？可想而知，若埃米莉·迪金森能亲临亚洲海啸或非洲干旱现场，她将会用文字绘制出怎样的一幅画卷。那华兹华斯呢？如果他有机会走在亚马孙雨林中，而不仅仅是在英国乡间小道徘徊，他的笔下会写出怎样的诗句呢？若小林一茶或李白能乘潜艇探访大洋深渊，他们诗作的意境又将是怎样的呢？

然而，诗人并非一定要身临其境。你不需要离开椅子才能去写沧海桑田。一本书可以带你去遨游，一张照片可以带你去穿越。如果你拥有的只是面前的一幅图，就像你手里的《最美自然诗集》中的任意一幅惊艳的美图一样，你能写出怎样的诗句呢？

更棒的是，去旅行，让眼睛成为你的照相机，让眼前的美景滋养你的大脑。去吧，去森林中历险，去探索一个洞穴，去勇攀一座高峰，去潜入海底，甚至去野地里和一只蚱蜢交个朋友，任夏风轻抚。你甚至可以去想象自己就是那只努力躲过雨燕的蜻蜓，或是那条幸运地游过灰熊两腿之间的三文鱼。

无论是借着照片观光还是身临其境，请尽早，赶在自然景观消失之前。每天，都有超过70种生物在地球上永远消失。《最美自然诗集》力图捕捉到大自然瞬息万变的属性，让逝去的不再被遗忘。同时，当有更多的人开始关心大自然时，便会有更多的人来拯救她。

无论你在哪里，用怎样的方式来向窗外的世界致敬，请你再一次，也是最后一次聆听梭罗先生的警世良言：

“重要的不是你眼前的，而是你心里的。”

——J. 帕特里克·刘易斯，美国童诗桂冠诗人

AURORA BOREALIS
北极光

The Thing Is the Thing Is Green

The thing is the thing is green and the green is green and by green I mean real mean green. I mean electric-eel green, alligator, iguana, anaconda green. I mean this thing has got all things green. It's got green turtles in turtle-green ponds and grasshoppers springing from groomed-green lawns and a green tree frog on a girl's left arm. It's got dark and dangerous greens. Greens you've never even seen greens. Ocean floor greens. Tornado sky greens. Tiger's eye greens. Eat-your-broccoli greens. Watermelons sparkling in the sun greens. Way beyond evergreen, this thing leaves green geckos on green leaves feeling green and green moths in the green dark and preying mantises on their thin green knees. It's a great and gorgeous green a light-bright-just-right-watch-it-grow-it-says-go shade of green. Have you guessed yet? Do you need another clue? Think rolling waves of grain green. Thick arms of vines climbing tall green trees. Mountains and mountains of green billions of waves reaching out of dark green seas all wrapped in one green ball and hung, an ornament in the sky. What a thing it must be to see the whole green thing floating by. It's true. The thing is the thing is green . . .

except when it's blue.

—Peggy Gifford

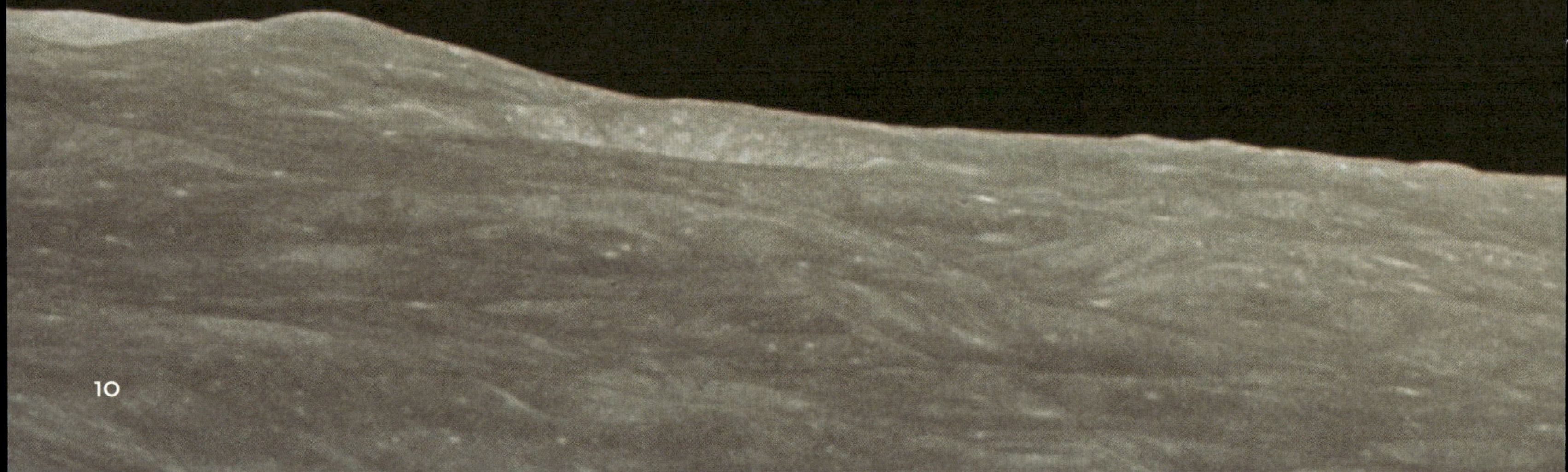

它要多绿就有多绿

要多绿就有多绿，绿就绿它个透心绿，就是这么绿，实打实的绿。我讲的是电鳗绿、鳄鱼绿、蜥蜴绿、蟒蛇绿，我说的这种绿把所有东西都染绿了。瞧那绿龟徜徉在龟绿色的池塘里，蚱蜢从刚修绿的草坪里一跃而起，一只绿树蛙停歇在女孩的左臂。有时候，它绿得阴森，绿得凶险，绿得其实你从未见过。大洋底的深渊绿，龙卷风的虐绿，老虎眼底的幽绿，“吃完西兰花”的郁闷绿，西瓜在阳光下的闪耀绿。比常绿植物更绿的，是绿叶上享绿的绿色壁虎、沉绿夜空的绿色飞蛾、紧绷双膝的绿色螳螂。它绿得伟大，绿得华丽，那“趁着阳光正好赶快生长说长就长”的一抹绿。还没有猜出来吗？还需要再来一点提示吗？想想那绿色的麦浪翻滚，想想那粗壮的藤蔓攀上绿色的参天大树。连绵不绝的绿色山峦，深绿海洋中的滔天巨澜，竟都被包在一个绿色的球里，独具一格地装点着天空。能亲眼看见这大绿球飘过该是一件多么大的幸事啊。没错，它要多绿就有多绿……

除非它变蓝了……

——佩姬·吉福德

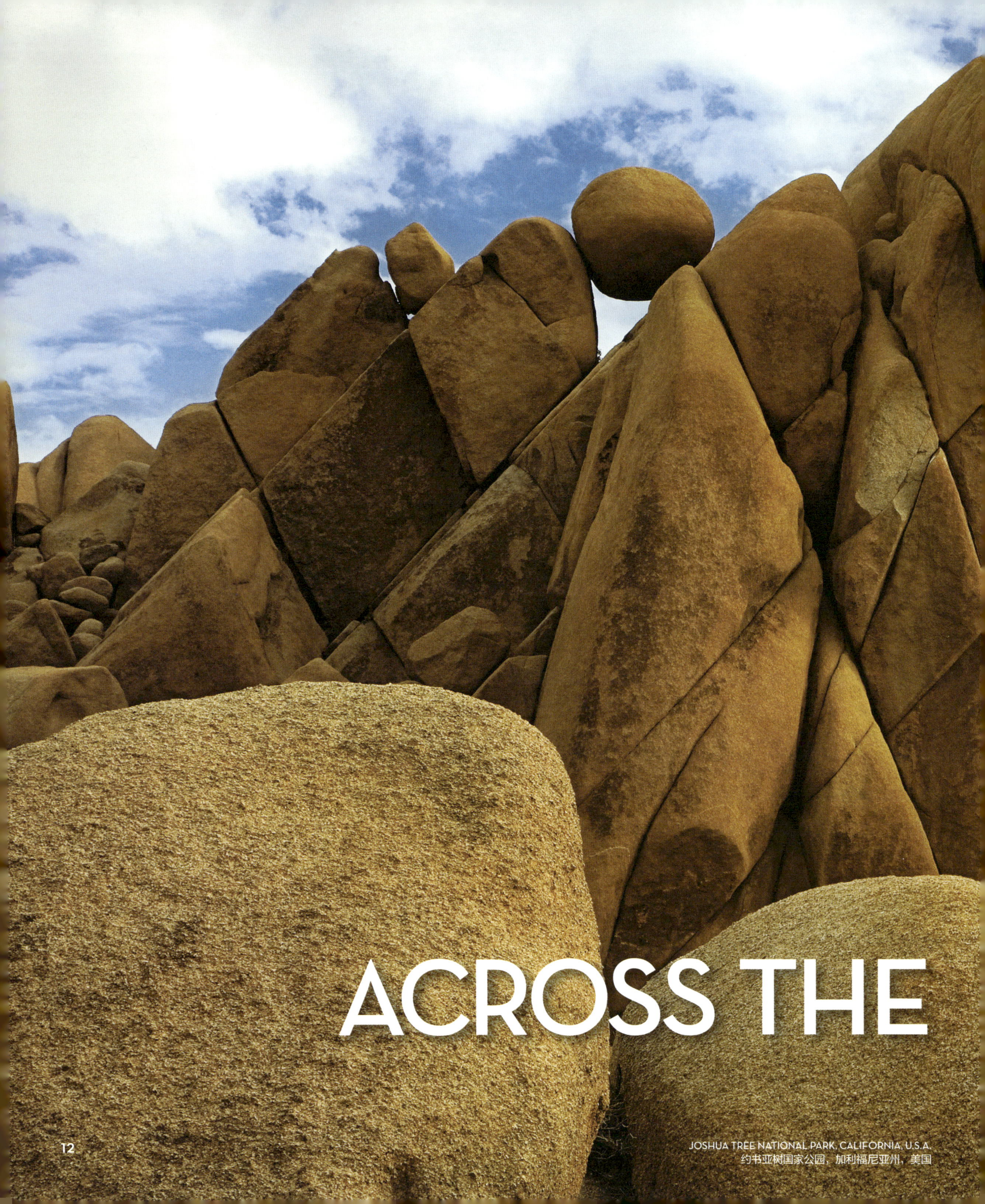

JOSHUA TREE NATIONAL PARK, CALIFORNIA, U.S.A.
约书亚树国家公园，加利福尼亚州，美国

LAND

You Ask Why

You ask why I make my home in the mountain
forest,
and I smile, and am silent,
and even my soul remains quiet:
it lives in the other world
which no one owns.
The peach trees blossom.
The water flows.

—Li Po

WRIGHT BROOK, MAINE, U.S.A.
赖特小溪，缅因州，美国

To Make a Prairie

To make a prairie it takes a clover and one bee,
One clover, and a bee,
And revery.
The revery alone will do
If bees are few.

—Emily Dickinson

An Indian Summer Day on the Prairie

(IN THE BEGINNING)
The sun is a huntress young,
The sun is a red, red joy,
The sun is an Indian girl,
Of the tribe of the Illinois.

(MID-MORNING)
The sun is a smouldering fire,
That creeps through the high gray plain,
And leaves not a bush of cloud
To blossom with flowers of rain.

(NOON)
The sun is a wounded deer,
That treads pale grass in the skies,
Shaking his golden horns,
Flashing his baleful eyes.

(SUNSET)
The sun is an eagle old,
There in the windless west.
Atop of the spirit-cliffs
He builds him a crimson nest.

—Vachel Lindsay

INDIAN GRASS
印度草

Afternoon on a Hill

I will be the gladdest thing
Under the sun!
I will touch a hundred flowers
And not pick one.

I will look at cliffs and clouds
With quiet eyes,
Watch the wind bow down the grass,
And the grass rise.

And when lights begin to show
Up from the town,
I will mark which must be mine,
And then start down!

—Edna St. Vincent Millay

Up on the Hill

I have been up on the side of the hill
And looked at the world till I looked my fill.

I walked and watched two distant showers,
Then sat and dreamed the hill was ours.

How does it feel to be on high?
Full as you hope to feel when you die.

—James Hayford

POPPIES AND WILDFLOWERS, CALIFORNIA, U.S.A.
罂粟和野花，加利福尼亚州，美国

Adlestrop

Yes. I remember Adlestrop—
The name, because one afternoon
Of heat the express-train drew up there
Unwontedly. It was late June.

The steam hissed. Someone cleared his
    throat.
No one left and no one came
On the bare platform. What I saw
Was Adlestrop—only the name

And willows, willow-herb, and grass,
And meadowsweet, and haycocks dry,
No whit less still and lonely fair
Than the high cloudlets in the sky.

And for that minute a blackbird sang
Close by, and round him, mistier,
Farther and farther, all the birds
Of Oxfordshire and Gloucestershire.

—Edward Thomas

from Bat Cave

The cave looked much like any other
from a little distance but
as we approached, came almost
to its mouth, we saw its walls within
that slanted up into a dome
were beating like a wild black lung—
it was plastered and hung with
the pulsing bodies of bats, the organ
music of the body's deep
interior, alive, the sacred cave
with its ten thousand gleaming eyes
near the clustered rocks
where the sea beat with the leather
wings of its own dark waves.

—Eleanor Wilner

MEXICAN FREE-TAILED BATS
墨西哥无尾蝙蝠

BEAVERTAIL CACTUS, CALIFORNIA, U.S.A.
海狸鼠尾仙人掌，加利福尼亚州，美国

Desert

I want to be there when the desert blooms
To see hot pink and shining gold
    interrupt the endless tan
To dance among the cactuses
    sporting flowers in their spiky hair
To celebrate the birth of tadpoles
    swimming in sudden pools

I want to be there when the desert blooms
To watch this serious span of earth
    grow festive for a day
To revel in rain as something
    sacred and rare
To honor this peculiar place
    where hope is not for fools

—Marilyn Singer

At the Un-National Monument Along the Canadian Border

This is the field where the battle did not happen,
where the unknown soldier did not die.
This is the field where grass joined hands,
where no monument stands,
and the only heroic thing is the sky.

Birds fly here without any sound,
unfolding their wings across the open.
No people killed—or were killed—on this ground
hallowed by neglect and an air so tame
that people celebrate it by forgetting its name.

—William Stafford

Former Barn Lot

Once there was a fence here,
  And the grass came and tried,
Leaning from the pasture,
  To get inside.

But colt feet trampled it,
  Turning it brown;
Until the farmer moved
  And the fence fell down.

Then any bird saw,
  Under the wire,
Grass nibbling inward
  Like green fire.

—Mark Van Doren

KENTUCKY BLUEGRASS
肯塔基蓝草

Red Rides West

Red buries green—*Autumn*.

*

Red marries yellow—*Sunset*.

*

Red rides west—*Sundown*.

*

Red hides soil—*Dust*.

*

Red burns orange—*Embers*.

*

Red turns gray—*Ashes*.

*

Red goes gold—*Evening*.

*

Red grows old—*Rust*.

—*Mariel Bede*

ARCHES NATIONAL PARK, UTAH, U.S.A.
拱门国家公园，犹他州，美国

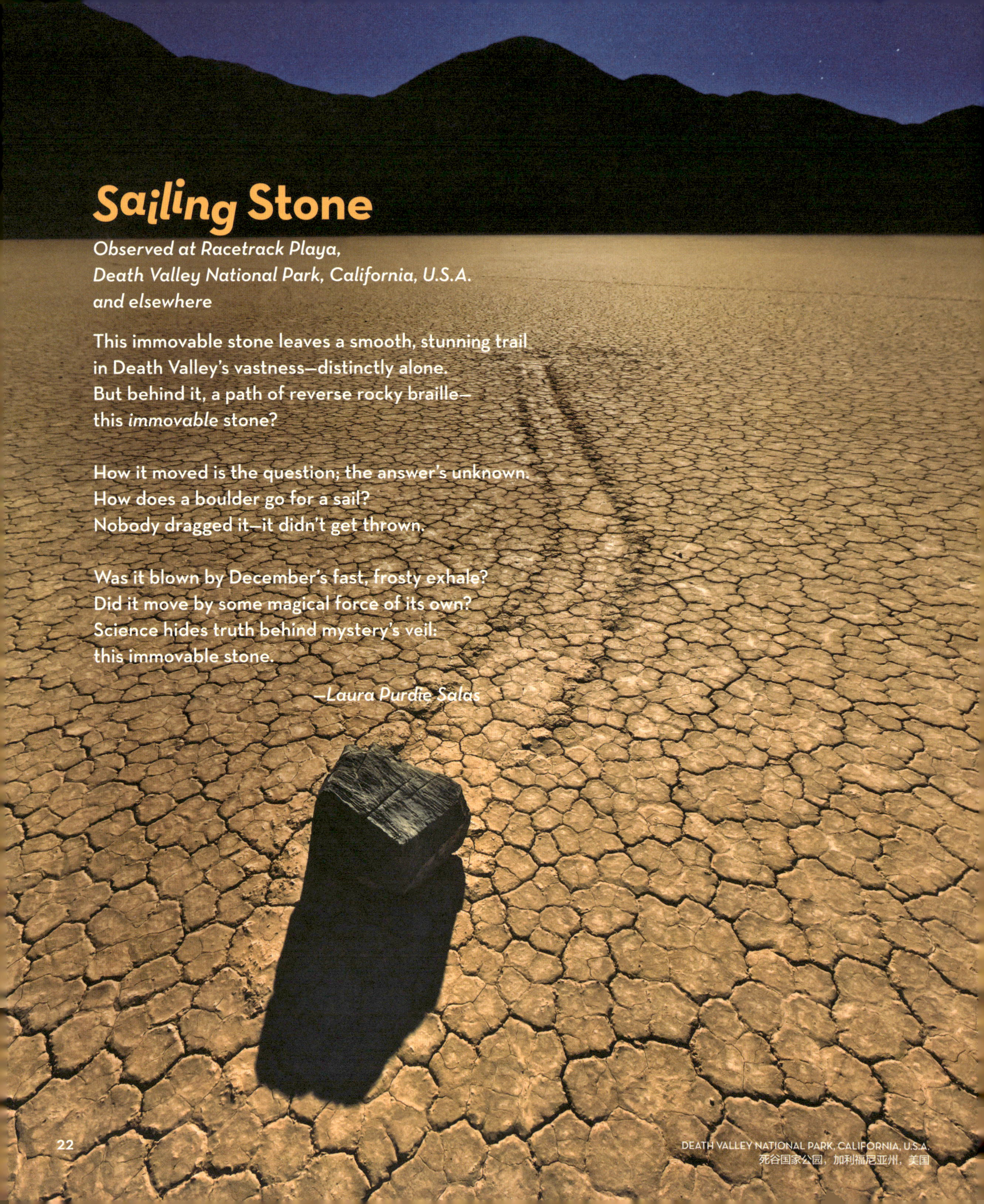

Sailing Stone

Observed at Racetrack Playa,
Death Valley National Park, California, U.S.A.
and elsewhere

This immovable stone leaves a smooth, stunning trail
in Death Valley's vastness—distinctly alone.
But behind it, a path of reverse rocky braille—
this *immovable* stone?

How it moved is the question; the answer's unknown.
How does a boulder go for a sail?
Nobody dragged it—it didn't get thrown.

Was it blown by December's fast, frosty exhale?
Did it move by some magical force of its own?
Science hides truth behind mystery's veil:
this immovable stone.

—Laura Purdie Salas

DEATH VALLEY NATIONAL PARK, CALIFORNIA, U.S.A.
死谷国家公园，加利福尼亚州，美国

In a Quiet Dark Place

The first drop leaves calcium—
a minuscule ring—
more molecules on the floor.

Drop by drop
fragile forms begin, stretch
down
up
an inch every 200 years.

Unknowable time,
from different places
moist tips draw near.

The moment comes,
inevitable union,
destiny sealed.

First touch in the dark,
gentle as a lover's kiss,
join them at last as one.

—David L. Harrison

ONONDAGA CAVE, MISSOURI, U.S.A.
奥农达加洞，密苏里州，美国

Thank You Note to the Gorge

At Watkins Glen State Park, New York, U.S.A.

Gorge,

You are like a Chinese brush painting,
all lichened rocks and crags,
jutting precipices, scraggly pines.
As tourists passed, I stood
and stared at a waterfall that tumbled
down your rocks in a spray of joy.

Halfway up your narrow stone path
I was out of breath. I stopped to watch
waters of yet another fall slide over you—
a transparent skin
that crashed in foamy froth.

Your cold air, deep shadows,
endless stone steps,
all shrouded in a strange green daytime light
made a mystery around me, and I felt
as though I were in some far and ancient land.

Thank you, gorge, for the wonder of my trip.

—Patricia Hubbell

WATKINS GLEN GORGE, NEW YORK, U.S.A.
沃特金斯峡谷，纽约州，美国

ROADS IN AUTUMN
秋日小径

A Late Walk

When I go up through the mowing field,
The headless aftermath,
Smooth-laid like thatch with the heavy dew,
Half closes the garden path.

And when I come to the garden ground,
The whir of sober birds
Up from the tangle of withered weeds
Is sadder than any words.

A tree beside the wall stands bare,
But a leaf that lingered brown,
Disturbed, I doubt not, by my thought,
Comes softly rattling down.

I end not far from my going forth
By picking the faded blue
Of the last remaining aster flower
To carry again to you.

—Robert Frost

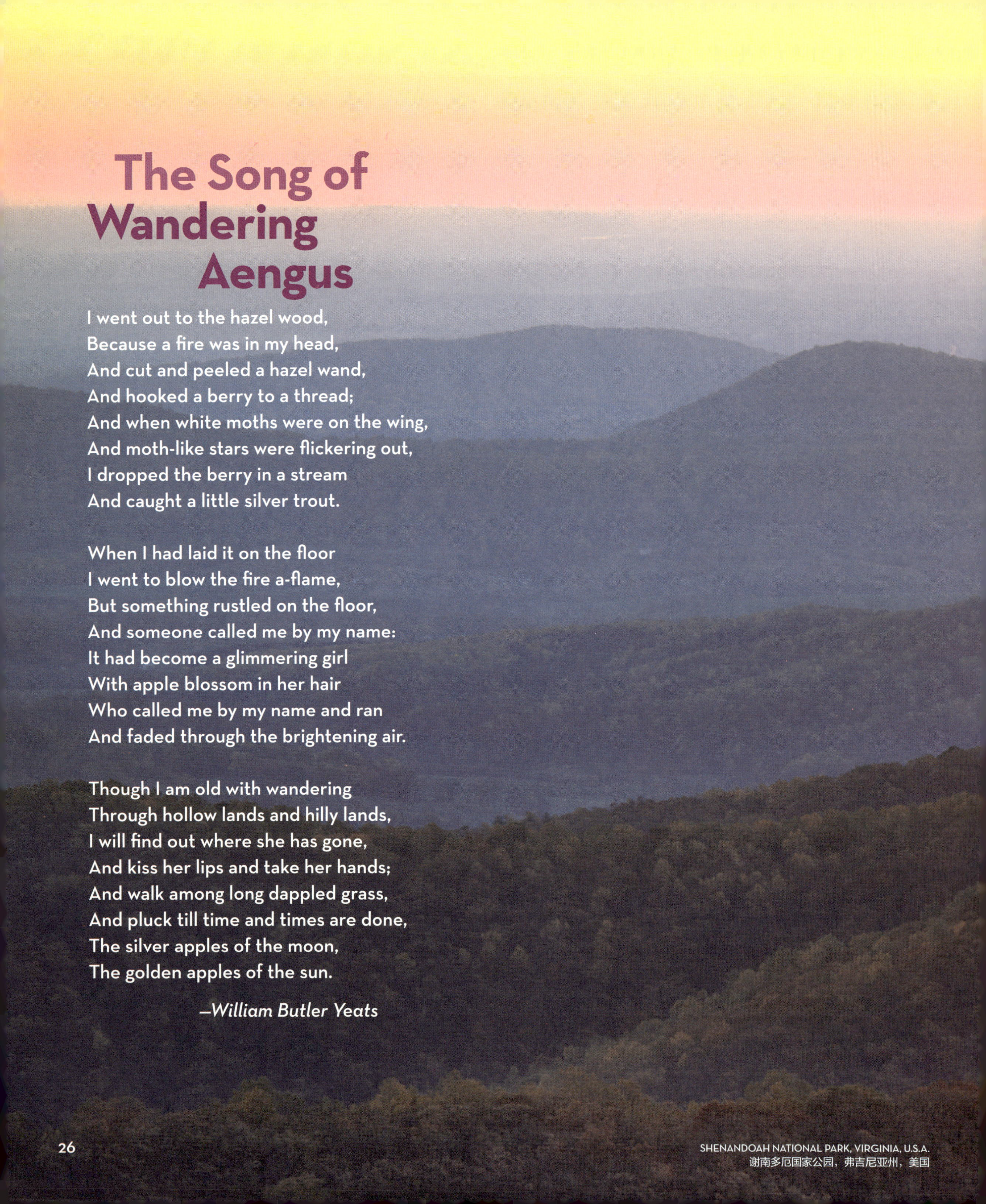

The Song of Wandering Aengus

I went out to the hazel wood,
Because a fire was in my head,
And cut and peeled a hazel wand,
And hooked a berry to a thread;
And when white moths were on the wing,
And moth-like stars were flickering out,
I dropped the berry in a stream
And caught a little silver trout.

When I had laid it on the floor
I went to blow the fire a-flame,
But something rustled on the floor,
And someone called me by my name:
It had become a glimmering girl
With apple blossom in her hair
Who called me by my name and ran
And faded through the brightening air.

Though I am old with wandering
Through hollow lands and hilly lands,
I will find out where she has gone,
And kiss her lips and take her hands;
And walk among long dappled grass,
And pluck till time and times are done,
The silver apples of the moon,
The golden apples of the sun.

—William Butler Yeats

SHENANDOAH NATIONAL PARK, VIRGINIA, U.S.A.
谢南多厄国家公园，弗吉尼亚州，美国

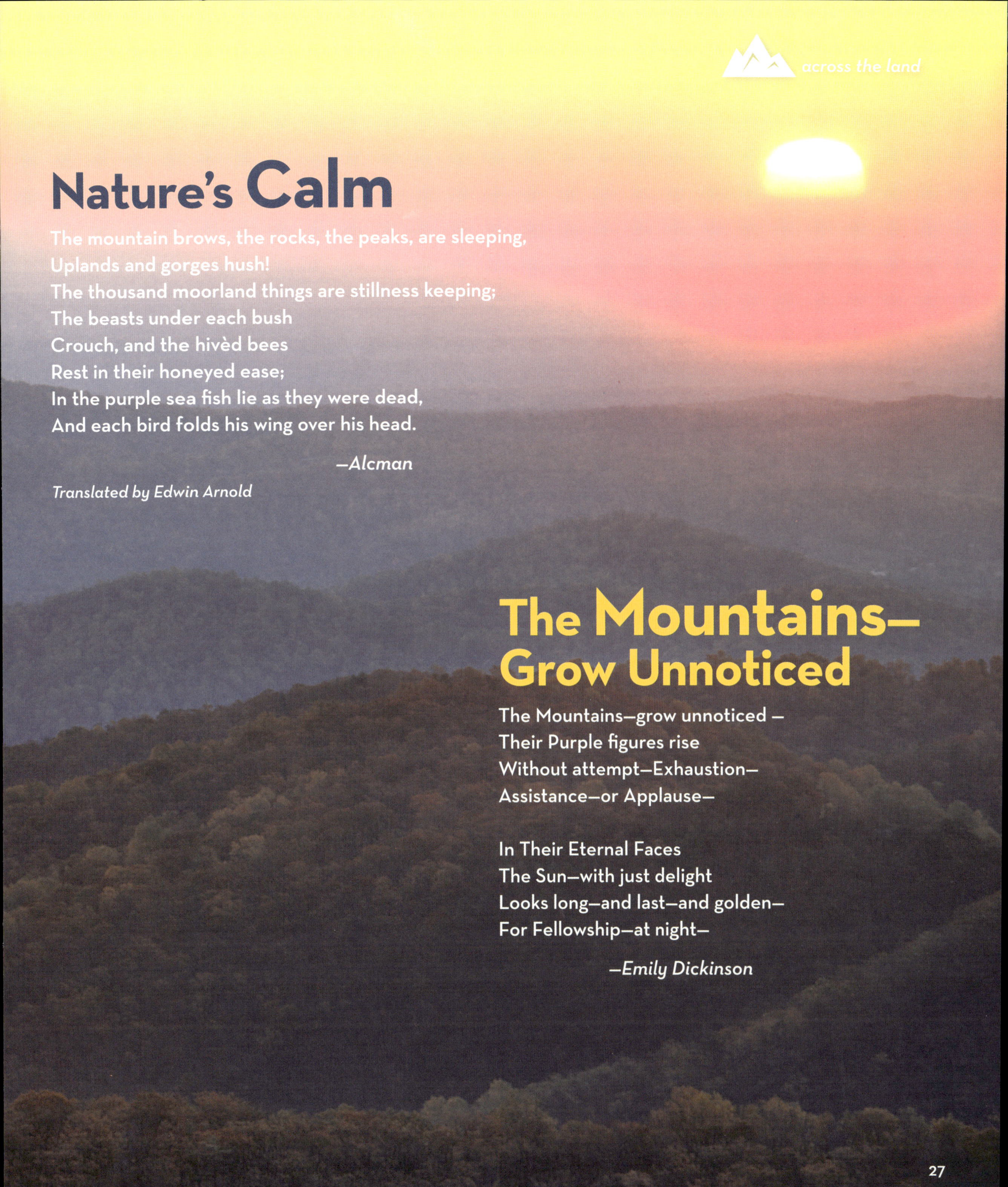

Nature's Calm

The mountain brows, the rocks, the peaks, are sleeping,
Uplands and gorges hush!
The thousand moorland things are stillness keeping;
The beasts under each bush
Crouch, and the hivèd bees
Rest in their honeyed ease;
In the purple sea fish lie as they were dead,
And each bird folds his wing over his head.

—Alcman

Translated by Edwin Arnold

The Mountains—Grow Unnoticed

The Mountains—grow unnoticed —
Their Purple figures rise
Without attempt—Exhaustion—
Assistance—or Applause—

In Their Eternal Faces
The Sun—with just delight
Looks long—and last—and golden—
For Fellowship—at night—

—Emily Dickinson

JOSHUA TREE NATIONAL PARK, CALIFORNIA, U.S.A.
约书亚树国家公园，加利福尼亚州，美国

山川
LAND

P14

You Ask Why

山中问答

问余何意栖碧山，笑而不答心自闲。
桃花流水窅然去，别有天地非人间。

——李白

P15

To Make a Prairie

如何造一个大草原

如何造一个大草原？
只要一株三叶草和一只蜜蜂就够了，
是的，一株三叶草和一只蜜蜂，
还有幻想。
如果没有蜜蜂，
只有幻想也行。

——埃米莉·迪金森

P15

An Indian Summer Day on the Prairie

草原上的印第安夏日

（清晨）
日出如年轻的猎手，
日出是绯色的欢愉，
日出像印第安少女，
来自伊利诺伊部落。

（仲晨）
阳光是微温的火焰，
蔓延穿过灰色平原，
晴空万里片云不留，
阳光普照雨花繁茂。

（正午）
艳阳如受伤的小鹿，
踏平天幕一片灰白，
他金色的鹿角摇曳，
他凶狠的目光闪烁。

（日落）
日暮正如雄鹰老去，
在风平浪静的西部。
在高高的峭壁顶端，
他建起红色的巢筑。

——韦切尔·林赛

Afternoon on a Hill

P16

山中午后

我会是阳光照耀下
最快乐的那一个！
我会抚摸一百株花，
却从不摘下一朵。

我会静静地凝望着
那些悬崖和云彩，
看大风吹弯了青草，
青草又直起身来。

当那城市中的灯火
开始在远处点亮，
我会记住属于我的，
开始下山去找寻。

——埃德娜·圣文森特·米莱

Up on the Hill

P16

在山顶上

我曾在山麓上
凝望着世界，
直到饱览所有风景。

我曾穿行于两场相距遥远的阵雨，
再坐下来，梦想整座山都属于我们。

在高山顶上是怎样的感觉？
你会感到充实，正如死去时希望的那样。

——詹姆斯·海福德

Adlestrop

P17

爱德斯托镇

是啊，我仍记得爱德斯托镇——
这个名字，因为在某个午后，
烈日灼心，
特快列车在这里偶然停下，
那是六月末。

蒸汽嘶嘶，有人清了清嗓子，
空无一人的月台上，
无人离开也无人到来。
我目光所及的只有
爱德斯托镇——只是这个名字。

还有那些柳树、柳兰和青草，
以及绣线菊和锥形的干草堆，
一点也不逊色于
天空中高悬的微云。

在那一刻，黑鹂高歌，
近旁，雾霭笼罩，
牛津郡和格洛斯特郡的鸟群
渐飞渐远。

——爱德华·托马斯

from Bat Cave

P18

《蝙蝠洞》节选

远远望去，
这个洞穴平淡无奇，
然而，只要我们靠近，
快走到洞口时，
就能够看到洞壁上斜成穹顶，
如黑色的肺剧烈拍打。
倒悬的蝙蝠，悸动的身躯，
涂满了洞顶，
身体深处合奏出的风琴乐，
生机勃勃。
在这神圣的洞穴里，
成簇的岩石边，
成千上万只眼睛炯炯发亮，
长着黑革翅翼的海涛啊，
拍岸而来。

——埃莉诺·威尔纳

P19

Desert

沙漠

我想到沙漠之花开放的地方，
去看那热辣的粉和璀璨的金
打破那冗长的黄沙。
我一定要在仙人掌间起舞，
看它们在尖刺中卖弄花朵。
我一定要为蝌蚪庆生，
看它们在天赐的水洼中游弋。

待到沙漠绽放之时，
我一定要去，
去看这块无垠的大地，
在一天之内变得洋洋喜气。
我一定要在雨中陶醉，
神圣而难得。
我一定要敬畏这奇特之地，
在这里，希望不会留给痴人。

——玛丽莲·辛格

P20

At the Un-National Monument Along the Canadian Border

在加拿大边境没有国家纪念碑的地方

在这片土地，战争未曾发生，
也没有阵亡的无名战士。
在这片土地，芳草连绵，
也没有纪念碑矗立，
天空是唯一的英雄。

群鸟飞过，哑然无声，
在旷野中展开翅膀，
无人杀戮——也无人牺牲——
在这片几乎被遗忘的神圣土地上，
平淡的气氛提醒人们：
忘记它的名字才是纪念它的方式。

——威廉·斯塔福德

P20

Former Barn Lot

旧谷仓

曾忆栅栏旧，
牧原草木长；
芳草何萋萋，
蔓蔓入谷仓。

雄驹蹴而过，
青草亦枯黄；
牧主迁而往，
唯余篱笆荒。

鸟儿线上停，
俯瞰旧谷仓；
荒草侵而入，
绿火幽幽上。

——马克·范多伦

P21

Red Rides West

红色在西方漂浮

当红色把绿色掩埋——秋天。
当红色与黄色联姻——日落。
当红色驰骋在西天——夕阳。
当红色把土地隐藏——尘土。
当红色把橘色燃烧——余烬。
当红色褪变为灰色——灰烬。
当红色幻化为金色——夜晚。
当红色渐变得古旧——锈迹。

——玛丽埃尔·比德

Sailing Stone

P22

风帆石

可在美国加利福尼亚州死谷国家公园的赛马场盐湖及其他地方观察到

这块静止的石头留下了一条光滑、绝妙的轨迹，
在广阔的死谷中孑然一身。
而在它身后，一串反写的盲文——
是这块静止的石头留下的吗？

它是如何移动的？答案无人知晓。
一块巨石如何扬帆远行？
没人拽它，也没人扔它。

是十二月凛冽的寒风吹的吗？
是靠自己的魔力移动的吗？
科学不能解释这块静止的石头，
这神秘面纱后的真相。

——劳拉·珀迪·萨拉斯

In a Quiet Dark Place

P23

在幽冥中

第一滴水留下了钙，
极微小的一环，
更多的钙分子落到了地面上。

一滴滴，
脆弱的外形开始形成，
向下拉拽，
向上伸展，
每二百年只长一英寸。

不知过了多久，
从不同方位，
湿漉漉的尖端越靠越近。

终于等到了，
那是宿命的相遇，
是久别的重逢。

幽冥中的第一次碰触，
像爱人的吻一般温柔，
最终融为一体。

——戴维·L.哈里森

Thank You Note to the Gorge

P24

献给峡谷的致敬辞

美国纽约州沃特金斯峡谷州立公园

致峡谷，
如水墨画，
苔痕碧岩，
峭壁嶙峋，
青松错节，
凝望瀑布，
飞流直下，
乐涛四溅。

石径斜上，
气喘欲绝，
驻足观赏，
水流漫延，
薄如蝉翼，
惊涛拍岸。

冷风暗影，
石阶无尽，
绿日葱茏，
神秘笼罩，
远古之地。

致敬峡谷，
旅途奇观。

——帕特里夏·哈贝尔

A Late Walk

P25

夜行

当我走上那刈过的青草地，
那片被斩的青梗，
沾着潮湿的露水，
像茅草一般平整，
半掩着花园小径。

当我走进花园，
鸟儿醒来，
回旋在纷乱的枯草上方，
言语无法描述的苍凉。

行道树孤独而立，
唯有一片枯叶流连树梢，
或被我的思绪干扰，
轻轻窸窣而下。

夜行不远我便停下脚步，
摘下最后一朵
凋谢的蓝色紫菀花，
再把它带来给你。

——罗伯特·弗罗斯特

The Song of Wandering Aengus

安格斯的寻爱之歌

我踱步在榛树林间，
因颅（炉）中有火在烧，
折一根细枝，剥皮，
挂一枚浆果，系线，
当白蛾展翅，
当星蛾扑闪，
我投浆果进小溪，
钓起银鱼一只。

当我把它放在地上，
前去把火点燃，
我听见沙沙声，
有人呼唤我的名字，
鱼儿变女孩，
浑身若明若暗，
发间花团锦簇，
是她唤我名字，
又转身即逝在泛白的空气中。

我垂垂老矣，却依然寻觅，
踏遍旷野，独步山地，
我要找寻你的去向，
执子之手，吻子芳唇，
行过那斑驳的长草，
采集，采集
月之银果，
日之金实，
直至天荒地老。

——威廉·巴特勒·叶芝

Nature's Calm

自然之静

山脊、岩石、顶峰，都睡着了，
高地、峡谷，一片寂静。
广袤荒野上万物静止，
每一片灌木丛之下，走兽蜷伏，
归巢的蜜蜂
在静蜜（谧）中休憩；
暗紫的海洋里，鱼群死寂，
鸟儿们将头埋进了翅膀。

——艾克曼

（原诗由埃德温·阿诺德译为英文）

The Mountains— Grow Unnoticed

群山悄然长

群山悄然长，
紫廓自然生，
无求亦无倦，
无助亦无赞。

山貌永留存，
日照欢愉久，
金辉长余世，
夜来相伴眠。

——埃米莉·迪金森

Who is mother nature?

When Mother Nature's near—in waterfalls, rivers, rainbows, meadows, or oceans—her admirers react with love, awe, curiosity, even fear, if she decides to reveal her grumpier side. The lady can be seen through telescopes or microscopes, from mountaintops or ravines, with the wind in our hair, soil in our hands, or sand in our toes. For those who aren't hopelessly city-bound, looking out a window will do.

Driven to explore the *science* behind the wonder of it all, Charles Darwin filled scores of notebooks about what was then the unexplored wildlife of the Galápagos Islands. Countless nature writers have followed his courageous example. Others have put themselves in nature, like naturalist John Muir, who once rode out a northern American windstorm by cocooning himself in the branches of a sky-high Douglas spruce. (Muir is famous—or should be—for saying, "The clearest way into the Universe is through a forest wilderness.")

Some humans, however, have no use for wild places, a view once expressed by Woody Allen with his typical wit: "I love nature. I just don't want to get any of it on me." For some, their love for animals extends only as far as Fido or Sweet Pea. That we share the Earth equally with other creatures is a notion as foreign and irrelevant to them as the disappearance of the rain forests or the melting of the ice caps.

But Mother Nature doesn't care who likes her. Nor is she bothered about being ignored. A midwife at the birth of creatures large and small, she will go on making waves by making waves, assembling forests, flowering deserts, and beautifying gardens. We can embrace her or resist her charms; it is of no concern to her.

Who is the mysterious lady known as Mother Nature? She is the material world, the environment of trees, plants, animals, everything under and over the sun. In short, she equals the world around us and includes whatever is not built by human hands.

Mother Nature is where we live. In other words, she is
a refuge to the lost,
a magnet to the curious,
a dare to the daring,
the cradle of rapture,
the university of the universe,
the glory of a morning and of a morning-glory,
not a whale but the idea of a whale,
a sign rewriter: I Welcome All No Trespassing,
the best cure for couch disease,
an opera performed by birds, bullfrogs on drums,
the sound of silence . . . amplified
to the symphony of the spheres, and ____________
____ .

Can you add another short description of Mother Nature to this poem?

The poets and photographers who have come together to produce National Geographic's *Book of Nature Poetry* would agree with John Keats, who defined their abiding faith: "The poetry of earth is never dead."

THREAD-WINGED ANTLION
线翅蚁狮

自然之母是谁？

当自然之母靠近的时候——在瀑布中，在河流中，在彩虹中，在草地或是海洋中——她的爱慕者用爱、敬畏、好奇来回应，甚至如果她显示暴躁的一面时，则用恐惧来回应。这位女士可以用望远镜或是显微镜来观察，从山顶到深谷，风在我们的发丝中穿过，泥土在我们手中漏出，沙在我们的脚趾中渗出。对于那些不喜欢住在城里的人来说，只要看一看窗外就行。

为了探索自然奇观背后的科学道理，查尔斯·达尔文把加拉帕戈斯群岛未知的野生动物记满了几十本笔记本。难以数计的自然主义作家跟随着他，以他为榜样。其他人则让自己融入自然。例如自然主义者约翰·缪尔，曾经用高耸入云的道格拉斯云杉的枝叶包裹着自己，经受住了北美的风暴。（缪尔由于下面这句话而知名——或应该知名——“融入宇宙最清晰的方式莫过于通过荒野森林”。）

然而，也有一些人，觉得野外毫无用处，这也是伍迪·艾伦用他特有的机智曾经表达的观点：“我爱自然，但是一点也别弄到我身上来。”而另一些人，他们对动物的喜爱只限于“菲多”或是“甜豌豆”。对他们来说，我们与其他生物平等地分享地球的观念，和雨林正在消失、冰层正在融化这样的概念一样，是未知而不重要的。

但自然之母并不关心谁喜欢她。她对这种忽视也毫不在意。她是大大小小各种生物出生时的产婆，她将不断在波浪中创造波浪，让森林遍地，让花朵在沙漠开放，让花园变得更美。我们可以接受或是抗拒她的魅力，她对此却毫不关心。

这位被人称为自然之母的神秘女士是谁？她是物质世界，也是植物、动物的环境和阳光下所有的一切。简言之，她就是我们周遭的世界，人类双手无法创造的世界。

自然之母在我们生活的地方。换句话说，
她是：
迷失者的庇护，
好奇者的磁石，
勇敢者的挑战，
狂喜者的摇篮，
宇宙的教化者。
她是：
清晨的光辉，
牵牛花的光，
并不是鲸鱼，
而是这创意。
她重新写了一个标记：我欢迎所有的非擅自闯入者。
她是：
沙发病的良药，
鸟儿、牛蛙在鼓上演奏的歌剧，
是寂静之声……被放大，
而成为万物的交响曲，
也是 ________________

你可以在这首诗后面加上一段描写自然之母的短句吗？

共同创作《最美自然诗集》的诗人和摄影家们会同意约翰·济慈的话，他道出了他们永恒的信仰：“地球的诗篇永远不会消亡。”

LOTUS AND BEES -WUQIANG
荷花与蜜蜂（吴强）

美国国家地理学会是世界上最大的非营利科学与教育组织之一。学会成立于1888年，以“增进与普及地理知识”为宗旨，致力于启发人们对地球的关心。美国国家地理学会通过杂志、电视节目、影片、音乐、电台、图书、DVD、地图、展览、活动、学校出版计划、交互式媒体与商品来呈现世界。美国国家地理学会的会刊《国家地理》杂志，以英文及其他33种语言发行，每月有3800万读者阅读。美国国家地理频道在166个国家以34种语言播放，有3.2亿个家庭收看。美国国家地理学会资助超过10 000项科学研究、环境保护与探索计划，并支持一项扫除“地理文盲”的教育计划。

Acknowledgments

To the entire National Geographic team for their enthusiasm and dedication in the making of this book, and to all the poets whose deserving work, regrettably, could not be squeezed into its pages.—JPL

The publisher gratefully acknowledges the heroic efforts of Natalie Turner in securing permissions, as well as the invaluable research assistance of Alyson Foster.

图书在版编目（CIP）数据

最美自然诗集 /（美）J. 帕特里克·刘易斯主编；Abby F. Yehenola，张原平，和览编译. —郑州：河南科学技术出版社，2018.1

ISBN 978-7-5349-8952-0

Ⅰ.①最… Ⅱ.①J… ②A… ③张… ④和… Ⅲ.①儿童诗歌-诗集-美国-现代 Ⅳ.①I712.82

中国版本图书馆CIP数据核字(2017)第269830号

出版发行：河南科学技术出版社

地址：郑州市经五路66号　　邮编：450002

电话：（0371）65737028　　65788613

网址：www.hnstp.cn

特邀策划：Abby F. Yehenola

策划编辑：马艳茹　韩雅楠　于凯燕

责任编辑：于凯燕

责任校对：徐小刚

整体设计：吴豆豆

责任印制：张　巍

印　　刷：北京盛通印刷股份有限公司

经　　销：全国新华书店

幅面尺寸：232 mm×276 mm　　印张：2.5　　字数：63千字

版　　次：2018年1月第1版　　2018年1月第1次印刷

全套定价：588.00元

To poets, nature, and nature poets everywhere.—JPL

献给诗人、自然和全世界写自然的诗人。

——J. 帕特里克·刘易斯

献给爱自然、爱诗歌的大小朋友们！

——Abby

美国童诗桂冠诗人［美］J.帕特里克·刘易斯　主编
Abby F. Yehenola ✿ 张原平 ✿ 和览　编译

NATIONAL GEOGRAPHIC
美国国家地理

book of nature poetry

最美自然诗集 5

（汉英对照）

200首诗歌
和会漂浮
会穿越，
会开花
的精彩图片

河南科学技术出版社
·郑州·

自然最美

千山鸟飞绝，
万径人踪灭。
孤舟蓑笠翁，
独钓寒江雪。

这是唐朝柳宗元的《江雪》。短短的20个字，便成功捕捉一幅美丽的风景画。当时的孤冷静谧与雪白世界，似乎透过这首诗被永久封存，美丽了好几千年，不曾消逝。

《最美自然诗集》的出版，重新带给我这样的震撼与感动。随着时代的变迁，生活节奏的加快，文字阅读耗费时间，致使读者更为钟情图像阅读。不过图像阅读与文字阅读所获得的乐趣，无法互相取代。纵使是对同个风景的描绘，使用新诗文字创作与照片图像创作，让读者感受到的乐趣亦是截然不同。若是舍弃文字的阅读，全都转向图像阅读，实在相当可惜。《最美自然诗集》却完美解决了这个问题：这本诗集的每首诗，都是一张照片加上一首诗，使得文字文本和图像文本相互合作对话，形成一支精彩的双人舞。

这本书真的让我重新认识美丽的地球！在大自然中，随着四季的交替、地形的差异、气候的更迭，每一刹那的风景都是独一无二、稍纵即逝的。照片是静态的叙事，透过摄影师的镜头，有意识地捕捉吉光片羽，所以一张张的美照，是摄影师透过自身的美学哲学与镜头的选择所决定的，也可以说照片是摄影师眼中的美景。

而诗的创作，则是透过诗人纤细善感的心思，触景生情，把当时的生命状态转化成诗句，以情寓景，让景物多了一股人情的芬芳，不少美景在诗句的化妆下，变得充满情韵，让人印象深刻。

除此之外，这本书的编者扮演着隐形创作者的角色，因为他们成功媒合了照片与诗句，让作品更有一层乐趣。诗句的意象让静态的照片翩然生动，仿佛可以听见照片中的潺潺流水声，让读者宛若身临其境，感受照片里的一草一木，让读者悠游在每幅照片之中。阅读《最美自然诗集》，需要最好的领航员同游，我们的译者充分领会了编者的匠心独运，十分用心地录制了200首音频，恰是《最美自然诗集》最好的导读。

这本诗集让读者感受到三种美学：文学之美、摄影之美以及想象之美。透过诗句，让读者感受到文字透过意象诠释的美学；透过摄影照片让读者感受到强烈的视觉盛宴。当今的科技，无论是手机、电视还是穿戴科技等等，均试图以科技的力量，让读者感受到身临其境的感官盛宴，增强读者的视觉与听觉震撼，产生娱乐感，但是与此同时，相对地也剥夺了读者想象之美的权利。而《最美自然诗集》在照片与文字当中，保留了相当多的空白，并分类为“感叹自然”“凌空”“渊洋”“生灵”“山川”“美植”“灾难”“四季”“奇景”“敬畏自然”，让读者可以发挥想象，感受编者所安排的想象之美。因此，阅读这本书让读者经历一场美学盛宴，沉醉在大自然的洗礼之中。

最后，从这本书中也可以看出编者对于环境保护的意识。人类过度开发，使得环境被破坏，导致气候异常，很多珍稀动物濒临灭绝，大自然也不再美丽。希望这本诗集，能唤起人类对于大自然的重新思考，思考如何与环境共生。

透过这本最美丽的诗集，让我们回忆起我们曾经的美好！伟哉自然，伟哉生命！

· 译者序 ·

植物与动物，一静一动，构成了整个世界的和谐。这本书中有25首诗专门来描写植物，一起来读读：

心里不平静的时候，来到林间，每一片树叶、每一只跳蛙都会让我们静下来。种一片树林，让我们和时间一起打造一个天堂。

你见过整个一棵树上面布满了帝王蝶吗？这个场景肯定会让你终生难忘，这两首诗可以帮助你。

这世界上的奇观不分大小，每个都会让你惊叹，无论是小小的睡莲，还是2000多岁的红杉，都宏伟得让人震撼。

世间有很多奥秘，花期是谜，卷藤是谜，小路也是谜，一首诗告诉你，谜即是美。

诗人把女人比作花，一个女人尚且好搞定，两个呢？三个呢？一群呢？诗人拿花束来解决这个问题。

菊花的出现，意味着凉气的逼近，有人爱菊花，如同这位韩国诗人，来听听我们韩国译者的讲解，你会越过英文版吮吸原文。

记得《最美动物诗集》中有一首诗是不可翻译的，我和原平重新写了一首补上，这次，在《最美自然诗集》中，又出现了一首，这次我用两种语言重写了一首诗，准保朗朗上口。

植物最美的除了形态，就数色彩了，四首诗中有西班牙的绿苔、彩虹色的桉树皮、绽放的粉白花和如粉色蝴蝶的三叶梅。

一朵花是怎么烘焙成的？你听得没错！如果用烘焙的手法做花朵，分几步呢？来读这首诗。

唱着《采蘑菇的小姑娘》长大的这一代，我们书中也有一首诗写了两个采蘑菇的小姑娘，她们的生活可谓闲适啊。

像乳草荚这样的植物能让迈克尔 · J.罗森这样重要的诗人为之写上一首诗是不是太荣幸了！来读这首诗，不太好读，但读懂了会让你惊喜。

华兹华斯仿佛可以把一切平庸的事物写得诗意无比，哪怕是他随便散个步也会有经典之作产生，例如这首诗。

有的树一千年不死，死了一千年不倒，倒了一千年不朽，这首诗中的玛士撒拉树就是这样的树，来读读诗人是如何描写的。

如果你的球掉在玫瑰丛中，你怎么办？这首诗把你去捡球的过程写了出来，太有意思了。

雪中冷冷的你，看到“挺且直”的松树会不会更冷？可是别忘了，诗里说了，树里还有红雀一家暖暖地依偎在一起。

Abby 2017年10月于昆明

IN SHADE

美植

J. PATRICK LEWIS HAS WRITTEN MORE THAN 95 PICTURE AND POETRY BOOKS FOR YOUNG READERS. IN 2011 HE WAS APPOINTED U.S. CHILDREN'S POET LAUREATE, AND WAS GIVEN THE NATIONAL COUNCIL OF TEACHERS OF ENGLISH AWARD FOR EXCELLENCE IN POETRY FOR CHILDREN.

HENRY DAVID THOREAU was one of America's truly Big Thinkers on a little pond—Walden Pond. It was there in 1853, in a self-built cabin not far from his Massachusetts family home, that he wrote: "I have a room all to myself; it is nature."

From his tucked-away cottage, Thoreau produced some of the most profound thoughts on Mother Nature. But poets from centuries past rarely wrote about the more exotic natural wonders. They never saw them, never knew they existed. Many of the most fascinating phenomena that we often take for granted today—thanks to the convenience of travel, books, or photographs—were seldom brought to the attention of the classical poets.

How would William Shakespeare or John Keats have described in a poem the grandeur of the Grand Canyon? One can only imagine Emily Dickinson, transported to the scene, painting on an easel built of words a picture of an Asian tsunami or an African drought. What immortal verse might William Wordsworth have written after a day's walk in the Amazon rain forest instead of the English countryside? What picture would Kobayashi Issa or Li Po paint after a submersible dive to the ocean deep?

And yet a poet does not have to be there! You needn't leave your chair to write a poem about the wilder shores of creation. A book is your ticket to ride; a photograph is rapid transit to the brain. What kind of poem would you write if all you had in front of you was an image, like one of the breathtaking pictures in the *Book of Nature Poetry* you are now holding?

Better yet, let your eyes be your camera, taking incredible pictures your brain will thank you for. Get up and go there! Explore the woods, a cave; climb a mountain; go scuba diving; or simply make a friend of a grasshopper in a field on a windy summer day. You might even imagine you *are* that dragonfly trying to escape a swift, or a lucky salmon that has wiggled through the legs of a grizzly bear.

Travel by photograph or on foot, but go quickly before nature disappears. Every day more than 70 animals, plants, or other living things, like fungi, roots, and molds, vanish forever. The *Book of Nature Poetry* seeks to capture the ever changing nature of nature, so that gone is not forgotten. Besides, when more of us care for nature, more can help save it.

However and wherever you greet the world outside your window, listen again to Mr. Thoreau for the last and best words of advice:

"It's not what you look at that matters. It's what you see."

—J. Patrick Lewis,
former U.S. Children's Poet Laureate

MALACHITE BUTTERFLY
孔雀石蝴蝶

J. 帕特里克 · 刘易斯已经为孩子们创作了95部图画书和诗集。2011年，他荣获了美国童诗桂冠诗人奖，并被美国国家英语教师委员会授予杰出童诗奖。

·前 言·

亨利·戴维·梭罗是美国真正的大思想家之一，他曾隐居在瓦尔登湖。

1853年，在离马萨诸塞州家不远的自建小木屋里，他写道：“我有一个只属于我自己的房间——大自然。”

就在这世外桃源般的小木屋里，梭罗萌发出一些关于大自然的极其深刻的思想。但是这几百年来，诗人们却很少再去描写更独特的自然奇观。他们从来没见过，甚至都不知晓它们的存在。很多今天我们习以为常的，可以从旅行、书籍或照片中轻松获取的绝世美景，以前却很少能引起古典诗人们的关注。

试想，莎士比亚和济慈会怎样用诗歌去描绘大峡谷的壮美？可想而知，若埃米莉·迪金森能亲临亚洲海啸或非洲干旱现场，她将会用文字绘制出怎样的一幅画卷。那华兹华斯呢？如果他有机会走在亚马孙雨林中，而不仅仅是在英国乡间小道徘徊，他的笔下会写出怎样的诗句呢？若小林一茶或李白能乘潜艇探访大洋深渊，他们诗作的意境又将是怎样的呢？

然而，诗人并非一定要身临其境。你不需要离开椅子才能去写沧海桑田。一本书可以带你去遨游，一张照片可以带你去穿越。如果你拥有的只是面前的一幅图，就像你手里的《最美自然诗集》中的任意一幅惊艳的美图一样，你能写出怎样的诗句呢？

更棒的是，去旅行，让眼睛成为你的照相机，让眼前的美景滋养你的大脑。去吧，去森林中历险，去探索一个洞穴，去勇攀一座高峰，去潜入海底，甚至去野地里和一只蚱蜢交个朋友，任夏风轻抚。你甚至可以去想象自己就是那只努力躲过雨燕的蜻蜓，或是那条幸运地游过灰熊两腿之间的三文鱼。

无论是借着照片观光还是身临其境，请尽早，赶在自然景观消失之前。每天，都有超过70种生物在地球上永远消失。《最美自然诗集》力图捕捉到大自然瞬息万变的属性，让逝去的不再被遗忘。同时，当有更多的人开始关心大自然时，便会有更多的人来拯救她。

无论你在哪里，用怎样的方式来向窗外的世界致敬，请你再一次，也是最后一次聆听梭罗先生的警世良言：

“重要的不是你眼前的，而是你心里的。”

——J. 帕特里克·刘易斯，美国童诗桂冠诗人

The Thing Is the Thing Is Green

The thing is the thing is green and the green is green and by green I mean real mean green. I mean electric-eel green, alligator, iguana, anaconda green. I mean this thing has got all things green. It's got green turtles in turtle-green ponds and grasshoppers springing from groomed-green lawns and a green tree frog on a girl's left arm. It's got dark and dangerous greens. Greens you've never even seen greens. Ocean floor greens. Tornado sky greens. Tiger's eye greens. Eat-your-broccoli greens. Watermelons sparkling in the sun greens. Way beyond evergreen, this thing leaves green geckos on green leaves feeling green and green moths in the green dark and preying mantises on their thin green knees. It's a great and gorgeous green a light-bright-just-right-watch-it-grow-it-says-go shade of green. Have you guessed yet? Do you need another clue? Think rolling waves of grain green. Thick arms of vines climbing tall green trees. Mountains and mountains of green billions of waves reaching out of dark green seas all wrapped in one green ball and hung, an ornament in the sky. What a thing it must be to see the whole green thing floating by. It's true. The thing is the thing is green . . .

except when it's blue.

—*Peggy Gifford*

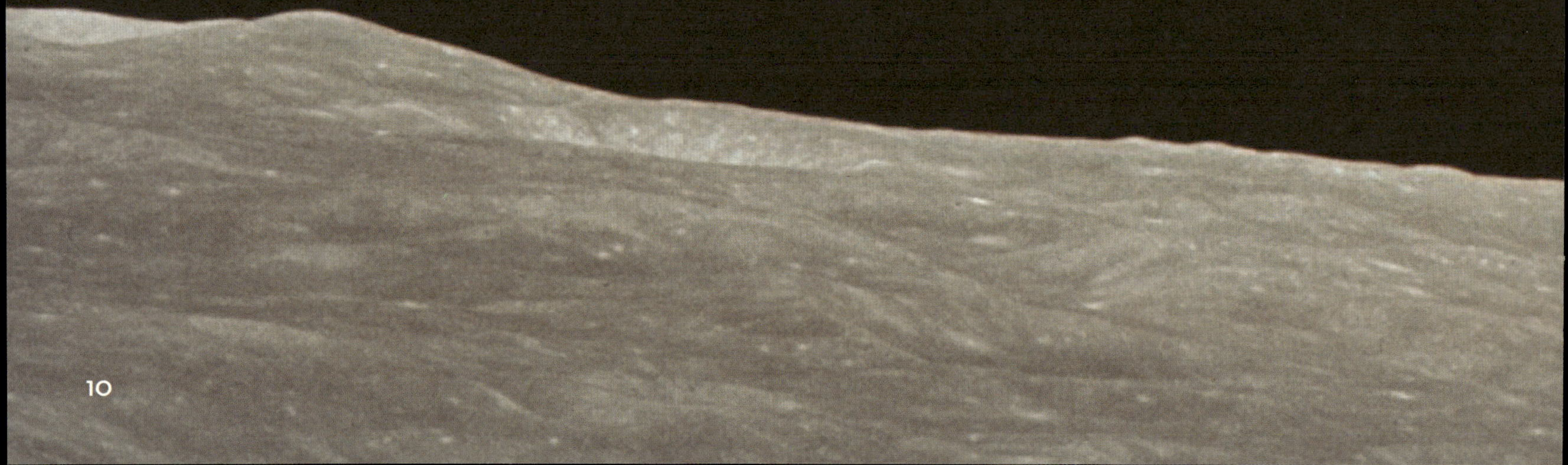

它要多绿就有多绿

要多绿就有多绿，绿就绿它个透心绿，就是这么绿，实打实的绿。我讲的是电鳗绿、鳄鱼绿、蜥蜴绿、蟒蛇绿，我说的这种绿把所有东西都染绿了。瞧那绿龟徜徉在龟绿色的池塘里，蚱蜢从刚修绿的草坪里一跃而起，一只绿树蛙停歇在女孩的左臂。有时候，它绿得阴森，绿得凶险，绿得其实你从未见过。大洋底的深渊绿，龙卷风的虐绿，老虎眼底的幽绿，“吃完西兰花”的郁闷绿，西瓜在阳光下的闪耀绿。比常绿植物更绿的，是绿叶上享绿的绿色壁虎、沉绿夜空的绿色飞蛾、紧绷双膝的绿色螳螂。它绿得伟大，绿得华丽，那“趁着阳光正好赶快生长说长就长”的一抹绿。还没有猜出来吗？还需要再来一点提示吗？想想那绿色的麦浪翻滚，想想那粗壮的藤蔓攀上绿色的参天大树。连绵不绝的绿色山峦，深绿海洋中的滔天巨澜，竟都被包在一个绿色的球里，独具一格地装点着天空。能亲眼看见这大绿球飘过该是一件多么大的幸事啊。没错，它要多绿就有多绿……

除非它变蓝了……

——佩姬·吉福德

A LONE TREE, VENDÉE, FRANCE
一颗孤独的树，旺代，法国

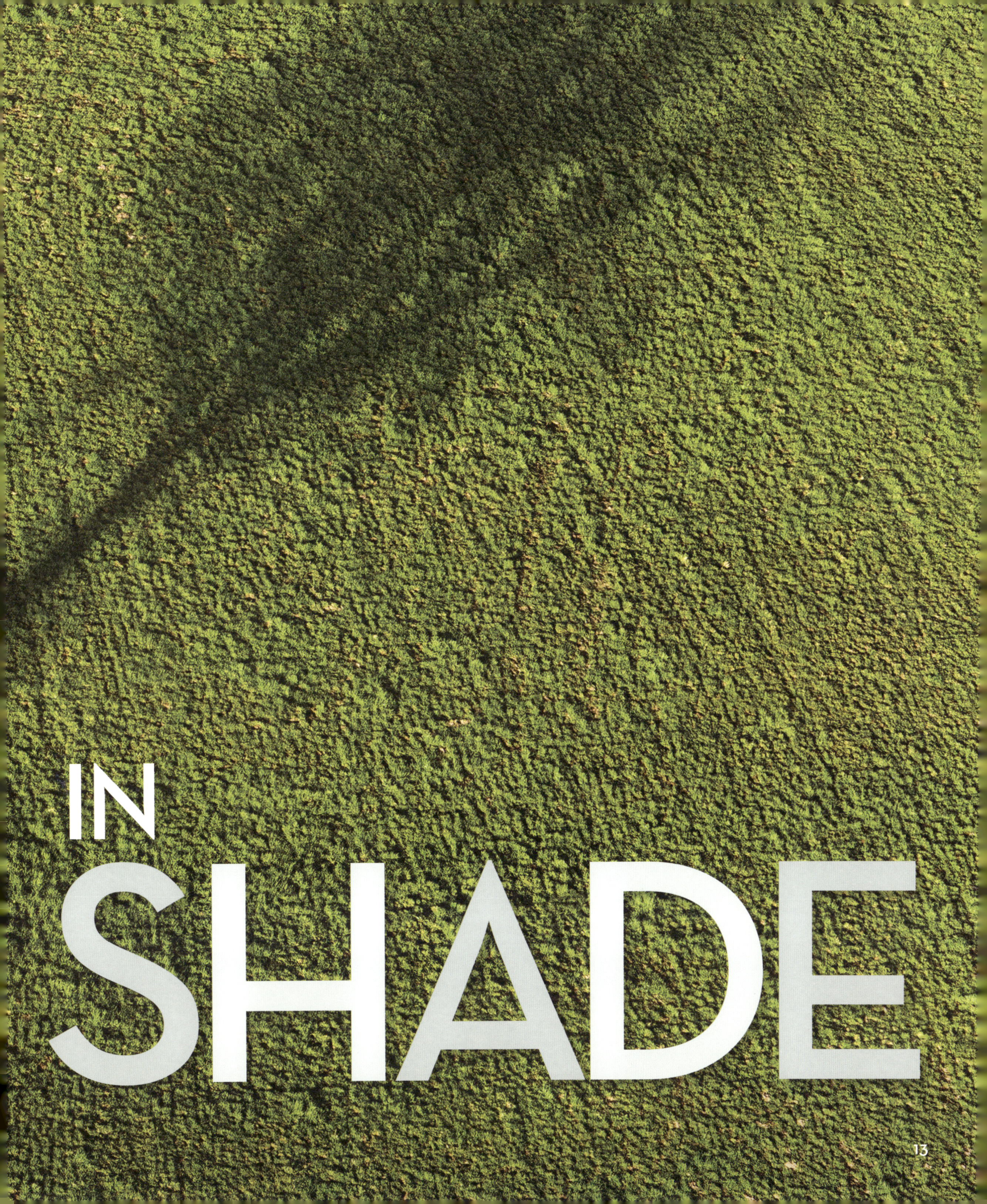

IN SHADE

Lessons in September

In the first golden hour of autumn
when light slants away from summer's angry eye
and the leaves, not yet blushing, mute and soften
I went to the woods
with nothing to tether me to this world—
to remember how to listen
to the wind cascade through leaves in cresting waves
to finches squabble like tetchy spouses
to the soft music of the creek.
To remember how to see
a spotted toad vault into the underbrush
a white caterpillar wend its way across the footbridge
a red-tailed hawk slide past the window of sky.
A birch tree, I've passed hundreds of times
without notice, stood sentinel all the same.
Someday, I hope to stay
who I am in the woods
when out of them—
Aware
Grateful
Awed

—Tracie Vaughn Zimmer

OAK SAPLING
橡树苗

Time to Plant Trees

Time to plant trees is when you're young
So you will have them to walk among—

So, aging, you can walk in shade
That you and time together made.

—James Hayford

Dew

Diamonds on the petals,
Silver on the stems,
Early morning sunrise
Turns dewdrops into gems.

—Charles Ghigna

BLUEBELLS
蓝铃花

Butterfly Tree

Like some
Hawaiian king
draped in a feathered robe,
eucalyptus reigns—resplendent
monarch.

—Joan Bransfield Graham

MONARCH BUTTERFLIES, SIERRA CHINCUA, MEXICO
帝王蝶，米却肯州，墨西哥

The Monarch's Flight to Mexico

Only a whisper from ancient roots
and cyclones of orange rise.
Good-bye to summer's sweet pursuits!
Only a whisper from ancient roots,
and billions dressed in brilliant suits
ride skyways billed for butterflies.
Only a whisper from ancient roots,
and cyclones of orange rise.

—Avis Harley

Haiku

lily:
out of the water . . .
out of itself

—Nick Virgilio

EGYPTIAN BLUE WATER LILY
埃及蓝睡莲

GENERAL SHERMAN TREE, SEQUOIA NATIONAL PARK, CALIFORNIA, U.S.A.
谢尔曼将军树，红杉国家公园，加利福尼亚州，美国

General Sherman Sequoia: World's Largest Tree

Giant Forest of Sequoia National Park, Tulare County, California, U.S.A.

General Sherman,
though elements
batter you—wind,
fire . . . storms—
you deflect them,
hold your ground.
For 2,500 years
you have watched
the rise and fall of
lives, civilizations.
At 275' tall, you
have captured a
corner of the sky.
Stand victorious:
we s a l u t e you.

—Joan Bransfield Graham

Sequoia

In the very middle
of the archaic woods
leaves browse on the sun
like gods, roots tongue
the dark below—who
needs words? I find
myself debating silence,
losing again.

—Leonard Nathan

The Mystery

The tree is the mystery,
its roots knotted
as surely as love.

The spring flowers are the mystery,
without calendar or clock
they announce the season.

The pond is the mystery,
holding trout in its deepest,
darkest heart.

The fern is the mystery,
knowing how to uncurl
with no teacher but the sun.

The path is the mystery,
worn down by many feet
yet still willing to support them.

The gate . . .
          the gate is no mystery at all
for we have put it there
to signal that house is near,

though dog has but to lift his snout
to know we are already home.

—Jane Yolen

FERN FROND
蕨叶

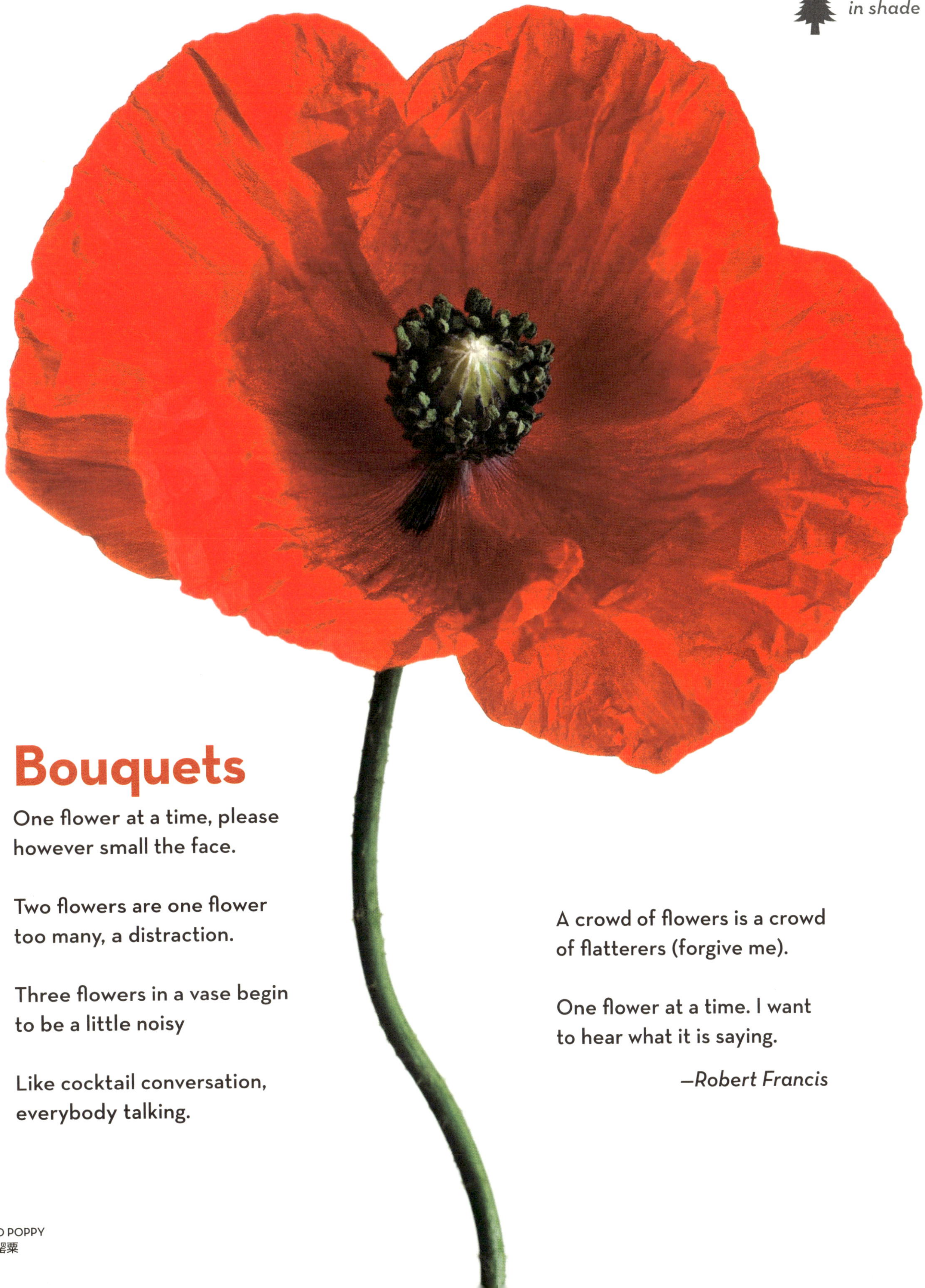

Bouquets

One flower at a time, please
however small the face.

Two flowers are one flower
too many, a distraction.

Three flowers in a vase begin
to be a little noisy

Like cocktail conversation,
everybody talking.

A crowd of flowers is a crowd
of flatterers (forgive me).

One flower at a time. I want
to hear what it is saying.

—Robert Francis

RED POPPY
红罂粟

Beside a Chrysanthemum

For one chrysanthemum to bloom
a nightingale
has sobbed since spring, perhaps.

For one chrysanthemum to bloom
thunder
has pealed in dark clouds, perhaps.

Flower! Like my sister standing
at her mirror, just back
from far away, far away byways of youth,
where she was racked with longing and lack:

last night's frost came down
to bid your yellow petals bloom, perhaps,
while I could not get to sleep.

—So Chong Ju

Translated by Brother Anthony of Taize

BUTTON CHRYSANTHEMUMS
纽扣菊

WHITE BIRCHES, COLORADO, U.S.A.
白桦树，科罗拉多州，美国

Counting-Out Rhyme

Silver bark of beech, and sallow
Bark of yellow birch and yellow
Twig of willow.

Stripe of green in moosewood maple,
Colour seen in leaf of apple,
Bark of popple.

Wood of popple pale as moonbeam,
Wood of oak for yoke and barn-beam,
Wood of hornbeam.

Silver bark of beech, and hollow
Stem of elder, tall and yellow
Twig of willow.

—Edna St. Vincent Millay

The Release

At sunset
the shadows of all the trees
break free and go running
across the edge of the world.

—Joseph Bruchac

Spanish Moss

A Southern Gothic,
A Live Oak lady,
Caressing limbs,
Secret and shady.

Wild and pale,
Curly and thin,
She's a tease in the breeze.
She sways in the wind.

—Charles Ghigna

SPANISH MOSS AND OAK
松萝凤梨和橡树

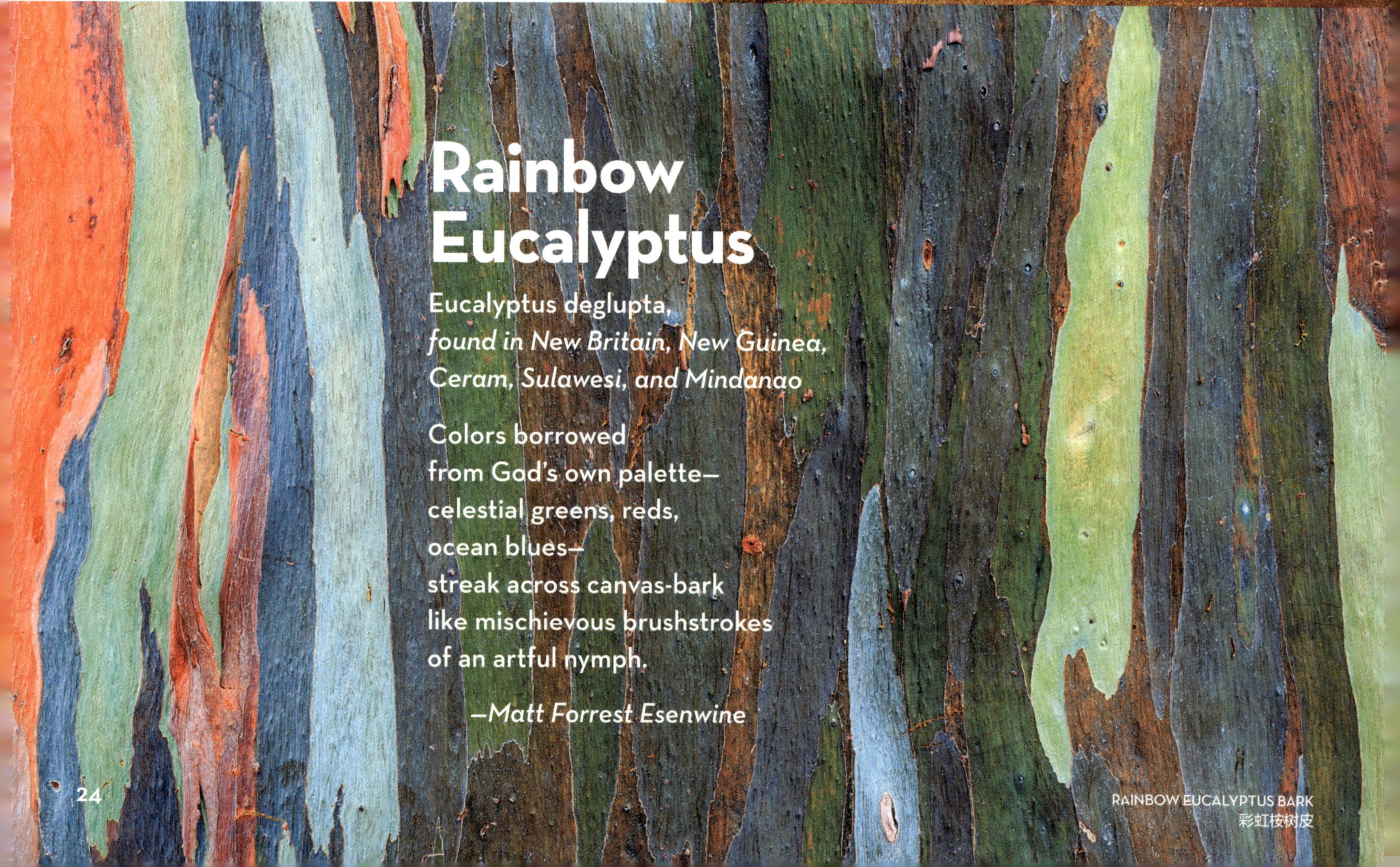

Rainbow Eucalyptus

Eucalyptus deglupta,
found in New Britain, New Guinea,
Ceram, Sulawesi, and Mindanao

Colors borrowed
from God's own palette—
celestial greens, reds,
ocean blues—
streak across canvas-bark
like mischievous brushstrokes
of an artful nymph.

—Matt Forrest Esenwine

RAINBOW EUCALYPTUS BARK
彩虹桉树皮

Blow-up

Our cherry tree
Unfolds whole loads
Of pink-white blooms—
It just explodes.

For three short days
Its petals last.
Oh, what a waste.
But what a blast.

—X. J. Kennedy

CHERRY BLOSSOM
樱花绽放

PINK BOUGAINVILLEA
粉色三叶梅

Bougainvillea

Tissue blossoms
bright as lips
start drifting with the breeze,

looping low and
twirling up
in between the trees,

a swath of color,
drooping slowly,
falling down to lie

on the ground.
Watch out! Don't step
on that pink butterfly.

—Ann Whitford Paul

How to Bake a Flower

Stir seeds into well-drained soil.
Fold in a half-cup live worms.

Sprinkle in occasional rain
until green shoots appear.

Blend in sun mixed with shade.
Add a dash of moonlight.

Simmer on low four to six weeks
in the unhurried oven of summer.

When the air starts smelling sweet
it's ready to be served—almost.

Swirl in butterflies.
Whip in bees.

—Ralph Fletcher

BEE ON COSMOS
波斯菊上的蜜蜂

TOADSTOOLS ON RAIN FOREST FLOOR, ECUADOR
热带雨林地面的伞菌，厄瓜多尔

Mushroom Hunting

Two girls bent in the wet woods wondering
why the heavenly mushrooms withered.
One said we have come at the wrong time
of year. One said nothing.

The one who said nothing said nothing
comes here.

A congress of clouds met just above:
The timothy bowed, the larkspur shied.
Miles away, a fox formed into a fox.

And the one who said nothing said nothing
comes here.

—Peter Kostin

Milkweeds, November

Now the brown and withered pods all break
into wide-mouthed grins. Each seed escapes
with a tuft of white for its body—if "body" can be
lighter than the waft of a monarch's lifting wing.

After the briefest flight, the seed heads drop
like the empty parachutes of dreams,
releasing—we called them "fairies" (finding no word
for what seemed equal parts wing and web

and wayward star from the Milky Way)—to float
across the asphalt and grass and into our rooms:
each an asterisk of air, a wish
the milkweed sent with hope's whispered breath.

Oh, to catch one
in a swat of your hand!

—*Michael J. Rosen*

COMMON MILKWEED
常见的乳草

I Wandered Lonely as a Cloud

I wandered lonely as a cloud
That floats on high o'er vales and hills,
When all at once I saw a crowd,
A host, of golden daffodils;
Beside the lake, beneath the trees,
Fluttering and dancing in the breeze.

Continuous as the stars that shine
And twinkle on the milky way,
They stretched in never-ending line
Along the margin of a bay:
Ten thousand saw I at a glance,
Tossing their heads in sprightly dance.

The waves beside them danced; but they
Out-did the sparkling waves in glee:
A poet could not but be gay,
In such a jocund company:
I gazed—and gazed—but little thought
What wealth the show to me had brought:

For oft, when on my couch I lie
In vacant or in pensive mood,
They flash upon that inward eye
Which is the bliss of solitude;
And then my heart with pleasure fills,
And dances with the daffodils.

—William Wordsworth

The Methuselah Tree: Ancient Bristlecone Pine Forest

Inyo County, eastern California, U.S.A.

Up here
on the slopes
of the White Mountains,
there is silence,
as if the world
is holding its breath.
When I was young,
pyramids rose
from the sands
of Egypt. Now,
almost 5,000 years old,
I am called
"living driftwood,"
awash in a sea of time,
sinew against sky
against century, I
am the oldest
living thing
on
earth.

—Joan Bransfield Graham

METHUSELAH, A GREAT BASIN BRISTLECONE PINE, CALIFORNIA, U.S.A.
玛士撒拉树，大盆地狐尾松，加利福尼亚州，美国

Rose

The story goes:
don't stick your nose
inside a rose
because of bees.
But knees,
bare toes,
and—ouch!—
elbows
are the parts
the prickles
hurt the most
when a ball gets thrown
in an overgrown bush
and you need to—
ouch!—
just reach an inch.
No one warns you:
roses pinch!

—Janet S. Wong

ROSE
玫瑰

Mirrorment

Birds are flowers flying
and flowers perched birds.

—A. R. Ammons

RED AND GREEN MACAW
红绿金刚鹦鹉

Pine Tree in January

A cone of green against stark white
Through wind and snow upright it stands,
Prickle point needle fingered hands
Spike sharp into the winter's night.
Remaining leaved once Autumn's been
Implies bristled tenacity.
Outwardly, an unfriendly tree,
Yet cardinals nestle warm within.

—Michael Salinger

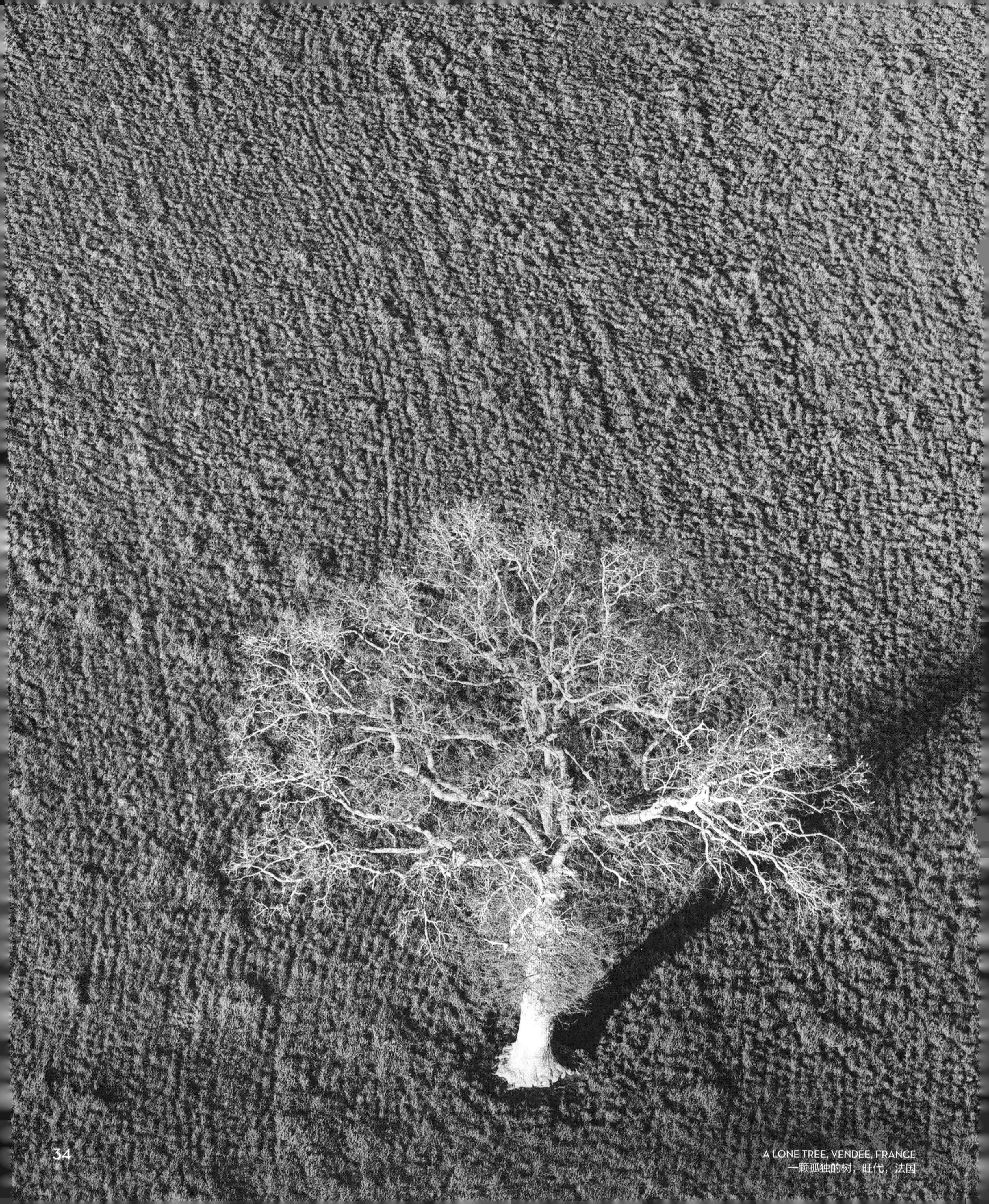

A LONE TREE, VENDÉE, FRANCE
一颗孤独的树，旺代，法国

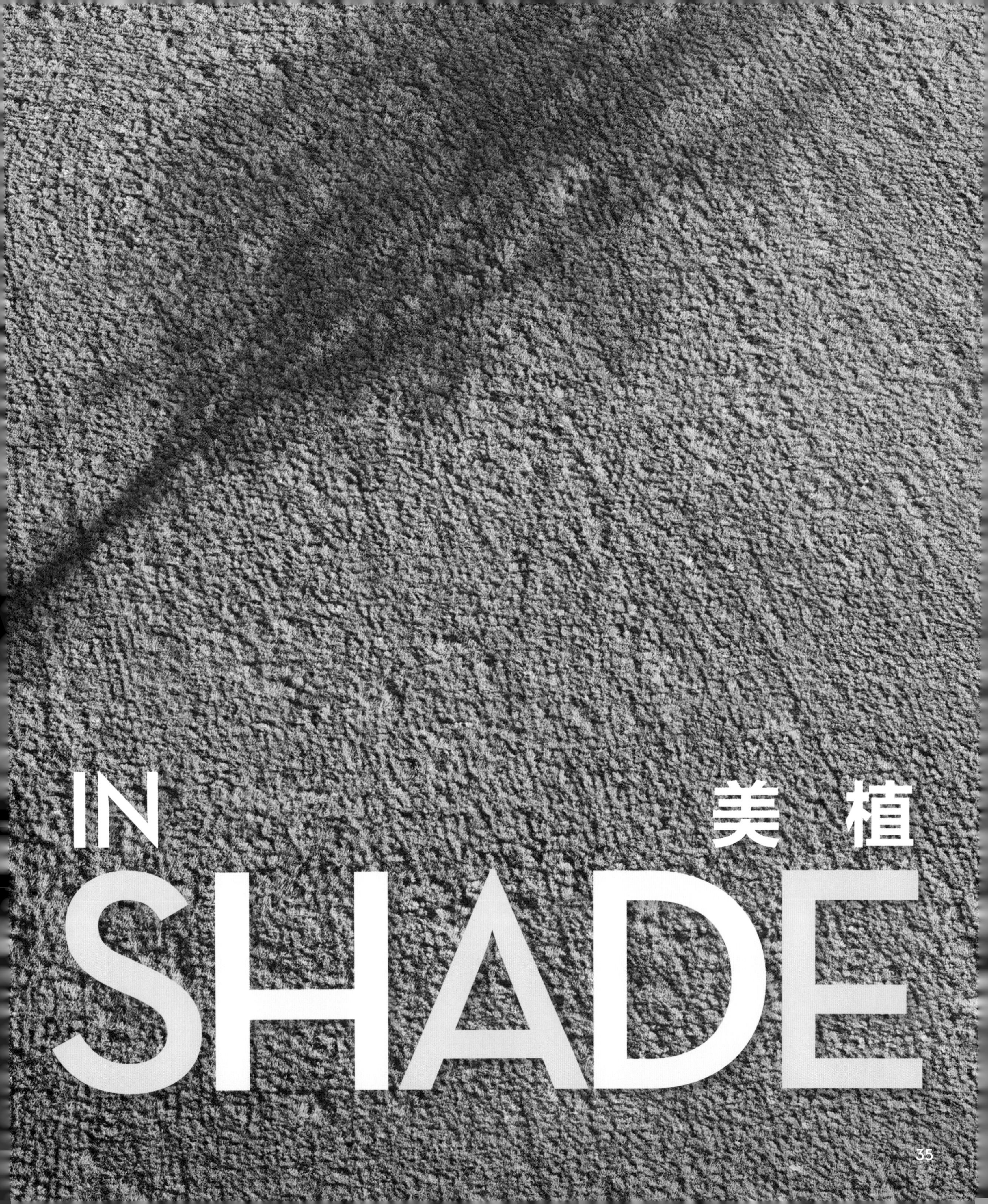

IN SHADE 美植

Lessons in September

P14

九月哲理

初秋黄金般的第一时间，
当阳光回避了夏日的怒目，
当树叶还未脸红，安静而温柔，
我走进树林，
心无旁骛——
记住如何去聆听，
听风狂奔于林海波涛，
听鸟夫妻动怒拌嘴，
听小溪轻奏旋律。
记住如何去观察，
看斑点蟾蜍藏进灌木丛深处，
看白色毛毛虫蜿蜒穿过步道桥，
看红尾鹰滑过天空之窗。
这白桦树，我虽已上百次经过，
却从未对它注目，它静静伫立，从未改变，
当有一天，我走出树林，
希望仍然保有那个
在树林里的自己——
明理，
感恩，
敬畏。

——特蕾西·沃恩·齐默

Dew

P16

露珠

花瓣上的钻石，
花茎上的银，
晨早日出，
化露珠成异宝。

——查尔斯·吉格纳

Time to Plant Trees

P15

种树佳时

趁年轻，抚土种树，
多年后，穿行林间。

当青春不再，仍可踱步
你与时光共筑的树荫之下。

——詹姆斯·海福德

P17

The Monarch's Flight to Mexico

君王飞往墨西哥

当远古的呼唤传来，
橙色飓风应声启程，
作别夏日的香甜！

当远古的呼唤传来，
百万舞者华服盛装，
蝴蝶筑路直奔天际。

当远古的呼唤传来，
橙色飓风应声启程。

——阿维丝·哈莉

P17

Butterfly Tree

蝴蝶树

宛如
夏威夷的国王，
身披五彩羽衣，
桉树国度——
辉煌之君。

——琼·布兰斯菲尔德·格雷厄姆

P18

Haiku

俳句一首

睡莲：
出淤泥不染……
绽放生命。

——尼克·维尔吉利奥

P19

Sequoia

红杉

原始森林深处，
树叶轻瞥太阳，
如神明般，
根系舔舐着黑暗。
何需言语？
我对抗沉默，
再次落败。

——伦纳德·内森

P19

General Sherman Sequoia: World's Largest Tree

谢尔曼将军：世界上最大的树

美国加利福尼亚州图莱里县红杉国家公园的巨红杉

谢尔曼将军，
任凭风吹雨打，
暴风山火，
你自屹立挺拔，
岿然不动。
两千五百年弹指一挥间，
你笑看人间冷暖，
世事浮沉。
二百七十五英尺之巅，
方圆天地，
尽收眼底，
丰碑铸就，
向你致敬！

——琼·布兰斯菲尔德·格雷厄姆

The Mystery

P20

神秘

大树是神秘的，
根系交织，
亦如真爱。

春花是神秘的，
无需日历，无需时钟，
花开即时节。

池塘是神秘的，
将鳟鱼藏匿
在那最深最暗的湖心。

蕨植是神秘的，
无师自通，
借着阳光，展开卷叶。

小径是神秘的，
众足纷踏，
依然诚意支持。

那大门……
大门一点儿也不神秘，
是我们在那儿将它放置，
让人知道，家马上就到。

狗儿扬鼻深嗅，
便知我们到家。

——简·约伦

Bouquets

P21

一束花

一次就一朵儿，好吗？
无论朵儿多小。

两朵花儿就太多，
另一朵成了搅扰。

三朵花儿插瓶中，
吵吵闹闹开了花。

宛如酒会上的闲聊，
众人都在侃侃而谈，

一簇花儿们
彼此溜须谄媚（抱歉如有冒犯）。

一次就一朵儿，
我想听它的故事。

——罗伯特·弗朗西斯

P22

Beside a Chrysanthemum

在菊花旁

或许，是为了一朵菊花的盛开，
杜鹃鸟，从春天开始啼叫。

或许，是为了一朵菊花的盛开，
天雷，撕开乌云。

那遥远的青春后巷
曾让人怀念、惋惜、揪心，
那花儿啊，
如姐姐站在镜前。

或许，昨夜下了一层薄霜，
就为催开四瓣黄色的花叶，
而我，居然毫无睡意。

——徐廷柱

（原诗由安善财译为英文）
（本诗中文版由王骏浩从韩文直接译出）

P23

Counting-Out Rhyme

背起篓篓打水歌（译者创作）

Sallow，yellow，willow，
看看竹篓一个不漏，
Maple，apple，popple，
打个招呼给树婆婆，
Moonbeam，barn-beam，hornbeam，
只有山泉无与伦比，
Hollow，yellow，willow.
若无其事怀里一搂。

——Abby F. Yehenola

译者注：Counting-Out Rhyme 这首诗有三段，每一段都押韵，但并没有逻辑。如果忠实地翻译原文为中文，不仅不押韵，还会让读者摸不着头脑。于是，我们取原诗押韵的意思并结合儿歌俏皮的特点，用中英文重新混排了一首新的诗，为了不让读者觉得和原诗距离太远，我们把原诗每一句的最后一个词提炼出来，挑选中文中相近似的音来与之押韵，形成了现在这首朗朗上口的小诗。

P23

The Release

逃跑

落日时，
所有树影
脱逃，
铺天盖地。

——约瑟夫·布鲁查克

Spanish Moss

P24

松萝凤梨

哥特小说
走出橡树女士，
轻抚树枝，
神秘而阴郁，

狂野又苍白，
卷曲又孱细，
她挑逗微风，
她摇曳风中。

——查尔斯·吉格纳

Rainbow Eucalyptus

P24

彩虹桉树

彩虹桉树，
长在新不列颠、新几内亚、
塞拉姆、苏拉威西和棉兰老。

颜色借自
上帝的调色盘，
星空绿、天际红、
海洋蓝，
就像那灵巧的仙女，
以调皮的笔触
把树皮画布用彩条布满。

——马特·福里斯特·伊森瓦恩

Blow-up

P25

绽放

我家樱花树，
挂朵满枝丫，
粉白花朵朵，
枝头大爆炸。

短短三天后，
花瓣飘满地，
唉，多可惜，
哇，多绚丽！

——X. J. 肯尼迪

Bougainvillea

P25

三叶梅

花叶如纸，
靓若红唇，
微风中
婀娜飘动，

回旋翻飞，
时高时低，
漫舞林间，

花色连片，
缓缓垂下，
恣意躺卧
在地上。

小心！ 不要踩到
那桃红蝴蝶。

——安·惠特福德·保罗

How to Bake a Flower

P26

如何“烘焙”一朵花

备好良土，种下花籽，
掺入半杯健康虫子。

时不时洒点雨，
待到绿苗冒出头。

拌入阳光，混合阴凉，
加上一抹白月光。

夏日烤炉悠悠燃，
文火慢炖四六周。

且闻风中蜜蜜甜，
上桌火候差点点，

蝴蝶添彩，
蜜蜂点睛。

——拉尔夫·弗莱彻

Mushroom Hunting

P27

采蘑菇

两个女孩俯身在潮湿的树林里，
琢磨为什么美味的蘑菇已枯萎。
一个说我们来的季节不对，
一个什么都没说。

什么都没说的那个说
这儿什么都没有。

一群云朵在聚首，
猫尾草点点头，飞燕草躲开了。
几英里外，一只狐狸长大了。

什么都没说的那个说
这儿什么都没有。

——彼得·科斯廷

Milkweeds, November

P28

乳草，十一月

如今那棕色干瘪的花荚炸裂，
咧着大嘴笑，种子纷纷逃走，
白色茸毛带起身体——如果“身体”可以
轻如帝王蝶翼。

短暂滑翔后，种子垂头下坠，
宛如梦想之伞空空，
释放——我们称乳草“精灵”（没有词语能更恰当比喻
它似翼似网，又似银河里那任性的星）。

飘过马路，
飘过草地，
飘进房间，
空气中的每一个星号，都是乳草送出的愿望，
伴着它那怀着希望的低语气息。

哦，抓一个，
拢在手中！

——迈克尔·J. 罗森

P29

I Wandered Lonely as a Cloud

我孤独地漫游，就像一朵云

我孤独地漫游，就像一朵云，
高高漂浮于山川河谷，
突然瞥见热闹的一群
金灿灿的水仙，
湖水边，树荫下，
摇曳风中，舞姿婀娜。

亦如繁星点点，
闪亮银河，
花儿尽洒湖湾之沿，
连绵成线无穷尽，
千朵万朵览入眼，
枝头摇曳，
轻盈起舞。

近旁湖水悦动，波光粼粼，
水仙得意更胜。
如此佳境为伴，
诗人怎能不欢喜，
望啊——望啊——竟未觉察
这场景给了我如此大的财富。

常常躺卧长榻，
或百无聊赖，或沉思冥想，
而独处之妙在于——
内观中总有那花那景，
于是我满心欢喜，
与水仙共舞翩翩。

——威廉·华兹华斯

P31

Rose

玫瑰

老话说：
别把鼻子，
伸进花里，
因为蜜蜂会蛰你。
但被刺被扎最厉害的是这里：
膝盖、
脚趾，
嗷！还有
手肘。
当球滚进恣意乱长的花丛里，
你要做的就是：
嗷！
哪怕只踏入一寸，
没人警告你，
玫瑰会扎你！

——珍妮特·S. 王

The Methuselah Tree: Ancient Bristlecone Pine Forest

P30

玛士撒拉树：古狐尾松树林

美国加利福尼亚州东部因约县

怀特山
　山坡
　　上面，
　　　四下沉寂，
仿佛世界
　　　都屏住了呼吸，
我小的时候，
　金字塔
在埃及沙漠
　　　升起。到如今
几乎已有五千岁，
　人们叫我
“活着的浮木”，
　　　　沉浮于时间之海，
　　与天比寿，
笑看沧桑，
　我是
　　地球上
　　　最高龄的
　　　　生物。

——琼·布兰斯菲尔德·格雷厄姆

Mirrorment

P32

镜像

鸟似飞翔之花，
花如栖息之鸟。

——A. R. 安蒙斯

Pine Tree in January

P33

一月的雪松

绿色锥松叫板严酷白雪，
风雪中，它屹立挺直，
针叶手指尖锐如刺
扎进冬夜，
历尽秋冬的考验，
仍留针尖的刚毅。
外表似乎拒人千里，
内里护佑红雀，温暖相依。

——迈克尔·塞林杰

Who is mother nature?

When Mother Nature's near—in waterfalls, rivers, rainbows, meadows, or oceans—her admirers react with love, awe, curiosity, even fear, if she decides to reveal her grumpier side. The lady can be seen through telescopes or microscopes, from mountaintops or ravines, with the wind in our hair, soil in our hands, or sand in our toes. For those who aren't hopelessly city-bound, looking out a window will do.

Driven to explore the *science* behind the wonder of it all, Charles Darwin filled scores of notebooks about what was then the unexplored wildlife of the Galápagos Islands. Countless nature writers have followed his courageous example. Others have put themselves in nature, like naturalist John Muir, who once rode out a northern American windstorm by cocooning himself in the branches of a sky-high Douglas spruce. (Muir is famous—or should be—for saying, "The clearest way into the Universe is through a forest wilderness.")

Some humans, however, have no use for wild places, a view once expressed by Woody Allen with his typical wit: "I love nature. I just don't want to get any of it on me." For some, their love for animals extends only as far as Fido or Sweet Pea. That we share the Earth equally with other creatures is a notion as foreign and irrelevant to them as the disappearance of the rain forests or the melting of the ice caps.

But Mother Nature doesn't care who likes her. Nor is she bothered about being ignored. A midwife at the birth of creatures large and small, she will go on making waves by making waves, assembling forests, flowering deserts, and beautifying gardens. We can embrace her or resist her charms; it is of no concern to her.

Who is the mysterious lady known as Mother Nature? She is the material world, the environment of trees, plants, animals, everything under and over the sun. In short, she equals the world around us and includes whatever is not built by human hands.

Mother Nature is where we live. In other words, she is
a refuge to the lost,
a magnet to the curious,
a dare to the daring,
the cradle of rapture,
the university of the universe,
the glory of a morning and of a morning-glory,
not a whale but the idea of a whale,
a sign rewriter: I Welcome All No Trespassing,
the best cure for couch disease,
an opera performed by birds, bullfrogs on drums,
the sound of silence . . . amplified
to the symphony of the spheres, and ____________
____.

Can you add another short description of Mother Nature to this poem?

The poets and photographers who have come together to produce National Geographic's *Book of Nature Poetry* would agree with John Keats, who defined their abiding faith: "The poetry of earth is never dead."

THREAD-WINGED ANTLION
线翅蚁狮

自然之母是谁？

当自然之母靠近的时候——在瀑布中，在河流中，在彩虹中，在草地或是海洋中——她的爱慕者用爱、敬畏、好奇来回应，甚至如果她显示暴躁的一面时，则用恐惧来回应。这位女士可以用望远镜或是显微镜来观察，从山顶到深谷，风在我们的发丝中穿过，泥土在我们手中漏出，沙在我们的脚趾中渗出。对于那些不喜欢住在城里的人来说，只要看一看窗外就行。

为了探索自然奇观背后的科学道理，查尔斯·达尔文把加拉帕戈斯群岛未知的野生动物记满了几十本笔记本。难以数计的自然主义作家跟随着他，以他为榜样。其他人则让自己融入自然。例如自然主义者约翰·缪尔，曾经用高耸入云的道格拉斯云杉的枝叶包裹着自己，经受住了北美的风暴。（缪尔由于下面这句话而知名——或应该知名——“融入宇宙最清晰的方式莫过于通过荒野森林”。）

然而，也有一些人，觉得野外毫无用处，这也是伍迪·艾伦用他特有的机智曾经表达的观点：“我爱自然，但是一点也别弄到我身上来。”而另一些人，他们对动物的喜爱只限于“菲多”或是“甜豌豆”。对他们来说，我们与其他生物平等地分享地球的观念，和雨林正在消失、冰层正在融化这样的概念一样，是未知而不重要的。

但自然之母并不关心谁喜欢她。她对这种忽视也毫不在意。她是大大小小各种生物出生时的产婆，她将不断在波浪中创造波浪，让森林遍地，让花朵在沙漠开放，让花园变得更美。我们可以接受或是抗拒她的魅力，她对此却毫不关心。

这位被人称为自然之母的神秘女士是谁？她是物质世界，也是植物、动物的环境和阳光下所有的一切。简言之，她就是我们周遭的世界，人类双手无法创造的世界。

自然之母在我们生活的地方。换句话说，

她是：

迷失者的庇护，

好奇者的磁石，

勇敢者的挑战，

狂喜者的摇篮，

宇宙的教化者。

她是：

清晨的光辉，

牵牛花的光，

并不是鲸鱼，

而是这创意。

她重新写了一个标记：我欢迎所有的非擅自闯入者。

她是：

沙发病的良药，

鸟儿、牛蛙在鼓上演奏的歌剧，

是寂静之声……被放大，

而成为万物的交响曲，

也是 ____________________

你可以在这首诗后面加上一段描写自然之母的短句吗？

共同创作《最美自然诗集》的诗人和摄影家们会同意约翰·济慈的话，他道出了他们永恒的信仰：“地球的诗篇永远不会消亡。”

LOTUS AND BEES -WUQIANG
荷花与蜜蜂（吴强）

美国国家地理学会是世界上最大的非营利科学与教育组织之一。学会成立于1888年，以“增进与普及地理知识”为宗旨，致力于启发人们对地球的关心。美国国家地理学会通过杂志、电视节目、影片、音乐、电台、图书、DVD、地图、展览、活动、学校出版计划、交互式媒体与商品来呈现世界。美国国家地理学会的会刊《国家地理》杂志，以英文及其他33种语言发行，每月有3800万读者阅读。美国国家地理频道在166个国家以34种语言播放，有3.2亿个家庭收看。美国国家地理学会资助超过10 000项科学研究、环境保护与探索计划，并支持一项扫除“地理文盲”的教育计划。

Acknowledgments
To the entire National Geographic team for their enthusiasm and dedication in the making of this book, and to all the poets whose deserving work, regrettably, could not be squeezed into its pages.—JPL

The publisher gratefully acknowledges the heroic efforts of Natalie Turner in securing permissions, as well as the invaluable research assistance of Alyson Foster.

图书在版编目（CIP）数据

最美自然诗集 /（美）J. 帕特里克·刘易斯主编；Abby F. Yehenola，张原平，和览编译. —郑州：河南科学技术出版社，2018.1
ISBN 978-7-5349-8952-0

Ⅰ.①最… Ⅱ.①J… ②A… ③张… ④和… Ⅲ.①儿童诗歌-诗集-美国-现代 Ⅳ.①I712.82

中国版本图书馆CIP数据核字(2017)第269830号

出版发行：河南科学技术出版社
地址：郑州市经五路66号　邮编：450002
电话：（0371）65737028　65788613
网址：www.hnstp.cn
特邀策划：Abby F. Yehenola
策划编辑：马艳茹　韩雅楠　于凯燕
责任编辑：于凯燕
责任校对：徐小刚
整体设计：吴豆豆
责任印制：张　巍
印　　刷：北京盛通印刷股份有限公司
经　　销：全国新华书店
幅面尺寸：232 mm × 276 mm　印张：3　字数：75千字
版　　次：2018年1月第1版　2018年1月第1次印刷
全套定价：588.00元

To poets, nature, and nature poets everywhere.—JPL

献给诗人、自然和全世界写自然的诗人。

——J. 帕特里克 · 刘易斯

献给爱自然，爱阅读的大小朋友们！

——Abby

美国童诗桂冠诗人［美］J.帕特里克·刘易斯　主编
Abby F. Yehenola ❁ 张原平 ❁ 和览　编译

NATIONAL GEOGRAPHIC
美国国家地理

book of nature poetry

最美自然诗集 6

（汉英对照）

200首诗歌
和会漂浮
会穿越，
会开花
的精彩图片

河南科学技术出版社
·郑州·

自然最美

千山鸟飞绝，
万径人踪灭。
孤舟蓑笠翁，
独钓寒江雪。

这是唐朝柳宗元的《江雪》。短短的20个字，便成功捕捉一幅美丽的风景画。当时的孤冷静谧与雪白世界，似乎透过这首诗被永久封存，美丽了好几千年，不曾消逝。

《最美自然诗集》的出版，重新带给我这样的震撼与感动。随着时代的变迁，生活节奏的加快，文字阅读耗费时间，致使读者更为钟情图像阅读。不过图像阅读与文字阅读所获得的乐趣，无法互相取代。纵使是对同个风景的描绘，使用新诗文字创作与照片图像创作，让读者感受到的乐趣亦是截然不同。若是舍弃文字的阅读，全都转向图像阅读，实在相当可惜。《最美自然诗集》却完美解决了这个问题：这本诗集的每首诗，都是一张照片加上一首诗，使得文字文本和图像文本相互合作对话，形成一支精彩的双人舞。

这本书真的让我重新认识美丽的地球！在大自然中，随着四季的交替、地形的差异、气候的更迭，每一刹那的风景都是独一无二、稍纵即逝的。照片是静态的叙事，透过摄影师的镜头，有意识地捕捉吉光片羽，所以一张张的美照，是摄影师透过自身的美学哲学与镜头的选择所决定的，也可以说照片是摄影师眼中的美景。

而诗的创作，则是透过诗人纤细善感的心思，触景生情，把当时的生命状态转化成诗句，以情寓景，让景物多了一股人情的芬芳，不少美景在诗句的化妆下，变得充满情韵，让人印象深刻。

除此之外，这本书的编者扮演着隐形创作者的角色，因为他们成功媒合了照片与诗句，让作品更有一层乐趣。诗句的意象让静态的照片翩然生动，仿佛可以听见照片中的潺潺流水声，让读者宛若身临其境，感受照片里的一草一木，让读者悠游在每幅照片之中。阅读《最美自然诗集》，需要最好的领航员同游，我们的译者充分领会了编者的匠心独运，十分用心地录制了200首音频，恰是《最美自然诗集》最好的导读。

这本诗集让读者感受到三种美学：文学之美、摄影之美以及想象之美。透过诗句，让读者感受到文字透过意象诠释的美学；透过摄影照片让读者感受到强烈的视觉盛宴。当今的科技，无论是手机、电视还是穿戴科技等等，均试图以科技的力量，让读者感受到身临其境的感官盛宴，增强读者的视觉与听觉震撼，产生娱乐感，但是与此同时，相对地也剥夺了读者想象之美的权利。而《最美自然诗集》在照片与文字当中，保留了相当多的空白，并分类为“感叹自然”“凌空”“渊洋”“生灵”“山川”“美植”“灾难”“四季”“奇景”“敬畏自然”，让读者可以发挥想象，感受编者所安排的想象之美。因此，阅读这本书让读者经历一场美学盛宴，沉醉在大自然的洗礼之中。

最后，从这本书中也可以看出编者对于环境保护的意识。人类过度开发，使得环境被破坏，导致气候异常，很多珍稀动物濒临灭绝，大自然也不再美丽。希望这本诗集，能唤起人类对于大自然的重新思考，思考如何与环境共生。

透过这本最美丽的诗集，让我们回忆起我们曾经的美好！伟哉自然，伟哉生命！

· 译者序 ·

四季的景象各不同，这是大自然的馈赠，四季中又藏有不同的秘密，我们不知道，但诗人们用这21首诗来告诉我们。

春天，

贵如油的春雨被诗人比作了蜂蜜，听着雨入眠也是一件妙事；卡明斯用看似凌乱的语句把春日孩子们的欢愉写得让你听得见；农场上的小牛在春日诞生，诗人罗伯特·弗罗斯特带你去轻抚它的脖颈。

夏天，

花园中的果实静静地长，耐心点，你会听见它们成长的声音；诗人让你来体验蒲公英满天的浪漫；华兹华斯的彩虹让所有人看到希望。

秋天，

主编专门用一首象形诗向我们展示了树叶到底是怎么变黄的，可是，醉翁之意不在酒啊；你有没有曾经纳闷大雁怎么知道要南迁了呢？诗人把秋天比作怪兽，它们不去，冬美人还不来呢，一首诗想向我们解释这个问题；秋天是个集市，树上的松树、天上的云朵和家里的热汤，都在忙忙碌碌；诗中的月亮仿佛比任何时候都懂事，安安静静地依偎在枝头；不知不觉，脚下清脆的踩踏落叶声提醒我们，霜降了。

冬天，

喜欢那首冬天的诗，天空暗沉的时候，蓝雀是我们唯一的蓝天；同样是冬天，诗人在冬日把一生对年轻一辈的祝福都写在了诗里；有没有想过窗上的冰花其实是一座森林？有许多的故事在里面；二月的冬日仿佛和其他月份的冬天都不同，因它酝酿着冬天的继承人——春天。

Abby 2017年10月于昆明

IN SEASON

四季

J. PATRICK LEWIS HAS WRITTEN MORE THAN 95 PICTURE AND POETRY BOOKS FOR YOUNG READERS. IN 2011 HE WAS APPOINTED U.S. CHILDREN'S POET LAUREATE, AND WAS GIVEN THE NATIONAL COUNCIL OF TEACHERS OF ENGLISH AWARD FOR EXCELLENCE IN POETRY FOR CHILDREN.

HENRY DAVID THOREAU was one of America's truly Big Thinkers on a little pond—Walden Pond. It was there in 1853, in a self-built cabin not far from his Massachusetts family home, that he wrote: "I have a room all to myself; it is nature."

From his tucked-away cottage, Thoreau produced some of the most profound thoughts on Mother Nature. But poets from centuries past rarely wrote about the more exotic natural wonders. They never saw them, never knew they existed. Many of the most fascinating phenomena that we often take for granted today—thanks to the convenience of travel, books, or photographs—were seldom brought to the attention of the classical poets.

How would William Shakespeare or John Keats have described in a poem the grandeur of the Grand Canyon? One can only imagine Emily Dickinson, transported to the scene, painting on an easel built of words a picture of an Asian tsunami or an African drought. What immortal verse might William Wordsworth have written after a day's walk in the Amazon rain forest instead of the English countryside? What picture would Kobayashi Issa or Li Po paint after a submersible dive to the ocean deep?

And yet a poet does not have to be there! You needn't leave your chair to write a poem about the wilder shores of creation. A book is your ticket to ride; a photograph is rapid transit to the brain. What kind of poem would you write if all you had in front of you was an image, like one of the breathtaking pictures in the *Book of Nature Poetry* you are now holding?

Better yet, let your eyes be your camera, taking incredible pictures your brain will thank you for. Get up and go there! Explore the woods, a cave; climb a mountain; go scuba diving; or simply make a friend of a grasshopper in a field on a windy summer day. You might even imagine you *are* that dragonfly trying to escape a swift, or a lucky salmon that has wiggled through the legs of a grizzly bear.

Travel by photograph or on foot, but go quickly before nature disappears. Every day more than 70 animals, plants, or other living things, like fungi, roots, and molds, vanish forever. The *Book of Nature Poetry* seeks to capture the ever changing nature of nature, so that gone is not forgotten. Besides, when more of us care for nature, more can help save it.

However and wherever you greet the world outside your window, listen again to Mr. Thoreau for the last and best words of advice:

"It's not what you look at that matters. It's what you see."

—J. Patrick Lewis,
former U.S. Children's Poet Laureate

MALACHITE BUTTERFLY
孔雀石蝴蝶

J. 帕特里克·刘易斯已经为孩子们创作了95部图画书和诗集。2011年，他荣获了美国童诗桂冠诗人奖，并被美国国家英语教师委员会授予杰出童诗奖。

·前　言·

亨利·戴维·梭罗是美国真正的大思想家之一，他曾隐居在瓦尔登湖。

1853年，在离马萨诸塞州家不远的自建小木屋里，他写道：“我有一个只属于我自己的房间——大自然。”

就在这世外桃源般的小木屋里，梭罗萌发出一些关于大自然的极其深刻的思想。但是这几百年来，诗人们却很少再去描写更独特的自然奇观。他们从来没见过，甚至都不知晓它们的存在。很多今天我们习以为常的，可以从旅行、书籍或照片中轻松获取的绝世美景，以前却很少能引起古典诗人们的关注。

试想，莎士比亚和济慈会怎样用诗歌去描绘大峡谷的壮美？可想而知，若埃米莉·迪金森能亲临亚洲海啸或非洲干旱现场，她将会用文字绘制出怎样的一幅画卷。那华兹华斯呢？如果他有机会走在亚马孙雨林中，而不仅仅是在英国乡间小道徘徊，他的笔下会写出怎样的诗句呢？若小林一茶或李白能乘潜艇探访大洋深渊，他们诗作的意境又将是怎样的呢？

然而，诗人并非一定要身临其境。你不需要离开椅子才能去写沧海桑田。一本书可以带你去遨游，一张照片可以带你去穿越。如果你拥有的只是面前的一幅图，就像你手里的《最美自然诗集》中的任意一幅惊艳的美图一样，你能写出怎样的诗句呢？

更棒的是，去旅行，让眼睛成为你的照相机，让眼前的美景滋养你的大脑。去吧，去森林中历险，去探索一个洞穴，去勇攀一座高峰，去潜入海底，甚至去野地里和一只蚱蜢交个朋友，任夏风轻抚。你甚至可以去想象自己就是那只努力躲过雨燕的蜻蜓，或是那条幸运地游过灰熊两腿之间的三文鱼。

无论是借着照片观光还是身临其境，请尽早，赶在自然景观消失之前。每天，都有超过70种生物在地球上永远消失。《最美自然诗集》力图捕捉到大自然瞬息万变的属性，让逝去的不再被遗忘。同时，当有更多的人开始关心大自然时，便会有更多的人来拯救她。

无论你在哪里，用怎样的方式来向窗外的世界致敬，请你再一次，也是最后一次聆听梭罗先生的警世良言：

“重要的不是你眼前的，而是你心里的。”

——J. 帕特里克·刘易斯，美国童诗桂冠诗人

AURORA BOREALIS
北极光

The Thing Is the Thing Is Green

The thing is the thing is green and the green is green and by green I mean real mean green. I mean electric-eel green, alligator, iguana, anaconda green. I mean this thing has got all things green. It's got green turtles in turtle-green ponds and grasshoppers springing from groomed-green lawns and a green tree frog on a girl's left arm. It's got dark and dangerous greens. Greens you've never even seen greens. Ocean floor greens. Tornado sky greens. Tiger's eye greens. Eat-your-broccoli greens. Watermelons sparkling in the sun greens. Way beyond evergreen, this thing leaves green geckos on green leaves feeling green and green moths in the green dark and preying mantises on their thin green knees. It's a great and gorgeous green a light-bright-just-right-watch-it-grow-it-says-go shade of green. Have you guessed yet? Do you need another clue? Think rolling waves of grain green. Thick arms of vines climbing tall green trees. Mountains and mountains of green billions of waves reaching out of dark green seas all wrapped in one green ball and hung, an ornament in the sky. What a thing it must be to see the whole green thing floating by. It's true. The thing is the thing is green . . .

except when it's blue.

—Peggy Gifford

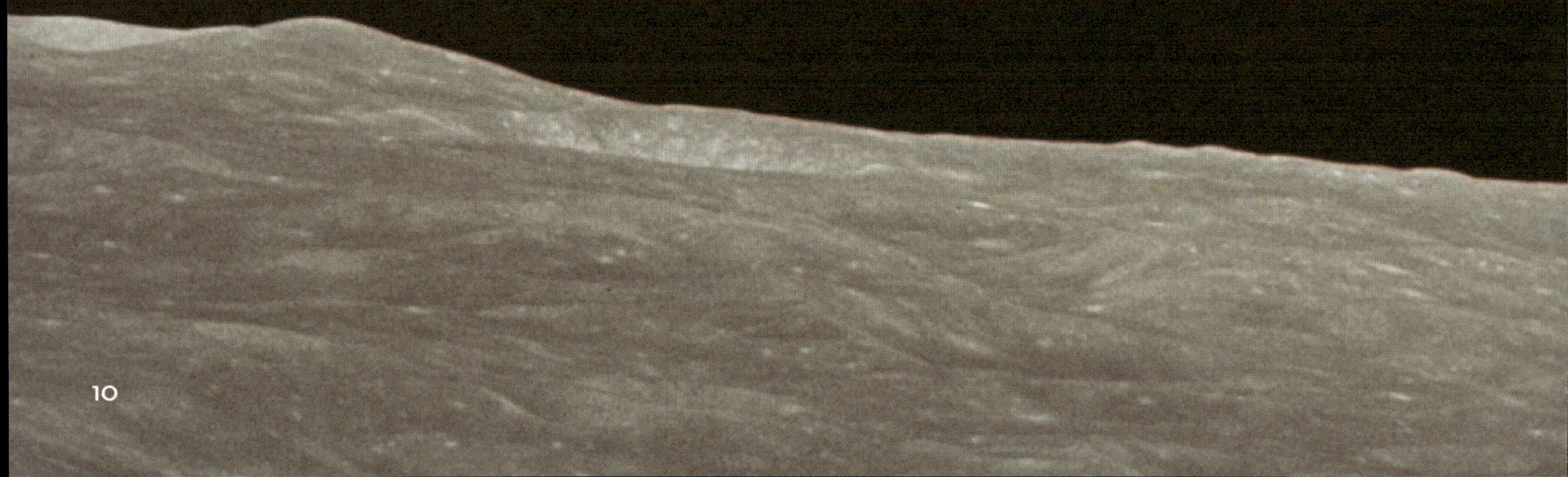

它要多绿就有多绿

要多绿就有多绿，绿就绿它个透心绿，就是这么绿，实打实的绿。我讲的是电鳗绿、鳄鱼绿、蜥蜴绿、蟒蛇绿，我说的这种绿把所有东西都染绿了。瞧那绿龟徜徉在龟绿色的池塘里，蚱蜢从刚修绿的草坪里一跃而起，一只绿树蛙停歇在女孩的左臂。有时候，它绿得阴森，绿得凶险，绿得其实你从未见过。大洋底的深渊绿，龙卷风的虐绿，老虎眼底的幽绿，“吃完西兰花”的郁闷绿，西瓜在阳光下的闪耀绿。比常绿植物更绿的，是绿叶上享绿的绿色壁虎、沉绿夜空的绿色飞蛾、紧绷双膝的绿色螳螂。 它绿得伟大，绿得华丽，那“趁着阳光正好赶快生长说长就长”的一抹绿。还没有猜出来吗？还需要再来一点提示吗？想想那绿色的麦浪翻滚，想想那粗壮的藤蔓攀上绿色的参天大树。连绵不绝的绿色山峦，深绿海洋中的滔天巨澜，竟都被包在一个绿色的球里，独具一格地装点着天空。能亲眼看见这大绿球飘过该是一件多么大的幸事啊。没错，它要多绿就有多绿……

除非它变蓝了……

——佩姬 · 吉福德

IN SEA

SON

When It Is Snowing

When it is snowing
the blue jay
is the only piece of
sky
in my
backyard.

—Siv Cedering

BLUE JAY
蓝雀

Storm Ending

Thunder blossoms gorgeously above our heads,
Great, hollow, bell-like flowers,
Rumbling in the wind,
Stretching clappers to strike our ears . . .
Full-lipped flowers
Bitten by the sun
Bleeding rain
Dripping rain like golden honey—
And the sweet earth flying from the thunder.

—Jean Toomer

PEA PODS
豌豆荚

You Never Hear the Garden Grow

Row on row,
you never hear the garden
grow.

Seeds split.
Roots shove and reach.
Earth heaves.

Leaves unfurl.
Stems pierce the
ground.

Peapods fatten.
Vines
stretch and curl.

Such growing
going on
without a sound!

—Lilian Moore

here is a poem of love and hope:

from a cold
de cem ber
a f t e r n o o n
out here in the flatland of e a s t ohio
and i am o u t in this considerable yard
u n d e r this h e a v y grey sky
pre s s ing on to my s h o u l d e r s
and s w e e t w o m a n
my head is bending l o w as the song goes
and my eyes are fixed on frozen patches of past
and future loves and deaths and dis re gards
and i am l i v i n g into my eight i eth y e a r
and i still address these poems to you to y o u r
eyes to that always welcoming smile to those
w e l c o m i n g a r m s

i am stripping away all that is not necessary
and this has been my p l a n m y pro cess
for m o s t of my conscious l i f e out here
discerning what is alive and what is almost
worth the mouth to mouth of the h e a r t
and i still believe in the power and force of love
as i can almost feel the land s h a k i n g with
the power and force of mindful des truc t i o n
and i shake under the daily drumbeat of death

please r e a d this poem with your o w n power and l o v e
and smile and r e r e a d and nod and be angry with resolve
these s t r u g g l e s must continue through h a r d w i n t e r
as we prepare for the new and g r e e n i n g s p r i n g

—ar n o l d a d o f f

frost

How does
The plain
Transparency
Of water

Sprout these
Lacy fronds
And plumes
And tendrils?

And where,
Before window-
Panes, did
They root

Their lush
Crystal forests,
Their cold
Silver jungles?

—Valerie Worth

PINES, WASHINGTON, U.S.A.
松树，华盛顿州，美国

April Rain Song

Let the rain kiss you.
Let the rain beat upon your head with silver liquid drops.
Let the rain sing you a lullaby.

The rain makes still pools on the sidewalk.
The rain makes running pools in the gutter.
The rain plays a little sleep-song on our roof at night—

And I love the rain.

—Langston Hughes

JAPANESE TREE FROG
日本树蛙

Metamorphosis

Dandelion!
Lowly, brilliant, friend of mine.
You bloom in grass,
through gravel, cracks,
stand alone or bunch in packs.
Stubborn, spindly, tell me why
you stretch your yellow toward the sky,
until you, furry, turn to seed,
come undone, let loose, and fly.

—Sara Holbrook

I So Liked Spring

I so liked Spring last year
Because you were here;—
The thrushes too—
Because it was these you so liked to hear—
I so liked you.

This year's a different thing,—
I'll not think of you.
But I'll like Spring because it is simply Spring
As the thrushes do.

—Charlotte Mew

Why Leaves
Change Color in the Fall

I was just about
to explain to the class that leaves
are nature's food factories taking water from the
ground and carbon dioxide from the air and using
sunlight to turn water and carbon dioxide into glucose
a kind of sugar that gives a tree its high energy through a
process called photosynthesis which is helped along by
a chemical known as chlorophyll that makes trees and plants
green though during autumn photosynthesis does not work
as efficiently due to less water and shorter hours of daylight so
trees begin to shut down their manufacturing and green
chlorophyll-filled leaves take a holiday by turning
themselves yellow and orange or like that sugar maple
for instance where the glucose trapped in the leaves
now that photosynthesis has stopped begins to turn
into an eye-delightful scarlet . . . but then I
thought why take the time to explain it
when they could all just sit here
with me to watch
that old tree
H o u d i n i
pull another
color trick
and send the
leaves like
feathers of a
dove falling softly
t o t h e g r o u n d

—J. Patrick Lewis

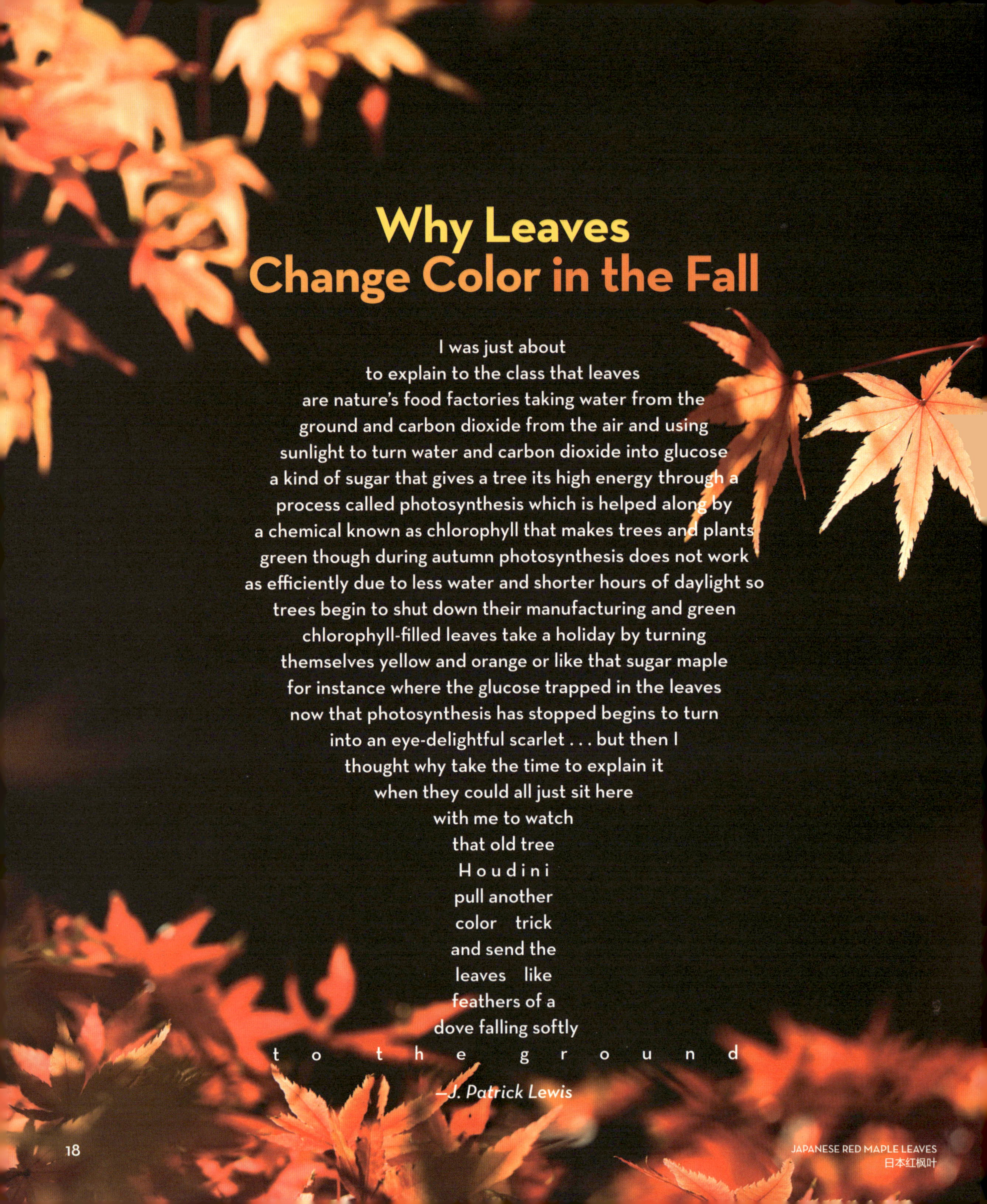

JAPANESE RED MAPLE LEAVES
日本红枫叶

CANADIAN GEESE
加拿大大雁

Something Told the Wild Geese

Something told the wild geese
It was time to go.
Though the fields lay golden
Something whispered,—"Snow."

Leaves were green and stirring,
Berries, luster-glossed,
But beneath warm feathers
Something cautioned,—"Frost."

All the sagging orchards
Steamed with amber spice,
But each wild breast stiffened
At remembered ice.

Something told the wild geese
It was time to fly,—
Summer sun was on their wings,
Winter in their cry.

—Rachel Field

February Tale

Above the earth
it's mitten-cold,
and children scurry,
rubber-soled.
Their icy breath
curls in the air
and every tree
is twig-thin bare . . .

Oh, February.

Yet far beneath
the frozen crust,
an eager bud
begins to thrust.
Another season's
written there;
another story,
winter's heir . . .

Ah, February!

—Renée M. LaTulippe

Sounds of Winter

The Old October Ogres come
without a fee-fi-fo or fum:
They lumber in *tum-tum-ti-tum.*

Nesting in trees forty feet tall,
they shake the leaves that fall in fall—
you hardly notice them at all.

But soon you hear the muffled snores
of Dark December Dinosaurs,
who wake to make the wind that roars,

The frost that bites, the ice that numbs,
the fee-fi-foes and dreadful fums . . .
when Ogres go and winter comes.

—Anonymous

SIBILLINI NATIONAL PARK, UMBRIA, ITALY
西比里尼国家公园，翁布里亚，意大利

November

The bottoms of autumn
wear diamonds of frost;
the tops of the trees rue
the sweaters they've lost.

Red squirrels, busy packing
oak cupboards for weeks,
still rattle their branches
with seeds in their cheeks.

Gray clouds go on promising
winter's first storm
while we stay inside by
the fire to keep warm.

Home biscuits are baking,
the gravy is stirred,
two pumpkin pies cool
by the thank-you bird.

—Mariel Bede

EURASIAN RED SQUIRREL
欧亚红松鼠

Autumn

A touch of cold in the Autumn night—
I walked abroad,
And saw the ruddy moon lean over a hedge
Like a red-faced farmer.
I did not stop to speak, but nodded,
And round about were the wistful stars
With white faces like town children.

—T. E. Hulme

FULL MOON
满月

November Night

Listen . . .
With faint dry sound,
Like steps of passing ghosts,
The leaves, frost-crisp'd, break from the trees
And fall.

—Adelaide Crapsey

FROSTED MAPLE LEAVES
霜冻枫叶

A Crack in the Clouds

How could
one slight
slit,
just a tiny bit
of a crack
in the cover
of clouds,
permit
such a pouring of sun
that engulfs
EVERYONE?

—Constance Levy

SMERILLO, ITALY
斯梅里洛，意大利

In Just

in Just-
spring   when the world is mud-
luscious the little
lame balloonman

whistles   far   and wee

and eddieandbill come
running from marbles and
piracies and it's
spring

when the world is puddle-wonderful

the queer
old balloonman whistles
far   and   wee
and bettyandisbel come dancing

from hop-scotch and jump-rope and

it's
spring
and
        the

                goat-footed

balloonMan   whistles
far
and
wee

—e. e. cummings

The Pasture

I'm going out to clean the pasture spring;
I'll only stop to rake the leaves away
(And wait to watch the water clear, I may):
I sha'n't be gone long.—You come too.

I'm going out to fetch the little calf
That's standing by the mother. It's so young,
It totters when she licks it with her tongue.
I sha'n't be gone long.—You come too.

—Robert Frost

My Heart Leaps Up

My heart leaps up when I behold
　　A rainbow in the sky:
So was it when my life began;
So is it now I am a man;
So be it when I shall grow old,
　　Or let me die!
The Child is father of the Man;
And I could wish my days to be
Bound each to each by natural piety.

—William Wordsworth

For All

Ah to be alive
on a mid-September morn
fording a stream
barefoot, pants rolled up,
holding boots, pack on,
sunshine, ice in the shallows,
northern rockies.

Rustle and shimmer of icy creek waters
stones turn underfoot, small and hard as toes
cold nose dripping
singing inside
creek music, heart music,
smell of sun on gravel.

I pledge allegiance

I pledge allegiance to the soil
of Turtle Island,
and to the beings who thereon dwell

one ecosystem
in diversity
under the sun
with joyful interpenetration for all.

—Gary Snyder

The *LONG* Summer

Then summer sat and smiled
As though to stay all year,
But then I was a child.

Now, given to good cheer
And glad to be beguiled,
I stay a child all year.

—James Hayford

UPPER BAVARIA, GERMANY
上巴伐利亚，德国

四季

IN SEASON

P14

When It Is Snowing

雪落时

雪落时，
蓝雀
是
我的
后院里
唯一一片
蓝天。

——西弗·塞德林

P14

Storm Ending

骤雨初歇

雷在头顶华丽绽放，
这些巨大的、中空、铃铛一样的花朵
在风中隆隆作响，
伸长响板到耳边，振聋发聩。
丰唇般的朵瓣
被太阳咬了一口，
流出雨来，
金金的蜜糖滴滴下落，
甜甜的地球渐渐飞远。

——琼·图默

P15

You Never Hear the Garden Grow

你从未听过花园在长

一排又一排，
你从未听过
花园在长。

种子裂开，
根茎舒展，
土壤隆起。

嫩叶打开，
枝茎
破土而出。

豆荚饱满，
藤条
卷曲伸长。

长啊长，
却寂静无声。

——莉莲·穆尔

P16

here is a poem of love and hope:

这是一首关于爱与希望的诗

在那寒冷的
十二月
下午，
在东俄亥俄的旷野中，
我站在这巨大的庭院里，
沉重无比，
苍穹压肩。
可爱的女子
歌唱时，我低下了头，
凝眸在那冰封的往事
和未来的爱与死以及漠视。
我已是耄耋之年，
但我仍要向你和你的眼睛吟诵这些诗，
向你那殷切的微笑和怀抱吟诵这些诗。

我揭开所有不必要的掩饰，除去所有缠累，
是我有生之年所要实现的计划
和要走的路。
去洞察什么是鲜活的，
什么才是值得惺惺相惜的。
我仍然相信爱的力量，
正如
我几乎可以感受到大地那
蓄意破坏的力量使得地动山摇，
而我自己则在死亡每日的鼓点中颤抖。

请用你自己的力量和爱
来阅读这首诗吧！
微笑并重读，点头、发奋自雄，
严冬中必有挣扎，
为迎接那崭新青翠的春天。

——阿诺德·阿道夫

P16

frost

霜冻

仅仅是
通透的
清水

如何生发出
蕾丝蕨植、
羽毛、
卷须？

窗棂前，
它们
何处生根？

那些茂密的
水晶森林，
那些寒冷的
银色丛林。

——瓦莱丽·沃思

P17

I So Liked Spring

我如此喜爱春天

我是如此喜爱去年春天，
因为有你
和画眉鸟，
因为你最爱听到画眉鸟的歌唱，
而我是如此喜欢你。

今年却大相径庭，
我不会再想起你。
但是我仍然喜欢春天，仅仅因它是春天，
就像画眉鸟一样。

——夏洛特·缪

P17

April Rain Song

四月雨中曲

雨，亲吻你。
雨，银色的雨滴，滴滴落在你头上。
雨，为你唱一首摇篮曲。

雨，在路边积成了静静的水洼。
雨，在水沟里哗哗流过。
雨，在夜晚的屋顶演奏一首小小的催眠曲。

我爱雨天。

——兰斯顿·休斯

P17

Metamorphosis

变形记

蒲公英啊！
我的朋友，你谦卑而美好。
你在青草中绽放，
穿过碎石、裂缝，
或傲然竖立，或成簇而居，
纤弱却倔强。
告诉我为什么
黄色的花朵直伸向天，
直到
茸茸飞花，变成种子，
脱落，
放手，
飞去。

——萨拉·霍尔布鲁克

P18

Why Leaves Change Color in the Fall

为什么叶子秋天会变色

我正要给全班讲解，
叶子是自然的食品工厂，它们从
土地中吸取水分，从空气中吸收二氧化碳，
再利用阳光来把水和二氧化碳变成储存着能量的
有机物，并且通过光合作用的过程为树木提供高能量
的糖类。光合作用需要一种叫作叶绿素的化学物质，它可以
让树木和其他植物变绿。在秋天，由于水分减少，日照时间缩短，
光合作用的效率减弱，因此树木开始停止生产有机物，而那些
绿色的充满了叶绿素的叶子也就放假了，变成了黄色、橘色
或是枫树般的颜色。有机物被锁在叶子里，光合作用也
停止了，叶子变成了悦目的深红色…… 但是我又想，
何必花时间解释这些，因为大家都可以和我一起
坐在这里，看着这棵古树像胡迪尼
的色彩魔术一般变换颜色，
让叶子像
鸽子
的
羽毛
一般

轻　轻　飘　落　到　地　上。

——J. 帕特里克·刘易斯

Something Told the Wild Geese

P19

听，是谁对大雁私语

听，是谁对大雁私语：
“该启程了。”
尽管田野一片金黄，
有人低语：
“要下雪了。”

绿叶翻飞，
浆果，闪着诱人的光泽，
但在那温暖的羽毛下面，
有人提醒：
“霜冻要来了。”

那些硕果累累的园子，
蒸腾着琥珀色的香气。
但那些大雁想到冰雪，
不禁涨紧胸口。

听，是谁对大雁私语：
“该飞走了。”
翅膀上还挥舞着夏日阳光，
叫声里却是一片冬日哀伤。

——雷切尔·菲尔德

February Tale

P20

二月物语

地上
冷得要戴手套，
孩子们匆匆跑着，
穿着胶底鞋，
呼气成冰，
卷在空气中，
每棵树
都枯枝瘦叶……

哦，二月啊！

但远在那冰封的地表下，
一株急迫的嫩芽
开始生发，
另一个季节
也被录入；
另一个物语，
冬之王储……

啊，二月！

——勒妮·M. 拉·图丽普

Sounds of Winter

P20

冬之声

十月妖怪们来了，
没有“嘿嘿喝哈”，
只有鼾声如鼓。

睡在树端，
震落秋叶
却毫无察觉。

但你很快听到十二月的黑色巨龙
传来沉闷的呼噜声，
醒来就使狂风呼啸。

霜寒刺痛人，冰冷麻痹人，
可怕的“嘿嘿喝哈”，
妖怪离去，冬天来临。

——无名氏

November

P21

寒月

秋日之尽，
钻石之霜。
丛林之冠，
落裘之伤。

松鼠之绯，
橡柜之盈，
碌碌而作，
周而复始，
摇枝木兮，
果实满颊。

灰云昭昭，
冬之初雪，
杜门不出，
取火炀之。

饼饵炙兮，
太羹滚滚，
金瓜双饼，
凉凉而食，
燕燕其声，
谢意不尽。

——玛丽埃尔·比德

Autumn

秋

秋夜，一丝凉意，
我走了出去，
看到那红润的月亮倚靠在树篱上，
好像一个红脸的农夫。
我没有停下脚步搭讪，只是点点头，
惆怅的星光环绕，
面色白皙，好像城里的孩子们。

——T. E. 休姆

November Night

十一月之夜

听……
那窸窸窣窣的声音，
像游魂的脚步，
叶子，被霜冻脆了，从树上脱落，
坠下。

——阿德莱德·克拉普西

A Crack in the Clouds

云之隙

一条如此微小的
狭缝，
只是云层上的
一丝缝隙，
是如何
使得
如瀑的阳光
湮没
所有人。

——康斯坦丝·利维

In Just

P23

大好春光

在这大好春光里，
世界散发着泥土的芬芳，
跛足的气球小贩
口哨声悠远微弱。

埃迪和比尔来了，
抛下玻璃珠和海盗游戏，
这正是大好春光，
世界充满了奇妙的水洼。

这古怪的、
年迈的
气球小贩
口哨声悠远微弱。

贝蒂和伊丝贝尔跳起舞来，
抛下跳房子和跳绳游戏，
因这正是大好春光。

而那
山羊脚的
气球小贩
口哨声悠远微弱。

——e. e. 卡明斯

The Pasture

P24

牧场

让我来清理一下牧场上的那口井，
只需要把落叶耙走就好
（当然还要看着它变清）：
我不会走太久——你也来吧！

让我把小牛牵过来，
它站在母牛旁边，真的好小啊！
连喝水都会踉跄一下，
我不会走太久——你也来吧！

——罗伯特·弗罗斯特

My Heart Leaps Up

P24

我心雀跃

我心雀跃，
因仰望那彩虹，
生命之初如此，
现已成人如此，
老迈时如此，
不然，让我死去！
这婴孩是人类之父，
愿我有生的日子，
每天被单纯的敬虔包裹。

——威廉·华兹华斯

For All

P25

致万物

啊，在这九月中的清晨，
活力四射，
光着脚、卷起裤腿
蹚过小溪，
拿着靴子，向前跋涉，
穿过阳光和浅滩中的冰层，
还有北方的岩石山脉。

冰冷的溪水潺潺闪烁，
碎石在脚下翻动，像冻僵的脚趾一般
又小又硬，
鼻子冰凉，
心里却歌唱着，
小溪的音乐、心灵的音乐，
而沙石上散发出阳光的气息。

我宣誓效忠，

我宣誓效忠，
这海龟岛的土地
和在这片土地上生活的一切。

同一个生态，
多姿多彩的生态，
在阳光下
快乐地彼此交融。

——加里·斯奈德

The *LONG* Summer

P25

悠长夏日

夏日静坐着，微笑起来，
似乎要在这里停留一整年，
但彼时我只是个孩子。

当下，我只想大声欢呼，
并乐意让自己相信：
整年我都不会长大。

——詹姆斯·海福德

Who is mother nature?

When Mother Nature's near—in waterfalls, rivers, rainbows, meadows, or oceans—her admirers react with love, awe, curiosity, even fear, if she decides to reveal her grumpier side. The lady can be seen through telescopes or microscopes, from mountaintops or ravines, with the wind in our hair, soil in our hands, or sand in our toes. For those who aren't hopelessly city-bound, looking out a window will do.

Driven to explore the *science* behind the wonder of it all, Charles Darwin filled scores of notebooks about what was then the unexplored wildlife of the Galápagos Islands. Countless nature writers have followed his courageous example. Others have put themselves in nature, like naturalist John Muir, who once rode out a northern American windstorm by cocooning himself in the branches of a sky-high Douglas spruce. (Muir is famous—or should be—for saying, "The clearest way into the Universe is through a forest wilderness.")

Some humans, however, have no use for wild places, a view once expressed by Woody Allen with his typical wit: "I love nature. I just don't want to get any of it on me." For some, their love for animals extends only as far as Fido or Sweet Pea. That we share the Earth equally with other creatures is a notion as foreign and irrelevant to them as the disappearance of the rain forests or the melting of the ice caps.

But Mother Nature doesn't care who likes her. Nor is she bothered about being ignored. A midwife at the birth of creatures large and small, she will go on making waves by making waves, assembling forests, flowering deserts, and beautifying gardens. We can embrace her or resist her charms; it is of no concern to her.

Who is the mysterious lady known as Mother Nature? She is the material world, the environment of trees, plants, animals, everything under and over the sun. In short, she equals the world around us and includes whatever is not built by human hands.

Mother Nature is where we live. In other words, she is

a refuge to the lost,
a magnet to the curious,
a dare to the daring,
the cradle of rapture,
the university of the universe,
the glory of a morning and of a morning-glory,
not a whale but the idea of a whale,
a sign rewriter: I Welcome All No Trespassing,
the best cure for couch disease,
an opera performed by birds, bullfrogs on drums,
the sound of silence . . . amplified
to the symphony of the spheres, and ____________
____.

Can you add another short description of Mother Nature to this poem?

The poets and photographers who have come together to produce National Geographic's *Book of Nature Poetry* would agree with John Keats, who defined their abiding faith: "The poetry of earth is never dead."

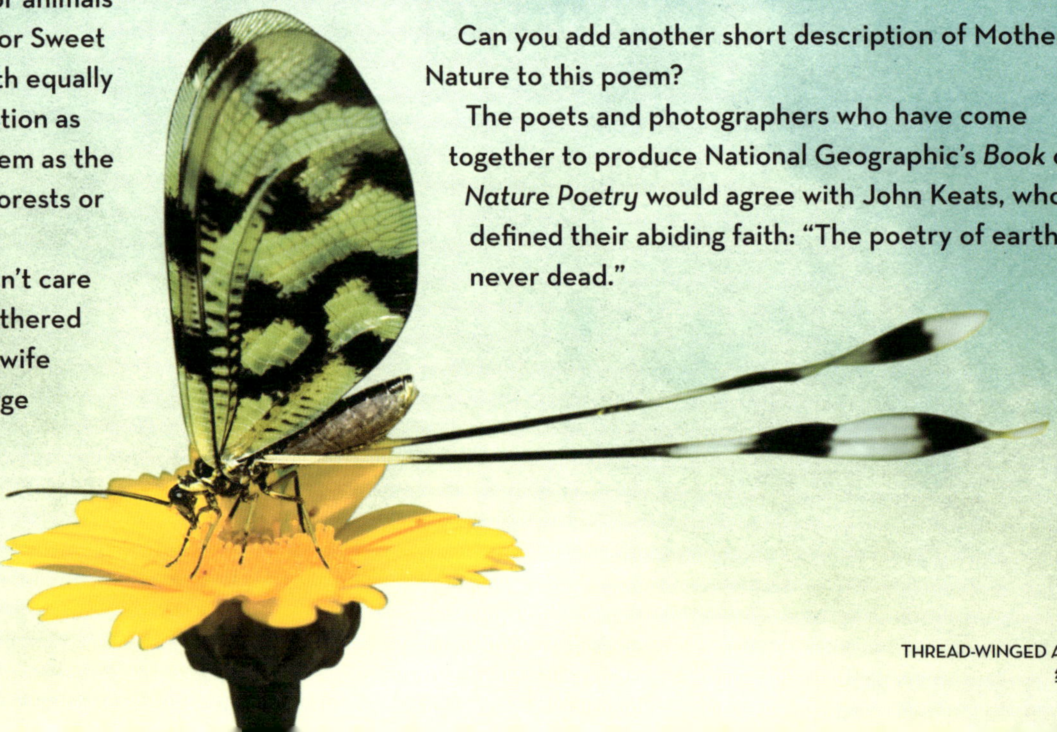

THREAD-WINGED ANTLION
线翅蚁狮

自然之母是谁？

当自然之母靠近的时候——在瀑布中，在河流中，在彩虹中，在草地或是海洋中——她的爱慕者用爱、敬畏、好奇来回应，甚至如果她显示暴躁的一面时，则用恐惧来回应。这位女士可以用望远镜或是显微镜来观察，从山顶到深谷，风在我们的发丝中穿过，泥土在我们手中漏出，沙在我们的脚趾中渗出。对于那些不喜欢住在城里的人来说，只要看一看窗外就行。

为了探索自然奇观背后的科学道理，查尔斯·达尔文把加拉帕戈斯群岛未知的野生动物记满了几十本笔记本。难以数计的自然主义作家跟随着他，以他为榜样。其他人则让自己融入自然。例如自然主义者约翰·缪尔，曾经用高耸入云的道格拉斯云杉的枝叶包裹着自己，经受住了北美的风暴。（缪尔由于下面这句话而知名——或应该知名——“融入宇宙最清晰的方式莫过于通过荒野森林”。）

然而，也有一些人，觉得野外毫无用处，这也是伍迪·艾伦用他特有的机智曾经表达的观点：“我爱自然，但是一点也别弄到我身上来。”而另一些人，他们对动物的喜爱只限于“菲多”或是“甜豌豆”。对他们来说，我们与其他生物平等地分享地球的观念，和雨林正在消失、冰层正在融化这样的概念一样，是未知而不重要的。

但自然之母并不关心谁喜欢她。她对这种忽视也毫不在意。她是大大小小各种生物出生时的产婆，她将不断在波浪中创造波浪，让森林遍地，让花朵在沙漠开放，让花园变得更美。我们可以接受或是抗拒她的魅力，她对此却毫不关心。

这位被人称为自然之母的神秘女士是谁？她是物质世界，也是植物、动物的环境和阳光下所有的一切。简言之，她就是我们周遭的世界，人类双手无法创造的世界。

自然之母在我们生活的地方。换句话说，

她是：

迷失者的庇护，

好奇者的磁石，

勇敢者的挑战，

狂喜者的摇篮，

宇宙的教化者。

她是：

清晨的光辉，

牵牛花的光，

并不是鲸鱼，

而是这创意。

她重新写了一个标记：我欢迎所有的非擅自闯入者。

她是：

沙发病的良药，

鸟儿、牛蛙在鼓上演奏的歌剧，

是寂静之声……被放大，

而成为万物的交响曲，

也是 ________________________

你可以在这首诗后面加上一段描写自然之母的短句吗？

共同创作《最美自然诗集》的诗人和摄影家们会同意约翰·济慈的话，他道出了他们永恒的信仰：“地球的诗篇永远不会消亡。”

LOTUS AND BEES-WUQIANG
荷花与蜜蜂（吴强）

美国童诗桂冠诗人［美］J.帕特里克·刘易斯　主编
Abby F. Yehenola ❁ 张原平 ❁ 和览　编译

NATIONAL GEOGRAPHIC
美国国家地理

book of nature poetry

最美自然诗集 6

（汉英对照）

200首诗歌
和会漂浮
会穿越，
会开花
的精彩图片

河南科学技术出版社
·郑州·

千山鸟飞绝，
万径人踪灭。
孤舟蓑笠翁，
独钓寒江雪。

这是唐朝柳宗元的《江雪》。短短的20个字，便成功捕捉一幅美丽的风景画。当时的孤冷静谧与雪白世界，似乎透过这首诗被永久封存，美丽了好几千年，不曾消逝。

《最美自然诗集》的出版，重新带给我这样的震撼与感动。随着时代的变迁，生活节奏的加快，文字阅读耗费时间，致使读者更为钟情图像阅读。不过图像阅读与文字阅读所获得的乐趣，无法互相取代。纵使是对同个风景的描绘，使用新诗文字创作与照片图像创作，让读者感受到的乐趣亦是截然不同。若是舍弃文字的阅读，全都转向图像阅读，实在相当可惜。《最美自然诗集》却完美解决了这个问题：这本诗集的每首诗，都是一张照片加上一首诗，使得文字文本和图像文本相互合作对话，形成一支精彩的双人舞。

这本书真的让我重新认识美丽的地球！在大自然中，随着四季的交替、地形的差异、气候的更迭，每一刹那的风景都是独一无二、稍纵即逝的。照片是静态的叙事，透过摄影师的镜头，有意识地捕捉吉光片羽，所以一张张的美照，是摄影师透过自身的美学哲学与镜头的选择所决定的，也可以说照片是摄影师眼中的美景。

而诗的创作，则是透过诗人纤细善感的心思，触景生情，把当时的生命状态转化成诗句，以情寓景，让景物多了一股人情的芬芳，不少美景在诗句的化妆下，变得充满情韵，让人印象深刻。

除此之外，这本书的编者扮演着隐形创作者的角色，因为他们成功媒合了照片与诗句，让作品更有一层乐趣。诗句的意象让静态的照片翩然生动，仿佛可以听见照片中的潺潺流水声，让读者宛若身临其境，感受照片里的一草一木，让读者悠游在每幅照片之中。阅读《最美自然诗集》，需要最好的领航员同游，我们的译者充分领会了编者的匠心独运，十分用心地录制了200首音频，恰是《最美自然诗集》最好的导读。

这本诗集让读者感受到三种美学：文学之美、摄影之美以及想象之美。透过诗句，让读者感受到文字透过意象诠释的美学；透过摄影照片让读者感受到强烈的视觉盛宴。当今的科技，无论是手机、电视还是穿戴科技等等，均试图以科技的力量，让读者感受到身临其境的感官盛宴，增强读者的视觉与听觉震撼，产生娱乐感，但是与此同时，相对地也剥夺了读者想象之美的权利。而《最美自然诗集》在照片与文字当中，保留了相当多的空白，并分类为“感叹自然”“凌空”“渊洋”“生灵”“山川”“美植”“灾难”“四季”“奇景”“敬畏自然”，让读者可以发挥想象，感受编者所安排的想象之美。因此，阅读这本书让读者经历一场美学盛宴，沉醉在大自然的洗礼之中。

最后，从这本书中也可以看出编者对于环境保护的意识。人类过度开发，使得环境被破坏，导致气候异常，很多珍稀动物濒临灭绝，大自然也不再美丽。希望这本诗集，能唤起人类对于大自然的重新思考，思考如何与环境共生。

透过这本最美丽的诗集，让我们回忆起我们曾经的美好！伟哉自然，伟哉生命！

林文宝

· 译者序 ·

大概你不会知道自然灾难和诗歌有什么关系，这里有15首诗，把自然灾害都写得时而幽默、时而俏皮、时而发人深省。

灾难篇的第一个对开页就让大家感受到了冰火两重天，诗人把雪崩比作苏醒的雪怪，另一位诗人把火山比作沉睡的巨龙，都非常值得一读。

海啸的力量是很难用言语去形容的，但是诗人用排山倒海的句子让我们心灵受到了冲击。

我最喜欢的诗人简 · 约伦借老百姓的表现写出全球变暖的严重性。

诗人把地震比作女人的生产，无法控制，来了就挡不住。

罗伯特 · 弗罗斯特借圣经中上帝用洪水毁灭人类的典故来问大家，下一次是降火，还是降冰?

谁也耐不住干旱，诗人告诉我们，在干旱中，只有干旱耐得住寂寞。

你没见过龙卷风没关系，只要你读这首诗，你就知道在龙卷风中掉下来几个人有多正常。

大气污染这么严肃的话题，诗人却用一首歌的形式把它写了出来，读完会陷入沉思。

野火其实并没那么可怕，其实它深爱着大地，所以才出来寻爱，这首诗写得好巧妙。

洪水摧毁的到底是什么？不仅仅是家园，还有承载着家园的情感。

Abby 2017年10月于昆明

IN DISTRESS 灾难

J. PATRICK LEWIS HAS WRITTEN MORE THAN 95 PICTURE AND POETRY BOOKS FOR YOUNG READERS. IN 2011 HE WAS APPOINTED U.S. CHILDREN'S POET LAUREATE, AND WAS GIVEN THE NATIONAL COUNCIL OF TEACHERS OF ENGLISH AWARD FOR EXCELLENCE IN POETRY FOR CHILDREN.

HENRY DAVID THOREAU was one of America's truly Big Thinkers on a little pond—Walden Pond. It was there in 1853, in a self-built cabin not far from his Massachusetts family home, that he wrote: "I have a room all to myself; it is nature."

From his tucked-away cottage, Thoreau produced some of the most profound thoughts on Mother Nature. But poets from centuries past rarely wrote about the more exotic natural wonders. They never saw them, never knew they existed. Many of the most fascinating phenomena that we often take for granted today—thanks to the convenience of travel, books, or photographs—were seldom brought to the attention of the classical poets.

How would William Shakespeare or John Keats have described in a poem the grandeur of the Grand Canyon? One can only imagine Emily Dickinson, transported to the scene, painting on an easel built of words a picture of an Asian tsunami or an African drought. What immortal verse might William Wordsworth have written after a day's walk in the Amazon rain forest instead of the English countryside? What picture would Kobayashi Issa or Li Po paint after a submersible dive to the ocean deep?

And yet a poet does not have to be there! You needn't leave your chair to write a poem about the wilder shores of creation. A book is your ticket to ride; a photograph is rapid transit to the brain. What kind of poem would you write if all you had in front of you was an image, like one of the breathtaking pictures in the *Book of Nature Poetry* you are now holding?

Better yet, let your eyes be your camera, taking incredible pictures your brain will thank you for. Get up and go there! Explore the woods, a cave; climb a mountain; go scuba diving; or simply make a friend of a grasshopper in a field on a windy summer day. You might even imagine you *are* that dragonfly trying to escape a swift, or a lucky salmon that has wiggled through the legs of a grizzly bear.

Travel by photograph or on foot, but go quickly before nature disappears. Every day more than 70 animals, plants, or other living things, like fungi, roots, and molds, vanish forever. The *Book of Nature Poetry* seeks to capture the ever changing nature of nature, so that gone is not forgotten. Besides, when more of us care for nature, more can help save it.

However and wherever you greet the world outside your window, listen again to Mr. Thoreau for the last and best words of advice:

"It's not what you look at that matters. It's what you see."

—J. Patrick Lewis,
former U.S. Children's Poet Laureate

MALACHITE BUTTERFLY
孔雀石蝴蝶

J. 帕特里克 · 刘易斯已经为孩子们创作了95部图画书和诗集。2011年，他荣获了美国童诗桂冠诗人奖，并被美国国家英语教师委员会授予杰出童诗奖。

·前　言·

亨利·戴维·梭罗是美国真正的大思想家之一，他曾隐居在瓦尔登湖。

1853年，在离马萨诸塞州家不远的自建小木屋里，他写道：“我有一个只属于我自己的房间——大自然。”

就在这世外桃源般的小木屋里，梭罗萌发出一些关于大自然的极其深刻的思想。但是这几百年来，诗人们却很少再去描写更独特的自然奇观。他们从来没见过，甚至都不知晓它们的存在。很多今天我们习以为常的，可以从旅行、书籍或照片中轻松获取的绝世美景，以前却很少能引起古典诗人们的关注。

试想，莎士比亚和济慈会怎样用诗歌去描绘大峡谷的壮美？可想而知，若埃米莉·迪金森能亲临亚洲海啸或非洲干旱现场，她将会用文字绘制出怎样的一幅画卷。那华兹华斯呢？如果他有机会走在亚马孙雨林中，而不仅仅是在英国乡间小道徘徊，他的笔下会写出怎样的诗句呢？若小林一茶或李白能乘潜艇探访大洋深渊，他们诗作的意境又将是怎样的呢？

然而，诗人并非一定要身临其境。你不需要离开椅子才能去写沧海桑田。一本书可以带你去遨游，一张照片可以带你去穿越。如果你拥有的只是面前的一幅图，就像你手里的《最美自然诗集》中的任意一幅惊艳的美图一样，你能写出怎样的诗句呢？

更棒的是，去旅行，让眼睛成为你的照相机，让眼前的美景滋养你的大脑。去吧，去森林中历险，去探索一个洞穴，去勇攀一座高峰，去潜入海底，甚至去野地里和一只蚱蜢交个朋友，任夏风轻抚。你甚至可以去想象自己就是那只努力躲过雨燕的蜻蜓，或是那条幸运地游过灰熊两腿之间的三文鱼。

无论是借着照片观光还是身临其境，请尽早，赶在自然景观消失之前。每天，都有超过70种生物在地球上永远消失。《最美自然诗集》力图捕捉到大自然瞬息万变的属性，让逝去的不再被遗忘。同时，当有更多的人开始关心大自然时，便会有更多的人来拯救她。

无论你在哪里，用怎样的方式来向窗外的世界致敬，请你再一次，也是最后一次聆听梭罗先生的警世良言：“重要的不是你眼前的，而是你心里的。”

——J. 帕特里克·刘易斯，美国童诗桂冠诗人

The Thing Is the Thing Is Green

The thing is the thing is green and the green is green and by green I mean real mean green. I mean electric-eel green, alligator, iguana, anaconda green. I mean this thing has got all things green. It's got green turtles in turtle-green ponds and grasshoppers springing from groomed-green lawns and a green tree frog on a girl's left arm. It's got dark and dangerous greens. Greens you've never even seen greens. Ocean floor greens. Tornado sky greens. Tiger's eye greens. Eat-your-broccoli greens. Watermelons sparkling in the sun greens. Way beyond evergreen, this thing leaves green geckos on green leaves feeling green and green moths in the green dark and preying mantises on their thin green knees. It's a great and gorgeous green a light-bright-just-right-watch-it-grow-it-says-go shade of green. Have you guessed yet? Do you need another clue? Think rolling waves of grain green. Thick arms of vines climbing tall green trees. Mountains and mountains of green billions of waves reaching out of dark green seas all wrapped in one green ball and hung, an ornament in the sky. What a thing it must be to see the whole green thing floating by. It's true. The thing is the thing is green . . .

except when it's blue.

—Peggy Gifford

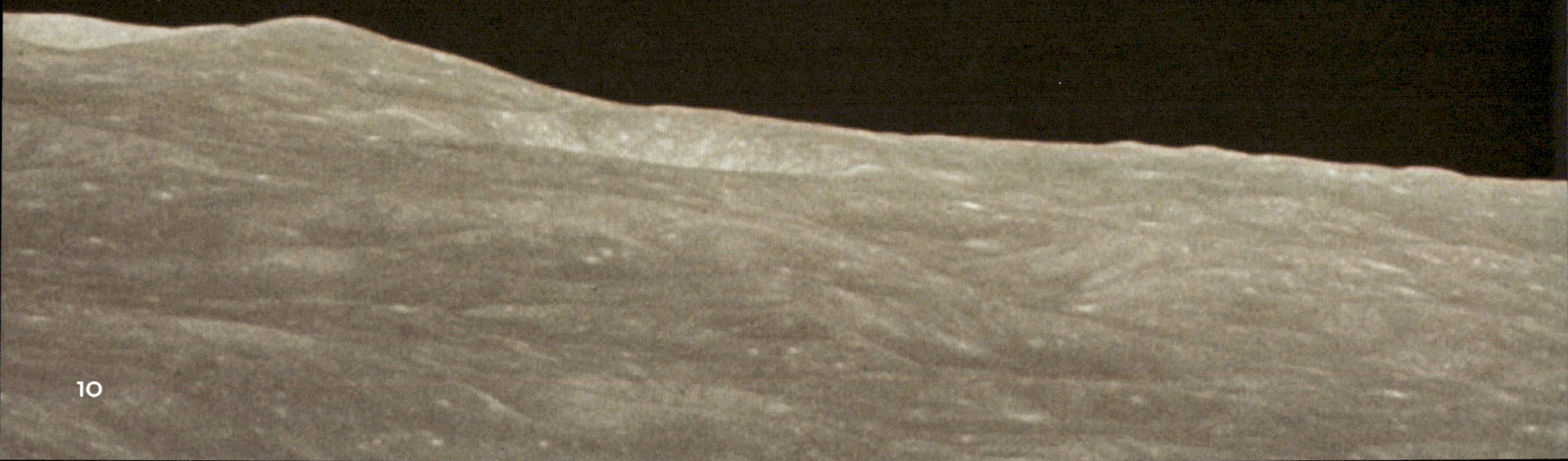

它要多绿就有多绿

要多绿就有多绿，绿就绿它个透心绿，就是这么绿，实打实的绿。我讲的是电鳗绿、鳄鱼绿、蜥蜴绿、蟒蛇绿，我说的这种绿把所有东西都染绿了。瞧那绿龟徜徉在龟绿色的池塘里，蚱蜢从刚修绿的草坪里一跃而起，一只绿树蛙停歇在女孩的左臂。有时候，它绿得阴森，绿得凶险，绿得其实你从未见过。大洋底的深渊绿，龙卷风的虐绿，老虎眼底的幽绿，“吃完西兰花”的郁闷绿，西瓜在阳光下的闪耀绿。比常绿植物更绿的，是绿叶上享绿的绿色壁虎、沉绿夜空的绿色飞蛾、紧绷双膝的绿色螳螂。它绿得伟大，绿得华丽，那“趁着阳光正好赶快生长说长就长”的一抹绿。还没有猜出来吗？还需要再来一点提示吗？想想那绿色的麦浪翻滚，想想那粗壮的藤蔓攀上绿色的参天大树。连绵不绝的绿色山峦，深绿海洋中的滔天巨澜，竟都被包在一个绿色的球里，独具一格地装点着天空。能亲眼看见这大绿球飘过该是一件多么大的幸事啊。没错，它要多绿就有多绿……

除非它变蓝了……

——佩姬 · 吉福德

HURRICANE IGOR AS SEEN FROM SPACE
从太空观测到的飓风“伊戈尔”

RESS

Avalanche

Hardpack buckles
Up from below.
Bare white knuckles

Jut through snow.
A yeti's paw
Begins to grow

Claw by claw.
And mountainside,
Softened by thaw,

Unearths a tide
For fractured slabs
Of snow to ride.

The monster grabs
At all in its path,
Heaves and jabs

With wintry wrath
Aspens bowed
In aftermath,

Leaving a shroud
Of powder cloud!

–Steven Withrow

AVALANCHE, PARADISE BAY, ANTARCTICA
雪崩，天堂湾，南极洲

Dormant Dragons

Volcanoes there are that sleep
the sleep of dragons
with cool heads and hot bellies
they crouch
solid and still
where the earth meets the sky
Till something wakes them
Then furious they breathe fire and smoke
hot spittle and wrath
to burn and choke
whatever lies in their path
leaving in their wake
an odd treasure
of stone sponges and glass
and an occasional lake

—Marilyn Singer

MOUNT ETNA, SICILY, ITALY
埃特纳火山，西西里岛，意大利

Tsunami

Five hundred miles per hour, the core
sweeps under every ship to shore,
unleashing megatons of sea-
floor-detonating energy

to flatten village, field, and road—
Mother Nature's mother lode—
at unsuspecting ports of call.
An ocean-blown Niagara fall.

—Anonymous

TSUNAMI, FUKUSHIMA PREFECTURE, JAPAN
海啸，福岛县，日本

Weather Deniers

How can you deny the change
when January has become
the very Florida of the year?
Thermometers perspire,
inspire walkers, who stride
across missing snowbanks,
arms bare.
Are you unaware
that this is no ordinary thaw?
There's a flaw in your thinking.
Mud and bud before March.
Even the daffodils are threatening,
raising their green shafts
like swords, and squirrels
digging up their buried nuts.

—Jane Yolen

Tsunami

The wave travels silently
without companions,
gathering them into itself.

Passing through
everything
like a ghost,

it rushes with something
to tell the shore.
But by the time it arrives

it can only roar.

—JonArno Lawson

Earthquake

Dakota, first to sense a change,
Begins to whimper—passing strange.

Here comes the catastrophic whine:
The loss is yours, the fault is mine.

Tectonic plates can only shake
A continental bellyache

By stretching several feet or more
To rearrange themselves before

The settlements of Earth lie bare
Among the rubble of despair.

—Mariel Bede

LAVIC LAKE FAULT, CALIFORNIA, U.S.A.
熔岩湖断层，加利福尼亚州，美国

Fire and Ice

Some say the world will end in fire,
Some say in ice.
From what I've tasted of desire
I hold with those who favor fire.
But if it had to perish twice,
I think I know enough of hate
To say that for destruction ice
Is also great
And would suffice.

—Robert Frost

NOVA SCOTIA, CANADA
新斯科舍，加拿大

Drought

Interminable
    Dynamo,
This dry disaster
    Takes it slow.

A random rain,
    Long promised, stops
The riverbeds
    And withers crops.

For those without
    A water source,
The famine runs
    Its tragic course:

First thirst, then fever,
    Endless sun . . .
The waiting for
    Oblivion.

—Peter Kostin

SOSSUSVLEI, NAMIBIA
索苏斯韦雷，纳米比亚

TORNADO SEASON

Wind went by with people falling out of it,
and hairpins,
and a barn door swinging without its hinges.
Grass rose in swarms along with nails.
A crow flew upside down,
his legs reaching skyward,
and growing longer.

—Adrien Stoutenburg

TORNADO, COLORADO, U.S.A.
龙卷风，科罗拉多州，美国

Punishing Conditions

For whipping winds and lashing rains the weather gods have hurri-canes

—Graham Denton

Where Will We Run To

Where will we run to
when the moon's
polluted in its turn

and the sun sits
with its wheels blocked
in the used
          star
              lot?

—X. J. Kennedy

The Merry-Go-Round Song

What shall we do with the ozone layer?
What shall we do, Daddy dear?
We'll knit the clouds into tight white shrouds
And stitch them with needles of fear.

The clock is striking, oh is it too late?
Have we run out of time, Mummy dear?
With our ladder of cars, we shall climb to the stars
To create a new atmosphere.

But when will we learn the lesson we must?
When will we learn, Brother dear?
We will learn how to fly like a plane in the sky
What a gas! (that won't disappear).

And is the earth leaking and what of her wounds?
Oh what of her wounds, Sister dear?
To plug up the hole, we shall fill it with coal
Though it bleeds with a dark oily smear.

What shall we do with the ozone layer?
Don't worry your head, my dear.
Now hide your tears and close up your ears
For nobody wants to hear.

—Andrew Fusek Peters and Polly Peters

Birds Have Left Without a Song

Birds have left without a song.
Morning light looks yellow and wrong.
Airports close, so does the town.
Winds pick up, trees blow down.
Radios go on and on.
Churches fill, church bells bong.
The people are listening, listening.

Born in a land Saharas away
Crossing an ocean to have its say
Crashing through town like a runaway train
Oh Breaker of Nations rain us your rain
Wind us your winds—of course we'll complain.
But leave us alive with reason to sing
When you are done chastening, chastening.

—John Barr

HURRICANE, ANTIGUA, WEST INDIES
飓风，安提瓜岛，西印度群岛

Wildfire

It's the earth I'm after,
the pungent taste of soil
sifted over time,
seasoned with moss and dried leaves,
perfectly stirred by
the undulation of worm.
I am grateful for the lightning
that struck the first tree
like a match.
I grew giddy,
my blue tongue licking
grass, timber, those strange boxes
men live in.
I rushed red, greedily devouring
all that stood between me
and the sweet delicacy of Earth.
And when only we two remained,
I licked her warm skin,
finally content to simmer,
to lie low, to die.

—Nikki Grimes

FOREST FIRE, CUSTER STATE PARK, SOUTH DAKOTA, U.S.A.
森林大火，考斯德州立公园，南达科他州，美国

Flood

Your levees break
And overflow
Like promises
Made long ago.

The city stop
Signs disappear,
Black water crests
At level: **FEAR**.

Old family photos
Float away
With furniture
And yesterday.

Then come the tears
Like rivulets:
A Mississippi
Of regrets.

—Peter Kostin

TURBULENT WATER
湍急的水流

灾难

IN DIST

HURRICANE IGOR AS SEEN FROM SPACE
从太空观测到的飓风“伊戈尔”

RESS

Avalanche P14

雪崩

结实的雪身
由上至下，

光白的指节
冲出雪面，

雪人的爪子
一步一步
已初露锋芒。

山麓
冰雪渐融，
湍流涌出，
势如破竹，
踏浪而来。

怪兽一路席卷，
翻天覆地。

雪兽的残酷
让山杨折腰，
余怒未消，

只留下一片
雪虐风啸。

——史蒂文·威思罗

Dormant Dragons P15

沉睡的巨龙

火山睡着了，
像沉睡的巨龙，
有着冰凉的脑袋和滚烫的肚子。
它们蜷伏着，
一动不动，
在天地交接的地方。
直到被吵醒，
接着大怒起来，
喷出烈焰和烟雾。
熔岩，爆发，
烧毁，窒息
面前的一切。
却紧跟着留下
奇珍异宝、
浮石和琉璃，
间或，一泊湖。

——玛丽莲·辛格

P16

Tsunami

海啸

以每小时五百英里的速度，
它卷起每艘船，摔向岸，
它释放百万吨级的能量
爆破海床。

踏平村庄、田野和道路，
自然之母的狂澜
在那毫无防备的港口，
如巨瀑一般倾泻而下。

——无名氏

P17

Tsunami

海啸

波涛潜行，
独自向前，
一路裹挟。

如鬼魅乎，
穿越万物。

激流勇进，
似有相告。

惊涛拍岸，
唯余怒号。

——琼阿诺·劳森

P17

Weather Deniers

气候变化？视而不见！

怎么可以对这变化视而不见！
当一月来临，
恍如一年中的度假时节，
连温度计都冒汗了，
让那些路上的行人，走在积雪消融的路边，
大步前行，露出手臂。

这不寻常的回暖，你若视而不见，
便是错了。
三月未到，
竟见冻土融化、蓓蕾初放，
水仙花举起
绿剑般的叶子示威，
松鼠也忙着挖出埋藏的果实。

——简·约伦

Earthquake

P18

地震

达科他州，先得震感，
大地开始啜泣，蔓延不安。

灾难般地悲鸣道：
失误是我的，可伤损你来包。

大地板块摇撼不止，
生拉硬扯好几尺。

闹痛大洲肚腹，
换得内部重组。

只留下一片荒凉，
断壁残垣的绝望。

——玛丽埃尔·比德

Fire and Ice

P19

火与冰

有人说世界将在火中毁灭，
有人说是冰。
因我了解欲望之猛烈，
故认可降火之论心切。
若世界必须毁灭两次，
据我对仇恨的领悟，
冰也能胜任摧毁的任务，
完全可以满足。

——罗伯特·弗罗斯特

Drought

P20

干旱

它精力旺盛，
没完没了。
这场旱灾，
不慌不忙，

从未兑现
哪怕零星雨点，
河流停滞，
庄稼枯干。

可怜的人们啊！
缺了水源，
饥荒盛行，
悲剧上演。

先焦渴，
后炎热，
无尽的烈日，
恍惚的神志。

——彼得·科斯廷

P21

TORNADO SEASON

飓风季

狂风卷袭，
人们，纷纷坠下，
发卡，随风散乱，
无樟的谷仓门，狂摆，
杂草，卷着钉子，团团升起，
乌鸦，头朝下飞着，
腿，向上空伸展，
越伸越长。

——阿德里安·斯托坦恩伯格

P22

Punishing Conditions

惩罚的方法

为了鞭挞风和抽打雨，天气之神制造了飓风。

——格雷厄姆·登顿

P22

Where Will We Run To

我们能逃到哪里去呢?

我们能逃到哪里去呢?
当月亮升起，
却被污染了。

而太阳被堵在
废旧的恒星停车场，
轮子动弹不得。

——X. J. 肯尼迪

P22

The Merry-Go-Round Song

旋转木马之歌

我们怎样才能拯救臭氧层?
我们要怎么做呢，亲爱的爸爸?
我们要把云朵织成厚厚的白布，
再用敬畏的针把它们缝好。

时钟敲响，哦，已经太晚了吗?
我们是不是没时间了，亲爱的妈妈?
把车子摞成梯，一定能爬到星星上，
就能造个新的大气层了。

我们什么时候才能吸取教训?
什么时候才能，亲爱的兄弟?
我们要像飞机一样飞翔，
好恶心!（而且永远不会消失。）

大地漏了吗? 她的伤口怎样了?
她的伤口怎样了，亲爱的姐妹?
洞要堵，可我们却用煤，
般出黑油的斑斑迹迹。

我们怎样才能拯救臭氧层?
别杞人忧天了，我亲爱的。
擦掉眼泪，堵上耳朵，
没人想听。

——安德鲁·福塞克·彼得斯，波莉·彼得斯

P23

Birds Have Left Without a Song

鸟儿，一声不响地飞走了

鸟儿，一声不响地飞走了，
晨光，面色焦黄，病了，
风起，树倒。
广播叫个不停，
机场关了，街头空了，
教堂满了，
听啊，听啊!
钟敲响了。

生于撒哈拉外，
漂洋过海
只为表个态，
如脱轨列车，踏破城镇，
哦，覆国之力!
雨，任你尽情下，
风，任你尽情刮，
我们当然要哭求
留一条活路吧!
因还要歌唱，
待你息怒，
快停吧，快停吧!

——约翰·巴尔

Wildfire

P24

野火

我在追捕大地，
那散发着浓烈气息的泥土。
被时光筛过，
被青苔和落叶腌过，
又被虫子的蠕动充分搅拌。

我感谢闪电，
点燃了第一棵树，
如划亮火柴。

我目眩神迷，
蓝色的舌头舔舐着
青草、树木和那些人类居住的
奇形怪状的盒子。

火红的烈焰驰骋，
贪婪地吞噬着
我和大地珍馐之间的一切。

最后只剩下我和大地，
我舔舐她温暖的皮肤，
在满足中，
退去，
倒下，
死亡。

—— 尼基·格兰姆斯

Flood

P25

洪水

你的堤已决口，
洪水泛滥，
就像很久以前
你许下的诺言。

大势所趋，
红灯消失，
黑色的大水已达
畏惧的峰值。

泛黄的家庭照片
和家具，
顺流漂远，
昨日不再。

眼泪
涓涓而下，
悔恨
已逆流成河。

——彼得·科斯廷

Who is mother nature?

When Mother Nature's near—in waterfalls, rivers, rainbows, meadows, or oceans—her admirers react with love, awe, curiosity, even fear, if she decides to reveal her grumpier side. The lady can be seen through telescopes or microscopes, from mountaintops or ravines, with the wind in our hair, soil in our hands, or sand in our toes. For those who aren't hopelessly city-bound, looking out a window will do.

Driven to explore the *science* behind the wonder of it all, Charles Darwin filled scores of notebooks about what was then the unexplored wildlife of the Galápagos Islands. Countless nature writers have followed his courageous example. Others have put themselves in nature, like naturalist John Muir, who once rode out a northern American windstorm by cocooning himself in the branches of a sky-high Douglas spruce. (Muir is famous—or should be—for saying, "The clearest way into the Universe is through a forest wilderness.")

Some humans, however, have no use for wild places, a view once expressed by Woody Allen with his typical wit: "I love nature. I just don't want to get any of it on me." For some, their love for animals extends only as far as Fido or Sweet Pea. That we share the Earth equally with other creatures is a notion as foreign and irrelevant to them as the disappearance of the rain forests or the melting of the ice caps.

But Mother Nature doesn't care who likes her. Nor is she bothered about being ignored. A midwife at the birth of creatures large and small, she will go on making waves by making waves, assembling forests, flowering deserts, and beautifying gardens. We can embrace her or resist her charms; it is of no concern to her.

Who is the mysterious lady known as Mother Nature? She is the material world, the environment of trees, plants, animals, everything under and over the sun. In short, she equals the world around us and includes whatever is not built by human hands.

Mother Nature is where we live. In other words, she is
a refuge to the lost,
a magnet to the curious,
a dare to the daring,
the cradle of rapture,
the university of the universe,
the glory of a morning and of a morning-glory,
not a whale but the idea of a whale,
a sign rewriter: I Welcome All No Trespassing,
the best cure for couch disease,
an opera performed by birds, bullfrogs on drums,
the sound of silence . . . amplified
to the symphony of the spheres, and ____________
____.

Can you add another short description of Mother Nature to this poem?

The poets and photographers who have come together to produce National Geographic's *Book of Nature Poetry* would agree with John Keats, who defined their abiding faith: "The poetry of earth is never dead."

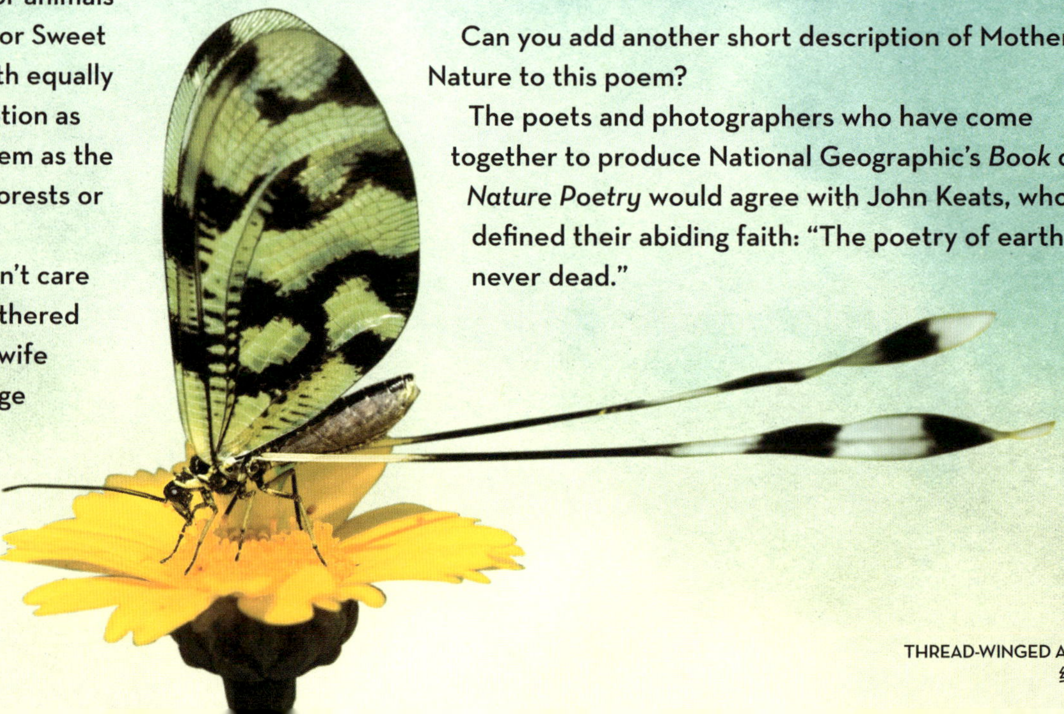

THREAD-WINGED ANTLION
线翅蚁狮

自然之母是谁？

当自然之母靠近的时候——在瀑布中，在河流中，在彩虹中，在草地或是海洋中——她的爱慕者用爱、敬畏、好奇来回应，甚至如果她显示暴躁的一面时，则用恐惧来回应。这位女士可以用望远镜或是显微镜来观察，从山顶到深谷，风在我们的发丝中穿过，泥土在我们手中漏出，沙在我们的脚趾中渗出。对于那些不喜欢住在城里的人来说，只要看一看窗外就行。

为了探索自然奇观背后的科学道理，查尔斯·达尔文把加拉帕戈斯群岛未知的野生动物记满了几十本笔记本。难以数计的自然主义作家跟随着他，以他为榜样。其他人则让自己融入自然。例如自然主义者约翰·缪尔，曾经用高耸入云的道格拉斯云杉的枝叶包裹着自己，经受住了北美的风暴。（缪尔由于下面这句话而知名——或应该知名——“融入宇宙最清晰的方式莫过于通过荒野森林”。）

然而，也有一些人，觉得野外毫无用处，这也是伍迪·艾伦用他特有的机智曾经表达的观点：“我爱自然，但是一点也别弄到我身上来。”而另一些人，他们对动物的喜爱只限于“菲多”或是“甜豌豆”。对他们来说，我们与其他生物平等地分享地球的观念，和雨林正在消失、冰层正在融化这样的概念一样，是未知而不重要的。

但自然之母并不关心谁喜欢她。她对这种忽视也毫不在意。她是大大小小各种生物出生时的产婆，她将不断在波浪中创造波浪，让森林遍地，让花朵在沙漠开放，让花园变得更美。我们可以接受或是抗拒她的魅力，她对此却毫不关心。

这位被人称为自然之母的神秘女士是谁？她是物质世界，也是植物、动物的环境和阳光下所有的一切。简言之，她就是我们周遭的世界，人类双手无法创造的世界。

自然之母在我们生活的地方。换句话说，

她是：
迷失者的庇护，
好奇者的磁石，
勇敢者的挑战，
狂喜者的摇篮，
宇宙的教化者。
她是：
清晨的光辉，
牵牛花的光，
并不是鲸鱼，
而是这创意。
她重新写了一个标记：我欢迎所有的非擅自闯入者。
她是：
沙发病的良药，
鸟儿、牛蛙在鼓上演奏的歌剧，
是寂静之声……被放大，
而成为万物的交响曲，
也是 ________________

你可以在这首诗后面加上一段描写自然之母的短句吗？

共同创作《最美自然诗集》的诗人和摄影家们会同意约翰·济慈的话，他道出了他们永恒的信仰：“地球的诗篇永远不会消亡。”

LOTUS AND BEES -WUQIANG
荷花与蜜蜂（吴强）

献给爱自然，爱诗歌的大小朋友们！

——Abby

美国童诗桂冠诗人［美］J.帕特里克·刘易斯 主编
Abby F. Yehenola ❁ 张原平 ❁ 和览 编译

NATIONAL GEOGRAPHIC
美国国家地理

book of nature poetry

最美自然诗集 7

（汉英对照）

200首诗歌
和会漂浮
会穿越，
会开花
的精彩图片

河南科学技术出版社
·郑州·

自然最美

千山鸟飞绝，
万径人踪灭。
孤舟蓑笠翁，
独钓寒江雪。

这是唐朝柳宗元的《江雪》。短短的20个字，便成功捕捉一幅美丽的风景画。当时的孤冷静谧与雪白世界，似乎透过这首诗被永久封存，美丽了好几千年，不曾消逝。

《最美自然诗集》的出版，重新带给我这样的震撼与感动。随着时代的变迁，生活节奏的加快，文字阅读耗费时间，致使读者更为钟情图像阅读。不过图像阅读与文字阅读所获得的乐趣，无法互相取代。纵使是对同个风景的描绘，使用新诗文字创作与照片图像创作，让读者感受到的乐趣亦是截然不同。若是舍弃文字的阅读，全都转向图像阅读，实在相当可惜。《最美自然诗集》却完美解决了这个问题：这本诗集的每首诗，都是一张照片加上一首诗，使得文字文本和图像文本相互合作对话，形成一支精彩的双人舞。

这本书真的让我重新认识美丽的地球！在大自然中，随着四季的交替、地形的差异、气候的更迭，每一刹那的风景都是独一无二、稍纵即逝的。照片是静态的叙事，透过摄影师的镜头，有意识地捕捉吉光片羽，所以一张张的美照，是摄影师透过自身的美学哲学与镜头的选择所决定的，也可以说照片是摄影师眼中的美景。

而诗的创作，则是透过诗人纤细善感的心思，触景生情，把当时的生命状态转化成诗句，以情寓景，让景物多了一股人情的芬芳，不少美景在诗句的化妆下，变得充满情韵，让人印象深刻。

除此之外，这本书的编者扮演着隐形创作者的角色，因为他们成功媒合了照片与诗句，让作品更有一层乐趣。诗句的意象让静态的照片翩然生动，仿佛可以听见照片中的潺潺流水声，让读者宛若身临其境，感受照片里的一草一木，让读者悠游在每幅照片之中。阅读《最美自然诗集》，需要最好的领航员同游，我们的译者充分领会了编者的匠心独运，十分用心地录制了200首音频，恰是《最美自然诗集》最好的导读。

这本诗集让读者感受到三种美学：文学之美、摄影之美以及想象之美。透过诗句，让读者感受到文字透过意象诠释的美学；透过摄影照片让读者感受到强烈的视觉盛宴。当今的科技，无论是手机、电视还是穿戴科技等等，均试图以科技的力量，让读者感受到身临其境的感官盛宴，增强读者的视觉与听觉震撼，产生娱乐感，但是与此同时，相对地也剥夺了读者想象之美的权利。而《最美自然诗集》在照片与文字当中，保留了相当多的空白，并分类为“感叹自然”“凌空”“渊洋”“生灵”“山川”“美植”“灾难”“四季”“奇景”“敬畏自然”，让读者可以发挥想象，感受编者所安排的想象之美。因此，阅读这本书让读者经历一场美学盛宴，沉醉在大自然的洗礼之中。

最后，从这本书中也可以看出编者对于环境保护的意识。人类过度开发，使得环境被破坏，导致气候异常，很多珍稀动物濒临灭绝，大自然也不再美丽。希望这本诗集，能唤起人类对于大自然的重新思考，思考如何与环境共生。

透过这本最美丽的诗集，让我们回忆起我们曾经的美好！伟哉自然，伟哉生命！

林文宝

· 译者序 ·

如果你想周游世界却没有钱，没关系，读完这本书，基本上你会把全世界最神奇的景色都看个遍，拥有这本宝书，坐在家里也可以“走”遍全“诗集”（世界）！

欢迎在太空游览可以清晰可见的生物建筑——大堡礁，不用沾湿身子，就可以在太空看到各种鱼类在大堡礁的生活，岂不惬意。

上帝是不是在天空画布上给人类换着画风地表演节目，乳状云你肯定没见过，这首诗不仅让你见识到这种云的美丽，甚至把乳状云的形成原因也给你科普一下。

听说过雨过天晴的彩虹，没听说过月光也可以形成虹吧！来美国的肯塔基州大开眼界。

你有幸经历过日食吗？一首小诗把日食科普一下，也告诉你日食的时候如何保护自己。

每天天上能下点吃的该有多好！别说，还真有下动物的，多数是小雨，诗里提醒你到时候别忘了把伞倒过来拿。

海滩上露出好几个没人要的月亮，你会来捡吗？这首诗带给你新西兰海滩奇遇记。

美国南达科他州有一片光秃秃的山，诗里说里面分层留着地球的历史。

加拿大艾伯塔省的平原上有一块大大的圆石头，谁也不知道它是怎么来的，至今仍是千古之谜，也许这首藏头诗能给你揭开谜底。

你见过三个日头当空照吗？四个呢？五个呢？不要惊慌，其中的秘密就在这首诗里。

委内瑞拉有一个地方，一年里有多数日子都在打雷，而且那个雷啊，可不普通，会让你觉得像世界末日一样，扫码听我讲给你听到底是怎么回事。

在深深的太平洋底，有一个马里亚纳海沟，据说它是世界的最低点，就连珠穆朗玛峰倒过来都碰不着底，但诗人要表达的却是人心。

美国的大峡谷可不只是石头，它的形成充满了神奇色彩，诗人说是格列佛捏塑出来的，你信吗？

位于中国和尼泊尔边境的珠穆朗玛峰是世界的最高峰，诗中的它傲慢至极，欲与天公试比高，听星星怎么回复它。

自从我给女儿读过这首关于粉色湖泊的诗，她就对澳大利亚充满了好奇，难道你不好奇吗？为什么这个湖泊的颜色可以跟泡泡糖一样？

当水遇到盐，再加上极低的温度，会发生什么现象呢？这首诗告诉你，它们会在海底铺一条银光闪闪的死亡之路。

下一个对开页中，你需要从美国大陆跳到热带雨林，再跳到尼亚加拉大瀑布，这个旅行实在太过瘾了，快来体验。

黄石公园一直是我儿时最向往的地方，虽然这首诗已经让我们仿佛身临其境，但有机会我一定要亲身体验。

贝加尔湖对于中国人来说并不陌生，因为歌手李健把同名歌曲献给了爱人，扫码来听这首诗的讲解，你还能重温那首浪漫的情歌。

马尔代夫的旅行中，如果你可以亲历诗中描写的荧光海滩就太幸运了。

巴西的大潮汐，让无数冲浪爱好者不顾生命危险来挑战，光读读诗就觉得心惊胆战了。

澳大利亚的艾尔斯巨石据说是石头中的大哥大，读读这首诗就知道它口气有多大了。

别光看赤潮漂亮，它可是十分危险的，扫码听译者讲解，会长知识哦。

美国亚利桑那州有一个奇幻森林，在那个森林中，树木都变成了化石，虽说没有了生机，漂亮就行啊。

北极光也许是自然界中最捉摸不定的现象了，这两首诗都给这个自然现象做了性格鉴定——顽皮的青少年！

本书最后七首诗是对大自然最后一次的讴歌，这七首诗每一首都值得大家铭记在心，因它们已经洗涤了我的灵魂，希望你们也有同样的经历。

Abby 2017年10月于昆明

IN SPLENDOR 奇景

LAST THOUGHTS

敬畏自然

J. PATRICK LEWIS HAS WRITTEN MORE THAN 95 PICTURE AND POETRY BOOKS FOR YOUNG READERS. IN 2011 HE WAS APPOINTED U.S. CHILDREN'S POET LAUREATE, AND WAS GIVEN THE NATIONAL COUNCIL OF TEACHERS OF ENGLISH AWARD FOR EXCELLENCE IN POETRY FOR CHILDREN.

HENRY DAVID THOREAU was one of America's truly Big Thinkers on a little pond—Walden Pond. It was there in 1853, in a self-built cabin not far from his Massachusetts family home, that he wrote: "I have a room all to myself; it is nature."

From his tucked-away cottage, Thoreau produced some of the most profound thoughts on Mother Nature. But poets from centuries past rarely wrote about the more exotic natural wonders. They never saw them, never knew they existed. Many of the most fascinating phenomena that we often take for granted today—thanks to the convenience of travel, books, or photographs—were seldom brought to the attention of the classical poets.

How would William Shakespeare or John Keats have described in a poem the grandeur of the Grand Canyon? One can only imagine Emily Dickinson, transported to the scene, painting on an easel built of words a picture of an Asian tsunami or an African drought. What immortal verse might William Wordsworth have written after a day's walk in the Amazon rain forest instead of the English countryside? What picture would Kobayashi Issa or Li Po paint after a submersible dive to the ocean deep?

And yet a poet does not have to be there! You needn't leave your chair to write a poem about the wilder shores of creation. A book is your ticket to ride; a photograph is rapid transit to the brain. What kind of poem would you write if all you had in front of you was an image, like one of the breathtaking pictures in the *Book of Nature Poetry* you are now holding?

Better yet, let your eyes be your camera, taking incredible pictures your brain will thank you for. Get up and go there! Explore the woods, a cave; climb a mountain; go scuba diving; or simply make a friend of a grasshopper in a field on a windy summer day. You might even imagine you *are* that dragonfly trying to escape a swift, or a lucky salmon that has wiggled through the legs of a grizzly bear.

Travel by photograph or on foot, but go quickly before nature disappears. Every day more than 70 animals, plants, or other living things, like fungi, roots, and molds, vanish forever. The *Book of Nature Poetry* seeks to capture the ever changing nature of nature, so that gone is not forgotten. Besides, when more of us care for nature, more can help save it.

However and wherever you greet the world outside your window, listen again to Mr. Thoreau for the last and best words of advice:

"It's not what you look at that matters. It's what you see."

—J. Patrick Lewis,
former U.S. Children's Poet Laureate

MALACHITE BUTTERFLY
孔雀石蝴蝶

J. 帕特里克 · 刘易斯已经为孩子们创作了95部图画书和诗集。2011年，他荣获了美国童诗桂冠诗人奖，并被美国国家英语教师委员会授予杰出童诗奖。

·前　言·

亨利·戴维·梭罗是美国真正的大思想家之一，他曾隐居在瓦尔登湖。

1853年，在离马萨诸塞州家不远的自建小木屋里，他写道：“我有一个只属于我自己的房间——大自然。”

就在这世外桃源般的小木屋里，梭罗萌发出一些关于大自然的极其深刻的思想。但是这几百年来，诗人们却很少再去描写更独特的自然奇观。他们从来没见过，甚至都不知晓它们的存在。很多今天我们习以为常的，可以从旅行、书籍或照片中轻松获取的绝世美景，以前却很少能引起古典诗人们的关注。

试想，莎士比亚和济慈会怎样用诗歌去描绘大峡谷的壮美？可想而知，若埃米莉·迪金森能亲临亚洲海啸或非洲干旱现场，她将会用文字绘制出怎样的一幅画卷。那华兹华斯呢？如果他有机会走在亚马孙雨林中，而不仅仅是在英国乡间小道徘徊，他的笔下会写出怎样的诗句呢？若小林一茶或李白能乘潜艇探访大洋深渊，他们诗作的意境又将是怎样的呢？

然而，诗人并非一定要身临其境。你不需要离开椅子才能去写沧海桑田。一本书可以带你去遨游，一张照片可以带你去穿越。如果你拥有的只是面前的一幅图，就像你手里的《最美自然诗集》中的任意一幅惊艳的美图一样，你能写出怎样的诗句呢？

更棒的是，去旅行，让眼睛成为你的照相机，让眼前的美景滋养你的大脑。去吧，去森林中历险，去探索一个洞穴，去勇攀一座高峰，去潜入海底，甚至去野地里和一只蚱蜢交个朋友，任夏风轻抚。你甚至可以去想象自己就是那只努力躲过雨燕的蜻蜓，或是那条幸运地游过灰熊两腿之间的三文鱼。

无论是借着照片观光还是身临其境，请尽早，赶在自然景观消失之前。每天，都有超过70种生物在地球上永远消失。《最美自然诗集》力图捕捉到大自然瞬息万变的属性，让逝去的不再被遗忘。同时，当有更多的人开始关心大自然时，便会有更多的人来拯救她。

无论你在哪里，用怎样的方式来向窗外的世界致敬，请你再一次，也是最后一次聆听梭罗先生的警世良言：

“重要的不是你眼前的，而是你心里的。”

——J. 帕特里克·刘易斯，美国童诗桂冠诗人

AURORA BOREALIS
北极光

The Thing Is the Thing Is Green

The thing is the thing is green and the green is green and by green I mean real mean green. I mean electric-eel green, alligator, iguana, anaconda green. I mean this thing has got all things green. It's got green turtles in turtle-green ponds and grasshoppers springing from groomed-green lawns and a green tree frog on a girl's left arm. It's got dark and dangerous greens. Greens you've never even seen greens. Ocean floor greens. Tornado sky greens. Tiger's eye greens. Eat-your-broccoli greens. Watermelons sparkling in the sun greens. Way beyond evergreen, this thing leaves green geckos on green leaves feeling green and green moths in the green dark and preying mantises on their thin green knees. It's a great and gorgeous green a light-bright-just-right-watch-it-grow-it-says-go shade of green. Have you guessed yet? Do you need another clue? Think rolling waves of grain green. Thick arms of vines climbing tall green trees. Mountains and mountains of green billions of waves reaching out of dark green seas all wrapped in one green ball and hung, an ornament in the sky. What a thing it must be to see the whole green thing floating by. It's true. The thing is the thing is green . . .

except when it's blue.

—*Peggy Gifford*

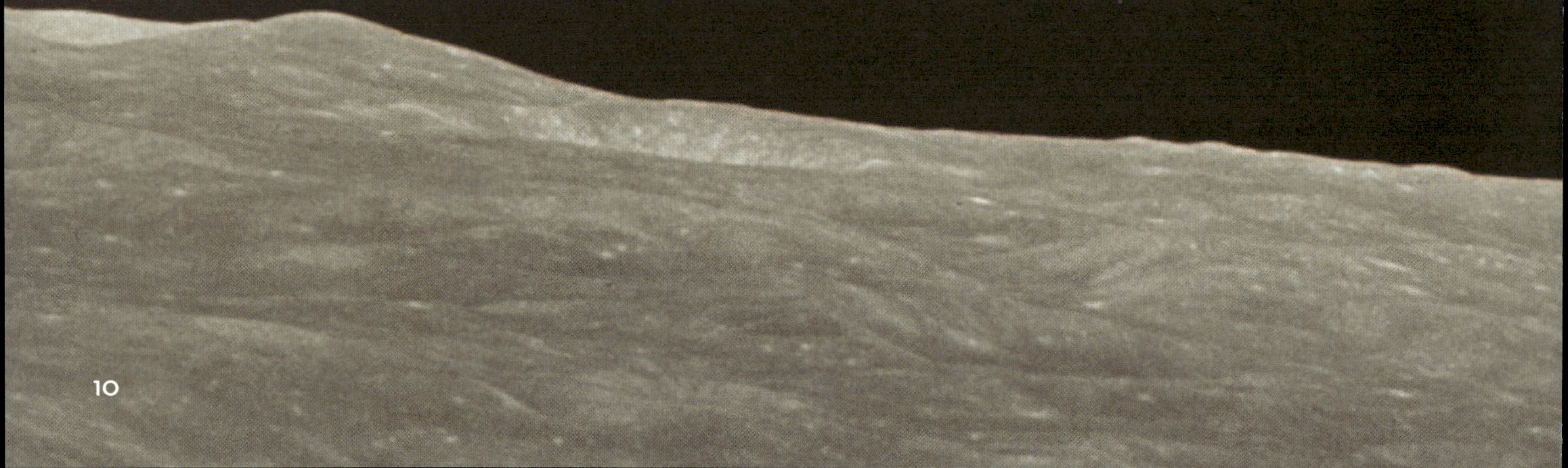

它要多绿就有多绿

要多绿就有多绿，绿就绿它个透心绿，就是这么绿，实打实的绿。我讲的是电鳗绿、鳄鱼绿、蜥蜴绿、蟒蛇绿，我说的这种绿把所有东西都染绿了。瞧那绿龟徜徉在龟绿色的池塘里，蚱蜢从刚修绿的草坪里一跃而起，一只绿树蛙停歇在女孩的左臂。有时候，它绿得阴森，绿得凶险，绿得其实你从未见过。大洋底的深渊绿，龙卷风的虐绿，老虎眼底的幽绿，“吃完西兰花”的郁闷绿，西瓜在阳光下的闪耀绿。比常绿植物更绿的，是绿叶上享绿的绿色壁虎、沉绿夜空的绿色飞蛾、紧绷双膝的绿色螳螂。它绿得伟大，绿得华丽，那“趁着阳光正好赶快生长说长就长”的一抹绿。还没有猜出来吗？还需要再来一点提示吗？想想那绿色的麦浪翻滚，想想那粗壮的藤蔓攀上绿色的参天大树。连绵不绝的绿色山峦，深绿海洋中的滔天巨澜，竟都被包在一个绿色的球里，独具一格地装点着天空。能亲眼看见这大绿球飘过该是一件多么大的幸事啊。没错，它要多绿就有多绿……

除非它变蓝了……

——佩姬·吉福德

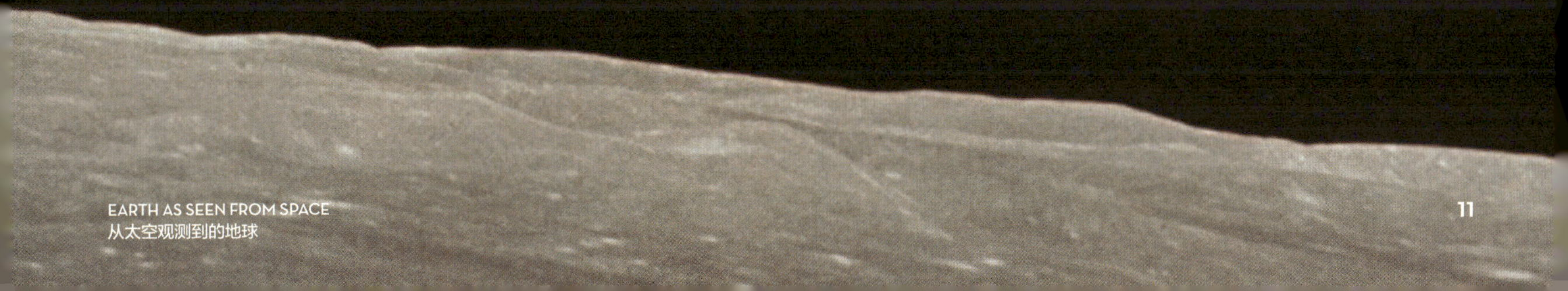

GRAND PRISMATIC POOL, WYOMING, U.S.A.
大棱镜泉，怀俄明州，美国

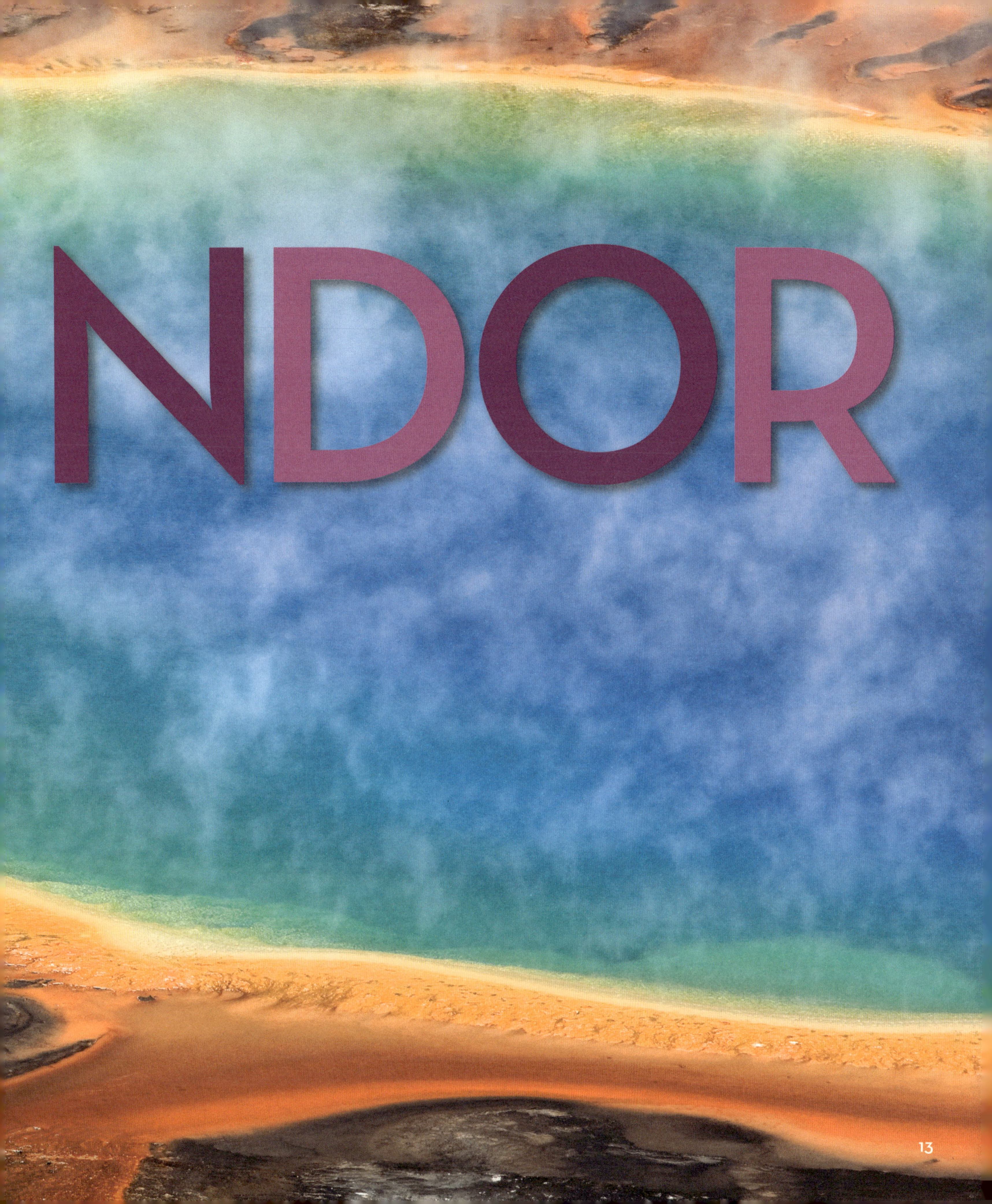
NDOR

GREAT BARRIER REEF MARINE PARK, QUEENSLAND, AUSTRALIA
大堡礁海洋公园，昆士兰州，澳大利亚

The Great Barrier Reef

In the Coral Sea, off the coast of Queensland, Australia

It's sixteen hundred miles long
along the Queensland coast,
the barrier reef whose name is "Great,"
and that's no idle boast.

It's sixteen hundred miles long
and every inch alive.
Perhaps you'd like to have a look?
You do not need to dive

or even get your swimsuit wet
to see this awesome place;
the reef's so huge it's visible
by astronauts in space.

To think, you can be orbiting
the earth while looking at
a teeming turtle, dolphin, whale
and porpoise habitat.

Your eyes will tell the story
and you will not doubt its moral:
There's hardly anything on earth
more beautiful than coral.

—Robert Schechter

Mammatus Clouds

Thunder coming with its usual heavy hammer
and the sky strange, bubbled
with clouds, the air humming
and warning us away.
Tornado coming today with its terrible trouble
and the sky pouched,
pockets of ice and water waiting
for their own best moment to burst.
Hard weather coming, for the worst reasons:
warm air, cool air, thermal instability,
wind shear, sublimation—
we cotton to the calmest explanations.
Something coming. Could be okay, could be misery—
who knows which or why?
Look at that sky, filled with question marks,
every mark cloud a mystery.

—Julie Larios

MAMMATUS CLOUDS, OKLAHOMA, U.S.A.
乳状的云，俄克拉何马州，美国

Moonbow at Cumberland Falls

In southeastern Kentucky, U.S.A.

Moonbow, moonbow made of mist and moonglow where the river flows over the falls
Full moon's moonshow how colors inside light glow where Cumberland cascades into falls
Red, orange, yellow, green waver on mist's silver screen where land level drops and river falls
Blue indigoes to violet where rivermist and moonbeam net Mystery among us yet:
Moonbow at Cumberland Falls

—*George Ella Lyon*

CUMBERLAND FALLS STATE RESORT PARK, KENTUCKY, U.S.A.
坎伯兰瀑布州立公园，肯塔基州，美国

Solar Eclipse

And owlets know it's nearing.
And hounds pretend it's night.
And Sun comes crowned in her corona.
    Stare—
    She'll steal
    Your sight.

And moonflowers yawn their petals.
And morning glories bind.
And earthworms glimmer in the gardens.
    Beware—
    She'll glare
    You blind.

—Steven Withrow

SOLAR ECLIPSE
日食

Fish Rain

Animal rain is an extremely rare
meteorological phenomenon.
Once in a weird while, it rains animals.
Not cats and dogs, but toads and frogs, always
the same species, and always the same size.
The most rained animals are tiny fish.
What makes live fish fall out of thunderclouds
many miles away from the nearest lake?
Are they whooshed up by fierce tornadic winds?
It has rained fish in Australia, India,
Louisiana, and Saskatchewan.
And in Yoro, a town in Honduras,
fish rain falls one or two times every year.
They celebrate it with a festival
thanking the fish rain for feeding the poor.
You'll probably never walk in a fish rain.
But, just in case, remember if you do,
to carry your umbrella upside down!

—Marilyn Nelson

Moeraki Boulders

Koekohe Beach, New Zealand,
between Moeraki and Hampden

Grown
like pearls,
deep in silt, these
globes began as bits of tooth
or shell that wrapped themselves
in trickling coats of stone and hardened
into fists. Slowly, over yawning time, their
silted seabeds lifted into cliffs. Now, the
pounding waves release these
treasures from their turf, splay
them like a spill of fallen
moons in sliding
surf.

—Joyce Sidman

MOERAKI BOULDERS, NEW ZEALAND
摩拉基巨石，新西兰

BADLANDS NATIONAL MONUMENT, SOUTH DAKOTA, U.S.A.
巴德兰兹国家遗址，南达科他州，美国

Fossil Beds at the Badlands

Badlands National Park, South Dakota, U.S.A.

Pass the RUSH-NO-MORE CAMPGROUND,
take a few turns, absorb the jagged shapes.
Saber-toothed cats sleeping,
wild horse dreams pressed into rock.
No quiet bigger than theirs.
Step gently, touch nothing,
does anyone remember?
Once they roamed the land of shining grasses,
owning sky. Tonight there's a bighorn sheep,
his back to the sunset, prairie dogs huddling
underground. How does so much disappear?

This kingdom holds lost hopes.
They are orange now. Some look like
fingers pointing to the sky.
Drop your own pain, no one will know.
Navigate soft sediment, whispering *Rhino*.
Everyone's emptiness made elegant,
even the bison and black-footed ferret,
even the woman, even the man.

—Naomi Shihab Nye

INGLEBOROUGH MOUNTAIN, UK
因格尔博罗峰，英国

Glacial Erratic

Big Rock, 15,000 tons, Alberta, Canada, and elsewhere

An open field surrounds a boulder so big, no

Giant could carry or move it. Who could have
Lifted it? Who set it down? Old people say it has
Always been here. Older than memory—
Could that be true? How did it get here, and why
Is it different from all other rocks for miles around?
Every mystery seeks its answer. See how this one,
Receding, drops a poem onto the field of this page.

—Helen Frost

SUN HALO
日晕

Sun Dogs

The sun made a special appearance
on his balcony, above the crowd,
surrounded by a halo
of diamond dust and clouds.

On either side of him there stood
two sun dogs, north and south,
keeping almost silent guard,
growls slipping from their mouths.

When the sun excused his audience
and disappeared in the dark,

he dismissed the sun dogs,
one and two, to guard the city parks.

—Janet S. Wong

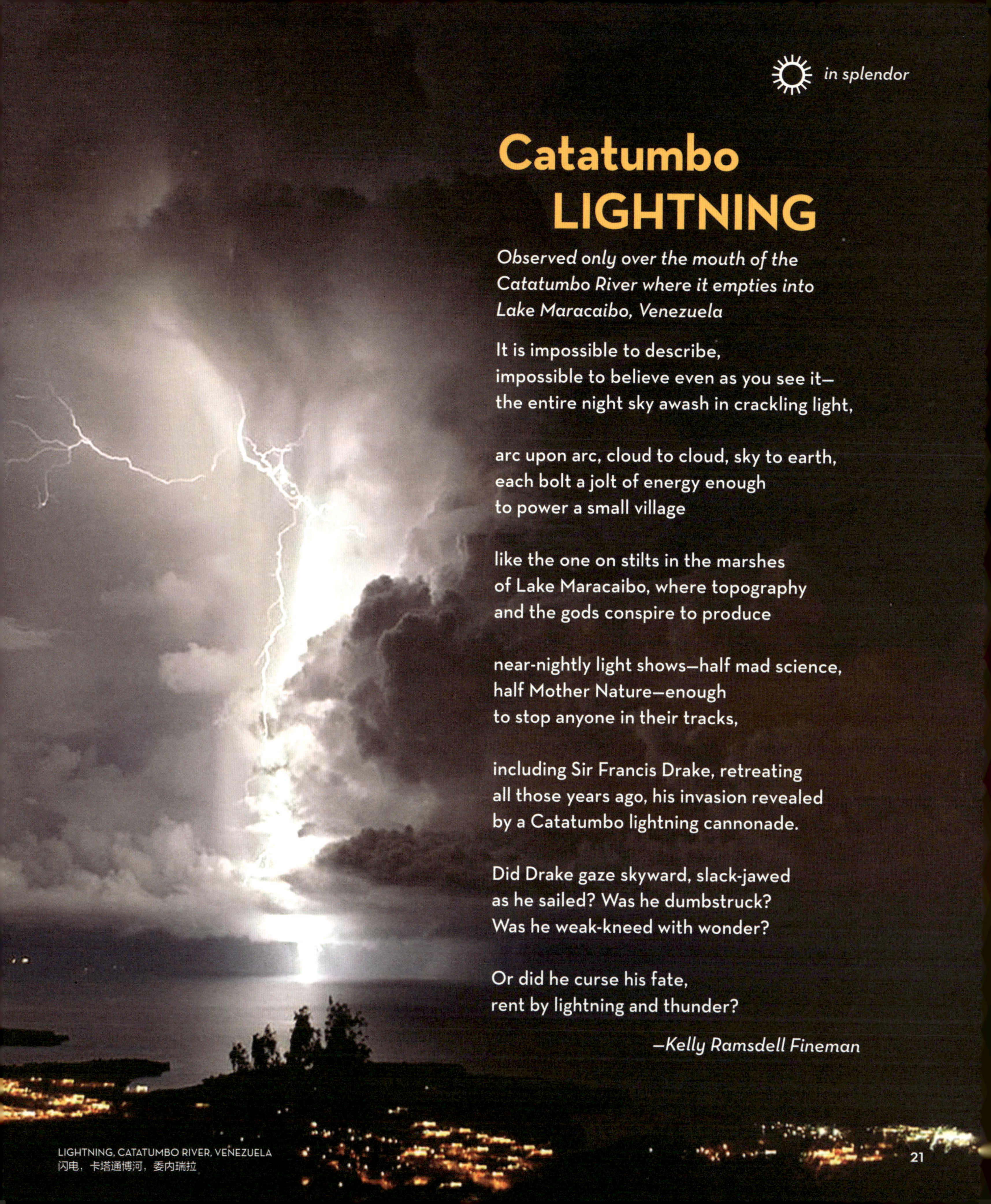

Catatumbo LIGHTNING

Observed only over the mouth of the Catatumbo River where it empties into Lake Maracaibo, Venezuela

It is impossible to describe,
impossible to believe even as you see it—
the entire night sky awash in crackling light,

arc upon arc, cloud to cloud, sky to earth,
each bolt a jolt of energy enough
to power a small village

like the one on stilts in the marshes
of Lake Maracaibo, where topography
and the gods conspire to produce

near-nightly light shows—half mad science,
half Mother Nature—enough
to stop anyone in their tracks,

including Sir Francis Drake, retreating
all those years ago, his invasion revealed
by a Catatumbo lightning cannonade.

Did Drake gaze skyward, slack-jawed
as he sailed? Was he dumbstruck?
Was he weak-kneed with wonder?

Or did he curse his fate,
rent by lightning and thunder?

—Kelly Ramsdell Fineman

LIGHTNING, CATATUMBO RIVER, VENEZUELA
闪电，卡塔通博河，委内瑞拉

The Mariana Trench

Western Pacific Ocean,
east of the Mariana Islands

In all the oceans, nowhere else so deep,
So dark with secrets men won't let it keep:
It yields to human eyes in submarines
And then, full of itself, goes back to sleep.

You wouldn't dream that hidden at its core
Life would go on as it has done for more
Than most of time, though seven heavy miles
Of water press down upon its floor.

To fathom it at last, to put on show
All that it holds, laid out in a neat row,
May happen sooner than to do that to
The mind of someone whom you think you know.

—X. J. Kennedy

MARIANA TRENCH, PACIFIC OCEAN
马里亚纳海沟，太平洋

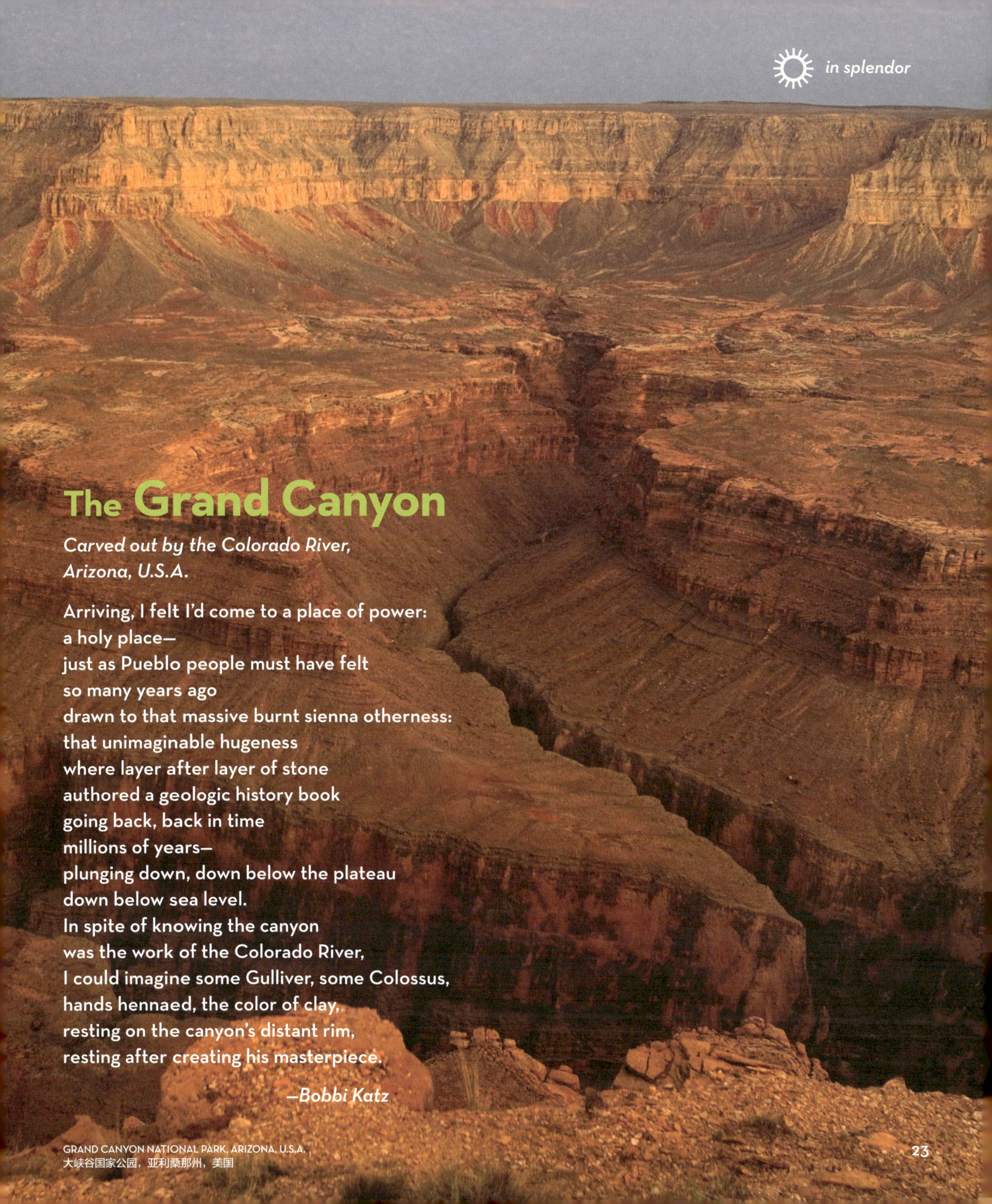

The Grand Canyon

Carved out by the Colorado River,
Arizona, U.S.A.

Arriving, I felt I'd come to a place of power:
a holy place—
just as Pueblo people must have felt
so many years ago
drawn to that massive burnt sienna otherness:
that unimaginable hugeness
where layer after layer of stone
authored a geologic history book
going back, back in time
millions of years—
plunging down, down below the plateau
down below sea level.
In spite of knowing the canyon
was the work of the Colorado River,
I could imagine some Gulliver, some Colossus,
hands hennaed, the color of clay,
resting on the canyon's distant rim,
resting after creating his masterpiece.

—Bobbi Katz

GRAND CANYON NATIONAL PARK, ARIZONA, U.S.A.
大峡谷国家公园，亚利桑那州，美国

MOUNT EVEREST, CHINA–NEPAL
珠穆朗玛峰，中国—尼泊尔

Mount Everest

Earth's tallest mountain, located on the border of Nepal and China in southern Asia, adds to its height each year.

Mount Everest calls out to the quiet stars,

"I am stronger than the wind,
I am immense,
noble,
King of the World!

As I lift my huge weight high, high above,
I see how tiny earth is.

Deeper and deeper into enormous spaces
I will climb and lay my shadow on all of it, everything.

Men call me 'Holy'
for I sail the skies,
and have now reached the crossing point
of heaven and earth . . .
I am coming!"

The Universe arches over,
and the stars, bending low,
whisper,
"We are waiting."

–Deborah Chandra

LAKE HILLIER, AUSTRALIA
希利尔湖，澳大利亚

Pink Lake

Middle Island,
Recherche Archipelago,
Western Australia

No natural site is sillier
than rosy-hued Lake Hillier.
You wouldn't be the first to think,
"This can't be real. That lake is pink!"
You'd not be first to ask, "How come
Lake Hillier looks like bubble gum?"
Ten times the salt found in the sea,
its waters are a mystery.

The tint may owe its genesis
to algae photosynthesis
which turns pink to attract sunlight.
But just in case that isn't right—
perhaps pink microbes halophilic,
who find salt water most idyllic,
have gathered in a massive group,
creating cotton candy soup.

Either one would cause the lake
to look like a strawberry shake.
You might be disappointed, though;
to find out we don't really know.
Salty Lake Hillier: Pink sensation.
Australian Barbie's dream vacation.
A pigment of imagination.

—Allan Wolf

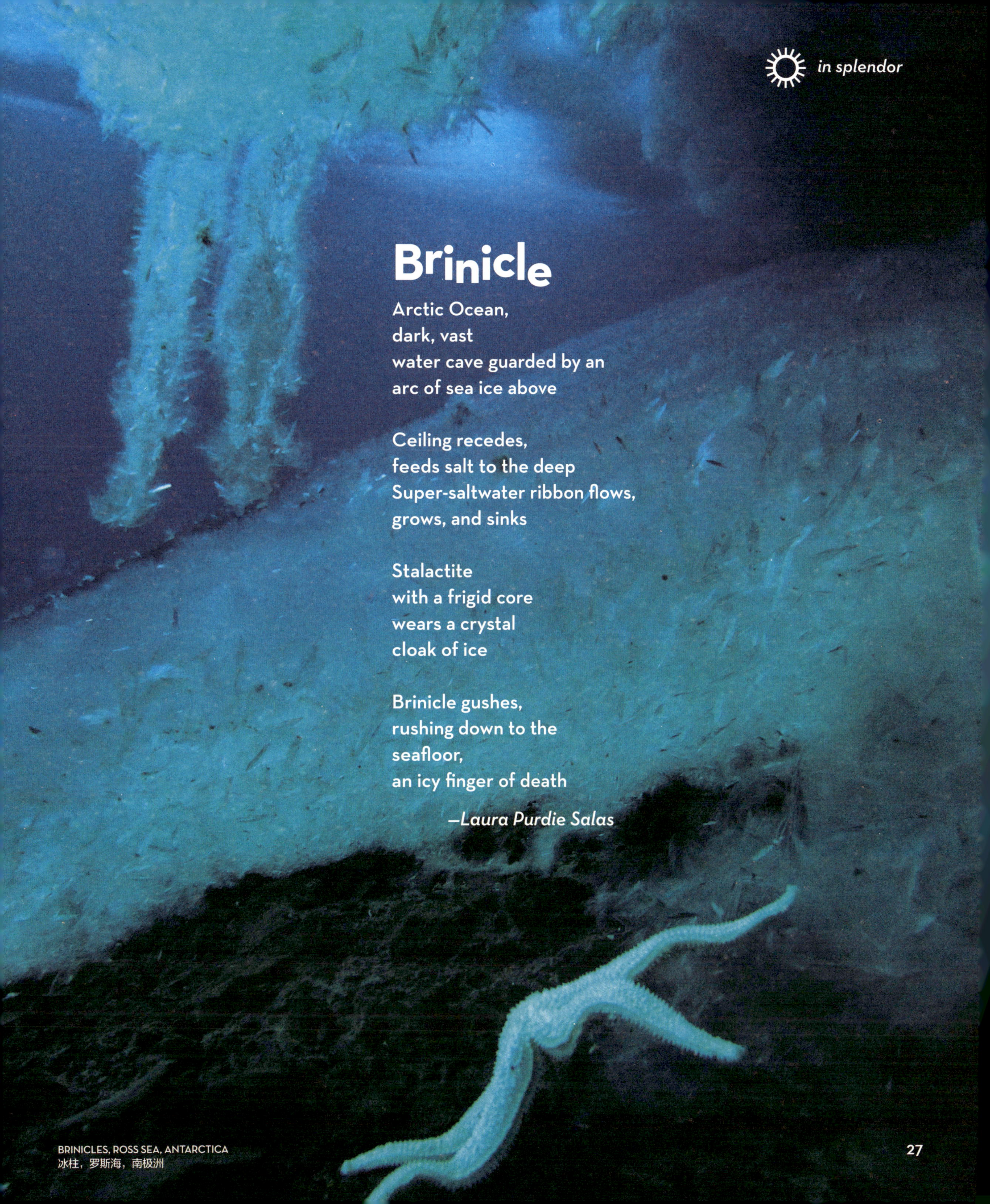

Brinicle

Arctic Ocean,
dark, vast
water cave guarded by an
arc of sea ice above

Ceiling recedes,
feeds salt to the deep
Super-saltwater ribbon flows,
grows, and sinks

Stalactite
with a frigid core
wears a crystal
cloak of ice

Brinicle gushes,
rushing down to the
seafloor,
an icy finger of death

—Laura Purdie Salas

BRINICLES, ROSS SEA, ANTARCTICA
冰柱，罗斯海，南极洲

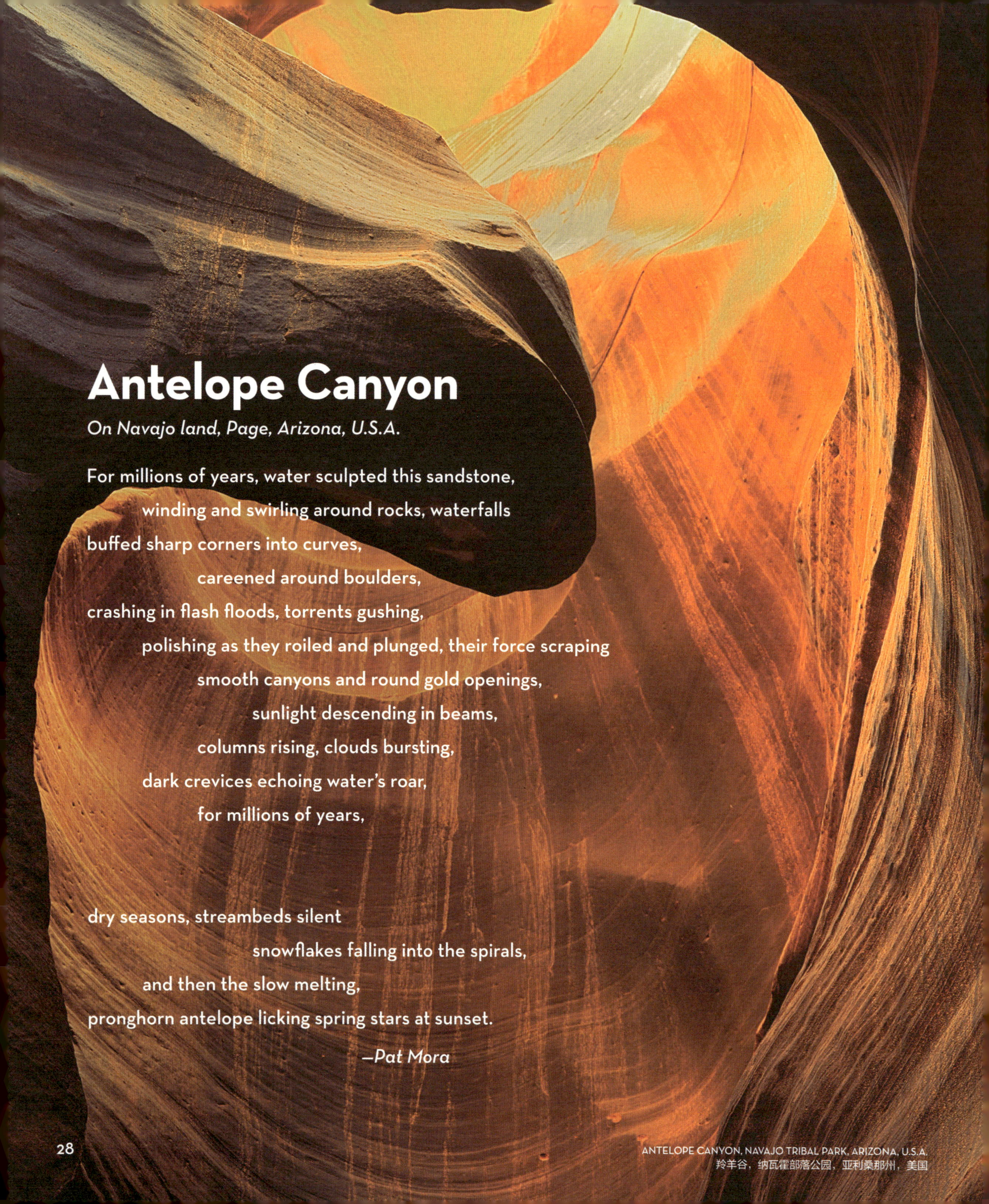

Antelope Canyon

On Navajo land, Page, Arizona, U.S.A.

For millions of years, water sculpted this sandstone,
winding and swirling around rocks, waterfalls
buffed sharp corners into curves,
careened around boulders,
crashing in flash floods, torrents gushing,
polishing as they roiled and plunged, their force scraping
smooth canyons and round gold openings,
sunlight descending in beams,
columns rising, clouds bursting,
dark crevices echoing water's roar,
for millions of years,

dry seasons, streambeds silent
snowflakes falling into the spirals,
and then the slow melting,
pronghorn antelope licking spring stars at sunset.

—Pat Mora

ANTELOPE CANYON, NAVAJO TRIBAL PARK, ARIZONA, U.S.A.
羚羊谷，纳瓦霍部落公园，亚利桑那州，美国

Rainforest

The forest drips and glows with green.
The tree-frog croaks his far-off song.
His voice is stillness, moss and rain
drunk from the forest ages long.

We cannot understand that call
unless we move into his dream,
where all is one and one is all
and frog and python are the same.

We with our quick dividing eyes
measure, distinguish and are gone.
The forest burns, the tree-frog dies,
yet one is all and all are one.

—Judith Wright

RED-EYED TREE FROG
红眼树蛙

NIAGARA FALLS, NEW YORK, U.S.A.
尼亚加拉瀑布，纽约州，美国

Niagara Falls

Between the province of Ontario, Canada, and the state of New York, U.S.A.

What a stage! What a play!
Thunder at its birth.
The longest running show around:
the greatest hit on earth.

USA and Canada
co-host this smashing show.
Don't miss the mist that nature kissed,
where double rainbows grow.

—Avis Harley

Yellowstone

Northwest Wyoming, U.S.A.

Forget all your troubles.
Forget all your cares.
And go to the park
With bisons and bears.
Moose go grazing.
Gray wolves stalk.
Great elk climb,
And pronghorn walk.
Rivers flow
And geysers spout.
Fir trees rise,
And lilies sprout.
Brown trout swim
And falcons fly.
All beneath a
Big Blue Sky.

—Douglas Florian

BISON, YELLOWSTONE NATIONAL PARK, WYOMING, U.S.A.
北美野牛，黄石国家公园，怀俄明州，美国

Lake Baikal

The oldest and deepest lake on Earth, Lake Baikal, in the south of the Russian region of Siberia, holds a fifth of the planet's unfrozen freshwater.

If Earth could fit within your cupped hands,
and the lands slipped free between the fingers,
and the skies' blue released between the thumbs,
and the oceans' tears seeped along your arms,

then you hold the planet's water in your palm.
Lift it to your lips. Sip that primal fresh.
And that crazed marble, that sapphire cat's-eye
in the rivulet that crosses your creased flesh?

That is Lake Baikal: frozen time.
Gaze into the blue. That glint?
It's Earth's beginning
staring back at you.

—Michael J. Rosen

LAKE BAIKAL, RUSSIA
贝加尔湖，俄罗斯

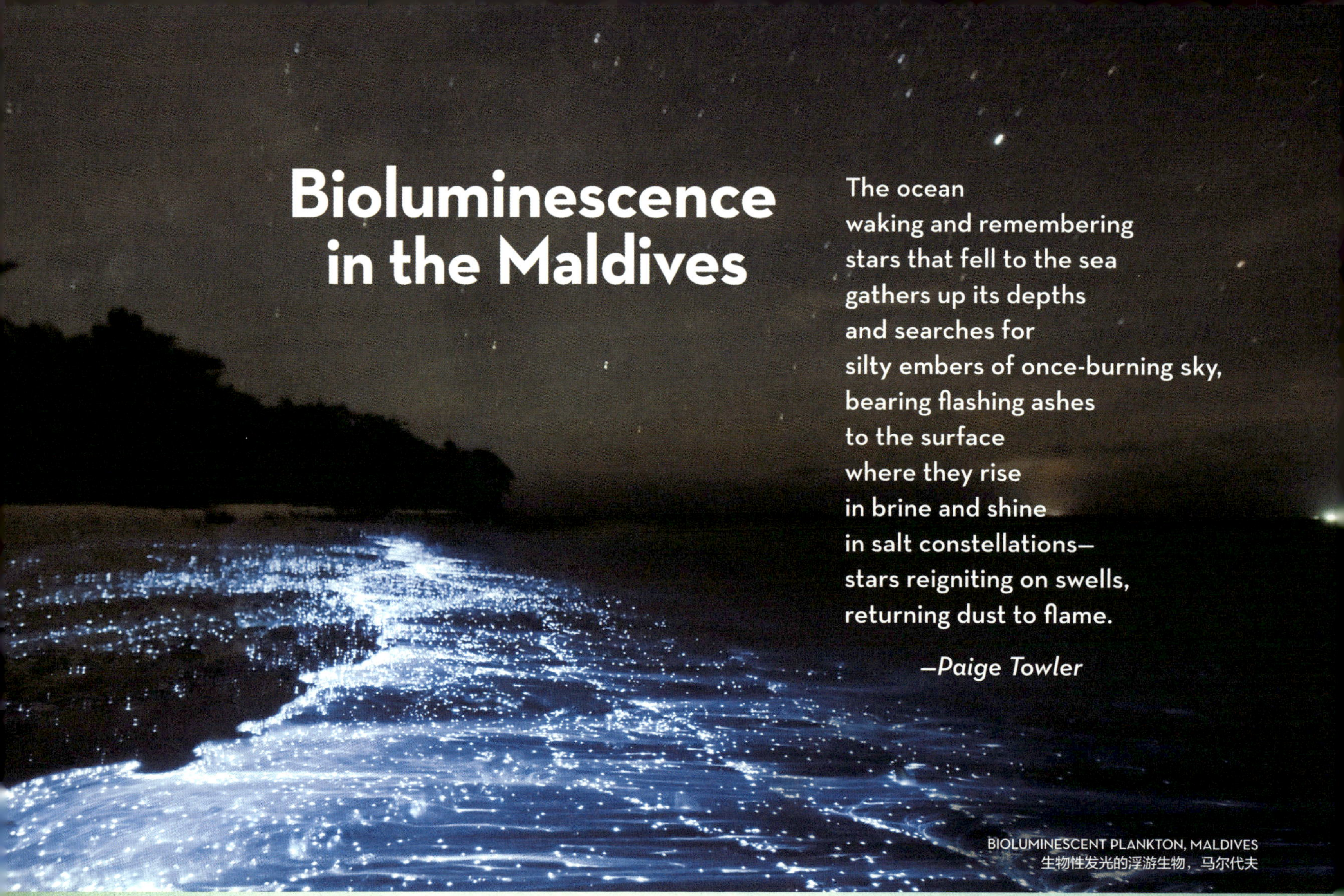

Bioluminescence in the Maldives

The ocean
waking and remembering
stars that fell to the sea
gathers up its depths
and searches for
silty embers of once-burning sky,
bearing flashing ashes
to the surface
where they rise
in brine and shine
in salt constellations—
stars reigniting on swells,
returning dust to flame.

—Paige Towler

BIOLUMINESCENT PLANKTON, MALDIVES
生物性发光的浮游生物，马尔代夫

Pororoca Tidal Bore

Araguari Pororoca,
Amapá state, Brazil

The Pororoca Tidal Bore
is the ocean at war with the river,
waves twice as tall as tanks
rolling, rumbling, roaring up the Amazon
delivering blast after blast after blast—

It lasts only days each year.
Ordinary people scurry away in fear
while surfers crazed as soldiers
surface from nowhere, eager
to navigate the battlefield of debris.

Trees: torpedoes. Rocks: grenades.
They choke on mud but they don't care.
When the *lunático* power of the pororoca
dissolves into nothing, these surfer-soldiers
will stuff their packs and head back home.

—Janet S. Wong

Wonder Down Under

Uluru (Ayers Rock), Australia

I'm known around the rockin' world by many,
enchanted by my ruddy, wrinkled dome.
But neighbors of my ilk? I don't have any.
The harsh and empty outback is my home.
My power is mysterious and mythic.
My people, the Anangu, understand
that I am more than simply monolithic—
I am a huge Australian rock star in the sand.

And though I love your awe and admiration,
applaud me from a distance, if you will.
I'm big enough for long-range observation,
and I can guarantee you'll get a thrill.
In photos or in person you will gawk,

even if you're not a fan of rock.

—Ted Scheu

ULURU (AYERS ROCK), ULURU-KATA TJUTA NATIONAL PARK, AUSTRALIA
乌鲁鲁巨石（艾尔斯岩石），乌鲁鲁-卡塔曲塔国家公园，澳大利亚

Red Tide

What if a tiny shred of alga,
a prosaic, single-celled seaweed,

which no one hears, no one sees,
a nothing caught in the Red Tide of life,

what if instead of wallowing in waves like a gutless jellyfish,
this helpless kelp gets a grand idea of its own,

if this lone wolf, this powerless thing,
bands together with other plankton in protest?

What if by day
the waters bleed,

and under the moon suddenly seen,
each alga burns blue-green,

now the machine of Algae United
waving its bioluminescent flag.

—April Halprin Wayland

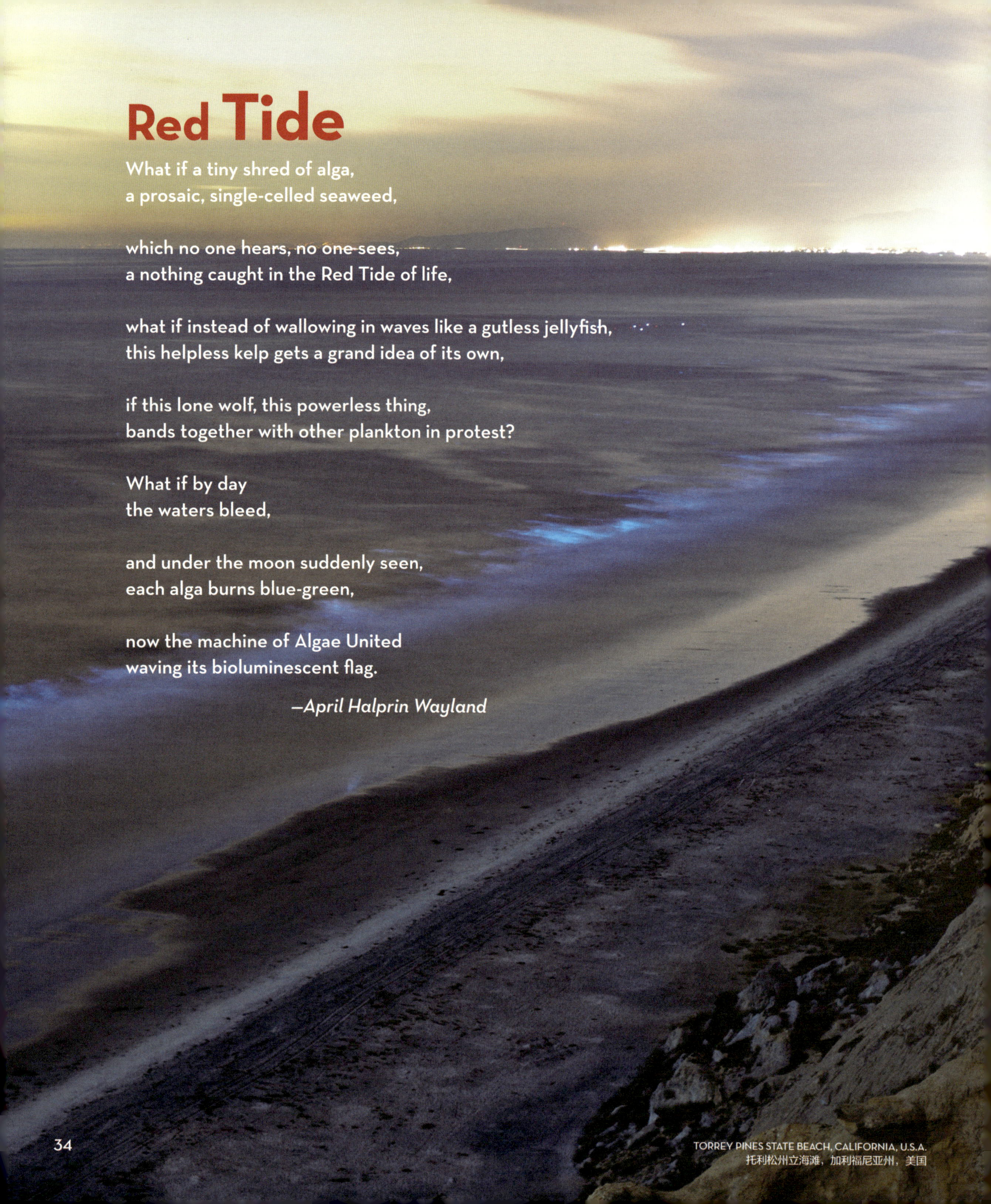

TORREY PINES STATE BEACH, CALIFORNIA, U.S.A.
托利松州立海滩，加利福尼亚州，美国

Petrified Forest

Navajo and Apache Counties, northeastern Arizona, U.S.A.

This is a place
where trees were buried.
This is a place
where water crept in.
This is a place
where minerals stayed—
where a stone tree looks
like a wood tree's twin.

Now the wood is gone
but the bark remains.
Rings of quartz spin
round and round.
These rainbow logs
that once were trees
tell ancient tales
without a sound.

—Amy Ludwig VanDerwater

PETRIFIED WOOD
石化木

Aurora Borealis

Over the shores of Labrador
a certain rippling purple curtain
scatters light throughout the night.
(Wait—the color's now a duller
hue of violet-turning-blue!)
This arctic veil, a breaching whale
could peer behind, and still be blind
as anyone. The northern sun
has bent to drape her gauzy cape
across the skies, and left my eyes
to stare and stare at the glittering air.

—Steven Withrow

Northern Lights

As self-absorbed and callow as a teen,
He never gave a thought to purple, blue,
Pink, red—or any color in between.

Amusements would appear but they were few
Till August heaved an easel in the sky
And *color*, modulating into *hue*,

Flew summer's spectral spectacle on high.

—J. Patrick Lewis

AURORA BOREALIS
北极光

Nothing Gold Can Stay

Nature's first green is gold,
Her hardest hue to hold.
Her early leaf's a flower;
But only so an hour.
Then leaf subsides to leaf.
So Eden sank to grief,
So dawn goes down to day.
Nothing gold can stay.

—Robert Frost

LAST

Nature

O Nature! I do not aspire
To be the highest in thy choir, —
To be a meteor in thy sky,
Or comet that may range on high;
Only a zephyr that may blow
Among the reeds by the river low;
Give me thy most privy place
Where to run my airy race.

In some withdrawn, unpublic mead
Let me sigh upon a reed,
Or in the woods, with leafy din,
Whisper the still evening in:
Some still work give me to do, —
Only—be it near to you!

For I'd rather be thy child
And pupil, in the forest wild,

Than be the king of men elsewhere,
And most sovereign slave of care;
To have one moment of thy dawn,
Than share the city's year forlorn.

—Henry David Thoreau

THOUGHTS

LOPEZ ISLAND, WASHINGTON, U.S.A.
洛佩兹岛，华盛顿州，美国

Swift Things Are Beautiful

Swift things are beautiful:
Swallows and deer,
And lightning that falls
Bright veined and clear,
Rivers and meteors,
Wind in the wheat,
The strong-withered horse,
The runner's sure feet.

And slow things are beautiful:
The closing of day,
The pause of the wave
That curves downward to spray,
The ember that crumbles,
The opening flower,
And the ox that moves on
In the quiet of power.

—Elizabeth Coatsworth

YELLOW CALLA LILY
黄色马蹄莲

Lessons of Nature

After Samuel Hazo

The darker the night, the wiser the owl.
The faster the hare, the smarter the fox.
The plumper the bird, the quicker the snake.
The hotter the day, the louder the bee.

The brighter the sun, the gladder the rose.
The stiffer the wind, the stiller the hawk.
The finer the flake, the lighter the snow.
The denser the fog, the thinner the tree.

The wetter the rain, the greener the frog.
The drier the field, the sadder the corn.
The higher the peak, the colder the air.
The deeper the gorge, the older the land.

The blacker the cloud, the whiter the wave.
The madder the sky, the fiercer the storm.
The flatter the sea, the sweeter the beach.
The farther the tide, the harder the sand.

—J. Patrick Lewis

GREAT GRAY OWL
大灰猫头鹰

the earth
is a living thing

is a black shambling bear
ruffling its wild back and tossing
mountains into the sea

is a black hawk circling
the burying ground circling the bones
picked clean and discarded

is a fish black blind in the belly of water
is a diamond blind in the black belly of coal

is a black and living thing
is a favorite child
of the universe
feel her rolling her hand
in its kinky hair
feel her brushing it clean

—Lucille Clifton

OWENS RIVER, CALIFORNIA, U.S.A.
欧文斯河，加利福尼亚州，美国

In Beauty May I Walk

In beauty may I walk
All day long may I walk
Through the returning seasons may I walk
Beautifully will I possess again
Beautifully birds
Beautifully joyful birds
On the trail marked with pollen may I walk
With grasshoppers about my feet may I walk
With dew about my feet may I walk
With beauty may I walk
With beauty before me may I walk
With beauty behind me may I walk
With beauty above me may I walk
With beauty all around me may I walk
In old age, wandering on a trail of beauty, lively, may I walk
In old age, wandering on a trail of beauty, living again, may I walk
It is finished in beauty
It is finished in beauty

—Anonymous (Navajo Indian)

Post-it Notes From the World

Is sadness the reason
for rainbows?

Are gardens why people
have knees?

Are bluebirds why houses
have windows?

Are geese the inventors
of V's?

A drought is the rain's inspiration;
a flood is a river's despair.

The sun is a storm on vacation.

A rose is a gift to the air.

The sky's a high-fashion designer.

The ocean's a bowl of fish soup.

Blue whale was the first ocean liner.

And seagulls made up the
word *swoop*.

Snowflakes are the
world's art collection.

Full moon's a firefly to the stars.

A canyon's a flatland's correction.

The wind's just a gust of guitars.

Would tides
like to skip daily practice
at filling the shore's hourglass?

Are porcupines cousins to cactus?

Are jellyfish breakable glass?

An orchard's the reason for ladders.

The tallest trees laugh at a stair.

A weed is indeed a
misunderstood seed.

But a rose, oh a rose
always wins
by a nose,
a rose is a gift to the air.

—J. Patrick Lewis

GRAND PRISMATIC POOL, WYOMING, U.S.A.
大棱镜泉，怀俄明州，美国

NDOR
奇 景

P14

The Great Barrier Reef

大堡礁

位于澳大利亚昆士兰海岸边的珊瑚海

绵延一千六百英里，
在昆士兰的海岸边，
这堡礁被命名为“大”堡礁，
名不虚传。

绵延一千六百英里，
每一英寸都如此鲜活，
若是你想看一眼，
都不用潜入水中，
也不用沾湿泳衣，
就能欣赏这壮丽之地。
堡礁如此巨大，
在太空里的宇航员都能看到。

想一想，
一边绕着地球转，
一边观赏，
充满了海龟、海豚、鲸
以及鼠海豚的栖息地。

眼见为实，
不言而喻，
地球上
最美不过珊瑚。

——罗伯特·谢克特

P15

Mammatus Clouds

乳状的云

雷声来临，响锤依旧，
天空充满了奇异的泡状云，
空中轰鸣着，
告诫我们走开。

飓风来临，灾难潜伏，
穹顶鼓鼓，
冰和水的袋子等待着
最佳的时机炸裂开来。

坏天气来临，其因也坏，
热气、凉风，温度不稳定，
狂风呼啸、升华——
我们只能接受最淡然的处理方式。

是什么来临，或好或坏，
谁知道会如何，又是为什么。
看那天空，充满问号的天空，
每个问号都云集着一个谜。

——朱莉·拉瑞奥斯

Moonbow at Cumberland Falls

P16

坎伯兰瀑布的月虹

美国肯塔基州东南

月虹——水雾与月光之虹，悬挂在河流溢成瀑布的地方。
满月透出月光的颜色，悬挂在坎伯兰瀑布倾泻而下的地方。
红、橙、黄、绿，在水雾的银幕上摇曳，由地面淌下随瀑布而落，
青、蓝、紫，河水的雾气和月光在我们的心中交织成谜，
坎伯兰瀑布的月虹啊！

——乔治·埃拉·莱昂

Solar Eclipse

P17

日食

幼枭知道它的逼近，
猎狗装作已是夜晚，
太阳戴上它的冕冠，
别看，
她会偷走你的视感！

月亮花瓣打起哈欠，
牵牛花也合拢困倦，
园中蚯蚓微光轻泛，
小心，
她会闪得你目眩！

——史蒂文·威思罗

Fish Rain

P17

鱼之雨

动物雨是一种极为罕见的
天气现象。
时不时地，在一些奇怪的时候，会下起动物雨。
不是下猫下狗，而是下蟾下蛙，
总是同一物种，同一大小。
最常下的是小鱼。
是什么让活鱼从雷雨中降落
数英里以外的湖泊？
被狂风卷来的吗？

澳大利亚、印度、路易斯安那州、萨斯喀彻温省
都下过鱼雨。
在约罗，洪都拉斯的一个小镇，
每年都会下一两次鱼雨。
人们像过节一样庆祝，
感谢鱼雨喂饱穷人。
也许你永远也不会见到鱼雨，
但是，万一遇见了，记得
一定要把雨伞倒过来！

——玛丽莲·纳尔逊

Moeraki Boulders

P18

摩拉基巨石

新西兰摩拉基与汉普顿之间的扣扣奇沙滩

如
珍珠般，
深植于淤泥，
这些圆球像牙一样冒出，
又像贝壳一样被石衣层层包裹，
坚硬如石拳。经年累月，布满泥沙的
海床上升，变成峭壁，波浪的拍打
让这些珍宝从覆盖的表层显露
出来，如一群坠落的月亮
展开在光滑的
水波中。

——乔伊斯·西德曼

Fossil Beds at the Badlands

P19

巴德兰兹的化石层

美国南达科他州巴德兰兹国家公园

穿过不急不躁的拉什莫尔营地，
转几个弯，忍耐那参差的路况。
长着剑齿的山猫长眠了，
疯马的梦境刻在岩石。
它们的寂静无与伦比，
轻轻走，什么也别碰。
有人记得吗？
他们曾逐水草而居，曾是天空的主人，
今晚，一只大角羊背对日落，
土拨鼠蜷缩在地下，
这一切是如何消逝的？

这个王国里装着失去的希望，
现在都变成了一片橘色。有些看上去好像
伸向天空的手指，
抛开自己的痛苦，没人会知晓。
搜寻着那些柔软的沉积物，悄声呼唤着犀牛，
每一位的空虚都如此优雅，
甚至野牛，甚至黑脚雪貂，
甚至女人，甚至男人。

——娜奥米·席哈勃·奈

Glacial Erratic

冰川漂砾

加拿大艾伯塔省及其他地方的巨石，重达15 000吨

只有一块空地围绕着巨石，
是哪个巨人能够举起、挪动它？
一块石头，却没人能撼动，
块垒堆积，是谁把它放在这里？老人说，
巨石一直都在这里，久远得记不清楚了——
大约这是真的吧？它从何而来，又为何到来？
的确和方圆几英里的岩石都不一样吗？
冰川的谜团在寻找答案。看这个谜题如何
川流解开，在纸上留下诗的答案。

——海伦·弗罗斯特

Sun Dogs

天狗

太阳闪亮登场了，
矗立阳台，俯视众生，
头顶环绕着
钻石般的灰尘和云雾组成的
光晕。

他的身旁站着
两只天狗，
一北一南，
安静守卫，
口中狺狺。

太阳向观众告辞，
在黑暗中隐没时，
他派出天狗，
一次两只，去守卫城市的公园。

—— 珍妮特·S. 王

P21

Catatumbo LIGHTNING

卡塔通博的闪电

只有在注入委内瑞拉马拉开波湖的卡塔通博河口可以观察到

即使你亲眼看见，
也是难以置信，
无以名状——
整个夜空都被爆裂的闪电吞没。

此起彼伏的闪电，劈云斩雾，上天入地，
每一波都可支持
一个村庄的供电。

就像打在马拉开波湖沼泽柱子上的闪电，
天时地利，一同孕育。

傍晚的光——半科学半自然——
让所有人止步不前，

哪怕是弗朗西斯·德雷克爵士，
多年前，他的进攻被卡塔通博的雷电炮击后，
只能落荒而逃，

德雷克航行时，是否仰望天空，张大嘴巴？
他是否目瞪口呆？
惊奇得膝软欲跪？

还是抱怨命运
已被雷电剥夺？

——凯莉·拉姆斯德尔·法恩曼

P22

The Mariana Trench

马里亚纳海沟

西太平洋，马里亚纳岛东部

所有洋底，这里最深，
诡秘莫测，人却要一探究竟，
投诚于潜水艇中的人眼，
海沟旁若无人，睡得深沉。

深藏其心，出乎意料，
生命如常，
无视七英里水压
对海床的干扰。

测度其深，
将海沟一一鉴明，
也快于鉴察
巨测的人心。

——X. J. 肯尼迪

The Grand Canyon

P23

大峡谷

被美国亚利桑那州的
科罗拉多河雕刻而成

我到了，有如置身于力量之地、
威力之地——
正如许多年前的普韦布洛人
被这巨大的焦赭色异象深深吸引。
那难以想象的浩大，
一层又一层的岩石
撰写地质的史书。
数百万年间，
在光阴中回溯——
骤跌，跌落高原，
跌破海平面。
都说大峡谷是科罗拉多河的鬼斧神工，
我却想象着格列佛啊，巨人啊，
手上染着陶土的颜色，
在峡谷遥远的边际休憩，
在完成了如此杰作之后休憩。

——鲍比·卡茨

Mount Everest

P25

珠穆朗玛峰

地球上最高的山峰，位于尼泊尔和中国边境，
每年高度都在增加

珠穆朗玛峰向寂静的群星呼喊：

“我比风更强，
我是伟大、
高贵的
世界之王！

我沉重的躯体高耸入云，
看到了地球的渺小。

深深刺入广袤的太空，
我将攀登，把影子投射在万物之上。

人们称我为‘圣山’，
因为我在天空遨游，
抵达了天与地
交接的地方……

我来啦！”

宇宙躬下身来，
星星低头悄声说：
“来吧，我们会等你。”

——德博拉·钱德拉

Pink Lake

P26

粉色湖泊

西澳大利亚
洛切切群岛
中央岛

自然景色中最傻不过
玫瑰色的希利尔湖，
“这不是真的。那个湖泊是粉色的！”
要是你这样想，也很正常；
“希利尔湖怎么像泡泡糖一样？”
要是你这样问，也不新鲜。
湖水的盐分是海水的十倍，
简直是个谜。

这色彩也许来自
水藻的光合作用，
变成粉色来吸收阳光。

不过这也难说——
也许粉色微生物喜欢盐分，
觉得这咸水最安逸，
于是就群聚于此，
成了一碗棉花糖汤。

这些都可能是让湖水
看起来像草莓奶昔的原因。
我们还真不确定，
让你失望了，
希利尔盐湖：粉红盛宴，
澳大利亚芭比的梦幻假期，
想象的色彩。

——艾伦·沃尔夫

Brinicle

P27

冰柱

北冰洋
深郁而广袤，
一拱海冰
守护着水洞，

冰顶下沉，
盐分填饱深渊的肚腹，
极咸的水带流动，
伸长，下沉。

虽如钟乳石，
却有一颗寒冷的心，
披着冰晶斗篷，

冰柱迸涌，
冲向
海底，
死神那冰冷的一触。

——劳拉·珀迪·萨拉斯

Antelope Canyon P28

羚羊谷

位于美国亚利桑那州佩吉市纳瓦霍原住民保护区

数百万年里，水流雕刻着砂岩，
蜿蜒岩石、瀑布，
磨尖锐成圆润，
巨石间横冲直撞，
洪流四溅，波涛滚滚，
搅动，抛光，倾泻，
切出光滑的峡谷和金色的圆洞口，
阳光一束束投下，
石柱直冲入云，
数百万年里，
黑暗的石缝回响着水的怒吼。

旱季，河床寂静，
雪花飘落螺旋峡谷，
渐融，
日落，叉角羚舔舐着
春夜的繁星。

——帕特·莫拉

Rainforest P29

雨林

雨林青翠欲滴，树蛙远远鸣唱，
他的声音平静，
青苔和雨水常年陶醉雨林。

我们无法理解树蛙的鸣唱，
除非潜入他的梦乡，
万物归一，一生万物，
树蛙巨蟒一样。

我们眼神敏捷，
测量，分辨，弃去。
雨林着了，树蛙死了，
一生万物，万物归一。

——朱迪思·赖特

Niagara Falls P29

尼亚加拉瀑布

位于加拿大安大略省和美国纽约州之间

好个舞台！好个演出！
雷霆降生。
最经久不衰的出演，
世上最伟大的杰作。

美国和加拿大
联合出品推出这一举世震惊的大片，
别错过自然轻吻的水雾
催生双胞彩虹。

——阿维丝·哈莉

P30

Yellowstone

黄石公园

美国怀俄明州西北

忘却烦恼，
抛开忧虑，
走入公园，
野牛熊罴，
驼鹿牧草，
灰狼潜伏，
麋鹿攀岩，
羚羊漫步。
河流滚滚，
喷泉间歇，
枞树高耸，
百合抽芽，
鳟鱼游弋，
猎鹰高翔。
同在一片
蓝天之下。

——道格拉斯·弗洛里安

P31

Lake Baikal

贝加尔湖

位于俄罗斯西伯利亚地区南部的贝加尔湖，是地球上最古老、最深的湖泊，拥有世界上1/5的未冻结淡水

如果地球刚刚好被你捧在手心，
如果土地能够从你的手指间流泻，
如果天空的蓝从你拇指间释放，
如果海洋的泪沿着你的双臂淌出，

就请你捧星球之水在掌心，
轻靠唇边，吮下那古老的清凉。
那有裂纹的珠子、蓝宝石般的猫眼
全都流淌在你皮肤褶皱的溪流里。

这便是贝加尔湖：冰封的时光。
凝视那蓝色湖泊的闪闪烁烁，
那是创世之始的
回眸一望。

——迈克尔·J. 罗森

P32

Bioluminescence in the Maldives

马尔代夫的生物光

这片海
醒来，忆起
坠落的星星，
尽其所深
寻找
淤泥中天空燃烧的余烬。
闪耀的灰烬
被翻至海面，
咸咸的星云
上升，
夺目。
波浪起伏中，
繁星复燃，
归尘土于烈焰。

——佩奇·陶勒

P32

Pororoca Tidal Bore

波波罗卡潮涌

巴西阿马帕州
阿拉瓜里河潮涌

波波罗卡潮涌，
大海和河流开战，
巨浪越坦克双倍，
沿亚马孙河卷袭、跌撞、怒吼，
一浪一浪又一浪——

每年只有几天，
却让众人畏惧地避让，
唯有冲浪者勇如战士，
腾空而出，乘风破浪，
巡航在战地废墟。

树木成了鱼雷，岩石成了榴弹，
他们呛到泥沙
却毫不在意。
当月相平复了波波罗卡的狂躁，
冲浪的勇士们才
整装踏上归途。

——珍妮特·S. 王

Wonder Down Under

P33

天下奇观

澳大利亚乌鲁鲁巨石（艾尔斯岩石）

在岩石界我无人不晓，
人们为我红色起皱的圆顶着迷，
我有远亲近邻吗？一个也没有。
严酷空旷的内陆是我的家。
我的力量神秘莫测，
我的人民，阿南格族人知道
我可不只是一块巨石——
我是澳大利亚荒漠中的岩石巨星。

尽管我喜欢你们的敬畏，
还是请你们在远处为我喝彩，
远远看去，我是如此巨大，
足以让人震撼不已。

无论照片还是实景都会让你目瞪口呆，
哪怕你根本不喜欢岩石。

——特德·朔伊

Red Tide

P34

赤潮

若撕一小片海藻，
一块普通的单细胞海草，

无人知晓，无人发现，
在生机勃勃的赤潮中毫不起眼。

不想像空空的水母随波逐流，
无助的海藻想出一条妙计，

如果这头独狼，这无力的小东西
和其他浮游生物联合示威，
会怎样？

光天化日之下，
海水如血流，

月亮升起才惊觉，
海藻泛着蓝绿色的光。

看那海藻联合国的机体上
飘扬着生物光的旗。

——阿普里尔·哈尔普林·韦兰

P35

Petrified Forest

石化的森林

美国亚利桑那州东北
纳瓦霍及阿帕奇县

在这个地方，
树木被埋葬。
在这个地方，
水缓缓流淌。
在这个地方，
矿物质存留。
石头树看去，
好像树木的
孪生的兄长。

森林已消亡，
树皮留此间，
石英环旋转，
一圈又一圈。
如虹般原木，
逝林犹可观。
沉默无语中，
述古老传说。

——埃米·路德维希·范德沃特

P36

Aurora Borealis

极光

在拉布拉多半岛的岸边，
涟漪般的紫色幕布
散布夜空，
（等等——现在颜色已从暗紫变蓝！）
这北极的面纱，一跃而起的鲸，
隔纱凝望时却似依然空无一物。
北极的阳光，
弯腰放下薄纱的披肩，
越过苍穹，我的视线
凝视许久那光彩夺目的高空。

——史蒂文·威思罗

P37

Northern Lights

北极光

像青春一样自恋而稚嫩，
他从不关注紫色、蓝色、粉色、红色，
或是任何中间色。

消遣时而有之，但并不多见，
直到八月在穹顶支起画架，
让色彩更有调调，
夏日的光谱奇观展翅翱翔。

—— J. 帕特里克·刘易斯

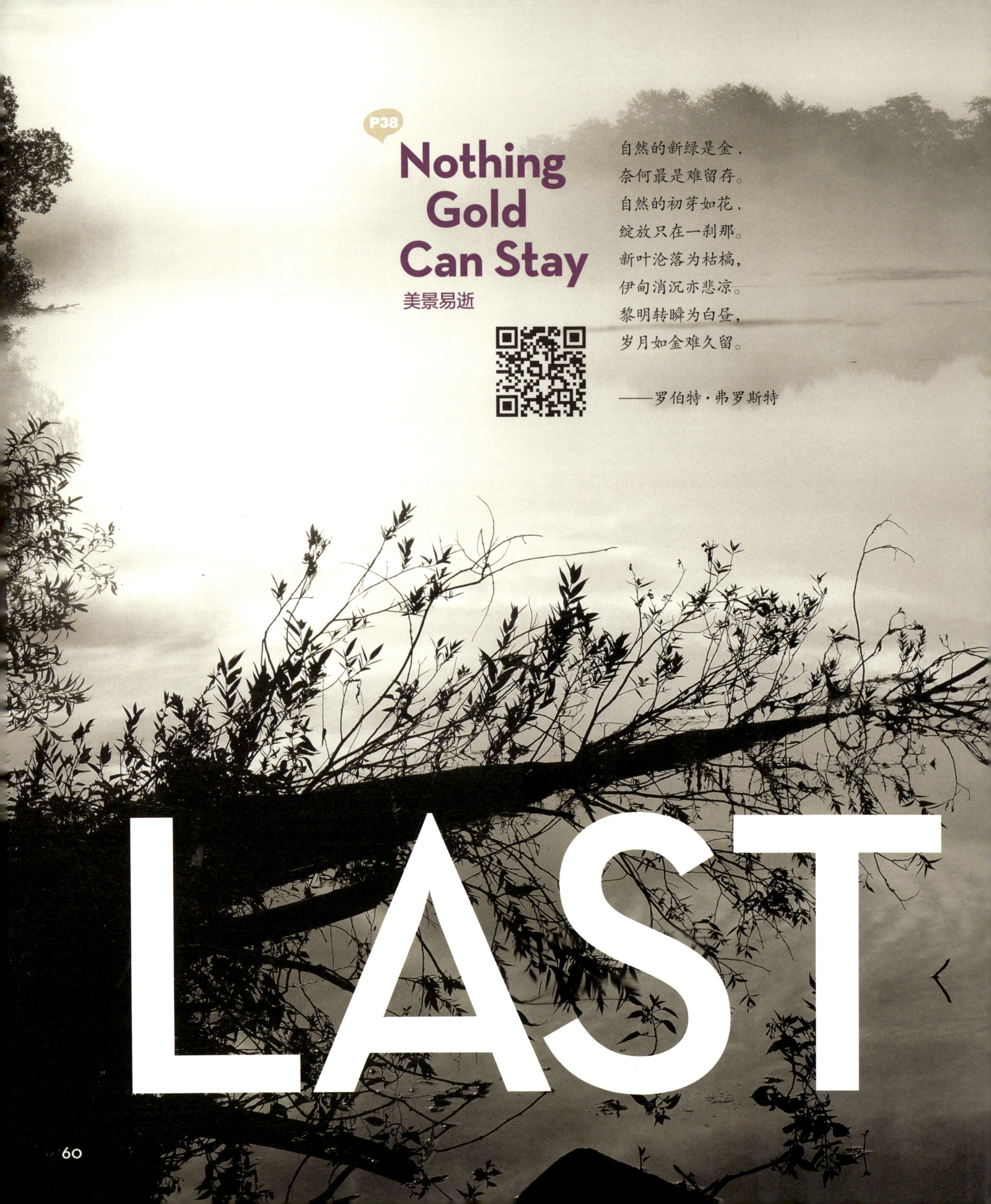

P38

Nothing Gold Can Stay

美景易逝

自然的新绿是金，
奈何最是难留存。
自然的初芽如花，
绽放只在一刹那。
新叶沦落为枯槁，
伊甸消沉亦悲凉。
黎明转瞬为白昼，
岁月如金难久留。

——罗伯特·弗罗斯特

LAST

P39

Nature
自然

哦，自然！我并不奢求
成为你诗班中的最高音，
或是你天空中的流星，
抑或是苍穹中逗留的彗星。

我只愿做一缕和风，
吹过低矮河岸边的芦苇丛，
在你给我的私密处所，
风一样地跑。

在那偏僻无人的草场上，
让我对那芦苇叹息，
或是在林中，在那绿叶的喧嚣中，
悄声呼唤寂静夜晚到来，
我要在这里安静地劳作——
只为靠近你！

我宁愿做你的孩子
和学徒，在这荒野的树林里，
也不愿做人间的君王，
或是荣极一时的臣仆。

我宁愿沉浸在你的片刻黎明，
也不愿分担城市终年的孤寂。

——亨利·戴维·梭罗

THOUGHTS
敬畏自然

LOPEZ ISLAND, WASHINGTON, U.S.A.
洛佩兹岛，华盛顿州，美国

Swift Things Are Beautiful

P40

敏捷即是美

敏捷即是美：
如雨燕野鹿，
似闪电乍现，
脉络清晰明亮，
如河川流星，
似风吹麦浪，
如强壮赛马，
似跑者如飞。

从容也是美：
如白日将尽，
似波涛暂缓，
浪花漫卷四溅，
如余烬成灰，
似蓓蕾初开，
如牛儿漫步，
沉静而有力。

——伊丽莎白·科茨沃思

Lessons of Nature

P41

自然的经验

致敬塞缪尔·哈佐

夜晚越黑暗，夜枭越聪明。
野兔越敏捷，狐狸越狡诈。
鸟儿越丰满，毒蛇越迅捷。
天气越炎热，蜜蜂越吵闹。

太阳越耀眼，玫瑰越开怀。
大风越强劲，老鹰越淡定。
雪花越纤细，风雪越轻柔。
雾气越浓厚，树木越消瘦。

雨水越稠密，青蛙越翠绿。
土地越干旱，玉米越悲伤。
山峰越高耸，空气越寒冷。
峡谷越深邃，土地越古老。

乌云越阴沉，波浪越惨白。
天空越狂暴，雷雨越猛烈。
海面越平静，海滩越怡人。
海潮越遥远，沙砾越坚硬。

——J. 帕特里克·刘易斯

P42

the earth is a living thing

地球是生灵

是一只蹒跚的黑熊，
弓起它狂野的背来，
将山峦扔进海洋。

是一只黑鹰，
盘旋在墓地上空，
绕着白骨，
已啄净，遗弃。

是水底目盲的鱼儿，
是炭中埋藏的钻石。

是一只黑色的生物，
是宇宙最爱的孩子，
手过乱发，
梳理顺滑。

——露西尔·克利夫顿

P43

In Beauty May I Walk

我愿美中行

我愿美中行，
从日出到日暮，
从春天到冬季，
美中行。
轮回中我欣然收获，
鸟儿们，
欢愉的鸟儿们，
我愿在花粉装点的小径上，美中行，
我愿随蚱蜢环绕脚周，美中行，
我愿露水轻落足际，美中行。

我愿美中行，
愿随身前的美丽，前行，
愿随身后的美丽，前行，
愿随顶空的美丽，前行，
愿随周遭的美丽，前行。
虽已垂暮，我愿徘徊在美的踪径，神采奕奕，
虽已垂暮，我愿徘徊在美的踪径，涅槃重生，
一切，都在美中完结。

——无名氏（纳瓦霍印第安人）

Post-it Notes From the World

P44

来自世界的便签

彩虹因忧伤而生吗?

膝盖因园艺而长吗?

窗户因蓝鸟而开吗?

V 字是大雁发明的吗?

干旱是雨的灵感。

洪水是河流的绝望。

太阳是暴风雨去度假。

玫瑰是给晴空的礼。

天空是名“高端”时尚设计师。

海洋是一碗鱼汤。

蓝鲸是第一艘远洋班轮。

海鸥让你知道什么叫“冲”。

雪花是世界的艺术展。

满月是星星的萤火虫。

峡谷矫正了平原。

风儿只是吉他在拨弦。

潮水会不会偷懒
不要每天去填海岸的沙漏？

豪猪是不是仙人球的表亲？

水母是不是易碎的玻璃？

梯子为果园而造。

高耸的树却来嘲笑楼梯。

野草是被委屈的种子，

但，玫瑰啊，玫瑰，
你是花中之最，
是给晴空的礼。

——J. 帕特里克·刘易斯

Who is mother nature?

When Mother Nature's near—in waterfalls, rivers, rainbows, meadows, or oceans—her admirers react with love, awe, curiosity, even fear, if she decides to reveal her grumpier side. The lady can be seen through telescopes or microscopes, from mountaintops or ravines, with the wind in our hair, soil in our hands, or sand in our toes. For those who aren't hopelessly city-bound, looking out a window will do.

Driven to explore the *science* behind the wonder of it all, Charles Darwin filled scores of notebooks about what was then the unexplored wildlife of the Galápagos Islands. Countless nature writers have followed his courageous example. Others have put themselves in nature, like naturalist John Muir, who once rode out a northern American windstorm by cocooning himself in the branches of a sky-high Douglas spruce. (Muir is famous—or should be—for saying, "The clearest way into the Universe is through a forest wilderness.")

Some humans, however, have no use for wild places, a view once expressed by Woody Allen with his typical wit: "I love nature. I just don't want to get any of it on me." For some, their love for animals extends only as far as Fido or Sweet Pea. That we share the Earth equally with other creatures is a notion as foreign and irrelevant to them as the disappearance of the rain forests or the melting of the ice caps.

But Mother Nature doesn't care who likes her. Nor is she bothered about being ignored. A midwife at the birth of creatures large and small, she will go on making waves by making waves, assembling forests, flowering deserts, and beautifying gardens. We can embrace her or resist her charms; it is of no concern to her.

Who is the mysterious lady known as Mother Nature? She is the material world, the environment of trees, plants, animals, everything under and over the sun. In short, she equals the world around us and includes whatever is not built by human hands.

Mother Nature is where we live. In other words, she is
a refuge to the lost,
a magnet to the curious,
a dare to the daring,
the cradle of rapture,
the university of the universe,
the glory of a morning and of a morning-glory,
not a whale but the idea of a whale,
a sign rewriter: I Welcome All No Trespassing,
the best cure for couch disease,
an opera performed by birds, bullfrogs on drums,
the sound of silence . . . amplified
to the symphony of the spheres, and ____________
____ .

Can you add another short description of Mother Nature to this poem?

The poets and photographers who have come together to produce National Geographic's *Book of Nature Poetry* would agree with John Keats, who defined their abiding faith: "The poetry of earth is never dead."

THREAD-WINGED ANTLION
线翅蚁狮

自然之母是谁？

当自然之母靠近的时候——在瀑布中，在河流中，在彩虹中，在草地或是海洋中——她的爱慕者用爱、敬畏、好奇来回应，甚至如果她显示暴躁的一面时，则用恐惧来回应。这位女士可以用望远镜或是显微镜来观察，从山顶到深谷，风在我们的发丝中穿过，泥土在我们手中漏出，沙在我们的脚趾中渗出。对于那些不喜欢住在城里的人来说，只要看一看窗外就行。

为了探索自然奇观背后的科学道理，查尔斯·达尔文把加拉帕戈斯群岛未知的野生动物记满了几十本笔记本。难以数计的自然主义作家跟随着他，以他为榜样。其他人则让自己融入自然。例如自然主义者约翰·缪尔，曾经用高耸入云的道格拉斯云杉的枝叶包裹着自己，经受住了北美的风暴。（缪尔由于下面这句话而知名——或应该知名——“融入宇宙最清晰的方式莫过于通过荒野森林”。）

然而，也有一些人，觉得野外毫无用处，这也是伍迪·艾伦用他特有的机智曾经表达的观点：“我爱自然，但是一点也别弄到我身上来。”而另一些人，他们对动物的喜爱只限于“菲多”或是“甜豌豆”。对他们来说，我们与其他生物平等地分享地球的观念，和雨林正在消失、冰层正在融化这样的概念一样，是未知而不重要的。

但自然之母并不关心谁喜欢她。她对这种忽视也毫不在意。她是大大小小各种生物出生时的产婆，她将不断在波浪中创造波浪，让森林遍地，让花朵在沙漠开放，让花园变得更美。我们可以接受或是抗拒她的魅力，她对此却毫不关心。

这位被人称为自然之母的神秘女士是谁？她是物质世界，也是植物、动物的环境和阳光下所有的一切。简言之，她就是我们周遭的世界，人类双手无法创造的世界。

自然之母在我们生活的地方。换句话说，

她是：
迷失者的庇护，
好奇者的磁石，
勇敢者的挑战，
狂喜者的摇篮，
宇宙的教化者。

她是：
清晨的光辉，
牵牛花的光，
并不是鲸鱼，
而是这创意。

她重新写了一个标记：我欢迎所有的非擅自闯入者。

她是：
沙发病的良药，
鸟儿、牛蛙在鼓上演奏的歌剧，
是寂静之声……被放大，
而成为万物的交响曲，
也是 ____________________

你可以在这首诗后面加上一段描写自然之母的短句吗？

共同创作《最美自然诗集》的诗人和摄影家们会同意约翰·济慈的话，他道出了他们永恒的信仰：“地球的诗篇永远不会消亡。”

LOTUS AND BEES -WUQIANG
荷花与蜜蜂（吴强）

美国国家地理学会是世界上最大的非营利科学与教育组织之一。学会成立于1888年，以"增进与普及地理知识"为宗旨，致力于启发人们对地球的关心。美国国家地理学会通过杂志、电视节目、影片、音乐、电台、图书、DVD、地图、展览、活动、学校出版计划、交互式媒体与商品来呈现世界。美国国家地理学会的会刊《国家地理》杂志，以英文及其他33种语言发行，每月有3800万读者阅读。美国国家地理频道在166个国家以34种语言播放，有3.2亿个家庭收看。美国国家地理学会资助超过10 000项科学研究、环境保护与探索计划，并支持一项扫除"地理文盲"的教育计划。

Acknowledgments
To the entire National Geographic team for their enthusiasm and dedication in the making of this book, and to all the poets whose deserving work, regrettably, could not be squeezed into its pages.—JPL

The publisher gratefully acknowledges the heroic efforts of Natalie Turner in securing permissions, as well as the invaluable research assistance of Alyson Foster.

图书在版编目（CIP）数据

最美自然诗集 / （美）J. 帕特里克·刘易斯主编；Abby F. Yehenola，张原平，和览编译. —郑州：河南科学技术出版社，2018.1
ISBN 978-7-5349-8952-0

Ⅰ.①最… Ⅱ.①J… ②A… ③张… ④和… Ⅲ.①儿童诗歌–诗集–美国–现代 Ⅳ.①I712.82

中国版本图书馆CIP数据核字(2017)第269830号

出版发行：河南科学技术出版社
地址：郑州市经五路66号　　邮编：450002
电话：（0371）65737028　　65788613
网址：www.hnstp.cn
特邀策划：Abby F. Yehenola
策划编辑：马艳茹　韩雅楠　于凯燕
责任编辑：于凯燕
责任校对：徐小刚
整体设计：吴豆豆
责任印制：张　巍
印　　刷：北京盛通印刷股份有限公司
经　　销：全国新华书店
幅面尺寸：232 mm × 276 mm　　印张：4.25　　字数：96千字
版　　次：2018年1月第1版　　2018年1月第1次印刷
全套定价：588.00元

To poets, nature, and nature poets everywhere.—JPL

献给诗人、自然和全世界写自然的诗人。

——J. 帕特里克 · 刘易斯